NITIN NANJI

LALJI'S
NAIROBI

Lalji's Nairobi
Copyright © 2023 Nitin Nanji

Cover design by Jessica Bell
Interior design by Amie McCracken

To My Wife, My Friend and My Rock

FORWARD

LALJI'S NAIROBI, BASED in Gujarat and Kenya at the beginning of the 1900's, is a story that is familiar to many Gujarati families. Oral accounts of their emigration for economic reasons are recounted in many families and communities. There has been a paucity of literature about their experiences and this novel intends to fill a tiny bit of that gap.

The courage of people to move from one colony to another under the same ruler is an unusual event. Commonly, that was with little knowledge about their destination across a hazardous ocean crossing. Often it was a one-way trip as returning was not an option.

Historians have largely ignored the Gujarat-Swahili Coast connection. Conventional history of the colonies was written by the conquerors. Too often it was written for popular consumption at home. Glorifying the colonialists and diminishing the conquered came naturally. European colonisation of Africa and India was the catalyst for the most heinous of man's conduct upon fellow man, that of subjugation through slavery and indentured labour. Land grabs and displacement soon followed.

Lalji's Nairobi tells the story of how with ability and persistence it is possible to find a way through the mire and succeed. It is a human story of man's faith in himself. It is a story of man's faith in others, even those from across political and cultural divides. It is a story of human triumph in adverse environments. But it is also a story about man's weaknesses from within.

This is my first novel. I was born in Nairobi when it was still a British Colony. The story is based on the life of my grandfather who left Gujarat at a young age for similar reasons and settled in Nairobi. It has had a long incubation since my teens when I decided to write it. I hope it lives up to your expectations and that you find its historical context alive and enjoyable. I have tried to make the context accurate and relevant to the focus of the story. At no stage has there been any desire to misrepresent any person or persons. I have tried to write fairly about the characters in the novel, being sensitive to their cultures and traditions of the time.

A small word of caution. I have used many words in vernacular language to add relevance and authenticity. To make it easier for those not familiar with the words I have added the English translation next to the word in parenthesis. In places, the English translation is deliberately omitted, where for example the word is repeated soon so as not to irritate the reader or interrupt the flow of the book.

Similarly, I have adopted the Gujarati conventions for titles. For example, "Bhai" means brother and can be used as a title of respect at the end of a forename or on its own. Likewise, "Bhabhi" means brother's wife and can also be attached at the end of a forename or used alone. Used at the end of a name can sound more formal and respectful. There are similar suffixes for other relationships, for example for uncle or aunt.

I would like to thank those who have helped in making this novel a reality. My copy-editor Jo Hall for her input and encouragement. Jessica Bell for the cover design and formatting.

My beta-readers and good friends, Elmein and Willem Le Roux, Amit Shah (actor), Usha Bahl and Johan De Waal all deserve a very special mention for their sharp reading, helpful suggestions and encouragement.

Nitin Nanji
June 2023

CHAPTER ONE

LALJI SENSED HE was different from those around him. He seemed to understand what the world was about. He was a thinker, but more than that he was a doer. He often saw things differently from others. He was confident in expressing his views on a situation, offering these with a degree of diplomacy which was rare for his young age of eighteen. He was aware he was listened to like an elder.

He put these qualities down to being 'different' from early childhood. His father had run a general supplies store having inherited it from his own father, a tiny cabin of tacked timber with a rusty tin roof. It was the main source of the family's income and all that his father Parshottam had to show for his achievement in life. Their village, twenty-two miles from Porbander on the coast of Gujarat, had been home for four generations.

"I am getting tired of this life," he once said to Lalji. "I feel I have done two lifetimes of work and worrying: first for my parents and siblings; now it's for my own family."

"You need not worry about us Bapa. We are old enough to take responsibility," said Lalji trying to reassure his father, whose eyebrows were almost touching in a frown.

"What you have not seen is how severe the drought can become. The Raj still wants taxes even when there is no trade. There is little here for you in Gujarat except for the dust; you should make your future elsewhere," said Parshottam.

Lalji had heard the statement before. His father held out hope that a move to Africa for one of his two sons would start them on a road of prosperity. What he also meant but did not say, was that a successful start elsewhere would also free him of his perennial worry of providing for the family. But

Lalji was unconvinced, concerned the family would end up in more debt paying for an expensive passage. There were stories of failure as well as success in starting anew in Africa.

Lalji knew that investigating a passage to Africa had become a pre-occupation for his father.

Lalji ran the small shop with his brother Naran, younger by three years. His father spent time reading newspapers or talking with others about the passage to Africa. The fact that no one from his village had ventured that far made him hesitate in trusting the stories. Lalji was the more confident one while Naran was introverted and quieter. Lalji was constantly looking out for new opportunities and was not averse to putting his foot into a door having spotted a niche. He would approach an established business or trader with a new idea and be willing to advise for a cut in the profit or a benefit of some kind.

Four years previously Lalji's friend Babu was being pulled out of school by his father to help in his shoe business. The bullocks which pulled the cart for transportation were getting older and slower. This meant for Babu's father that he could not run his shop single-handedly anymore. He hand-crafted shoes and *chappals* (open slippers) himself, and went out with his bullocks to pick up carcasses. He had told Babu that his own schooling of two years had not helped him in his craft and so he remained illiterate. In his view, school was a drain on money for someone like Babu who required the use of his hands to make a living.

Babu had been distraught at the prospect of not attending school where he had a happy existence. He enjoyed studying, especially maths, as well as the daily games of *gilli-danda* (game played with a hitting stick and peg) with his friends. There was always plenty of time to linger home after school with his friends, arms around each other's necks, singing, laughing, mock fighting. He had long decided he would never want to be a cobbler like his father.

When Babu told Lalji what was being planned for him, Lalji smiled.

"What have you got to worry about in your dad's trade?" asked Lalji. A puzzled Babu asked what he meant, and Lalji began an explanation of how Babu's father could run the whole business better without the bullocks.

"Your father needs to sell those ageing bullocks while he can. With the money he needs to buy a bicycle and get you to learn how to ride it. That way, when a carcass needs picking up, you could go after school on the bicycle and secure the animal as yours."

"How do we get it back to the shop without a bullock cart?" inquired Babu.

"Simple. When you have secured the carcass, you would need to hire someone to collect the carcass, skin it and deliver the hide to your father's yard. First, you must agree a price. Get someone to do it for a good rate."

Babu nodded.

"Think about the money you would save from not having to feed those old bullocks. The savings would pay for the bicycle. That's not even considering the usefulness of the bicycle as transport for the family. You could still go to school and be able to help your father after school," announced Lalji.

Babu was surprised how matter-of-factly Lalji had given the advice. He admired Lalji's ability to understand his father's business in an unfamiliar way.

"What you said sounds clever. Can you repeat it for me, slowly?" asked Babu. Having grasped the points, Babu's problem now was how to present it to his father as an option. But he knew his father would never entertain any advice about the business from him.

"Will you talk to my father?" he asked.

"Sure, I will. But I would like to be able to use the bicycle whenever I need it. Only then will I convince your father, but that must be a secret between us."

Babu felt nervous about making a secret deal but was also excited that it was a deal with Lalji, whom he trusted. He knew that Lalji was also clever in making things work. He felt safe with Lalji and so he agreed.

Lalji went to see Babu's shoemaker father. Addressing him as "*Sethji*" (title for a successful man), which embarrassed the cobbler coming from a higher caste *Lohana* boy, Lalji broached the subject. First, they chatted about the number of businesses that had disappeared after the famines. The old-established village *lohar* (blacksmith) who had decided to move the family and take up residence with a distant cousin in Rajkot. There he hoped to find piecemeal work for the English Cantonment. Then there was the case of the village barber who disappeared overnight owing rent.

"Different for me," said the cobbler, "there will always be dead animals and people always need shoes and *chappals* (open slippers). But the money is tight with fewer people paying for new shoes. Then the beasts need feeding and the cost of fodder has multiplied."

Lalji was right on cue to take the conversation from there with his formula for the business. He sat on the floor opposite the cobbler and spoke slowly and carefully, outlining his view of how the business could be better run.

With a raised eyebrow Babu's father asked, "So who will teach my son how to ride a bicycle?"

"I will," said Lalji, without hesitation although he was not prepared for the question. His only experience of bicycles amounted to having sat on the crossbar as a passenger, which did not matter to Lalji at the time. It also served as a way of assuring he would be getting his hands on the bicycle often enough.

After some convincing, the old cobbler agreed and sold his bullocks. Lalji went with the cobbler to buy the bicycle.

The boys learnt to ride within a week and Babu continued school. Lalji started to borrow the bicycle and landed odd jobs for himself, like delivering clothes for the village tailor to customers. Once a month he rode into the nearest town to the *marwari* (moneylender from Rajasthan), and collected small outstanding debts from customers. He was good at this, taking advantage of his age as the customer was often too embarrassed to argue with a youngster.

One day Lalji found his father sitting alone, thinking.

"Lalji, we have to consider another way to improve our situation," said Parshottam.

"We have discussed this before. Selling up and moving to Porbander is not an option. Jobs are scarce there."

"It's something else. Hear me out. We can ask for help from the Islamic Society. But there are conditions."

"You mean convert to Islam?" asked Lalji.

Looking away Parshottam replied, "So many have joined the *Bohras* who are Shias. But those who join don't seem to talk much about the experience. They have a different way of life and pray five times every day."

"It's not only about getting help and prayers Bapa. You know that."

Parshottam averted his eyes again, "Well, yes. Men wear skull caps and women wear *burkhas* (long garment worn by Muslim women). They don't have religious symbols except for a fabric illustration of their holy Kaaba in Arabia."

"Isn't that a big change?" asked Naran who had joined them.

"They still keep some of their customs like before," replied Parshottam. "But I agree, it may be too big a change for us, at present."

"What does *Baa* (Mother) say?" asked Lalji.

"Oh, I have not asked her yet. I am not sure she would hear of it. She is always hopeful things will change after the rains arrive."

"You realise Bapa, people have to change names, start eating meat, fast for a whole month every year," said Naran, adding, "you can't come back when times improve."

Lalji agreed.

"Many of our *Lohana* families have been turning to a less strict form of Islam led by someone called Aga Khan," said Parshottam. "They have convinced many in Kutch, where the famine has been more severe and longer. They even provide financial support."

Lalji got straight to the point, "Would you change your name and take up a foreign religion, turning your back on your ancestral faith? In the land of Krishna's ancient Kingdom?"

"You put it well. I guess I can't."

"If the rains come and things improve, we will be fine as you often told us," suggested Naran.

"What if they don't?"

"Then I will head to Africa as you desire," was the instant involuntary response from Lalji.

There was silence. Lalji wished he could take back the words; he never made decisions on a whim. His father and brother were studying him, aware he would not go back on his word.

CHAPTER TWO

FOR PURSHOTTAM, THE promise of Africa for his son was seductive. He would sit down in the backyard near the cow shelter with his sons and relay what he had learnt from his reading.

"So many different European *sarkars* (governments) are looking for young men to travel to the new colonies in Africa, to settle and work there," he announced. "But there are differences in how they operate."

"How?" asked Lalji.

"Most provide a free passage. Not all give you the choice of going where you wish. They have local jobs for migrants which are fixed up by agents before you get on the ship."

"Can you say no?" asked Naran.

"Not really, since the passage is free. You must sign a bond."

"But you can move on if you are unhappy?" asked Lalji.

"Not if you have signed a bond, which usually restricts movement for ten years. After ten years, you can stay on or return home," Parshottam said.

"Meanwhile, be a slave, living and working where it is decided for you," said Lalji.

"Slavery is banned surely?" asked Naran.

"This is one better. A newer model was designed by those who abolished the old one. But you still belong to them, for a wage and the passage," said Lalji.

Parshottam was getting uncomfortable at the direction of the discussion.

"Is there danger in the voyage?" asked Naran.

"I don't know about that. These are big modern ships with heavy machinery which drives them," responded Parshottam.

"I have heard people die on the journey from becoming ill. Those who do are thrown into the sea," said Naran.

No one commented. A strong whiff of fresh cow dung hit them like a slap across the face.

"Some *Lohana* families from other villages reached *Mumbasa* (Mombasa) safely and have done well in Kenya. They say the British *sarkar* (government) is a better choice as they have more colonies near there," said Parshottam. "The land is said to be more fertile and they have built a new railway using Punjabi labourers."

"Well then, the only other choice is to pay for your passage in an Arab vessel, a *vaan* (dhow) and head to British Africa. I don't know how we can afford that," announced Lalji, stamping his feet on the ground while getting up from his charpoy and walking off.

***

Parshottam's friend and confidante, Dhiraj, was also engaged in obtaining information. Dhiraj had a son, Bhasker who was older than Lalji by five years. Bhasker was idle and never helped at home or in his father's shop which was also in decline.

Bhasker's favourite pastime was to sleep. When he was not sleeping, he could usually be found under the village peepal tree sitting on its low wall surround. He would be chatting to passers-by or making a nuisance of himself with the women of the village.

For Dhiraj, the possibility of getting his good-for-nothing son off to Africa with Lalji would be an unmissable opportunity.

"Parshottam, you can't send your son all that way in an Arab *vaan*," he stated.

"Why is that, Dhiraj?"

"Well, the danger of course. Even with the most well-recommended *vaan* master, your son travelling alone could be in danger."

"Yes, I know. I can only send Lalji as his younger brother needs to stay here."

"That is why we should send my son along with Lalji!" announced Dhiraj.

"Oh. I will have to speak to Lalji," said Parshottam, averting his eyes.

***

The *vaans* came to the Gujarati ports as they had done so for centuries. They traded between the Indian Ocean ports of Western India, Arabia and East

Africa. Dependent on the trade winds of the monsoon, the traffic went one way before returning after the change in wind direction months later.

Choosing a *vaan* and its master was tricky. The skills and reputation of the *vaan* master had to be researched. A skilful master could sail with goods for trading along the shores of Arabia and Africa as far as *Jungbar* (Zanzibar) or beyond. They could exchange passengers at any of the ports along the way. Porbander and Mombasa were on the main route.

Parshottam had written to his cousin in Somnath asking if he could inquire in Veraval, a seaport in Gujarat where the *vaans* were built. He had asked for his recommendation of a reputable Arab *vaan* master, whose passage costs were reasonable. Unscrupulous *vaan* masters were known to throw passengers overboard when rations got scarce.

Within days he heard back from his cousin, recommending a *vaan* master called Dawood. He was due in Porbander to pick up supplies on his way to Mombasa on the Kenyan coast. He was well recommended by families from Somnath and Rajkot who had used him and charged a fair rate.

Dawood was in his mid-forties. He had been sailing the Indian Ocean from the age of eighteen and hailed from Oman. His two wives and nine children saw him twice a year when the monsoon trade winds changed direction between *Hindustan* (India) and Africa. He sailed with two *vaans*, the second led by his younger brother Yusuf. The brothers always sailed together as it meant they were safer from pirates. It also meant larger loads shared between the two increased their profits. Yusuf had a wife and five children and like his elder brother only saw them twice a year. He was the expert navigator using a *kamal* (navigation instrument) and knew the night sky for navigation better than most. He had a limp from childhood but that did not stop him from being an expert climber on the masts.

Purshottam made his inquiries about Dawood and Yusuf. He went to see Jethadas, Porbandar's well-known Gujarati *soni* (jeweller) who dealt with many Arabs. His family had traded with the Arabs for generations and he had family running jewellery shops in many of the ports on the trade route. They changed gold into local currency or silver. Gold was the currency of the Indian Ocean, with long-established *sonis* providing a service of currency exchange. Gold came in many shapes and sizes, from blocks and coins to cables and shavings. Any currency could be converted using the *soni's* weights.

Jethadas looked surprised to see Parshottam, having last seen him when he sold some of his mother's gold after her death.

"What brings you to me today Parshottambhai?" asked Jethadas. He was seated on an elevated platform near the entrance of his shop. His chubby, clean-shaved face exaggerated a smile that bunched up his cheeks below both eyes. He was always clad in new white silk shirts.

"I am looking for some information about an Arab seafarer I want to use to send my son to Africa."

"You have come to the right place! Fares have gone up but fortunately, the price of gold is better so now might be a good time to exchange old gold."

"Yes. I need to know if you know two brothers from Oman called Dawood and Yusuf?" asked Parshottam.

"Yes, I know them well. They have been customers of mine ever since they came to Gujarat, and their father before them. They are due here any day now on their way to Africa."

"Do you know people who have travelled with them?"

"Sure, I do. Many families have travelled with them, and some both ways."

Parshottam was immediately reassured and beamed a friendly smile before asking, "Are they honest?"

"Sure they are. They trade in fabric and spices from Gujarat and dried fruits and perfumes from the Arabian Peninsula. From Africa they bring ivory, gemstones and cloves. From what I know, they don't owe any money to anybody. Oh yes, Dawood also speaks Gujarati like some of his crew."

"That's good to know. Are their fares reasonable?" asked Parshottam.

"I will speak to them for you. I would not hesitate to send my son or family with them. But like I say, the price of old gold may drop again and now might be the right time to use it for the fare."

"Yes, yes. I need to discuss it with the family before coming back to you on that," Parshottam said. "I will also want to take advice from our village *Panchayat* (elected council)."

"Good, that's fixed then. Can I offer you some tea or sherbet?"

"Thank you but I need to be getting along."

"Shall I let you know when he arrives?"

"That would be very helpful. *Jai Shri Krishna.*"

Parshottam headed home to talk to Lalji.

"You will not be alone as Dhiraj's son Bhaskar can go with you," said Parshottam nervously.

The mention of Bhasker sent a shiver up Lalji's spine.

"I don't know Bhasker well. You know he has never done a day's work in his life. He is the last person I need with me! He would be a liability," said Lalji, irritated.

"Yes, I know. But travelling alone is no safe thing either. It's better to be with someone."

"You said the *vaan* master had a good reputation."

"Yes, I did. But suppose if you became unwell on the voyage, how would you cope? Most young men go with others. You would support each other."

Lalji's mother Rambai listened thoughtfully before asking when she would see her son again. Parshottam looked awkward before saying people returned if things did not work out. Lalji listened to the discussion, aware of an air of nervousness in his father's demeanour. To his surprise, it was his younger brother Naran who was most concerned about the risks. It had clearly dawned on Naran that until his brother made good in Africa, he would most likely shoulder more responsibility. He felt they could only afford the passage if they borrowed from the moneylender. With business as poor as it was, it would not be long before Lalji would need to send funds from Africa.

"We will work all that out my son," announced Parshottam confidently, which Naran perceived as a putdown. Naran's eyes met Lalji's and both knew their father had probably not considered the wider aspects of the plan.

Everyone realised that Lalji had not said anything and his father turned to him.

"What are your thoughts, son?" inquired Parshottam.

"I want to give it some more thought and will give you my answer tomorrow," was Lalji's response.

There ended the family conversation until Parshottam and his wife Rambai found themselves alone at bedtime. He asked for her opinion, knowing she must have other concerns.

"It's his decision," she replied. "I want to make sure he will be safe and can come back when he wants to. He must come back to get married and take his bride back with him."

"Are you worried things will not work out and he will fail?" inquired Purshottam, echoing his own anxiety.

"No. Because he will be successful. Very successful," she replied.

Bemused and surprised, Parshottam looked at his wife and asked, "How can you be so certain?"

"Because the first *Sadhu* (ascetic monk) who came to our door asking for alms after Lalji was born told me he was going to travel far and become very successful at a young age."

Parshottam had forgotten the *Sadhu's* words but was surprised his wife had kept her faith in the remark after all these years. "How different we all are," he thought. "Some of us push and toil to change life's lot while others are calm and assured in the faith that the future holds promise."

CHAPTER THREE

THE NEXT MORNING brought an early visitor to their door in the shape of the village *Sarpanch*, Thakorbhai. The *Sarpanch* was the elected head of the village and led the *Panchayat*. His role was to officiate over disputes, collect fines and enforce the law with the help of the police.

Thakorbhai was a large man with short legs and a bull neck. He sported a moustache that was long and curled upwards at the ends, like two cobras poised to strike. When he sat on a chair, he folded his legs under him and they disappeared under his enormous belly. The children of the village were thrown into fits of giggles at this sight as he looked like an overgrown hen sprawled over her eggs. For that reason, he was also known unkindly as '*Murgiben*' (mother hen).

He invited himself into the yard and sat down on Parshottam's charpoy. He had come about the story going around that Parshottam's son was to head out to Africa. He knew Parshottam had been making inquiries about the next meeting of the *Panchayat* and thought the two matters may well be connected.

"You are right, I was hoping to have the matter considered at the *Panchayat*," said Parshottam before calling out for Lalji to join them. Rambai appeared with a tumbler of salted buttermilk for the *Sarpanch* and joined in the chorus calling for Lalji.

"What does the boy say?" inquired Thakorbhai.

"He hasn't made up his mind. See, I was thinking with the lack of prospects here after the famines and with the tax situation…."

"You leave the tax situation to me, Parshottam," bellowed Thakorbhai. "We need to know if the boy is willing to go and take his chances!"

At that instance, both Lalji and Naran appeared. They paid their respects to the *Sarpanch* by bowing to him and gesturing to touch his feet hidden under his belly.

"So, what's your decision young man?" he inquired of Lalji. "Are you ready to cross the big ocean and arrive at the opposite shore to start a new life, away from your family?"

Lalji seated himself down in a squatting position and looked straight at the *Sarpanch*. Without hesitation announced, "Yes, I willl be taking the *vaan* and see what destiny has in store for me. It is my role as the eldest son."

"*Shabbash* (well said), my boy! That's the right answer." The cobras parted to reveal pink gums.

"The son of Dhiraj will be accompanying him, so as he is not alone," interjected Parshottam.

Thakorbhai waved the idea away as being of no consequence. He told Parshottam his son was in a different league from many and he was supportive of the idea. He mentioned others had considered it before but no son of the village had made the journey.

"The reasons are many but the fact is no one has had the strength of character to take the step. If I was twenty years younger, I would have given the same answer as Lalji here," he said.

Turning to Lalji he asked, "Would you lead a group of three others from here to go with you?"

Lalji was taken aback by the question, having never considered himself as taking on such responsibility. He didn't feel unable to lead, but he wanted to know whom the *Sarpanch* had in his mind.

"It would be you as their leader with Nizar the hardware merchant's son, and Ramji the eldest son of Karsan the builder. Then there's that idle son of Dhiraj your father has been talking about."

"But I hardly know them. Will they follow my wishes?" inquired Lalji.

"Leave that to me. I have spoken to Karsan and Noormohammed about that and they have both pledged their sons will do as you say. They have been waiting for such an opportunity for a long time to get their sons to Africa. They are good boys and want to succeed for their families. They need sound advice and guidance from someone who is mature and responsible. None of them are capable of it on their own. They all need to be led by someone sensible and smart."

"But I am eighteen and I think they are older," responded Lalji. The words seem to stop the *Sarpanch* in his tracks momentarily. He retorted dismissively, "*Arre!* When I was your age, I ran both the shop and farmed the land. And I did the accounts for my elder brothers. *Ability trumps age!*"

Having gulped the buttermilk in one long action with his head tossed back. Then he got up briskly to leave, adding, "I hear you have an Arab sea master in mind, Parshottam. For my part, I will speak to my contacts in Porbander to find out who they should contact in Africa. I suggest you start putting together enough food and grains for the journey for him." The two cobras were drowned in buttermilk.

For Lalji, events started to turn fast. That evening Nizar and his parents arrived to see Parshottam and his family. They wanted to talk about the journey and the future. Most of all they wanted to meet Lalji. The family lived in the Bohra Muslim Lane of the village and recognised each other from sight but had never talked before.

Nizar was tall and thin with ribs and collar bones visible under his white cotton kurta. He wore a skull cap and a well-trimmed beard. He had six younger siblings, four sisters and two brothers. His parents appeared more traditional and were not recent converts to Islam. His mother had pale forearms covered in blue polka dot tattoo patterns, visible when her sleeves pulled back. His father Noormohammed had a dark *zebiba* (prayer bump) in the centre of the forehead and a greying long beard. Noormohammed's eyes were friendly and warm, an air of dignity around him. Parshottam felt a sense of comfort meeting him. The two mothers embraced and introduced themselves, studying each other's faces.

Noormohammad spoke first. "We have come to make our acquaintance with you as our sons will be travelling to Africa together as brothers, sons of this village. We wanted to meet him and learn what his plans are. We must ensure the two of them can be of help to each other."

"You are most welcome *Bhai* (brother) and this must be Nizar. He and Lalji must talk and get acquainted. They also need to meet up with the other sons of the village going with them," advised Parshottam. Noormohammad agreed, asking who the other two companions were.

The mothers saw things differently from their husbands. There was an instant pact of understanding, communicated when their eyes met. Theirs was not a language of men. It came from being a woman, the homemaker with experience of withstanding the harsher times of life. They were lifelong understudies of their husbands. Both were aware of what the future could hold in store for their sons. There could be success and happiness or there could be tragedy and misfortune.

"Yes, soon they will be looking out for each other," announced Noormohammed.

"Indeed. They need to work out what they must do when they arrive and where they might stay. It's a journey I would have done myself at their age. There is much danger but also much to gain. *Prabhu-Kripa* (by God's mercy), they will illuminate the name of our village in that distant land," said Parshottam.

"*Inshallah!* (If Allah wills it!)" agreed Noormohammed.

Lalji and Nizar met the other two fellow travellers the next day. Ramji, the son of Karsan the builder, had little formal education. He could read Gujarati but writing was out of the question. He blamed it on the stiff thickened skin of his palms from years of working in the dust with his father. Yet, his percussion skills on *tablas* (pair of percussion instruments, played together) and the *dhol* (two sided drum) belied this excuse. He was much in demand for his musical talent at *bhajan* (religious song) and *dayro* (religious concert) evenings. There he was known for his dexterity when playing complicated *taals* (formula of beats). The eldest of six, he had his life's work cut out for him. He also knew his responsibilities extended to his siblings as well as to his parents. Life had become hard after the famines. Like the village river, work had almost dried up. The dust got into his eyes and ears and he had a constant cough.

The idea of travelling to Africa came from Ramji's father. He had heard how those who had ventured there in the last ten years were ready to return home laden with wealth. Ramji had built a house for a family whose sons returned regularly with enough wealth to keep the family back home comfortable. He heard they had gone into supplying provisions from the coast to towns inland in Tanganyika, a German part of Africa.

Ramji had met both Nizar and Lalji before but barely knew them. To him, they were also taking on the task of lifting their families out of the cycle of debt, poverty, and famine. From what little he knew of them he felt they were sensible companions to have going with him. He had heard the *Sarpanch* talking of Lalji's intelligence and of Nizar's level-headedness and felt comfortable joining them. Ramji's aim was to get to Africa and work in construction, earning enough to return home every year with his gains, before heading back. His comfort and pleasure were his *tablas* and *dhol* and they were going to go with him.

Bhasker, the last of the foursome, was there by virtue of his father's friend-ship with Parshottam. No one knew what skills he brought with him or how he would manage the expedition. From the perception Lalji had of him, he was nervous about handling Bhasker. Especially after the *Sarpanch's* reaction when he heard Bhasker was also going. His fears were not allayed after the three of them met up with Bhasker. Bhasker had an air of confidence and opti-mism around him. For Lalji this meant the young man either had little idea of what was in store for them or he had a matter-of-fact way of looking at things. Either way, he did not see Bhasker losing much sleep over tricky matters. But that could also be his strength thought Lalji.

At their first meeting, Ramji asked Bhasker, "What are your plans after you reach Africa?"

"I will do all I can to help you all and find work for myself. I will arrange rooms for us to stay and our meals. If required I will prepare the food myself," replied a confident Bhasker.

"And what is it you intend to do for a living?" asked Nizar.

"I would join up in any kind of work that's suitable for any of you. I know I have little experience of working but I will start earning as soon as possible and save enough to send back home. I know my responsibilities," Bhasker said pointedly.

Lalji was impressed at Bhasker's confidence. Something told him it was not false bravado, that it was genuine. He seemed to have in mind more pragmatic matters. Somehow, despite his constant chatter and laughing he came across as a determined individual.

"That's all very well but how are you intending to feed us? We don't want you learning on the job!" a bemused Ramji teased, before adding, "And what of Nizar's diet of meat and fish? What can you do there?"

"We are all going to be required to do things and act in manners we have not experienced before. It's Africa, far from home and a little wild. None of us should be going if we don't understand there will be challenges ahead, not knowing if things will work out. But we need to be ready to change plans because of circumstances and be ready to adapt," Bhasker replied. "And if I need to learn to cook for Nizarbhai in different ways, I will."

Everybody fell silent after that, absorbing Bhasker's comments.

"There will be no need for that Bhaskerbhai," reassured Nizar, "I am almost vegetarian as it is. Anyway, who can afford meat in these times? Whatever you can do will be accepted by us all, I am sure."

"Well said," agreed Lalji. Ramji nodded in approval.

"Tomorrow, we meet the *vaan* (dhow) master and plan things further," announced Lalji.

***

Dawood came with Yusuf after his cargo had been unloaded at the *bandar* (harbour) in Porbander. They all met at Parshottam's house with the fathers of the four passengers present. Dawood sported a greying goatee. His light hazel eyes with a hooked nose made him look like a character from the Arabian Nights. His manner was straight, he wanted to inform them about the passage, how long it would take. He said that unless they got blown off course, they would be arriving at the Sultanate of Mombasa in three to six weeks. He let it be known that all passengers sooner or later became seasick but that would pass.

Dawood's tall and thin stature was at odds with that of his brother Yusuf. Yusuf was darker in complexation with short, curly hair and a stocky shape which looked awkward balanced on his limp. He had wide, rounded shoulders and muscular arms. Lalji could not help wondering if they had different mothers.

The plan was to load more cargo in Yusuf's *vaan* and all passengers to be in the leading vessel of Dawood. They would have a minder for the journey who would guide them and cook for them. The loading should be completed within a few days and then they would wait for a favourable wind before setting off. Dawood gave the passengers a list of items to take along and informed them that there was malaria on the East African coast. Although hot and humid, they would be safe sleeping in nets once there.

"Smoking is prohibited on board at all times," added Dawood, which provoked a wince from Bhasker. "And if we are in difficulty, we will call for all hands on deck."

Dawood then explained he expected half the passage fare now and the other half in Mombasa. He suggested lodging the second half of the fare with Jethadas the jeweller. Jethadas had a cousin with a jewellery shop in Mombasa. His cousin would complete the transaction in Mombasa on the production of the relevant paperwork from Jethadas. Reassuringly, the full fare was to be paid only after the safe arrival of the passengers in Mombasa.

Lalji was relieved that the details were finally in place and they had met the two *vaan* masters. They seemed experienced and competent. At the same time, he suddenly had a feeling of dread at the prospect of going so far away to a foreign land and starting work there. He had never been on a boat before and the full weight of responsibility as a leader of the group dawned on him. Both thoughts filled him with self-doubt until he told himself that others had done it before. While the men had sat and chatted, the mothers and sisters had been listening from an adjacent bedroom window, out of sight from the Arabs. They had sat in statue-like silence, their saris pulled low over their heads as veils, hanging on every word spoken by the men outside. When the two *vaan* masters had taken their leave, the ladies emerged into the yard. Lalji's mother announced there should be a special prayer and *havan* (ritual fire used in Hindu ceremonies) for the seafarers before they left. All the 'boys' would take part, including Nizar if that was approved by his father.

"Allah's blessings upon you, *Bhabhijaan* (Urdu for brother's wife), for such a noble thought," responded Noormohammed to Rambai. "And I must arrange for the boys to attend a prayer with the Mullah for their safe passage," he added. There were nods of approval and a general buzz as everyone was energised into activity, like worker ants on a mission.

CHAPTER FOUR

JANKI WAS TWO years junior to Lalji, her fiancée. They had been betrothed to each other at the age of eight and ten. The families knew to each other and for years had traded in the same business. Lalji provided regular supplies to Janki's father in the next village, twenty minutes by foot.

Lalji had not developed any sense of attachment or responsibility for Janki. Everybody got married and every couple worked together to set up a family and a home. The roles of man and wife were different but complementary. After marriage, the bride came to live in the husband's family home, living in an extended family. She would be tutored by her new family in the ways of marriage. Her biggest responsibilities being running the kitchen and bringing up the children.

Most young brides were well versed with their expected roles and harboured dreams of having large families and good homes. Most had expectations of wealth in the form of jewellery and sons who would bring wealth. Gold jewellery was the currency of wealth and of savings. In good times it was sought as insurance against future downturns or major calamities.

Janki was still not mature enough to have set in her mind many wishes for her future. She had spent three years in school and afterwards had started to stay at home under the watchful eye of her mother and aunt. She helped with the daily chores and milked the family cow. She spent a lot of time with the calf and playing with her friends in the neighbourhood. Learning to cook and manage the kitchen was her aunt Lalbai's domain. Being the most recently married she was perfecting her skills. She was a patient teacher and fond of Janki. She was getting Janki to start estimating quantities, sift pulses and mix the dough for the *rotis* (flat bread). She did not trust Janki with the frying yet. Janki and her aunt had a secret pact of disappearing to the river every afternoon when her mother had a nap. They would go for a swim or pick berries along the trees of the banks and gossip. They would return to prepare tea for the family and start planning the evening meal.

Lalji had known that marriage and bringing Janki home was likely to be in the next few years. The plans for going to Africa put a different complexion on things. He felt a sense of responsibility to speak to his father-in-law, Gopalbhai, about his plans and to have words with Janki. The former was straightforward as he knew and conversed with his future father-in-law often. As regards Janki, he had never had a serious conversation with her before. He was not sure she would understand. He felt she was young and naïve. When he did tell Gopalbhai of his plans, adding he would be returning once he had set up something in Africa, he felt a burden lift. This was something which he had not been conscious of before. Gopalbhai was encouraging, citing the families he knew whose sons had ventured to Africa. He only gave one word of advice: not to leave his marriage too long into the future.

"A man is going to need two cooked meals a day and someone to keep home, a companion," he added. Lalji agreed and suggested it would be something to consider on his first return. He then popped into the home behind the shop to seek out Janki and his future mother-in-law.

They were both sitting on the ground in the shade, sifting moong grains, checking for grit. There was a soft murmur of an intimate conversation between mother and daughter. He announced his presence somewhat clumsily and greeted both.

The women greeted him with *'Jai Shri Krishna'*, and Gopalbhai's wife, Valbai, invited him to take a seat. "What a surprise to see you," exclaimed Valbai as Lalji's usual visits were to the shop.

"I wanted to come and give you some news," responded Lalji with an eye on Janki, who appeared taller since the last time he had seen her. "I am going off to Africa to find work and explore opportunities."

Janki had a fixed, wide smile as always but he noticed her look down at his announcement. "That is good news and when are you going?" asked Valbai after a thoughtful pause.

"I am leaving by *vaan* in the next few days. I will be returning next year to see the family and make more plans," he said, looking at Janki for a reaction.

Janki had made little eye contact but Lalji had noticed the dark mascara outlining her eyes which made her eyes look bigger and fixed his gaze. He realised, perhaps for the first time, that she was maturing into a beautiful, young woman. She bent lower to collect more grain and Lalji noticed for the first time a fullness of her chest, her breasts supported by her tight-fitting *choli* (bodice-like upper garment).

He was overcome by a feeling of excitement and noticed his breathing was faster. His throat had become dry and he was unsure what to say next.

"—that is good thinking," Valbai had been speaking in the background. "I am sure with your good nature and hard work you will be successful wherever you go. Just don't get too used to the lonely ways of life or lose yourself in too much work," she added.

"I thank you for your advice, *Baa* (Mother). I am going with three others from the village," responded Lalji.

"I will make some tea for us," uttered Valbai as she got up and disappeared into the kitchen. She needed a moment to reflect on the news. She also sensed that Lalji would appreciate the private time with Janki.

"So, what do you think?" he asked Janki as if he had been conversing with her all the time. He tried not to stare at her chest.

"You have made a decision for the future and by Krishna's grace everything will go well," Janki replied. Lalji noticed her left foot and ankle sticking out under her long dress. It was a pretty sight, her pale skin next to the colourful fabric. There were three tattooed dots just above the ankle, arranged like an upside-down triangle.

"*Our* future" emphasised Lalji, in a reflex. That brought out a small giggle from Janki and a flash of admiration for her future husband. It was the first time she had felt needed by someone else, of having a link to that person.

"What will you bring back for me?" she asked teasingly, but immediately felt childish for saying so.

Lalji laughed out loud at her question. "I don't know what there is that I can bring back for you but I promise I will have a lot to discuss about Africa and us," he answered.

Janki gave a small nod and took his hand into both of hers and said, "Go safe. I will be here waiting." Lalji noticed an impatience in Janki's eyes that reflected his own feelings in her presence.

When tea was served, Valbai was more inquisitive. "Where will you land and do you know anyone there? What work will you look for? Has the *vaan* done the journey before and is it a strong vessel?" Valbai fired off the questions without waiting for an answer; a sure sign the announcement had sunk in and her anxiety had surfaced.

Lalji was honest and answered as best as he could. He explained there were many unknowns and who the others going with him were. He told her he was going to be responsible for them and they would take up any reasonable jobs at first. Between them they hardly had any contacts to connect with there, but the *vaan* and the captain came recommended and sailed the route often. There were heading for the Sultanate port of Mombasa on the edge of British East Africa where they would seek work or head inland.

The British East African Railway had started construction in 1895. From what Dawood had told him the construction was moving further inland. Lalji was aware that all along the route there was a need to start settlements and businesses. Farming was being developed by the whites of the British Raj. According to Dawood, the old trades of ivory and animal skins still flourished but newer farmed crops meant a growth in trade. He explained the Raj maintained an Army inland to keep order which had to be sustained with supplies.

"If we are lucky to be at the right place at the right time, it should all go well," he said.

"You have a sound business mind so you should be able to spot something good," was his future father in law's observation, having joined them for tea. "Make sure you work for someone with a trustworthy reputation. If you are successful, you will want your younger brother to join you later," he added.

"Yes indeed," was Lalji's response. What was unsaid was that Janki would need to join him when circumstances allowed. It seemed to Lalji that now he had more clarity, and the more he talked of the prospects, the more impatient he became to get there.

***

The time leading up to setting sail had been frenetic with purchasing grains and dried fruits for the voyage. The families of all four travellers had arranged for them all to take part in their own traditional prayers.

All four were present for the visit to the tomb of Haji Osman Peer Baba and tied prayer ribbons to the window vents of the tomb for luck. All went to the *Devi Mandir* (Devi Temple) on the hill for prayers at dawn and brought back a coconut each to offer the great Ocean at the crossing of Socotra. Family *havans* (ritual fire used in Hindu ceremonies) were held and prayers were said in the mosque where the Mullah talked about the courage of youth venturing far afield. Lalji felt blessed, perhaps too well blessed as he had not been to so many religious events in such a short time. It was as if events had taken their own role in moving on and he soon lay to rest any notion of trying to control them. He realised what was happening also provided comfort for the folks they were leaving behind.

The night before sailing there was a noisy and jovial evening of *bhajans* and *dayro* (concert of religious songs) at Parshottam's yard where all four families attended. Almost the entire village came by at some stage of the evening. Everyone wanted to know what the four young men had planned, when they had planned it, and how they would manage the journey across the ocean.

Ramji was playing his *dhol* (two-sided drum) and *tablas* (pair of percussion instruments, played together), and all the musicians who were asked to come along attended. As a rule, the musicians did not charge for their service for *bhajan* (religious songs) evenings and held out their contribution as an offering to the service of God. Badru and Gulbanu from next door sang Krishna *bhajans* (religious songs for Lord Krishna) with great passion. The duo always guaranteed a healthy turnout with their fast beats and repetitious long chords. Badru was formerly known as Bhimji and he had converted to becoming a *Bohra* Muslim while his wife Geeta was now known as Gulbanu. Their enthusiasm for the *bhajans* (religious songs) had anything but dampened after converting to Islam. The bonds of culture, language and fraternity were no match for any religious ideologies to erode.

Janki and her family came and left early for their journey back. Parshottam kept repeating he was very happy to see them attend. Lalji was glad for another chance to see his fiancée. She looked more mature for her years with her hair tied up higher, revealing dangly earrings to match her colourful *chania-choli* (bodice-like upper garment with long skirt). He noticed her feet were decorated with henna patterns which added to the attractiveness of her long legs and slender body.

Thakorbhai, the village *Sarpanch*, decided he wanted to speak a few words at the event. On announcing his intention to do so, he sprung up from his seat to soft mumbles of protest and whispered jibes amongst the audience. The ladies present took the cue to disappear to the back of the yard where tea and snacks were being freshly prepared. There they could gossip out of earshot of the men.

On their return with the refreshments, the *Sarpanch* was in full flow. He was talking about Lord Ram having left home for a long exile, drawing inappropriate comparisons with the voyage of the 'four sons of this village'. Everyone was too polite to argue and sat in silence with long faces and heavy eyelids. All except the musicians who were engrossed in tuning and re-tuning their instruments. It surprised Lalji how the musicians always seemed to assume a licence to do as they wished. Even seasoned speakers managed to talk through their fiddling and tuning of their instruments. What seemed like an incompetent tuning up was belied when they burst into full gusto at the first sign the speaker had finished. Any semblance of applause intended for the poor *Sarpanch* was drowned out by the music. The audience awakened into a general buzz of low voices and stretches of backs, legs and necks. Teas were slurped and snacks hastily passed around.

The evening continued until the singers had exhausted their repertoire for all the Deities and Saints they could praise. Hasty goodbyes were said with arrangements to see the voyagers at the *bandar* (harbour) the day they sailed.

The next morning Dawood sent word that they would set sail in the evening. It was the 12th December 1904. All four passengers and crew from the two vessels sported fresh haircuts. By mid-afternoon there was a hive of activity around the two *vaans* as last-minute purchases of fresh produce were completed by the crew. The passengers were allowed a basket of personal foodstuffs and a large water container.

The four passengers arrived with their families and were introduced to Jaana, their minder for the journey. Jaana was a *Siddhi,* a man of African descent born and raised in Gujarat, near Gir. His father had been a sailor before him. Jaana was of medium build, had a boyish face with puffed cheeks which parted into a ready smile, revealing a wide gap between the two upper incisor teeth. His complexion was the darkest that Lalji had ever seen and became the talk of the four of them instantly.

All boarded the *vaan* to load their belongings. What looked like a high and giant structure from the ground suddenly felt restricted. Once on board they heard the groans of the ships timber heaving with the rocking of the vessel. The floor was uneven and soft with dampness. An unpleasant sweet smell percolated the air on board, changing from place to place according to the cargo.

"Have you seen how dark he is?" spurted out Ramji at the first opportunity when Jaana was out of sight.

"Enough to put the fear of demons in you," added Bhasker.

"He's the darkest man I have ever seen but he seems fine. He helped clean the berth when I arrived and brought me fresh water," said Nizar.

"He is who he is. He is here to help us. Remember he does this *safar* (journey) twice a year and is going to be our guide and friend. He speaks Gujarati and Arabic very well and I am told he will cook for us," said Lalji. "And as far as demons go you are going to a place largely unknown, where you may have much more to be afraid of."

The others nodded in nervous agreement, unrolling their mattresses and making good their bunks.

When Jaana returned he was carrying a small basket of dates for them. He sat down on the floor opposite them and started to inform them of the *vaans* daily activities. It did not amount to much and it seemed that there would be long periods of inactivity and sleep even for the crew. Catching the wind for the sail was always a top priority and the opportunity was never missed, day or night. It sounded as if there would be equally long stretches of continuous activity.

Ground rules were relayed. They were to move in twos until they were accustomed to the movement of the boat. No fire or naked light was allowed other than what was provided. Everybody was responsible for clearing up their own vomit and he advised against fatty and full meals. It was compulsory to hold the strap provided in the toilet box. Similar precautions of using the straps when bathing. The alarm for man overboard, fire, and vessel damage required everyone on deck to help. Fever had to be reported immediately so the person could be isolated.

Jaana had a unique way of relaying his messages that showed he had done it many times before. His voice would be low and sentences slow to introduce a new danger and then hasten into an excited pace ending with a giggle or laugh as he finished. All four hung on his every word and were mesmerised by his changing facial expressions and voice. Bhasker kept staring at the gap in his teeth, appearing and disappearing as he spoke.

He then took them to the cargo area which acted as ballast where the air was rancid and full of dust. Then he showed the middle living deck where everyone slept and where they would have to eat during rough weather. Lastly the top deck where there was the cooking area under a small tin roof. He showed them the tiller wheel and demonstrated the straps and ropes to hold onto when moving around. He showed them the toilet box and the shower area before demonstrating how to use them.

Back on the ground, goodbyes were said and packets of *mishri* (crystallised sugar) wrapped in red cloth were presented to the travellers. Each packet contained a coin for good luck. Hugs were exchanged, and the feet of elders were touched in exchange for slaps of blessings on their backs. Little was spoken as what was important had already been said before. Solemn mothers and sisters started to weep quietly while the men held their nervous silence. Within minutes the whole contingent of ladies had been overcome with a contagion of weepiness and sniffling.

There was a light breeze as they set sail into the evening twilight. All four passengers stayed on deck and watched as Porbander receded very slowly in the distance. Ramji remarked it was as slow as an oxcart and the others agreed with a giggle. Dawood and his tillerman were locked in conversation, following Yusuf's *vaan* which was ahead. Yusuf was busy studying the early stars of the evening and taking measurements on his *kamal* (navigation instrument).

Darkness fell quickly and the sky lit up with hundreds of stars. Jaana suddenly appeared with a dim lantern from below.

"We will sail at this speed until we get to the high seas. You may want to start thinking about retiring early for the night. On board, there's little to do after sunset. I suggest you sleep with empty stomachs tonight as it's your first night," he said. "Tomorrow we will talk about the ocean, the *vaans*, the traders and of Africa." The last word was said with a mysterious look on his face and bulging eyes, a loud chuckle exposing the teethy gap again.

They followed him into the sleeping cabin and made themselves comfortable. Bhasker looked unhappy with the listing and creaking of the boat. Jaana passed him a wooden pail, a quarter full of water and said sternly, "In case you need it, but don't go emptying it until full light."

Bhasker thanked him and looked relieved to have the pail near him.

"If you have any problem in the night, just shout out my name," said Jaana before leaving.

Just as everyone had settled down, Bhasker announced: "There may be mice and rats here but at least there are no ghosts on board!"

"How do you know that?" an intrigued Nizar asked.

"Because Bhasker's best friends are ghouls!" interjected Ramji, producing a laugh all around.

"I was told ghosts do not like the water," replied Bhasker in a serious tone.

"Maybe they don't like being sea-sick," added Lalji to further laughs. "Let's get a good night's rest. Tomorrow will be a very long day."

"*Shubh ratri (good night)*, everyone," from Ramji invited a chorus of the same from the others.

CHAPTER FIVE

THE NIGHT PASSED quickly enough despite the hard bunks, the listing, the groans and creaks of the boat. Bhasker appeared to have calmed down after he was presented with the bucket. Dawn arrived like a veil lifting over the eastern sky.

They were taken on deck by Jaana and met Dawood who greeted them in Gujarati and asked if they had a comfortable night. They were shown how to gather water for washing which was a two-man job. Nizar put a prayer mat down and prayed in the direction advised by a crew member. The others took turns to have a wash first before saying their prayers. Ramji led them with morning chants and slokas. Breakfast was served in a large metallic plate around which the five of them sat and ate together. Jaana had prepared a rice pudding with milk and dates. There was weak tea after.

The boat seemed to have picked up speed and Lalji noticed the full sail was up and was getting taut. The sea had lost its blue hue and was almost black. Dawood had a smile on his face and kept a constant eye on Yusuf's boat which was a safe distance alongside. Jaana cleared up and showed the four men where they could wash their plates and clean up in the future.

He then sat on a box and beckoned the four of them to sit.

"I am going to give you more information. Listen carefully and you will be safe," he began, breaking into his now-familiar grin. "We are now on the Indian Ocean and will be travelling westwards towards the Arabian Sea. The winds this time of the year allow straight sailing in the direction we want and we will pick up speed. You see that the colour of the ocean is black, like me," he laughed. He went on, "It's called *Kaala Paani* (black water) which you may have heard about. This is the deepest part. I know you can't swim so you need always be careful on the sides of the *vaan*."

"Has anyone fallen from this boat?" inquired Ramji.

"Once a sailor fell off the side in bad weather when he slipped on the deck. Luckily, he could swim and was seen."

"Do you know this is the only ocean in the world named after a people and their country?" asked Jaana with bulging eyes.

"No, I did not know that," replied Lalji and the others shook their heads.

"Then you won't know why. Let me tell you. For centuries these waters have been sailed by sailors from Arabia, India and even China. These countries have traded with each other and with Africa which was made possible by the monsoon trade winds. The boats are either heading to or away from *Hindustan* (India)."

"What about the Europeans?" asked Nizar.

"The Portuguese, British, French and Dutch competed in a race to reach India from Europe. They had to cross two oceans and only a few were successful at first. The Portuguese won the race but then the British sent the Company which started trading on a large scale from Calcutta. The others were slow and soon the Company was followed by bigger ships and then troops. Within a few decades, the Company controlled not just the trade but *Hindustan* itself." A mysterious tone had entered his voice. "Everything was turned upside down and the *firangi* (derogatory term for a foreigner) took over *Hindustan* as if it had always been theirs," he added, almost in a whisper.

"And they brought with them not just the guns but also their taxes. If you didn't die from the first, then the second killed you off slowly like poison," said Lalji. "Add to that our crops failing. When the famines came it meant that the people could not pay the taxes or feed themselves. This we all know from Porbander."

"And so, you are here to start a new beginning in Africa," announced Jaana with eyebrows raised.

"Tell us what Africa is like. And the people. Are there taxes like at home? Are there famines?" inquired Bhasker.

"Africa is largely unexplored by outsiders. There are few roads or towns. The weather is good on the coast but I have heard it is cold inland, where I haven't been," responded Jaana. He continued: "The people live under the Sultan's Raj on the coast. Inland there is much wildlife, including lions, elephants, snakes and crocodiles. Most of them are dangerous. The people of the coast are like elsewhere. Inland, the people belong to various tribes. Many wear little. They have strange languages and no knowledge of the rest of the world."

"How do they relate to outsiders?" asked Nizar.

"Most have never seen a white or brown man before so they will stare and examine you, sometimes for a long time. A few grow food, some keep livestock and some are hunters. There are few towns except where the Europeans started settlements. The Raj took a lot of Indians to these lands to build a railway which was dangerous because of the lions and elephants. But now the railway has started there is more movement of people into the interior."

"Are the Indians still there, the ones who built the railway?" asked Ramji.

"Many died during the building of the railway from disease or being eaten by lions. Most returned home at the end of their time and some stayed back to work the railways or start businesses," replied Jaana.

"And taxes or famines?" asked Bhasker again.

"On the coast, you pay tax to the Sultan. It is a fair tax. He taxes businesses and people for arriving there. You will need to put your name down in his *darbar* (administrative office) after you land. You are required to pay on arrival. I don't know what happens inland. I think the European *sarkar* (government) is fair with the taxes as they want people to stay," Jaana said.

"And the Africans inland, do they pay taxes also?" asked Lalji.

"The African people live amongst themselves. They don't know or understand money. They have only traded in goods or livestock in the past. And I have not heard of famines. The place is lush and has many jungles. The main danger is wild animals and disease."

"What are they growing as produce?" asked Lalji.

"The Europeans have started farms after clearing land. It has been slow as they need to teach the locals how to use tools. Many locals have held on to their old ways and don't see the point in changing," answered Jaana. "Some will grow their own crops and many have cattle and goats which need to be grazed."

"Do you have relatives there?" inquired Bhasker.

"Me?" answered back Jaana before bursting out into a roar of a laugh. "I was born and raised in Gir. My father was a sailor from the Swahili Coast and settled in Gujarat. I don't know anyone there and I can't speak their strange languages. They stare at me like I am a freak!"

The *vaan* was speeding up and pitching more forcefully, causing splashes of water to wet the deck. There was a commotion as Dawood busily barked orders to his men to adjust the sail. Jaana jumped up and disappeared in the direction of one of the sailors struggling to tie a wet cord to a hook.

The four passengers had lost all sense of time. When they thought only an hour had passed, Jaana looked at the sun in the sky and informed them it had been more than three hours. Suddenly, with a violent pitch and a roll, everyone's stomachs shifted skywards. The four passengers raced to the side of the boat to expel their breakfasts. Jaana could not stop laughing aloud. They decided to take to their cabins and lie down. The flat hard plank on their back provided solid support from all the rolling and pitching, calming their stomachs.

***

Life on board started to become familiar over the next few days. All four passengers had managed to train their stomachs to accept food and drink according to what was convenient or necessary. Hunger as a sensation seemed to have largely disappeared. Everyone seemed to have developed a tendency to lightly rock their bodies when sitting upright, even during calm sailing. Lying flat on the back gave the best relief from nausea. Lying down on their bunks was also a welcome respite during the afternoon sun, even though it could be stifling in the middle deck. The cowls provided a refreshing but damp breeze most of the time. Initial inquisitiveness and observation of the strange ways of life on board had led to a feeling of familiarity. This gave everyone a sense of security. Dawood knew misplaced confidence in non-swimmers on board could be dangerous. The sea and the weather were good reminders of the dangers and any sense of complacency faded.

The four passengers, or '*jehaji bhais*' (brotherly travellers) as Jaana referred to them teasingly, had started to add to the life on board in small ways. Ramji liked to lead prayers in the morning, and between him and Bhasker they became quite a duo singing *bhajans* (religious songs) in the evenings. Bhasker had an unrealised talent for singing. They soon became popular with the sailors who joined in after evening *namaaz* (prayer). They loved the intense fast beats of the *dhol* (two sided drum) and revelled in dancing to the beats. The Arab sailors went into raptures of laughter when Bhasker sang notes aloud and Ramji followed with identical sounds of the *dhol*. Ramji would often tease them on deck by mimicking the sounds and intonations of their shouts on his *dhol*. In the end, they started to call him the 'talking drum master'.

Nizar spent time with Jaana and a young sailor called Majid from Aden. Majid was fascinated by Nizar's decision to go to Africa and wondered how things might pan out. Although they could only converse with Jaana acting as interpreter, they were often discussing the duties of a Muslim man in a new country. Bhasker helped Jaana in preparing food such as chopping potatoes or advising him on how to use his spices better. His knowledge of spices and perfumes from his father's shop gave them something to talk about. It was soon clear that the food on board had started to taste different.

Nizar and Majid did their *namaaz* together. Majid would advise on the direction of Mecca and talk of his wish to go on the *Hajj* (Islamic pilgrimage to Mecca). *Namaaz* on board was staggered so that there was always someone managing the tiller with one lookout. Everyone seemed to be engaged with some sort of daily religious activity except Jaana. He usually joined in the *bhajans* (religious songs) playing cymbals and was occasionally seen whispering to the evening sky with his eyes shut.

"Jaana, who do you talk to in the sky?" asked Ramji one day.

"I talk to my ancestors. I ask them for answers to my problems," replied Jaana.

"And do you get answers?"

"Sometimes."

"What if you don't?" asked Ramji.

"Then I will ask *Kaali* (Godess Kaali) to take the problem away."

"Do you mean *Kaali Mata*?"

Laughing out loud Jaana replied, "Yes, the same Mother Goddess you know."

"But how come …."

"My father only ever talked to his ancestors. He would become quiet and unhappy when something kept bothering him. My mother started going to a *Kaali Mata Mandir* (Kali Mata Temple) after she saw her long hair and black face. She prayed there and found much peace. She told my father to do the same. She said *Kaali* was from Africa like us, and carried weapons like African people."

"How do you ask her to help?" inquired Ramji.

"I light a *diya* (lamp) and pray to her. Let me show you her image," said Jaana and produced a small image of *Kali Mata* from a folded leather holder in his pocket. Ramji was barely able to identify the familiar image of the Goddess on the fading picture.

From then on Ramji and Jaana were often engrossed in conversations about religion. Ramji took it on himself to explain to Jaana the relationships between *Kaali Mata* and *Shiva*. Then with *Ganesh* and *Kartik*. Then *Amba Mata* and *Kali Mata*. Jaana had been to *Somnath Shiv Mandir* (Temple of Lord Shiva in Somnath) but had little idea of the relationships. He was fascinated that *Shiva* was the consort of *Kali Mata*. The more he learnt, the more he wanted to know about these deities.

One day Lalji asked Jaana how he felt as the only non-Muslim on the crew.

"Dawood and Yusuf like it. They ask me to pray when times are bad. They tell me to start praying while they attend to the *vaan* if there is danger," replied Jaana.

"Why is that?" asked Lalji.

"There was a time some years ago during a heavy storm when it felt like the sea was going to swallow up both *vaans*. We got separated from Yusuf and we thought we had lost his *vaan*. Dawood had lost all his colour and was scared. I had never seen him like that. We had a Hindu Priest with us going to Africa and he told Dawood not to worry. Then he recited some prayers for an hour and when he finished the sea had settled down. It was as if there had been no storm that night. The next morning, we spotted Yusuf's *vaan*. Ever since then, Dawood and Yusuf like prayers to be said on board. They say it does not matter whose God saves us if the prayers are heard."

***

Over the following days, Lalji spent more time on deck talking with Dawood. One day he was peering into the distance when he thought he saw a shiny object in the expanse behind them. The sun was out but the visibility was hazy. It was early morning and most people were engaged in preparing or eating breakfast on both the *vaans*. Dawood noticed him observing a point and pulled out his looking glass. Once again there was a momentary glimmer of light which they both saw. Suddenly there was pandemonium as Dawood started shouting orders to his men and sails were rigged to increase speed. A series of signals were sent to Yusuf ahead to do the same. Within minutes the haze cleared to reveal a small Arab vessel with no identifying features. It was too small to be carrying much cargo and seemed to be heading straight at them.

"Who are they and what do they want?" inquired Lalji.

"They are pirates," replied Dawood. "Thankfully you spotted them in time and I think we can outrun them."

"Pirates this far out and in a small boat?" asked Lalji.

"Yes, it's usually a small crew and they are looking for ivory or gold. They will be armed and can catch up with us easily as they are a lighter vessel. But we have a head start now and if we get into choppy seas, they will have to give up the chase," said Dawood.

Up ahead, Yusuf had already altered direction southwards and was sailing full sail. The pirate vessel was also at full sail and Lalji could make out the shape of someone in the front pointing a musket. It looked to Lalji that they were gaining speed faster but Dawood seemed unperturbed. He had clearly been in this position before.

A few shots rang out from below the stern. Large plumes of white smoke appeared. Three of Dawood's sailors reloaded and fired again. Yusuf's men also followed with a ring of shots. The pirate vessel was gaining speed with the gap between Dawood's *vaan* and it getting smaller. More shots rang out from below deck but there was no return of fire. They saw only one musket and the rest of the pirates were armed with swords. With less than fifty yards between the two vessels the shouting from the pirates could be heard. Further shots rang out in unison from below deck. The pirates appeared to duck and the shouting stopped. The show of firepower seemed to have a sobering effect on the pirate vessel. Suddenly the main sail was lowered and the chase was given up. Everybody on board cheered and Dawood was relieved and sported a big smile. The four *jehaji bhais* (brotherly travellers) were jubilant having seen the spectacle. A couple of the musket-waving sailors started dancing and Bhasker was quickly on deck with Ramji's *dhol* (two sided drum) to add to the celebrations.

Dawood walked up to Lalji and said, "*Shukran* (Thank you)," in a loud voice and embraced him. Lalji was not quite sure why his intervention was deemed so valuable.

From then on whenever Lalji appeared on deck Dawood would take time to speak with him. Very soon they started discussing trade. Lalji was fascinated by the riskiness of Dawood's business but saw the reward of conveying high-value items as a decent trade-off.

One day Dawood asked him: "What do you intend to start doing when you get to Mombasa?"

"I will find some work in one of the newer businesses. That will start me off. Then I want to start my own business, by moving inland along the new railway. I am told there are many trading posts along the new railway where it is possible to start trading."

"Yes, the taxes inland will be less. What about your friends?" asked Dawood.

"We intend to stay together whether we do the same work or not," replied Lalji.

"Yes, it is safer to go in numbers. There is much that is different there. The place to do business is with the new settlers along the railway. I am told the weather is more pleasant inland."

***

Socotra was a halfway point and a good trading post to pick up fresh supplies. Where vessels did not have business in Aden, they would berth at Socotra, saving some sailing days. The small island was a curiosity for Europeans who had envisaged it as a strategic location on the route to India. The Portuguese and later the British used it as a staging point. It seemed to lack any other purpose. The British leased the Island from the Omanis and it became a 'flag-pole island'.

It was a busy little place with smaller vessels mooring and larger ones heading to and from Aden. Aden on the southern tip of Arabia, was the commerce capital of the region. Many Gujarati sonis were established for generations, dealing in gold and silver as the ocean trade currency. Nizar mentioned he had not seen so many vessels with different markings. Some were sailing vessels made from wood and others were European steamships, made partly or fully of metal.

Dawood was watching supplies being loaded on board when Nizar and Bhasker joined him. Bhasker asked him about the many vessels present. "How come so many seafaring nations are here?" he asked.

"Trade and supplies with Europe, everything comes here, from *Hindustan* (India), China and the East."

"Some of these ships are massive."

"In one direction comes fabrics, silk, spices, ornaments, jewellery, gold, silver. The other way there is little to trade, especially after the end of the slave trade. There is a small trade in muskets and cannons, and the new African Colonies provide some ivory and animal hides."

"So how can they afford to trade?" asked Bhasker.

Dawood laughed at the question, raising his eyebrows. "How do you think?" he asked.

Bhasker shrugged his shoulders.

Dawood continued, "By shipping back to the source the finished product, like cloth. The East India Company bans anyone from producing locally or competing with them. And of course, it collects taxes."

"What about slaves? Do they still deal in slaves?" inquired Nizar.

Dawood smiled. "After opposition at home, the slave trade slowed down, then stopped. Although slavery continues. They now have a new form of cheap labour for the plantations of the colonies, bonded people known as indentured labourers. For a free passage and a small wage, they work seven days a week, living in harsh conditions. The length of the contract is usually ten years before one is free to leave."

"Is this what the Raj called the *'Great Experiment'?*" asked Lalji, who had arrived and had been listening.

"Yes, and so successful it is that the other European powers have started their own. The Arab slave traders lost the slave trade and continued trading other goods along local routes. We also started to bring more passengers who wanted to travel to start new ventures in Africa, free from the indentured ticket."

"So how do the indentured recruits select their destinations?" inquired Nizar.

Dawood chuckled and went on, "Having little knowledge of their destination, the illiterate *'coolies'* (derogatory term for Indian people, porters or labourers) thumb-printed their agreement to the contract. It was never a choice of whether you were going to Africa, the Caribbean, Malaysia or Fiji. You were landed where there was a need. Families would be split up on the route, to satisfy the demand for labour at landing points. Tens of thousands died on their fateful journeys from lack of food, water or disease. Many were children sent by desperate parents who thought they might be a better future across the seas."

Dawood pointed out the marked mooring spaces for the bigger *coolie* steamships. Names such as *Zenobia, Peterborough, Gainsborough, Suffolk, Malabar, Umvoti, Carnatic* and *Copenhagen*. "Their destinations are as different as their names and many of these ships transported slaves in the past," he added.

Lalji fell silent contemplating the enormity of the trade. The deceit and the hopelessness of those who had made the choice to sail for an unknown destination despite the risks. An inhospitable destination, that was all too often a one-way passage.

With a sharp yell, one of the sailors announced the loading was complete. Dawood and Yusuf allowed everyone a two-hour break before heading off on the next leg to the East African Swahili Coast. This was an opportunity to check out the local shops and drink fresh coconut water. Supplies and drinking water were restocked.

For Indian *yatris* (travellers), Socotra held a special significance. It was a halfway point to East Africa and was soon to be followed by the equator. The sea here and the changeable winds of the equator demanded healthy respect from both sailors and travellers alike. Vessels could become stationary for days. Equally, strong winds with changeable directions could be whipped up with the risk of being blown off course.

All had their way of paying respects to this sea. On reaching the appropriate point between Socotra and the equator, the four *jehaji bhais* said a special *shanti path* (Hindu prayers for peace). They offered their coconuts as an offering to the sea of Socotra, having first painted Hindu Swastikas in red vermillion on the coconuts. As always, Ramji led the prayers and all on board joined in.

A special *namaaz* (prayer) was said by Yusuf on behalf of the two vessels with everyone present. There was anticipation in the air as the halfway mark had been reached and within another few weeks, they would be setting foot on African soil.

CHAPTER SIX

THE PASSAGE BETWEEN Socotra and the horn of Africa was uneventful. Closer to the equator the sailors became anxious, and were hoping for a passage that would allow the *vaans* through unimpeded. The sail had been flagging at times and the acceleration felt with a full head of sail had disappeared.

On the day of crossing the equator a storm had been building up from the northeast, and the winds it brought gave them that extra push to get further south. A few streaks of lightning followed, causing concern to the sailors, but before dawn it was all over. The four *jehaji bhais* had been told that the most feared things at sea were the *rukudon* (doldrums) and then fire. At least with fires you could take your chances, but a lame *vaan* stuck without wind was at risk of running out of supplies. When the winds picked up it was easy to get lost because of their erratic directions.

Daylight brought a fresh feeling of hope and the sun shone brightly in the blue, morning sky. Everybody took courage from the speed and acceleration the *vaan* was gaining. Bhasker sang some folk songs about the coming of the dawn and of boatmen who took travellers across to the other side.

Jaana was his usual happy soul and had struck up a good friendship with Bhasker. Music and rhythm were strong reasons for their friendship. When time allowed Bhasker would put the *dhol* (two sided drum) around Jaana's neck and stand opposite him, playing a few beats of a *taal* and then ask Jaana to do the same. After a few attempts and failures, Jaana would revert to his own beat and start to sing off-key, much to the disgust of Bhasker and laughter of all around.

Lalji was either reading old newspapers or magazines in English or Gujarati. His command of English suffered from a big gulf between comprehension and speaking or writing. He understood almost everything in the English newspapers he had brought from Porbander. His fluency in Gujarati was without fault. He liked the straight language of the newspapers to the flowery language of the magazines.

Occasionally Dawood would seek out Lalji and talk to him about trade. He confided in Lalji that when he had more capital, he was interested in trading silk and china from the Far East. At present, he owed money for his *vaans* and the transition was too risky.

"Who in Africa wants silk?" inquired Lalji. Dawood explained it was not for the African market but for the Arabian market. From there he would continue acquiring nuts, dried fruits and wooden furniture to trade in Africa. Dawood seemed to look better after his chats with Lalji.

One day Lalji asked Dawood if he should remain on the coast or head inland when they reached Mombasa.

"Inland my friend. I know you must shepherd your friends and you all need to work. There will be more to do inland than at the coast where businesses are already running," replied Dawood. "I also think the coast is unstable politically. The Sultan of *Jungbar* (Zanzibar) ceded his territory on the mainland when the Germans surrounded his Island twenty years ago. He has been given a small strip of land along the coast by the British and Germans. He is not a happy man."

Dawood informed Lalji that Mombasa was still in a state of flux after the changes. The British were interested in its value as a seaport with their focus on the new territories inland up to the Uganda Protectorate. Their investment had been in the Uganda Railway which had been completed three years ago.

Lalji nodded thoughtfully.

"Start discussing your plans with your friends. The progress we are making means we should be stopping at Lamu in the next seven to ten days and then head to Mombasa," advised Dawood.

***

The crew and passengers remained well throughout the voyage. Most complained of frequent loose stools and always suffered if they had taken in more than the minimal at meals. Ramji showed signs of weight loss but remained cheerful. Bhasker was quicker to vent his discomfort. Nizar had an unfortunate disagreement with a curried fish when temptation took the better of him. The bout of vomiting lasted almost three days and his already slim body started to shrivel away under the drab fabric of his oversized clothes. Jaana was a good nurse and fed him molasses water and lemon to get fluid into him and give him energy.

Most of the issues that arose with the passengers on board were to do with being confined to a small space and adapting to constant movement. Sooner or later, someone would become complacent and suffer the consequences. On one such occasion, Ramji had decided to attend to his toilet needs without an escort. It was a relatively calm day and he had decided not only to go it alone but also dispense with the need to use any ropes or harnesses. A gust of wind almost blew the basket horizontal from its hanging position over the side of the *vaan,* with a nude Ramji about to fall into the sea. He managed to grab hold of a rope and shouted for help. One of the sailors heard him and burst out laughing at the scene. Ramji was holding on for dear life, at the same time trying desperately to grab his *dhoti* (traditional attire for men) from the side of the basket. All on board saw the spectacle and couldn't stop laughing. It became a repeated joke about the look on Ramji's face, trying to decide between holding the rope or grabbing his *dhoti*.

The brief stopover at Lamu hardly caused any delay. Fresh food was picked up and they were on their way again. On a cloudy morning of Sunday, the 19th of February 1905, land was spotted and soon they saw the tell-tale signs of the white minarets and the Fort at Mombasa. They had been at sea sixty-nine days. The *azan* (call to prayer) from the Mosque was heard intermittently when the wind allowed its direct transmission to the *vaans*. All the sailors except Dawood and Yusuf bent down in prayer towards Mecca.

Dawood and Yusuf were studying the winds and taking note of the current while looking for a break in the canopy of clouds. The Lamu stop had been much more straightforward, with not much in the way of hazards. The Mombasa coral reef was a different matter. A mile off the coast they were met by a small boat of local Arab fishermen who were available for a price to pilot them through to Mombasa harbour. Negotiations were entered into and the payment was to be a mixture of spices and dried fruits. It was planned to go through a reef break later in the morning when the light would be better. Each *vaan* would be guided by one of the fishermen and Yusuf would take his *vaan* through first.

With the *vaans* at the mercy of the wind and coastal currents, it required the full concentration of the crew to manoeuvre the boat through the gap. There were a lot of orders and shouting as sailors tried to make themselves heard. One was perched high on the mast with his left leg hooked on the top of the sail. His job was to look out for small jutting areas of coral below the surface.

It seemed to take forever to navigate the first *vaan* through the gap. Once they were through there was loud cheering by all from both *vaans*. Then Dawood's pilot asked for the sail to be hoisted just enough to command a speed to allow control over the force of the current. This allowed a slow and careful passage through the gap, guided by the first *vaan's* wash. Once through, they headed towards the whitewashed buildings of the old town with the ghostly image of Fort Jesus on the left of the harbour.

A feeling of excitement leapt inside Lalji's chest and he sensed he was staring at the land of his future, his destiny and his fate before him.

As soon as the *vaans* came through the reef they were surrounded by a few small boats of scouting traders, asking what was being brought in. By the time the harbour formalities had been finished and taxes paid there would be the appropriate traders waiting on shore to make deals. Yusuf had already mentioned there were four young men, settlers from Porbander who would need a room and meals.

By the time they reached the Old Mombasa harbour, it was stifling hot and the sun high in the sky with large breaks in the clouds. The atmosphere felt oppressive with the humidity of the old town. Dawood informed the *jehaji bhais* that he would be in Mombasa for the next four days before moving on to *Jangbar*, (Zanzibar). They should make their way to the accommodation hostel after docking. He said he would catch up with them the next day to settle their fares. He would be staying in the *vaan* all the time.

There was a lot of commotion at the old harbour with teams of men pulling ropes to dock the *vaans* into their berthing positions. Once there, the four passengers went into their living quarters to gather their belongings. Then followed a series of handshakes with the sailors. Jaana was in no hurry to say goodbye, having got accustomed and close to the four for whom he felt a sense of responsibility. He said he was coming along to see them settle into their hostel.

A small, tubby Gujarati man, sporting a thick curly moustache, was waiting at the harbourside for the new arrivals. His clothes and turban needed a good wash but he had a cheery smile. He called out in Gujarati at the four before they disembarked: *"Jai Shree Krishna.* I am Premlal Joshi and I run the vegetarian hostel where we have rooms. How many of you are there?"

"Four," replied Lalji.

"That's fine," was the reply. "We are not too far from here and you can walk with me."

"Namaste Premlalbhai! (Greetings Premlalbhai!)" bellowed Jaana who had appeared, the gap in the teeth showing like an absent door.

"Namaste Jaanabhai. Good to see you again. Come and help these four young men get to my place and join us for a proper hot VC meal!" ordered Premlal.

"You know I could never refuse that," chuckled Jaana.

Bhasker, Nizar and Ramji were asking each other what 'VC' stood for when Lalji overheard them. "It stands for *vegetarian cuisine* usually provided by a Brahmin cook," he informed them. A Brahmin serving his vegetarian food meant everybody could eat it, without any concern about contamination from meat.

After introductions, Premlal told Jaana he would set the four youngsters on the route to Nairobi.

"There is no work in Mombasa unless you have money to start a new business," he informed them.

Hostel rates were not mentioned at this stage. It was understood that despite being the only VC hostel for men, there was unlikely to be any excessive charging.

Carrying their belongings the four found walking on the ground slow and tricky at first as their brains were still in *vaan* mode. They were led through the narrow streets of Mombasa, past carved ornate front doors of living quarters. They passed small dingy shops with sparkly dust floating in the air, lit up by shards of sunlight.

They passed small warehouses full of bags of dried fruits and others where arcs of ivory were lined up on the floors, numbered in black lettering. They came across old men chatting, seated on mats on the ground, sipping hot black coffee poured from a brass *kahvah* (coffee) dispenser. The dispenser was strapped to the back of the *kahvah* man, a pouring pipe reaching just above one shoulder. Holding a cup to the spout, the man would bend his spine to get the hot coffee to dispense.

"They say the *kahvah* keeps you cool on a hot day," said Premlal. He was full of questions and information, barely pausing for an answer or even a breath. How long were they going to stay in Mombasa, did they have relatives or friends who were waiting for them up country, had they any jobs in mind? He proceeded to explain some local procedures and customs. He pointed out the vegetable market and completely ignored the fish market next to it. He also pointed out provision stores and introduced the owners to them. Before long they reached the 'Premlal Joshi VC and Hostel'. The name was emblazoned above the two-door entrance in red Gujarati letters.

Premlal's hostel had a shop front from where he sold freshly cooked snacks to passers-by. There was seating on a couple of tables for customers who wanted to eat in. Most of his regulars preferred to go through to a small hall at the back, next to the kitchen where they could sit in rows on the floor. There they would be served directly from the kitchen. The hostel guests also ate there.

Their rooms were off a small corridor and Premlal opened two for them. Each was neat and immaculately clean with no furniture apart from a chair. The floor was large enough for two sleeping mattresses to be rolled out in each room. There were two small windows on one side and the tin roof was pitched on wooden joists. The bathing facility was a standpipe and a bucket in the yard outside, next to a clothesline behind a fabric screen. All guests were responsible for washing their own clothes.

Premlal invited everyone to come and be seated so that lunch could be served. His wife was baking hot *rotis* (flat breads) on a wood fired stove and welcomed everyone. The food was served by an African maid. Everyone ate well, happy to have the taste of home cooking again.

"You will find your appetite will come back quickly now you are on land," said Premlal.

***

The next morning the four set out for the *vaan* at the harbour. They had to complete the arrival registration and pay Dawood. The Soni counted the Indian Rupee notes and coins, which was the legal currency in British East Africa. He counted out what Dawood had requested in cash and then paid the balance in gold.

At the Registration of Aliens Office, also known as the old Liwali's Office, there was a wiry bespectacled Goan clerk. He wrote their names in a thick ledger book. All their names and where they came from, their ages and where they were heading next. All said Nairobi was the destination. The clerk assigned each of their forenames with "*bhai*" after their forename, meaning "brother" as in Gujarati tradition.

Lalji noticed that Nizar had been assigned '*bhoy*' instead of '*bhai*' and asked if it was a mistake. The clerk replied in broken Hindi that all Muslims preferred to spell it that way. Nizar stepped up saying he preferred the same spelling of '*bhai*' like his friends, much to the annoyance of the clerk.

A telegraph message was sent to Lalji's father from the Post Office. It stated the date of the telegraph and Mombasa Telegraph Office at the top. They abbreviated their message to the least so as not to incur higher costs. The telegraph message read: 'REACHED MOMBASA GOING NAIROBI ALL WELL STOP'. The news would spread like wildfire in the village in four hours.

They walked the narrow streets of old Mombasa and before long were completely lost. Hot and sweaty, they came across a small commercial area with an assortment of shops from grocery and provision shops to fabric shops. The fabric shopkeeper realised they were young settlers and called out to them, asking if they wanted a drink of cool water. Everyone accepted willingly and sat on the step outside the shop.

The shopkeeper introduced himself as Narshidas Bhogani from Jamnagar in Gujarat. He asked them what their plans were. He confirmed that going inland was better for opportunities compared to staying in Mombasa. His shop was double-fronted and manned by Narshidas and his two younger brothers. They had started as a small retail shop importing cheap cotton fabric from India. Later, they realised the potential for supplying up-country. They remained in Mombasa to receive the imported goods. One of the three brothers travelled inland with new stock to sell to retailers.

Lalji noticed so many of the larger shops were family businesses shared by brothers or father and sons. They came across Karimjee and Sons, Hardware Merchants. Alibhai and Sons were a provision store that also supplied kitchen wares. Lalji Jethwa was also a family shop owned by four brothers supplying homeware items and small items of furniture.

Narshidas invited them to lunch at his home but the four politely declined, citing they had a meal arranged at the hostel. He asked if anyone could read English and Lalji volunteered he could but not very well.

"Oh good!" he exclaimed. He brought out an old, tatty flyer from a drawer and asked if Lalji could read aloud from it. The flyer was advertising services of established businesses in Mombasa.

There were names of businesses like Sorabjee M, Mody Brothers and A Alladina Visram who were forwarding agents in Mombasa. All were available to receive or send goods to India or Europe. Narshidas nodded his head as if he was acquainted with them. Then there was also Smith McKenzie and Company but Narshidas shook his head and said they were a European store that only imported from Europe.

Lalji asked if the European businesses were successful.

"Not always," replied Narshidas. "There is a lack of skills in most places. Small European businesses cannot manage the responsibility that goes with becoming chief agents. Even the larger ones cannot grow because of a lack of skilled staff," he added.

"Are there no new Europeans coming?" asked Lalji.

"There are, but as many return as arrive. They prefer to set up farms inland but that can be a headache because of land disputes with the local tribes. Then there is the issue of the heat and diseases, which does not suit their women and children," replied Narshidas. He went on, "See, there is a new hotel here in Mombasa for Europeans called 'Hotel Cecil' which opened last year. Its business is so unpredictable that rarely has it been full since it opened."

"What about those on contracts, like in the Civil Service and police, do they not stay longer?" asked Lalji.

"Some do as they are on a steady income. They get paid in English Pounds and Shillings if they are from England while everyone else deals in Indian Rupees. Many children are sent back to Europe to boarding schools and only return once a year. That causes a lot of frustration for the wives. It's a tough time for most Europeans."

Lalji mulled over the conversation at great length in bed at night. "There is opportunity here which needs exploring," he thought. With that recurring thought and after the trumpeting of mosquitoes in his ears stopped, he fell asleep, wondering what Janki would be doing.

CHAPTER SEVEN

NIZAR HAD GONE out early the next morning to pray at the Mosque and returned to find Bhasker sitting outside the hostel, practising his *tablas* (pair of percussion instruments, played together) . He had gathered half a dozen children who stared at him from a distance.

"So how was *namaaz*?" asked Bhasker.

"It was good to attend. The place was crowded. Someone asked me something in Swahili or Arabic and when I could not reply they all had a good laugh. I think they thought I was deaf," said Nizar. "Where are the others?"

"Ramji is still in bed; he thinks he has a fever and his cough is back. Lalji was talking to the owner."

Lalji had been thinking and planning that morning after his conversation with Premlal. The railway journey to Nairobi was overnight and Premlal had recommended a friend's hostel in Nairobi for young men.

Premlal had asked Lalji directly, "Have you any idea what job you and your friends want to do?"

"I will start with something in the retail area as I have some experience. Most of us are traders from Gujarat and can adapt. Ramji was in the building business, but I would need to start some trade of my own at some stage," said Lalji.

"I think that sounds good but be careful as many have failed here. So many of the railway construction workers went back to India as they saw no long-term future in small businesses. They were mainly from Punjab, and in their case a lifetime of commerce was of little interest to them. They would probably have stayed on as farmers but the Colonial Office has reserved the best land for whites only, in the Highlands beyond Nairobi," explained Premlal. "But with determination and teamwork, someone with a mind for business can do well here. There are opportunities which are waiting to be spotted."

Lalji was glad to hear that as it confirmed his thoughts from the night before. "What about you Premlal? Have you no desire to do more?" asked Lalji.

"You misunderstand my work here," replied Premlal. "I am a Brahmin and my father and uncles were always *Pujaris* (Hindu priests) working in *Mandirs* or *Havelis* (Hindu temples). I am not interested in business but came here at the request of the *Pujari* in Jungbar (Zanzibar) who is a cousin of mine. He said there was a need for a hostel with VC food in Mombasa because of the rise in numbers of young men coming to start a life here. One day I will be going back to my own *Mandir* in Gujarat when I am not required here anymore."

Lalji wondered if that ambition would ever get fulfilled. To his mind, this was a land where the needs of the settlers and populace were greater than could be met. The structures for governing the country seemed undeveloped compared with the civic organisations back home. Yet it was precisely this which attracted Lalji.

After lunch, the four *jehaji bhais* (brotherly travellers) sat down to discuss the next leg of the journey. Lalji led the discussion by asking if they were still of the same resolve as when they set off from Porbandar. Everyone confirmed they were, much to his relief. Ramji, who was feeling and looking better after his rest was keen to set off at the earliest.

They discussed getting on with finding work after reaching Nairobi. Lalji suggested trying the retail trade first as they all had some experience of it. Ramji could also look for any possible openings in construction.

***

The Mombasa-Nairobi train was due to leave at six in the evening. Premlal had prepared a light meal they could have for supper and a bag of mangoes with bananas for breakfast. He provided the details of his friend Raman Bhatt who ran a guest house for vegetarian travellers in Nairobi.

The ticket office sold first, second and third-class tickets. First was for whites only, Second had bunks and accommodated three to a compartment while Third Class was hard bench seating with barred open windows. Being on a budget they opted for Third and were relieved to see three other groups of new immigrants on the platform. One was a newly married couple. The husband had been in Nairobi a year and just returned by a European steamer with his bride.

Lalji was intrigued to see the contrast between the man and his wife. He was dressed no different from most who wore either a *dhoti* (traditional attire for men) and shirt with a *pugdi* (turban), or substituted the *dhoti* with a cotton *patloon* (trousers). The wife, however, was wearing a scarlet and gold sari pulled down at the front into a veil so no more than her mouth and nose stud were visible. She was heavily bedecked with gold bangles and a *Mangal Sutra*, her matrimonial necklace. She could have been wearing her wedding outfit, thought Lalji. They were clearly going to be received in Nairobi by relatives and he wondered when he would be bringing Janki here the same way. To his surprise, the newlyweds had also purchased third-class tickets.

Goodbyes were exchanged on the platform after the carriages rolled in alongside the platform. The engine driver was a middle-aged Sikh dressed in black overalls. His turban was blackened with soot and grease but a glint of orange showed in each fold on one side revealing the original colour. The noise from the steam vents and valves from the engine roared deafeningly and the black steel wheels, almost as tall as a man, slowly ground to a halt. Anyone about to board the train was struck in awe of the Raj who could not only make the machinery but transport it across the world, then commission it to run in a new country. Ramji noticed a group of white soldiers smoking on the platform. Like in India they were on duty for train security and would accompany the guard in his compartment.

Nizar and Ramji were in deep conversation with Premlal about stopping and praying at the tomb of Seyyid Baghali located two hours out of Mombasa. Seyyid Baghali was a Muslim indentured labourer who had worked on the railway when it was constructed. He was well known for his physical strength and various miraculous feats were ascribed to him. It was becoming customary for the train to stop on request at the place of his tomb. The place was known as "McKinnon Road," and passengers were allowed off the train to pray for a safe journey. If no stop had been requested the train drivers would slow down to a crawling pace and blow a long whistle in salute. Premlal suggested the four travellers should stop and pray at the tomb. Lalji reflected on the prayers said at the Socotra crossing a few days earlier for the same purpose. At precisely six o'clock, the whistle was blown by the station master. The guard was dangling out of his compartment with his green flag ready to wave it once everyone was on board. The engine driver blew two loud and long whistles to encourage any stragglers to get on board.

Once on their way, the train seemed to linger at a man's walking pace for some considerable time. There was an immediate incline to start with and it would remain much the same all the way to Nairobi, sitting at an altitude of five and a half thousand feet. The journey took between 13 to 14 hours; much depended on wild animals on the tracks.

The sun had gone down quickly and it had become pitch dark, with a cool breeze blowing in their faces. On reaching McKinnon Road they, along with a few others, were escorted by two soldiers to the tomb of Seyyid Baghali where they bowed in respect. Nizar led the prayer asking for a safe journey to Nairobi. Within minutes they were back on the train, the soldiers stubbing out their cigarettes on the side of their wagon.

The carriage was quiet, each one lost in their thoughts or dozing off. Lalji found himself thinking more of Janki, her eyes and her anklets. Bhasker was humming a tune absent-mindedly.

A few hours after the McKinnon Road stop there was a sudden screeching of the brakes and whistle blowing from the engine, outside a place called Voi. All in the third-class compartment had been asleep, some with blankets covering bodies and faces to keep out the mosquitoes. They looked like corpses lined up in a morgue. Startled, everyone sat up as the guard and two soldiers rushed up to the front of the train on the outside. Someone in the dark asked the guard what the matter was and he whispered back, *"Elephants!"*.

After remaining stationary for a good half hour, they heard a rifle shot, the whistle was blown and the engine started puffing back into life. This time the speed was slower as the driver and his assistant, aided by one of the soldiers, were peering in the darkness ahead for further elephants.

It was a quarter-moon night and soon after getting moving someone pointed out giant red shapes on the left side. They looked like massive ant hills, the same ochre colour as the soil, until a glint of reflection in an eye gave them away. It was impossible to tell if they were moving or not with the slow speed of the train. Everyone in the compartment had fallen silent, taking a lead from the elephants. Even the baby elephants did not make a sound. Bhasker had been counting and once the train picked up speed, he announced his tally of thirty-three elephants and six babies.

Now it was impossible to sleep from the clattering of the tracks. Every now and then the brakes were urgently applied and the whistle blew to warn any animals sighted. Thankfully the offenders dispersed to safety and there were no further unplanned stops. Dawn revealed a vista of straw-coloured grass-land as far as one could see, acacia thorn trees scattered randomly. Soon they spotted giraffes, zebras and wildebeest. Occasionally they saw women, children and goats in small clearings next to mud huts. The children stood frozen at the sight of the noisy train, squinting their eyes from the sun to get a look at the passengers. They wore little or no clothes; the women had necks adorned with colourful jewellery. Many wore multiple glass or wire bangles as earrings in what were massive holes on the rims of their ears.

The odd male youth, donning a long blanket, was spotted alone tending to goats. With stick or spear in hand, one foot resting upon the inside knee of the other leg. There was no acknowledgment from anyone but an unblinking stare which followed the train. Nizar tried waving at the children without eliciting any response.

"Not friendly, are they?" remarked Ramji.

"It's all strange and mysterious to me," said Nizar.

"I guess we are strange and mysterious to them," said Lalji.

The train slowed down at a point where railway workers had been changing a track. About a dozen Punjabi men, with a similar number of locals, were engaged in a heavy lift and pull of an iron track using ropes. The Sikh foreman got everyone's effort synchronised by chanting *"Har Ambee,"* after the Goddess Durga. All the men responded in unison shouting *'hey'* at which exact time they pulled with all their might. The Punjabi men looked up and some waved back at the friendly faces waving to them.

Within minutes they passed a collection of vultures and hyenas scrapping over a picked skeleton of a large beast, either a hippo or rhino. This had been the night's kill for lions. There was a sense of urgency amongst the foragers who were fighting off each other to protect their meagre share. A short distance up the track was a pride of lions resting in the shade of trees, their faces visible through the blades of straw-coloured grass. They were over fed with many lying prostrate, bellies tight. All were panting to compensate for lungs squashed by over-full abdomens.

All the passengers sat rooted, staring at the spectre of the African stage playing out before them. None of the animals, especially the lions, showed any desire to make eye contact. Nor were they distracted by the large train carrying humans whose gazes were fixed upon them.

As Nairobi approached the grassland became greener. More ponds and small lakes were visible and the soil had changed in colour from ochre to a blood red. The engine was struggling with the final pull uphill, but soon the tin roofs of the town, reflecting the morning sun, became visible.

Pulling into Nairobi Railway Station there was evidence of a busy hub. The town rested on flat country with hills visible in most directions around. For the first time they saw local Africans dressed in shirts and shorts, but none wore shoes. Even those carrying loads on muddy tracks walked barefoot.

Soon they saw some Europeans and their *Memsaabs* in long dresses carrying parasols. Some sprayed Eau de Cologne to keep themselves cool and smelling sweet, although the sun had not risen enough to make it feel warm. The temperature at that time of the morning was pleasant and a few scattered clouds near the hills threatened to close the sky over.

Then they spotted more Sikh workers around the shunting tracks, their attire and turbans soiled from a mixture of Nairobi red earth and black grease. They were engaged in the heavy work around the main station, their body frames exhibiting their superior strength. Other Indian figures could be made out from the platform. There was a wedding party carrying marigold garlands to greet the newlyweds. There were other men with long black coats over white *dhotis* with a Gujarati black *toppee* (hat) on top. They had also come to receive someone important from the second-class carriage. Others wore traditional *dhotis* and shirts, standing with hired porters alongside. The porters pulled two-wheeler carts to transport goods arriving in the town.

Lalji surveyed the scene and felt his heart flutter from anticipation and excitement. Here was the epicentre of commerce of an embryonic country he thought. It was unlike Mombasa which looked like an established port, facilitating goods in and out like it had always done. In comparison Nairobi was like a blank sheet of canvas; nothing had been determined and there was no outward sign of order. Everyone was new to the place, some more than others, but all were involved in establishing their futures and building a new home. Lalji was quiet, content to observe and take in the scene, studying all that was going on.

On the platform a tall Gujarati man who was there to receive goods approached them. He asked where they were heading. He knew the VC Hostel of Raman Bhatt. He explained it was at one end of the Indian Bazaar and he was going there with his goods. He indicated they could load their luggage on his goods cart and spoke in a local language to the African porter pulling it. He collected three massive bundles of white cotton fabric from one of the goods carriages. The man then introduced himself as Magan Dewji, an employee of a Gujarati importer. They set off walking into the town in the cool Nairobi breeze.

The town of Nairobi had a few tarred roads where the Colonial Administration offices were based. The government offices were stone built with tin roofs. Along the Government Road were also a few large shops, selling imported European goods. Most had European names like 'The Colonial Stores', 'L. Besson & Co' and 'C. Roberts & Son' advertising their European Agencies and goods. A few had Indian names like 'Rattansi and Sons' and 'Hamid Brothers' who seemed to sell local produce to the European market. They were also agents for a few European goods. Magan Dewji pointed out the few important roads and buildings to the newcomers.

Soon they turned left into the Indian Bazaar which was a long straight dirt road, narrower and a hive of activity. The four travellers smelt fried cooking and saw a small queue for *masala chai* (spicy tea) at a catering shop. The atmosphere was abuzz with activity like in Porbander, but at a more sedate pace. They were stared at and asked where they had sailed from.

They arrived at their hostel and the porter helped them with their luggage. They thanked Magan Dewji for his help, who asked if they were going to stay or move 'up country'. Ramji replied they intended to stay in Nairobi for the time being. Magan Dewji told them he would put the word out that they were here and available for work. All four expressed their gratitude for his unsolicited help. Magan Dewji called out to the owner of the hostel and two small children appeared. A girl with a half-tied trailing ribbon on one side of her head and the other a small boy with a thick sweater with a snotty nose. Both rushed back inside announcing the arrival of new guests.

They were greeted by the owner Raman Bhatt who looked like he was in the middle of cooking. He exchanged pleasantries and asked an African employee to take their luggage and show them to two rooms and went back to cooking breakfast. Their rooms were like the place they had stayed in Mombasa. They asked for hot water for a bath. It would take ten minutes to get a bucket of hot water from the wood-fired copper urn. The "bathroom" was in the backyard consisting of a square stone floor and fabric draped around sticks making a small cubicle.

Breakfast followed soon and a few local regulars who had come in for their daily breakfast left. It was then that Raman Bhatt came over to talk. He asked when they had arrived in Mombasa and where they were from. He wanted to know if they had any laundry and how long they intended to stay. The four travellers asked him to put the word out that they were available for work. They checked with him the local arrangements to register with the authorities.

Ramji found the courage to ask him if he knew anywhere they could stay for less, saying it did not matter if they had to cook themselves. Raman Bhatt said he would ask around. In the meantime, he invited them to stay with him until they had settled into jobs. He said he would charge them his lowest rate as the hostel was not busy.

***

After breakfast, Lalji and Nizar decided to take a walk and check out the neighbourhood. The town was quiet compared to Porbander. With a few lamp posts along Government Road, with its grand width, suggested this was the heart of the British Administration. Occasionally, a motor vehicle clanked past at a slow pace and stopped outside one of the government buildings. They caught sight of a few lawyers, in black gowns with white shirts, in deep conversation outside the court building. They were European and engrossed in a discussion with two other lawyers dressed similarly who looked Indian.

A lot of the shops along Government Road were selling European goods. Many advertised they were agents for specific products from Europe. The occasional notice announced new items: 'Just arrived. Top quality French Table Wines. Reserve yours now while stocks last.'

Outside a large Emporium called 'Donaldson & Co' was a sign which said:
Male Sales Assistant required
Monthly Salary
Apply to the Manager
(only Europeans or Goans need apply)

Lalji had realised from the ticket master at the train station and the administrator at the Sultans Office in Mombasa that Goans had a special status, unlike other Indians. He was to learn later that this was because as Christians they were perceived to be more trustworthy. Many had a better command of English. Some had knowledge of Portuguese customs and practices, considered 'Europeanised.'

By the time they returned for lunch they had gathered plenty of information. Lalji had also bought a copy of '*The African Standard, incorporating Mombasa Times and Uganda Standard*'. He read the business advertisements and government notices; the local news being uninteresting. By the time they had walked along Government Road and Victoria Street, they had spotted most of the businesses advertised in the paper.

At the hostel, they were met by a beaming Raman Bhatt who announced they had all been asked to go and meet a certain Samji Lalvani. Lalvani was a prominent businessman and importer. He required more workers for his shop which he planned to expand to stock more supplies from India and England.

They reached 'Lalvani & Sons' at the beginning of Duke Street. The triple-fronted shop was full of stock, placed on the floor and on the shelves in random order. Wooden crates of crockery from England were stacked next to coffee beans and jute bags. A stale smell of spices lingered in the air and the sight of mice droppings near corners. There were two large cats who wandered the place at their leisure, jumping off shelves onto bags of goods.

Samji Lalvani recognised the four travellers and introduced himself, inviting them to sit down. He relayed his own story of having arrived twenty years before from Surat, to provide supplies from India for the Raj.

Lalvani and his son Mohan manned the store. He asked what experience each had in retail or business before proceeding to describe his needs. He stated he was looking for one individual, to travel up country to his customers and take orders. He also required someone to help serve in the shop and someone else to book-keep, keeping track of debtors and creditors. Ramji interrupted and asked if he had the need for a builder or carpenter. The answer was positive as he needed to expand the yard and the *godown* (warehouse).

Having satisfied himself that the four had the potential and were hungry for work he suggested they could start immediately. Lalji asked about registering with the authorities and Samji Lalvani said his son Mohan would go with them to the Labour and Settlers Office. Lalji asked about wages and Samji Lalvani said he would meet all their boarding and lodging costs and pay them more depending on how the business picked up. Lalji and Nizar looked at each other and both realised the answer was deliberately vague. They decided no further questions were necessary, in case Samji Lalvani decided they were too smart and withdrew his offer. They were in it to learn the ropes and where better to start than at an established 'retail and wholesale' business.

Nizar asked Samji Lalvani if he could help them open bank accounts. Mr Lalvani suggested opening accounts at the Post Office Bank so they could send money orders back home.

Having arranged to start work the next day, the four travellers decided to take a tour of the town before heading back to the Indian Bazaar. They passed 'R. Ayres & Co' where a notice in the window announced all prescription drugs were dispensed under the supervision of *Dr.Ribiero, LM & S.* Lalji wondered why the Goan doctor was not working as a doctor instead of supervising the dispensing of drugs.

Soon they passed the offices of London buying agents called 'Haddon & Co'. There was no information in the window but behind the front glass was a black venetian blind and a European secretary sat at a desk typing at a slow pace. As they appeared and looked through the window, she caught their eye and stared at them after lowering the rim of her glasses on her nose. Lalji tried to smile, at which she stood up, walked over to the window and briskly turned the blinds shut. Ramji saw the whole episode and laughed out loud.

"I think your smile scared her!" said Ramji after he had stopped laughing. A bemused Lalji walked on. Bhasker asked what buying agents were and Nizar suggested they might be importers who obtained specialist tools and machinery.

"They would have the contacts in Europe and act as middlemen for the buyers here" said Lalji, realising their function for the first time himself.

They walked towards a large store of 'Sorabjee M, Official Broker, Auctioneer, Stevedore, Shipping and Railway Clearing Agent and Commissioning Agents'. Clearly, businesses had multiple roles while the market was small, forced to branch out to provide diverse services.

A few doors down were 'AM Jeevanjee & Co, General Merchants, Contractors, Commissioning Agents, House and Landowners, Stevedores'. They boasted they had branches in Bombay, Karachi and Mombasa. Nizar wondered how such businesses managed with multiple sites in different countries. Lalji remarked that since there were so many partnerships based on untried businesses there were likely to be failures and disputes. His suspicions were confirmed later when he looked at the newspaper. There the Court Listings were full of individuals suing established businesses, or businesses suing each other. Notices in the paper announced cancellations of Powers of Attorney. These were after trusted individuals had left their employers or after partnerships had broken down.

Soon they passed a new stone building with a tile roof. It was the 'Norfolk Hotel', advertising itself as Nairobi's first 'stone-built hotel with a tiled roof'. The *rickshas* ("rickshaws") parked outside indicated it was an exclusive European establishment. The red flowerpots outside were immaculate. They contrasted with the white-washed steps they adorned.

Next was a small office of the 'Kikuyu Trading Syndicate, Direct Importers and Export Merchants'. The office was closed and the window advertised the few hours it opened and which managing individual would be in attendance. The syndicate was a white farmers co-operative set up to try and cut out the middleman. White settlers were finding the set-up costs needed controlling, despite the generous grants of land and cash.

"There is risk all around in the commerce here," Lalji thought. But he also realised there were a few common patterns. There was a desperate need for skilled labour — and those with basic commerce skills. No serious attempts to get indigenous people trained had started. Secondly, a lot depended on the railway to keep supply lines open.

The four *jehajis* (travellers) got back to the hostel and Raman Bhatt handed old copies of the 'Mombasa Times' to Lalji to read. Having read a few issues of the newspaper Lalji was building up a picture in his mind of the Colonial Administration. He realised that although the Indians could fill a lot of the skill gaps the official policy was to try and manage without them.

There was rivalry between the East India Company and the Colonial Office. The latter tied to distance itself from the old practices of the Company. To Lalji it seemed the Indian currency was a point of contention. The Colonial Office and the white settlers resented the Indian Rupee as the currency. The Company wanted it as it streamlined trade throughout the Indian Ocean.

There seemed in parallel some antipathy towards Indians. Although they could fill the skills gap, they were excluded from major commerce. These Indians, like the four from Porbander, had volunteered to emigrate to the Colony. They had entrepreneurial aspirations, unlike the indentured labourers preceding them. A constant complaint was that business permits were issued under Indian Colonial Law, which favoured Europeans. There was a third group from India: civil servants, teachers, nurses and doctors. These groups were recruited in quotas and many came from Goa.

The shortage of skilled European settlers was proving to be a major issue for the Colony despite the boost provided by the new railway. Keeping the railway solvent was a challenge. No sooner had the railway (and the ferry boats on Lake Victoria) started to carry goods, freight charges rose beyond the reach of settler farmers. This led to a clamour from the farmers for subsidised rates from the Colonial Office.

The four read the latest newspaper together that evening, with Lalji translating what he understood. The paper said that the government in London had in mind to take over the administration of the Colony in response to the demands of white settlers. It was felt that rule from the India Office was not responsive enough to the needs of a new developing colony, a country that was different from India.

Lalji was surprised that he understood most of the newspapers. There were shortages of seeds, lack of equipment and limited access to export markets for farmers.

The government of Britain had come up with a novel idea to inject a skilled non-Indian workforce by starting a large Jewish settlement in the Uganda territory. Known as the *'Zionist Scheme'*, an area of four hundred square miles was identified for the formation of a Jewish state in Uganda. Leaders of the Jewish race were invited to come and see. It would provide two solutions for Britain: get the labour force British East Africa needed, and remove Jews from Britain and Europe. The opposition labelled it a re-invention of the 'Australian formula'.

The paper stated that ninety percent of the white settlers were against the scheme. It was held by the settlers that 'the pulpit, parliament and public' was against the scheme. They voiced that 'dumping these pauper aliens in our midst' was not an option and the settlers started protests. It was alleged that soon after being settled the Jews 'would stop agriculture work as they had no inclination for it and start small businesses and compete directly with the white settlers'.

The four *jehajis* had no idea what kind of person a Jew was. It seemed the race was undesired from their reading. The Jews seemed to have a flair for business but were not trusted. "That's like us," said Nizar with a laugh.

"Are they white, brown, black or Chinese?" asked Bhasker. There was silence all around as no-one knew the answer.

"Why is there so much suspicion of Indians?" asked Nizar. Lalji shrugged his shoulders.

It was Ramji who responded. "I guess we are no longer trusted after the revolution of 1857, which almost drove the British out of *Hindustan* (India)."

CHAPTER EIGHT

THERE WAS NO doubt that the railway was a great boon for all. Roads had not been developed and dirt tracks were beginning to be resurfaced as murram roads, to prevent being washed away in the rains.

Those white settlers who took up land were demanding local boarding schools to avoid having to send children away to Europe for a year each time. But the remoteness of settlements and the lack of skilled labour were proving too much. Often, they had to put up with hostile locals and enrol themselves into a volunteer reserve for protection. This in turn made their relationship with locals more fraught.

Then there was the need for developing medical facilities. Some Christian Missionary groups had started to open their doors for the sick and mothers to deliver babies, nursed by resident nuns. Many grew disillusioned and decided to return to Europe, having given Africa their best shot.

Indian businessmen and philanthropists had started projects to help their growing communities, many along religious or community lines. Those communities that had more and better facilities opened their doors to others. But the stratification of society and businesses into European, Indian and African prevented any meaningful integration. Racial segregation was embedded in the laws and civic fabric of the country. 'White privilege' was constantly refined with further and newer restrictions on the others.

Residential and business areas were restricted according to race. Initially, the Indians had no land made available for residential purposes. They lived in crowded spaces behind their shops. The conditions that resulted in an outbreak of plague in Nairobi in 1903. Lalji realised that land was cheap but there was a lot of soul-searching by the authorities and white settlers about who they wanted to share it with. Land for Indians was held up. Vociferous white settlers wanted British Law to replace Indian Law. They demanded reductions in railway freight charges. The newspaper announced protests: '*White Colonialists, who are very powerful and essentially a progressive body of men, have arranged another protest*'. Lalji knew the future for Indians lay in becoming self-sufficient, from both the white settlers and the administration. He knew the regime remained adept at changing rules as they went along, as they had always done in India.

The next day the four *jehajis*, who would be deemed 'Settler Merchants' on registration at the Settlers Office, had risen early. Magan Dewji had a bounce in his step after his intervention had secured employment for the four young men. He was louder and more jovial than they had seen him, humming a happy tune.

There was a thick covering of cloud in the sky but the morning air was crispy cool. Magan Dewji's *masala chai* came as a welcome relief from the chill. The table was full of chat about what else needed to be done now they had accommodation and jobs.

They were at Lalvani's shop before it opened. Soon they met Mohan, the elder of Lalvani's sons who was going to take them to the Labour Office. Lalvani had other sons who were still minors and not in the business. Two further sons and three daughters of school age except for Laxmi, the oldest daughter. She had studied in Gujarati to the end of primary school. She helped her mother with daily household chores. All had studied at City Primary School, the only Indian School in Nairobi. There was no high school yet and those who aspired to go further went to India.

On their walk to the Labour Office, Mohan informed them, "You will all need to start learning Swahili. It is hard for the locals to learn our language. There are many local tribes and as many dialects. Up country they don't understand Swahili much so you may need to learn local dialects. Many Swahili words are from Arabic and some from Gujarati."

Soon they had arrived at the partial stone and timber office with a tin roof. The stone steps had been washed over with fresh red mud from the flower beds which had overflowed in the rains. Inside the main office was a middle-aged white man in khaki shirt and short trousers, stockings up to his knees and brown shoes. His hard sola topee sat nearby on his table. They could tell from his ruddy face and grey moustache that he was not a novice to Africa.

No sooner had Mohan explained the purpose of his visit, the man bellowed, "De Souza! Get these *kew lees* written up for registration, *pdq*!"

From a partially open door behind him, a bespectacled young Goan man with oily hair appeared. He bowed to his boss, then nodded his head to Mohan before disappearing into a side office, leaving the door open.

The Englishman bellowed again, this time in accented Hindi, "*Undaar jaho*, go in." He had to repeat himself as no one reacted at first to his incomprehensible accent. All filed into De Souza's cubby office. He asked them in broken Hindi to come forward in turn to give him their details. Lalji went first as no one else moved and everyone looked to him.

The formalities were straight forward and they were permitted to remain in the Colony for twelve months. At that time, they would need to pay a renewal fee of ten rupees each, although the first registration was free. They received paperwork to show they were now registered as *'British Colonial Citizens'*. With all the permits logged, De Souza went back to his chief who countersigned and stamped them. He did not acknowledge them as they left, despite Mohan thanking him.

The next stop was the Post Office to open their savings accounts. They had to queue up to see the clerk whose name was on a plate on his desk: S C Roberts, Chief Accountant. A ceiling fan hung above him, turning without effect and making a click at each revolution. He asked to see their registration permits and filled in a long form in triplicate for each of them. He took special care not to smudge the ink of the carbon paper onto the forms by holding the forms pinched at the edges. Once he had finished, a few hundred clicks of the fan later, he asked Mohan if they wanted to sign or use thumb prints. All signed their names in Gujarati except for Lalji who did so in English.

On the way back Mohan took them past the new stone-built Jamia Mosque to show them the architecture. It was massive with Arabic writing above the main entrance. Then they came to a Hindu *Mandir* (Temple), one of two small structures in Nairobi. In Gujarati above the door it announced, 'Shree Nathji Haveli, Nairobi'. Through an open window they saw the *Pandit* (priest) wiping the floor below a large black marble statue of Shree Nathji. Peering through the window from the outside were a few young local children. They looked fascinated by the toys at the feet of the statue and the offerings of fruit.

On reaching Lalvani's shop they were greeted by the boss himself who was busy unrolling fabric for an Arab customer. Lalvani asked if everything went well.

"Good. Let's get you all to the *godown* (warehouse) to unpack the goods brought in yesterday. Mohan will show you what needs doing."

Outside the shop they saw a couple of men deep in conversation, not noticing the small leper with a collapsed nose sitting on the ground. He was begging with one fingerless palm extended.

CHAPTER NINE

AFTER LALJI'S *VAAN* sailed, Janki realised that she would be taking the same route one day. She felt a tinge of nervousness, but also plenty of excitement. From having had no aspirations, she now felt an urgent need to learn new skills. She wanted to become more responsible around the house.

She realised Lalji's return would lead to their marriage and her heading off with him. She had a year to hone her skills. Both her Aunt Lalbai and her mother had started to spend more time in instructing her about the role of a woman. In matters of the kitchen both were involved, and when it came to religious observances it was her mother. Her aunt taught her sewing and needlework.

Janki already had a keen interest in home remedies which she had picked up from her friend Mukta. Mukta's father was the village *vaid* (herbalist). The two spent time with Mukta's father learning about herbs and Ayurvedic remedies.

When the telegram arrived from Lalji, with the news they had arrived safely, there was excitement in the village. Lalji's mother received the telegram by the postman, who told her what it said. Neither could read or write English so the postman had arranged a translation from the postmaster. Rambai, tears of relief dribbling down her cheeks, sought out her husband. Parshottam was overjoyed. He rushed to inform the other parents of the news. In the meantime, the postman stationed himself under the peepal tree in the centre of the village. From there he informed all and sundry of the good news.

Ramji's father burst into tears and hugged Parshottam. He headed to the village *Mandir* to express his gratitude. Nizar's father looked visibly relieved and sat down to drink some water, his hands shaking. It became clear that no matter how positive they had all been, the expedition and the unknown risks had weighed heavily upon those left behind. Three of Ramji's siblings started to dance. They started to throw coloured powder at one another and at passers-by in celebration. They then made their way to Janki's house where Parshottam was waving the telegram in the air and sharing the news with her father.

Janki had not heard the news when the three children ran into the yard behind the shop and found her.

"*Didi, didi,* (sister, sister) have you heard-telegram arrived-all the bhais (brothers) have arrived safely," they blurted out together. Before Janki could ask them to explain slowly, their hands, full of green, purple and red powders, flung the contents at Janki. She emerged from the cloud of colour with hair like a parakeet's feathers. Large blotches of coloured powder stuck to her clothes. A loud cheer with laughing followed and Janki realised it was her parents. Her aunt appeared, grabbed Janki's hands and started dancing with her.

Bhasker's father Dheeraj and his family were last to hear. They learnt directly from the postman, who was on his way to the next village and stopped by at their shop. The postman arranged to return in a few days in case anyone required him to write a response. He not only delivered letters, but also read them aloud for the illiterate. He was then available for writing replies. A pillar of society, he also sat on the *Panchayat*.

There followed over the next few days many conversations about what the four were likely to be doing. It became everybody's topic of conversation. Children of the village started to talk about moving to Africa one day. Toy boats were made from tree bark, with dried leaves for sails. Sand provided ocean waves for their delicate toy *vaans*.

***

Parshottam had busied himself after the four had left trying to find out more about British East Africa. He looked in newspapers and studied old magazines. The news was sparse about the opportunities for Indian settlers. All boasted the success of the railway built by Indian labourers.

His friend Pandyaji, the school headmaster liked to discuss current affairs. Pandyaji read widely and the two of them met fortnightly to discuss developments. Having taught each of the four *jehajis*, he was keen to know how they were doing. The topic often moved to Mohandas Karamchand Gandhi, an ex-Porbander lawyer. He challenged the colonial powers over their treatment of Indians in Southern Africa. In hushed tones they discussed the latest about Gandhi's fight against the *sarkar* (government) on behalf of indentured labourers. Gandhi's successes inspired both Pandyaji and Parshottam. But they did not think of Southern Africa as being a suitable destination for Gujaratis. In comparison, British East Africa seemed better. At least Indians could emigrate on non-indentured permits. The distance from Gujarat was shorter and the currency was the Indian Rupee.

Gandhi was not a topic for discussion, after his successes against the British *sarkar* (government) of Southern Africa. Having started the 'Natal Indian Congress', he remained a person of interest to all the *sarkars* under the British Raj. The risk of being discovered discussing him would be arrest on suspicion of sedition. Yet, recently in the eyes of the British, he had become a likeable figure. He had managed to recruit over a thousand Indian volunteers for the British Medical Corps, to aid them in their war against the Boers.

Pandyaji and Purshottam had long conversations trying to understand the mind of the 35-year-old Gandhi. He changed strategy in his dealings with the *sarkar* when least expected. The former thought Gandhi was cleverer than the *sarkar*. Pandyaji had once attended a talk by him in Porbander on 'Life in Africa'. After that he concluded the younger generation could make a success of their lives there. The two men also discussed the state of the country under the British Raj, again in soft voices. The taxes levied during the famine times were hated most. They saw no return for the tax they paid. It was accepted that it went into running the army and the government. Whatever was left, went to the monarch of Britain who was also amassing the wealth of the Rajahs and Maharajahs. After all, it was the British monarch *'who wears the Koh-hi-noor diamond,'* as Pandyaji put it.

Inevitably these discussions led to wondering how the *firangi* (foreign) *sarkar* could be removed. Pandyaji would read from magazines or newspapers stories or poems which were written about everyday things. Many had hidden political meaning to get past the censors. Their meetings would end with Pandyaji reading aloud patriotic poetry. The two friends, their nationalistic fervour satiated, would then part company.

CHAPTER TEN

THE FIRST SIX months passed quickly. The four *jehajis* had become accustomed to Nairobi and had started building a life for themselves. They had moved out of Magan Dewji's hostel and paid him their rental arrears out of their first salaries. They continued to have one meal a day there and had breakfast and supper at home. Home consisted of two small rooms to share, with a small hallway and bathroom, behind a shop in River Road. The toilet was outside.

Bhasker was keen to cook and started showing off his culinary repertoire from the beginning. Ramji had started smoking cigarettes which he said helped his dry cough which still troubled him, especially at night. Their jobs were easy and they all became accustomed to being able to take each other's places in the shop if required. The accounts side was Lalji's domain with help from Nizar who was keen to learn. They received occasional help from Mohan although he preferred to be on the shop floor.

Nizar had been to Mombasa by rail to collect goods and textiles from the *SS Sultan* which had docked from Mumbai. He spent two nights at Premlal's hostel while the goods were cleared by customs. Bhasker had taken the train in the opposite direction to a place called Eldoret to deliver goods and show samples to the local traders. He described Eldoret as wet and cold, after being caught up in a hailstorm. Ramji had helped a local contractor extend the *godown* (warehouse) at Lalvani's shop. The contractor, Karsandas from Bhuj, was particularly pleased with his work and had asked Ramji to join him as his right-hand man. Having discussed the proposal with Lalji, Ramji declined. There was not enough work for them both but they had agreed that Karsandas could call Ramji for help if he became busy.

Three months after starting their jobs, Samji Lalvani became ill with abdominal pains and episodes of vomiting. Local doctors had suspected an ulcer and prescribed strict diets and pills without much relief. In the end, on his wife's insistence, he booked a trip to Mumbai to get himself seen at a clinic.

Mohan was in charge at the shop and his sister Laxmi minded their house and cooked for the family. Before leaving, Lalvani had extended his gratitude to the four settlers for their service. He said it was a load off his mind that they were there to help during his absence. He called Lalji one day and spoke to him about keeping an eye on the business. He asked him to be on the lookout for new opportunities.

The shop closed on Sundays and the four settlers went out together to explore new places. There was a new bus service in Nairobi and they started to mix into the local communities. They had been to a theatre production of '*Mirabai*' by Trumbak Lal performed on stage, the first such play from India. The place was sold out and full to the brim. All the Indian communities came including Sikhs and Ismailis, despite the play having a Hindu story. There were two representatives from the Colonial Office as observers. They were there to check the content of the play was not seditious and to observe the behaviour of the audience. Granting the licence to the Indian Community to put up the show was a first for the administration.

The four often ventured out to a *bhajia* (snack) house for a Sunday teatime treat with masala tea. This soon became a tradition followed every Sunday afternoon.

Nizar had started to attend prayers at the *Ismaili Khoja Khana* (Ismaili Mosque) as the Jamia Mosque was far and poorly served by transport. He did not mind the emphasis of the service meant for the benefit of the Aga Khan, as he attended to listen to the readings from the religious texts.

Bhasker had started to play *tablas* (pair of percussion instruments, played together) with Ramji. They had teamed up with a small group of *bhajan* (religious song) singers attached to the *Mandir*. Although there was no time for rehearsals, they attended requests for *bhajan* (religious song) evenings at peoples' homes.

All four had started to write home to their families using Lalvani's shop as their postal address. The arrival of a letter for anyone met with questions from the others to share information about the state of things back home.

One day out of the blue Lalji received a letter from Janki which surprised him. They had hardly ever shared a private conversation together before he left. He ripped open the letter. The contents were a bit matter of fact with news about the village, her family, and the lack of rains. Her writing was small and written beautifully. Immediately he felt she should have studied more.

Having read the letter, Lalji kept reading over and over her last line asking him to '*take care of himself*'. The tenderness of the sentiment made him feel happy and not alone. For him, that constituted the letter. There was no request for a response or question of when he might return. Nor any inquiry of any plans he might have considered for their future.

The four had started picking up the local Swahili language. The basic words were not difficult as many of them were repeated syllables making up words, like '*sasa*, now', '*mimi*, me' and '*wewe*, you'. The numerology was also not difficult. With regular conversations with locals they became more fluent. What was difficult was to write anything down as the locals had no school education and were illiterate as far as reading or writing went. Many locals who worked in shops started picking up words or numbers, from export boxes and packages. But writing was a remote skill for most.

Ramji had a huge issue with communicating time when he started working in the *godown* (warehouse). He had not been aware that the locals read the clock face using diametrically opposite numbers of the hour hand. He had hilarious misunderstandings at first. He would ask someone to come at 8 am only to find they turned up at 2 pm. Similarly, midday was '*saa sita*', meaning 6 o'clock. When Samji Lalvani learnt of Ramji's plight, he could not contain his laughter before explaining the local way to read the time.

What was clear to them was that the locals were loyal and hard-working. One trait was their readiness to learn. Lalvani also told the four early on about cultural differences. He narrated the story of a white farmer who allowed a worker time off to attend his mother's funeral. The same request was made to the farmer's wife later the same year when the farmer was away. A year later he made a third request to attend his mother's funeral and both the farmer and his wife refused permission. Upset but unable to work he absconded and returned days later with an elderly uncle to help resolve the issue. It transpired that he had indeed lost two mothers, as his father had three wives, which the farmer was not aware of. The third was in fact an elderly aunt referred to as 'Mother'.

The two locals who worked at the shop were Njenga and Kijana. The former had worked on a construction site and Njenga was his nickname, meaning 'fixer'. He particularly liked working alongside Ramji who spent more time in the *godown* (warehouse). He was always on hand to observe Ramji whenever he called for his toolbox so he could pick up more tips. He would try out the tools himself after Ramji had left.

'Kijana' was also a nickname, meaning 'young one', as he looked like a teenager despite his 28 years. He liked to dress boldly, often turning up in a bright red hat, contrasted with a yellow shirt.

The only other individual was the *askari* (night watchman), who sat outside the front of the shop next to a wood fire through the night. He wore a heavy khaki coat which almost reached his ankles. His ears were pierced with long holes which went halfway down the ears, wire earrings of different colours laced through the holes. He carried a long, heavy, ebony stick. The watchman also had a nickname, known by all as 'Pembo,' which meant 'alcoholic beverage.' A wicked tease as he detested drunkards. It was never known if he enjoyed a drink himself. But he chased away anyone passing in front of him with a slight stagger. Shouting and swearing at them, he would hasten their escape with sharp blows from his stick to their legs.

Despite his age of sixty, Pembo was fit and strong. He once ended up spending a night in a police cell after he had beaten a drunk man unconscious with his stick. The man survived and luckily no charges were pressed, Pembo getting away with just a warning.

***

Samji Lalvani was away in India for three months. Medical treatment was not successful for his ulcer. He ended up having surgery to have part of his stomach removed. Lalji was at his happiest in those three months. Trade seemed to be increasing with the growth of Nairobi town. He accepted more responsibility and enjoyed a good relationship with Mohan. Although he did all the banking, he insisted Mohan check all the transactions.

Lalji often ended up talking to any European customers which helped increase his English skills. He had a good relationship with the Bank Manager, Mr Lloyd Edwards. Mr Lloyd, as Lalji referred to him, was friendly and always inquired how the business was doing. On learning that Samji Lalvani was away for medical treatment, he always asked after him. Lalji enjoyed these conversations and he found his English was improving. Mr Edwards had a way of gently correcting him on his grammar. He later told Lalji he had come to Kenya to teach in Secondary School but there were not enough schools or jobs then so he joined the bank. Lloyd Edwards often reminded Lalji his bank also lent money at favourable rates. He thought well of Lalji and started to refer to him overseas sales agents looking to engage with local businesses.

Once he had sent a representative from Bristol in England who was looking for a sole agent in Nairobi to import brown paper bags, paper and glued tape. Another time someone who wanted an East Africa agent for tinned condensed milk and cream. Lalji worked out when the approach to him had come after the representative had not had any joy with the bigger stores. Usually, the goods were either not competitively priced or had a small market. In the case of the brown paper and bags, Lloyd Edwards assured him the agent had not done the rounds and there was a real opportunity. Also, the Bristol factory wanted an agent with a large storage capacity, which Samji Lalvani now had following the expansion of the *godown* (warehouse).

Lalji saw the Bristol representative with Mohan and pressed him for more favourable credit terms. When he had negotiated these, they wrote to Samji Lalvani in Mumbai for his permission to close the deal. Three weeks later they had a positive reply; they took all the samples the representative had and shook hands on the deal. Their first cargo would be dispatched from Hargreave Paper Mill in Bristol and arrive in Mombasa four weeks later.

The railway became the artery of business in the emerging colony. No other service had become as central a commodity as the railway. It was the means of transport for trade, supplies, export, settlers, merchants, passengers, security forces and exploration. It was glorified as: *'Uganda Railway, the gateway to British East Africa, the brightest gem in Britain's Cluster of Colonies'*. It had cost the Colonial Government six million pounds sterling. There was an intense controversy ongoing about the amount paid out and the actual building cost of three and a half to four million pounds. Questions were being asked about where the surplus had disappeared. The Railway authority was under pressure to perform to justify the investment.

It was administered by Governor Sir Charles Eliot's office. The Central Committee of Supplies dictated freight charges. These depended not only on the weight and volume but also on the nature of the goods. Under 'martial law', produce prices were fixed and were only varied centrally. Reduced freight charges were promoted for foods produced locally and markets began to thrive up and down the railway.

Lalji had started to read the *African Standard* and the *Nairobi News*. Ironically, there was resentment among the white settlers that the Indians were not natural farmers. Their skills, unlike 'the European' or 'the Goan', was in trading and small businesses.

Lalji saw that the Protectorate often contradicted itself. On the one hand, they wanted small businesses to open in remote places to promote commerce, which the Indians were good at. On the other hand, the administration believed that the Indians did not seem to engage in developing the agricultural sector. The land laws restricted farming land to European settlers only. The protectorate had declared the fertile highlands inland for white settlers only. These became known as the *'White Highlands'*. These contradictory stances towards the Indians created unusual tensions. Their natural talent for trade was not encouraged. There were those who felt the dice was loaded against the Indians forever. Many tried to disinherit their Indianness and blend into a different people. The Goans claimed they were Portuguese and referred to by the administration as 'exceptionally superior men'. Similarly, the Gujarati-speaking Parsees claimed to be Persian. This was despite having settled in India for generations.

Lalji translated the following letter from an older edition of the African Standard for the others :

'TO THE EDITOR AFRICAN STANDARD MOMBASA dated Nairobi 15th March 1905.

Sir, As most of the newly arrived 'white men' do not seem to know who the Parsees are, and therefore, take them for Indians only because they come from India, I beg to request that you would be so good as to publish the following, in the next issue of your widely circulated paper along with this letter.

My card is enclosed for your information.

Yours, &c.

A PARSEE'

The piece to be printed was as follows:

'It is true they come from India, but India is their country of adoption: their native country being **Persia** of which they were once the **Rulers**. They left Persia some 1300 years ago, **rather than give up their sacred religion.** They have up to now zealously preserved the purity of their **blue-blood**, never allowing any admixture by intermarriages with Indian races, of which they are justly proud. In India theirs is the most advanced community in every respect. They enjoy many high posts in the Government Service. **They are most cleanly in their habits**. They are admitted in the **best of hotels** in India, and **their children** can be seen learning side by side with English Children in such schools as the Cathedral and the Alexandra, in Bombay. They are well known for their **loyalty to the British Taj** *(crown)* **and their law-abiding quality**. They are very sensitive and can be ill-brook to be taken for, or treated as Indians. They also think it is a slight to be called **baboos.**'

But Parsees and Goans got their recognition in different ways. In Nairobi, it was the Parsee and Goanese Cricket Clubs who were invited to play in the local league against settler clubs. Characteristic of British Empire Dominions, cricket had been introduced earlier. Only the worthy were invited to play in the gentleman's league.

In contrast, the Aga Khan, religious and community leader of the Ismailis, was welcomed by his own followers from Gujarat and Kutch. Other Indian communities joined in. The Administration referred to him as 'a British Subject of immense influence.' There was no formal invitation to meet the Governor. His visit to the Protectorate was reported for the 'enormous funds collected for his benefit.' No reference was made of his philanthropy or his social projects.

Lalji realised that the greed for land and the revenue from it was the chief driver of the colonial administration. This provided the Empire with taxes, produce and profit. He thought their unwillingness to share, especially with the locals, would store up trouble for the future. With so many restrictions on Indians and the locals, he decided to keep his sights firmly on his trade. In his view the British East Africa Protectorate could only advance with the skills and the labour of Indians from across the Ocean. There were skilled craftsmen and traders to be attracted if the conditions were fair. Training the locals could take a generation he thought. Christian missions were providing education for new converts, which swelled their congregations.

CHAPTER ELEVEN

THE BROWN PAPER products had taken off well. Orders were coming in from all kinds of businesses including the Post Office, the railway, stationers, police and the army. They were getting inquiries for other related materials and especially for cardboard boxes that had started to be used in Europe. Lalji added jute sacks to the list. Soon they had to hire a small *godown* (warehouse) for extra stock and employed a second night watchman for it. Lalji invested in a bicycle with a front-loading basket and within a fortnight had taught Kijana how to ride it. It would be one of his duties to deliver orders.

Kijana was a transformed man with his new skill. He turned up to work in a new shirt and a tatty but clean peaked cap. Overnight he had adopted an air of officialdom. When speaking to clients or strangers he kept his line of vision just below the rim of his cap, hiding his eyes and speaking with authority. When riding the bicycle, the neighbourhood children chased him as he sped along, ringing the bicycle bell non-stop. Every day ended with a wash down to keep the machine gleaming, like on the first day it arrived.

Samji Lalvani returned from Mumbai in good spirits. H had lost weight which he put down to having to eat smaller meals after his operation. He had a gauntness around his eyes which suggested something more serious. He lacked stamina but his pride and joy of seeing his business flourishing was obvious. He saw Lalji as the catalyst who had kept the business afloat in his absence.

Six months after his return from Mumbai, Samji had become weaker and lost his appetite. The weight started to drop off him dramatically.

"Samjibhai, you should consider returning to Mumbai to see your doctor," Lalji advised.

"Yes, Bapa, something is wrong," said Mohan.

Samji looked at the door to his room to make sure nobody else was around. Then he spoke in hushed tones. "This is to be expected. My specialist told me the ulcer was cancerous," his voice faltering. Addressing Mohan, he said, "Your mother is unaware. It is better this way, otherwise she would make herself ill with worry."

"Is that serious?" asked Mohan.

"It is a matter of a few months…..there is no cure," replied Samji, not looking at Mohan.

Mohan broke down and started sobbing.

Samji looked at Lalji and spoke. "I think it would be better if you could remain a while. I mean afterwards, after my departure. Make sure things are ticking over."

"Of course, we will stay to make sure everything is working well," said Lalji. Lost in the enormity of the news, Lalji's mind was juggling thoughts about Samji, his family and the business. He realised their own plans had become linked to the fortunes of the Lalvani family.

"Good. I knew I could count on you and your friends. I know you will want to spread your wings one day and move on. That is understandable. Would you assist Mohan here if things get too much for him?"

"You need not be concerned about that. But surely one more trip to the doctor in Mumbai, it does not have to be what you think," said Lalji.

"It's of no use. Everything the doctor said is happening just as he told me. I prefer to be here."

Samji Lalvani had stopped coming into the shop within a couple of weeks after his conversation with Lalji and Mohan. He had developed an irritating, dry cough which he blamed for giving him daily headaches. His wife had changed the household routine to revolve around his needs, encouraging him to eat despite his loss of appetite.

The four *jehaji bhais* (brotherly travellers) agreed they would remain and help the family through their difficult period. Samji Lalvani had opened his doors and employed them all at their first meeting. The strength of their bond with him was evident, despite the brief time they had known him.

***

There was a debate surrounding selling residential land to Indians. The formula of living above or behind the shop was leading to overcrowding as families expanded and put pressure on utility services. Lalji had words with his three compatriots and had insisted they should get ready to buy land at short notice. Indeed, it was not long before the administration released 'Indian Residential Plots.' These were in areas across the Nairobi River in Ngara, Pangani, Eastleigh and Parklands. The plots were a standard five thousand square feet sold on a ninety-nine-year lease. As in schools and businesses, the *sarkar* (government) designated 'Native Areas', 'Indian Areas' and 'European Areas' for residential purposes. For reasons more to do with their policy of dividing people, the *sarkar* even specified 'Goan Residential Plots.' These were in locations close to Indian areas. If that was designed to attract more settlers from Goa it failed. It never mustered up enough interest to create viable Goan communities outside of Nairobi.

Land was also made available for community projects, such as schools and hospitals. Capital to build was the responsibility of the communities. For schools, there was help available for those who adopted English curricula, like that from Cambridge. Help was also available for those that used English as the medium of teaching. Others who chose to teach in Indian languages had less help, if any.

***

There was quite a buzz amongst the Indians when residential plots were eventually released. Many still opted to stay in their original habitats above or behind their shops. Theirs was a familiar area, more secure being close to friends and with manageable costs. Meanwhile, the price of commercial property in the town centre started to drop, from a lack of buyers. Seeing the Indians had started to buy residential plots, the *sarkar* responded by opening the commercial property market to everyone. It was clear to Lalji that staying still was not an option. The four had to acquire land and start their own ventures for the long term. The release of plots was an opportune time.

Lalji had struck up a good relationship with the Bank Manager, Lloyd Edwards, who had witnessed the fortunes of the business rising and had surmised it was the young emigrant that was responsible. Indeed, it was Mr Edwards who had approached Lalji asking if the business required a loan. Initially Lalji had been taken aback by the question. He did not know anyone who had borrowed from a bank. There had been no bank at home in Gujarat and even leaving money in one was a departure from normal practice.

"Thank you for the offer," he had replied the first time. However, the next time he asked, "What will it cost?"

Mr Edwards took him into his office and explained how the loan worked, the interest charged, the collateral required and the need for business experience. Lalji realised that purchasing a shop with living accommodation attached was the only option open to them.

When the plots were released Lalji approached Mr Edwards. Initially the four had wondered about getting into a large single business together until Mr Edwards advised them otherwise.

"A larger business would be competing against the established European businesses and require a larger loan," Mr Edwards said. "Also, I would have little say in the process as my head office handles large loans."

"Oh," Lalji said, looking disappointed.

"You see Lalji, head office in London has a higher lending bar which would be difficult for you to reach without a record of running your own business here. They have seen large European ventures fold up."

"I see. So, what can be done?"

"Well, if you had four smaller loans for each of you then I would have to be satisfied of your business case to approve them myself."

"And Head Office?"

"For smaller loans, they leave the decision for me to make," said Mr Edwards. "I must be satisfied with the business you have in mind and how you would meet the repayments. The four of you need to be sure of what you want to do and work as a partnership."

Lalji relayed the discussion to his friends.

Nizar was ready to invest in a commercial site. He had been thinking about a hardware shop having seen the surge in building in Nairobi. Ramji was interested in starting a workshop near the Industrial section close to the railway station to start a small carpentry and building outlet. Bhasker was happy to consider a small business. He preferred to work alongside one of the others.

Lalji was aware he had to manage the expectations of his friends, who each had ability but had not been exposed to business risks. Here Mr Edwards was going to be useful with the sort of conditions he would put forward to lend.

CHAPTER TWELVE

MOHAN HAD STARTED to spend time attending to his father who spent more time in bed. When Mohan came to the shop he was preoccupied and forgetful. Usually, he inquired about how things were before spending time chatting with Lalji about orders and deliveries.

Within a month Samji Lalvani passed away. He had developed pneumonia and lost a drastic amount of weight. His wife and children nursed him until the end. The family had Dr B K Shah come twice a day to give him painkilling injections. Eventually, he stopped coughing and his breathing sounded like a rattle. He became cold to touch, slipped into unconsciousness and died in his sleep. Those last few days of his life became a dark cloud overshadowing all activities of the shop and at home. Time seemed to have slowed at first, then speed up after his death. Suddenly there was a lot to do and organise and no one person could arrange it all.

The funeral was held the same day in the afternoon. The open-air cremation ground was a twenty-minute walk away. As was customary none of the women attended. Samji Lalvani's body, wrapped in brilliant white, was carried atop a hand-pulled cargo ricksha and the men followed chanting a *Ram Dhun* (repetitive chanting Ram's hymn). The priest chanted *Shlokas* (Hindu religious verses) during the prayers before the pyre was lit by Mohan.

Everyone who had known Samji Lalvani seemed to have come. Pembo the night watchman, came to walk alongside the mourners heading to the cremation ground. He stood outside the circle of men gathered at the pyre in his thick khaki coat with his stick in hand, not speaking to anyone.

The four *jehaji bhais* along with Njenga and Kijana helped organise the daily prayers after the funeral. Chairs and mats were borrowed from neighbours and people came to show support. A middle-aged lady wearing thick rimmed spectacles, sat alongside Samji Lalvani's widow and recited the *Bhagavad Geeta* (Hindu scripture, words of Lord Krishna).

The shop remained closed the next day. Mohan had suggested longer but Lalji advised him of honouring orders and being available for buyers who came from up country. Since his trip to India Samji Lalvani had been paying the four *jehajis* a fair wage. They discussed sending money back home to their families now they had savings in their Post Office accounts. Mohan advised it was safer to send money orders from the post office and it would be quicker than using the soni jeweller network. Each one asked Lalji how much to send and he suggested half of what they had, leaving the rest for investment in their own businesses.

Lalji was wondering about making plans to return to Porbander to get married and bring Janki back. But first he needed a place of his own to stay. Nizar and Bhasker had indicated they also wanted to travel back to see their families. They were in discussions about whether it would be by *vaan* (dhow) or a steamship this time. Lalji suggested steamship as they could now afford the fare. The scheduled departures and arrivals would mean they could plan their trips better.

News arrived of the Habib brothers, two of Nairobi's established businessmen, having perished at sea. Their *vaan* had sunk in high seas on their way to Hajj (Islamic pilgrimage) in Mecca. The two brothers, both in their forties were well known, having been in Nairobi fifteen years. They had traded in goods couriered across the ocean in Arab *vaans*. Their wives had remained back in Gujarat, not having made the crossing to Africa because the children were still young. Their chief products were ivory from inland bought at auction for export to India and the Far East. Cotton and spices from India were the items for the local market.

It was rumoured the *vaan* had sunk in a freak storm and no one had survived. The local Bohra community was in a state of shock and there was a small mention in the Mombasa Times. The wives had decided to stay in Gujarat and the estate would be handled through lawyers. When details of the estate were published it was realised there was little the two brothers had in savings. Instead, to the surprise of most, they owned almost twelve acres of land along the Nairobi River. The Administrator-General took charge of the land and appointed lawyers for the family. He decided to dispose of the land in one lot by auction.

Many were talking about the amount of land and how the brothers had kept their acquisitions secret, how no one was able to buy the whole lot. It was clear white settlers were more in favour of buying farms or residential plots in the suburbs. Lalji became interested in the land and saw opportunities. After thinking through all the angles of an acquisition he got the other three to sit down with him to hear his proposal. He also made an appointment with Mr Edwards at the Bank to discuss his plans.

What Lalji had developed was a vision of joint ownership of the land with the other three. He was aware Mr Edwards had suggested four smaller loans. He suggested the Land Title be divided in four ways defining each plot in individual names. Lalji wanted to use the land in several ways. Firstly, he felt they would need to downsize by selling off sub-plots or leasing them. That would initially help pay for the bank's large lending. Secondly, they would reserve for their own business what land they needed. He was not aware of other prospective buyers who could afford the high capital outlay. Most would only have use of smaller parcels of land.

In the eyes of the bank, the risk was divided between four parties. Lalji put forward a cogent case for the four of them by emphasising their experience in helping run Samji Lalvani's shop. Mr Edwards listened without interrupting. When Lalji had finished, he lit up his pipe and asked what businesses they had in mind. He wanted to know what the prospects were of selling off or leasing subplots. He asked what their total savings were and what they thought the price of the land would be at auction.

Lalji was prepared for the questions. He presented to Mr Edwards their Savings Books. Mr Edwards wrote down the amounts on a clean sheet of paper.

"We have in mind a workshop for Ramji who has construction experience. Nizar wants to start a hardware shop and import from England. It would stock house building supplies. He would work with Ramji who would have a better idea of the needs of the market," said Lalji. "As regards selling or leasing smaller plots, we know traders are always looking for smaller plots for their shops. I am confident we will be able to lease or sell smaller plots. Additionally, Bhasker and I would start a retail business while one of us still works for the Lalvanis."

"And the price?" asked Mr Edwards.

"That is the trickiest question of all," responded Lalji with a glint of excitement in his eyes. Mr Edwards recognised the same glint he had seen before when Lalji had come to him to discuss the sole agency for the brown paper products.

Lalji went on, "You see, the value of the land for the purchaser is always going to be different from what the Administrator General will ask for. The Administrator has decided to sell in one lot which makes his job a lot easier than splitting it up into smaller plots. The Habib family lawyer would also be keen for the lot to be sold once and not have to revisit the issue again and again."

Lalji looked at Mr Edwards as there was still the question hanging in the air like the curls of his pipe smoke. "With our savings, we could not afford a large loan so we would bid slightly below the reserve price. If there are other buyers interested at auction, we would be unlikely to be successful. But if not, then we still stand a chance if the temptation of having a single buyer for the whole lot is the Administrator General's aim."

"So, let me see now, Lalji," began Mr Edwards, looking straight at him. "You don't know the reserve price and you need me to agree to a loan for the four of you as a consortium but with individual liabilities to the bank. You think you are likely to be overstretched so you hope to sell or lease parts of the land to help repay the loan. Apart from your savings and some experience working for Mr Lalvani, there is little else you bring to the deal. Am I right?" he finished.

Lalji felt the opportunity slipping away. But he had not broken his eye contact. "If you look at it that way you would never be taking any risks," responded Lalji, evoking a rise of the eyebrows on Mr Edwards's face. He went on, "But with no risk you may have a safe and secure bank ticking over, affording only to pay the exorbitant rent for the bank. Nairobi is just taking on the role of a centre of commerce in this part of Africa, and there will be more happening in the future. The Raj is fully committed to it. It is the place for adventurous minds who are focused on their aims and willing to put in the effort to make things work. The four of us believe in our aims and we are confident of success."

There was a pause while everyone reflected on what Lalji had just said. Nizar having understood some of the conversation and Bhasker having studied the tone of it, both felt Lalji was too bold. He might have scuppered any chances they had.

Mr Edwards broke the silence. "How did you know the bank is paying a high rent for this place?" he asked seriously, before bursting into laughter. Everyone except Lalji laughed as it helped lighten their nervousness.

Lalji replied, "Mr Edwards you are renting from rich English nobility, someone who is a settler, who bought out land early. He is having a go at cattle ranching in the White Highlands. The bank needed him to provide a premium spot which he did. I suspect there was little negotiation of the rent as the conversations would have taken place in London. Right now, your head office is probably wondering how long it would need to continue supporting the rent."

Mr Edwards replayed Lalji's words in his mind. Then a look of satisfaction showed in his face. Without further comment, he asked to see where the auction land was on the map. He kept eyeing an area close to Government Road.

"Very well. Let me make inquires and think it over. Bring me the auction sale details when you get them and we can talk again," stated Mr Edwards tapping the ash from his pipe into his waste bin.

Outside, Ramji who had not said anything so far, went first. "*Laljibhai*, you did well to put your case straight to Mr Edwards. It shows we have ambition and guts. Even if we get a flat 'no' we have been at a place today we could not have thought possible a year ago," he concluded.

Nizar added, "It was your idea and you had him thinking about our determination as Ramji says. I agree we had to have a go. At worst he can only refuse."

"And if he agrees we will have a headache and a great deal of work!" quipped Bhasker which made everyone laugh.

Lalji sensed a lift in their morale and a new point in their relationship.

***

A fortnight went past with the four back to their usual roles in the Lalvani shop. Mohan had asked Lalji how the meeting at the bank had gone. Lalji replied they had done their best but could not predict the outcome.

"Well at least you met Mr Edwards and he listened. Most of our people start by borrowing from each other. Nobody that I know has borrowed from the bank. But it makes sense to do what you have planned. The old way would have people giving opinions and interfering with your plans. Having been here a short while you are less well known which helps."

Janki had written again asking how Lalji's plans were working out. She sent news from Lalji's mother who was inquiring about his health and well-being. Purshottam, Lalji's father was having second thoughts whether they had done the right thing by sending the youngsters to Africa. His anxieties receded when he met the village *Sarpanch* (elected leader) who reassured him he had full faith in the mission. He had said to Purshottam, "Remember we sent four of them together. There is safety in numbers. If anything goes wrong, they will all be able to handle it together. Just await their return and you will see."

Since then, Purshottam had regained his smile and started recounting to people how the voyage came into being. Outside his shop three or four customers would gather, sitting on their haunches, sucking at tobacco *bidis (Indian cigarettes)*. They would listen to him, *bidi* held between the front teeth, moustaches stained yellow from the smoke. Just like the dust stains on their white clothes. It was a strange ritual as many came back to hear the story again, which was recounted with the same enthusiasm after the purchase of *bidis*.

'*Remember your brother is now anxious to join you as well,*' Janki had written. '*Your father's store is just ticking over.*' Lalji took that as a cue that funds were needed. He reflected at how gently Janki had put it. In his reply he confided in her that soon the four families would receive funds from their sons.

The others had similar stories from home. Nizar's father had sent news of the rains starting and hoped they would continue for at least three weeks to make the soil fertile again. Bhasker's father sent news of his family and cousins but omitted all reference to how they were managing. Ramji's father had injured his hand with a woodcutter but was doing 'fine' he wrote.

Then one morning Mr Edwards had sent word he wanted to see all four of them.

When they met, he had a business-like air about him and got right to the point. "I have been considering your proposal and although it is unusual there is merit in the project. I have made my own inquiries with the Administrator General's Office. He is intending to list the property for auction within a fortnight. First, of course it must follow the formalities of notice of sale in the *Mombasa Times*. Allow inquiries to be addressed from potential buyers."

"Anyone showing interest?" asked Lalji.

"No one so far, I am told. If it remains the same then you may have a chance," replied Mr Edwards.

"And the price?" asked Lalji.

"Well, I have let the Administrator General know there is a party interested. I informed him the Bank will be funding the purchase. But it all depends on the price," was Mr Edwards' reply, a fixed stare at Lalji's face. "Of course, when we know of the kind of figure they may be willing to accept, they will inform me and we will then know what the bank can do for you. I will keep you posted."

Already the other three were looking weary and downcast, but Lalji had understood the position very well.

"Mr Edwards, let us see what news you get back from the *Administrator General's office*," he emphasised. He was already wandering what Mr Edwards' ultimate agenda was when they left, a friendly smile exchanged between the two of them.

***

The four resolved to send a quarter of their saving each to their families. The Post Office made four telegraphic transfers and said the funds would be there in 48 hours. Sure enough, four days later they received a collective telegram back from Purshottam:

"LALJI PURSHOTTAM FOUR PARCELS RECEIVED SAFELY STOP"

CHAPTER THIRTEEN

JIVAJI VELJI HAD been in British East Africa since 1894. A stonemason and builder, his birth and childhood were in a small village near the town of Bhuj, in Kutch. Like all in his family, working with stone was his skill. Whether it was quarrying, cutting or building, the dwellers of Kutch were in demand all over *Hindustan* (India). But the famines had led to a disastrous downturn in their fortunes.

Added to that was the harsh climate of Kutch, most of which was desert. Sandstorms and dust contributed to the daily ration of misery. Jivaji was only twelve when his uncle had converted to the Khoja-Ismaili faith and become a follower of the Aga Khan. He remembered his father and grandfather agonising over his uncle's decision and the atmosphere of gloom in the house. His uncle still came to visit them and tried to make the family understand his decision. He narrated his difficulties from having little work, a young family to feed and the famine. He had seen no other way to ensure his family's future. He could now get support from his new community; support that came directly from the Aga Khan, their spiritual leader.

Jivaji was sixteen when he went to British East Africa. His father had sent him along with a close friend who was also going for the first time to find work and settle there. Already equipped with good masonry and building skills for his age, Jivaji had also picked up basic carpentry. He worked with his father's friend in Nairobi and they gained a reputation for being good builders. Apart from shops and homes, they were often asked by Municipal departments to provide services. Four years after arriving in Nairobi, Jivaji returned to Kutch and got married.

His first child, was born in Nairobi after a difficult pregnancy for his wife. When his wife became pregnant again, he decided she needed to be with her mother back in India to give birth. When a suitable space was available on a steamer, he booked his wife and son Chagan on it. His wife delivered a healthy girl and Jivaji decided to travel to Kutch to fetch her and the two children. Work was busy but nothing too difficult for his partner to handle alone for a short spell.

They boarded the *SS Sultan* in early July for their return journey to Mombasa. Jivaji's wife remained pale and weak after the delivery. She found eating difficult because of the seasickness. When the steamer sighted Mombasa, Jivaji felt happy. The journey's end was in sight and his wife had come through the difficult voyage. She had managed to feed the new baby despite her poor appetite. Jivaji planned to take the overnight train to Nairobi.

He had packed up the few possessions of the family and called out to his son Chagan, who had been playing on deck. The deck was a narrow walkway linking the second-class cabins. Theirs was the first second-class cabin after the European class accommodation, separated by a large wooden board. Chagan had become an occasional playmate of his first-class neighbour Rodney. Rodney was travelling with his parents for the first time to Mombasa. They were going to be heading inland past Nairobi to the White Highlands to a small village called Naivasha. There Rodney's father, Captain Morgan Chadwell, was being posted as the new Superintendent of Police. After two years in India, Captain Chadwell fancied a return to Africa, having worked in the past in Southern Africa. He thought his wife would be better suited to the cooler climes of the East African highlands.

Chagan and Rodney often played at shooting each other with imaginary guns or bows and arrows. Not able to communicate in a common language they made do with signs and pointing. The barrier between the first and second-class cabins served as a good obstacle to hide behind during their shooting matches. Occasionally Rodney appeared with a cowboy hat and pistol in hand. When his mother called him, he had to go indoors and he would later re-appear to continue the game minus the pistol and hat. Chagan could not understand why that was but he was grateful for the company and the game. Chagan's parents had seen him playing with Rodney and his mother had expressed her reservations.

"You should not play like that with strangers," she would tell him.

"Why can't I play? He is my friend."

"Because it's not good. Pointing guns and shooting is not a game."

"But it's just a game *Baa* (Mother*)*. *Bapuji* (Father) doesn't stop me. He opens the door so I can go out."

"What will happen if you upset the white boy and make him cry? What will we do if his mother complains? Do you think your *Bapuji* (Father) will be able to protect you?"

"Why don't you let the boy play?" Jivaji would say upon hearing the commotion.

"I don't like it. It's not right," she would conclude.

Captain Morgan Chadwell had initially been reluctant to take a post in a remote area. It meant his wife would spend much time alone and his son would need to attend a boarding school near Nairobi. In the end his commanding officer had written to the Chadwells and informed them that there was an active Settlers Club in a nearby town of Nakuru. There a new school for settlers' children was being built. The climate was temperate and the captain would oversee an area the size of Wales. All the local white community were looking forward to welcoming the new Superintendent of Police.

After accepting his commission, Captain Chadwell had received a personal handwritten letter from the Administrator General. He would meet his counterpart at Mombasa on arrival. They would be guests of the local Superintendent before boarding the Uganda Railway. Chadwell felt honoured and couldn't wait to get to Naivasha.

When the steamer sighted Mombasa, Mrs Chadwell had already packed the family's belongings. Captain Chadwell had laid out his khaki uniform on his bunk bed and had busied himself polishing his tan belt, shoes and holster. While his wife showered he attended to the *dhobi* (washerman) who had ironed his wife's dress for the welcoming ceremony. Rodney, on seeing his father talking to the *dhobi*, had picked up his father's pistol lying on a pillow. He went out onto the deck inspecting the heavy pistol like he had seen his father do. He saw Chagan on deck and pointed the pistol at him. Trying to get his fingers around the butt to reach the trigger the heavy pistol kept slipping in his small hands.

Chagan initially thought it was a new toy but soon realised it was a real pistol and froze. He started to cry and screamed out *"Bapuji!* (Father!)*"* On hearing the alarm in his son's voice Jivaji stepped out onto the deck at which point there was an almighty bang. Both Jivaji and the pistol fell to the deck. Rodney rushed into his cabin and collided with his father who had seen the pistol missing as he heard the bang.

"You are not allowed to touch my pistol, I have told you before!" a beetroot red Captain Chadwell shouted at his son, who broke down in tears. His mother had appeared in a bath gown and grabbed her son. While her husband was recovering the pistol off the floor, she alerted him to the deck next door where a man lay on the floor. On realising what had happened Captain Chadwell stormed out and entered the neighbouring cabin. The man's wife was sitting next to him on her haunches and yelling out to him, shaking his shoulder.

Morgan Chadwell's heart sank at the sight and he turned the man over onto his back amid the screaming of the woman and her two children. There was a gun shot wound in the centre of the chest and the man was lifeless, with his eyes open. Chadwell shouted at his wife to get help.

***

As soon as the *SS Sultan* docked word was sent to the Police Captain waiting for Captain Chadwell to be brought on board. In the meantime, Captain Chadwell had changed into full uniform which partly helped to calm the tempers of other passengers. Captain Robert Braithwaite came on board with three *askaris*(contables). He greeted Morgan Chadwell, introducing himself.

"Hope you had a pleasant journey, Chadwell?"

"The journey was satisfactory but we have hit a bit of a snag."

"Oh?"

"Please come to my cabin," said Captain Chadwell, leading the way.

THE AFRICAN STANDARD, Saturday July 29, 1905.
FATAL ACCIDENT
An accident which resulted fatally occurred on board the SS Sultan this morning. It would appear that before the steamer entered the harbour, a gentleman on board whilst handling a revolver accidently let it off; the bullet after passing through a wooden partition struck an Indian sitting on the other side, killing him. We understand that after investigation the magistrate here found the matter to have been purely accidental.

CHAPTER FOURTEEN

THE NEXT TIME Mr Edwards sent for the four he had some drawings from the Acting Land Officer on his desk. A green area outlined the land for sale in the general area of central Nairobi. Another drawing, a blow up of the area, showed utility services from the water and sewage department of the Municipality. There was an outline of a red area next to Government Road which Mr Edwards proposed his bank would buy.

"This is where we intend to construct our new building and offices," he announced, keeping all four in his sight.

The four looked at each other and Lalji spoke, "There would be no objection from us. There is plenty of land. If the bank needs land, we would be pleased to let you have it. Is there any reason to talk about it now?"

"Yes, there is, Lalji. The funds you hold are not going to be enough to secure the kind of loan you will need to purchase the land."

"Purchase, meaning …?" inquired Nizar, looking at Lalji.

Lalji took that as his cue to explain to his friends in Gujarati what Mr Edwards was saying, about needing more capital. All looked concerned.

"The loan…." started Lalji and explained further in Gujarati.

Mr Edwards continued, "I don't know what price the sale will be. I know the Administrator General does not want to split up the land into smaller plots. The family's lawyer also wants a single sale. Your strength is you are looking to buy the full plot, and then split it up to sell off what you do not need. I have had communication with our head office in London and we would like to purchase and build on suitable land for our future expansion. We also need a prime site for which, I am pleased to say, we would pay well," ended Mr Edwards with eyebrows raised, signalling something unsaid.

"Mr Edwards sir, first if we don't have enough money for a good loan then nothing works, isn't it so?" asked Lalji.

Edwards nodded. "I would be able to accept in *principle* that you have the funds from the bank's purchase of its plot of land. With the increased amount, in *principle*, the bank would be willing to arrange a larger loan," explained Mr Edwards, a mischievous glint in his eyes.

Before Lalji had a chance to answer Ramji, who had looked out of it and far away, interjected: "Yes, yes, it's good. *Principle* is good. Very good," with a wide smile on his face.

The other three looked at Ramji with surprise and amusement as they didn't think he had understood much of the conversation.

Lalji asked Mr Edwards, "So the upset price is important for this working out, no?"

"Lalji, the upset price may still be above your reach. Maybe we can do better than that. I have met the Administrator General recently on a different matter and we have discussed around this subject. With this other way it may be possible to pay less than the upset price. But it carries more risk as it could attract other purchasers."

"I don't understand, sir," said Lalji.

"When we know what the upset price would be, we will see if the bank's loan, your savings and our purchase price for the land will be enough. If it is, you would need to put your bid at no more than the upset price. That's straightforward, yes?"

"Yes, sir."

"If you can't reach the upset price, then provided there are no bidders at auction the sale would be withdrawn. It would be put up for private bidding at a future date by the Administrator General. That will need a notice to be printed in the newspaper to give the public another chance to bid."

"And if there are still no other buyers, we can buy with what we have? Even if we are short of the upset price..." Lalji stated, realising the smartness of the plan.

"Yes, but there is the risk you may lose it all if there is interest from other buyers," stated Mr Edwards.

Lalji nodded but doubted Mr Edwards would let matters get that far. Especially as he wanted the land for building his new bank. Additionally, the loans to the four stood to bring him to the attention of his bosses in London.

Lalji explained the second option to the others. Ramji stated that, it was better to go for the upset price, and not below. "If we miss that we will lose our grip on the land and the scheme will fall into dust," he said. Lalji smiled at the comparisons from his building work.

There seemed to be a consensus amongst the four that Ramji was right. Lalji agreed but could not dismiss the alternative plan straight away. He explained to Mr Edwards they would consider both options. "We will keep our eyes and ears open in case others are also interested," he said, bringing a smile on Mr Edwards's face.

Auction day came. Once the lawyers of the deceased's family had calculated the upset price, the Administrator General's office informed Mr Edwards. The four *jehajis* (travellers) were going to be short. They had discussed the option to forgo the auction and hope for a private bid afterwards which seemed the only way.

Some of the land fronted Government Road and the rest sprawled towards Nairobi River. The upset price was set at 35,000 rupees. The price was already discounted by thirty percent on the usual going rate the administration sold plots for commercial use. Mr Edwards's bank required half an acre and was offering a generous 7,500 rupees. The four *jehajis* had saved just over 3,000 rupees in total. The bank was willing to lend 20,000 rupees which left a short-fall of 4,500 rupees.

Mohan had inquired how their plans were progressing. Although matters were confidential, the four felt he was trustworthy and shared their difficulty with him. The following day Mohan approached them and said he could loan them the 4,500 rupee shortfall as a loan. His father's death had released life insurance funds which he could lend. The arrangement would be that if the four were unable to pay him back after a year, they would forfeit one acre to him as a penalty. He wanted his cash back and the penalty would encourage the four *jehajis* to pay him back on time.

Mr Edwards saw the four with Mohan and to go over the whole proposal. He knew Mohan was good for the shortfall as his deceased father's life insur-ance money had recently been lodged at the bank. He finally announced the formula was sound. But they would need to secure their own agreement with Mohan. The bank would draw up the paperwork for the loan and the sale of the land that it required. Mr Edwards would also speak to the Administrator General and inform him of the gist of the transactions so the auction would not be held up. All four of the *jehajis* and Mohan signed forms for Mr Edwards to make the final money transfer to the auction if their bid was successful. There would be further costs like taxes, auction fees, legal and registration fees. Mr Edwards undertook to provide a further small loan to cover these.

On the morning of the auction the four *jehajis* and Mohan entered the auction room. There were chairs at the front of the room which were designated for white settlers. Only one occupant sat in the middle, a Mr Mario Cassini who had come to bid on farm machinery sold by customs. Mr Mario, as he liked to be addressed, had a small farm north of Nairobi. There he was growing grapes, olives and coffee having worked in vineyards in his native Italy. Behind him were a couple of rows for 'British Subjects and Goans' which were empty. Then came the non-designated seating for Indians and others. Lalji wondered if the bidding followed a similar pecking order.

None of the five had ever been to an auction before. Lalji was surprised by the informality of the room. Bhasker complained about the smell, a mixture of old wooden furniture and mineral oil. The floor had been swept, revealing giant rings of oil stains, wood chipped in places. Although it dealt with sales of high value, to Lalji it was still a market stall. There were a few other people scattered here and there, but no one that Lalji or Mohan recognised. At precisely 10 am the auctioneer came in, a middle-aged Englishman with a monocle in one eye, wearing a beige cotton suit, white shirt and striped tie. He wished everyone good morning and proceeded to read out the rules of the auction in English, politely nodding in reassurance to Lalji. Lalji had met him briefly beforehand when registering as a participant; Mr Edwards had introduced them.

A small list of the lots was passed around and posted on a wall. The first few items were from the Uganda Railway of unclaimed goods including ten bags each of rice, *masoor dahl* (lentil) and sugar. All three lots were secured by an Indian man standing at the back of the room. Next came a second-hand bicycle for which there was furious bidding between three Indian men. Then came the farm machinery of interest to Mr Mario. There was no other interested party so he put in a very low bid which prompted the auctioneer to threaten to withdraw it. There then followed a long argument between the auctioneer and Mr Mario. It soon became clear that the machinery was originally intended for Mr Mario. He had failed to have it released at customs because all his documentation was in Italian. He claimed he was being denied the option to await further documents in English from Italy. The auctioneer withdrew the lot and informed Mr Mario to have further dialogue with customs. That seemed to partly satisfy the furious Mr Mario who proceeded to put on his jacket, babbling in Italian under his breath on his way out.

A 'wireless' radio came next which was bought by the same Indian man who had picked up the foodstuffs. Then the auctioneer turned to the last item: the various plots of land bundled up into the sale of the estate of the Habib brothers. He introduced the lot and announced the reserve price, which he said had been offered already, looking at Lalji and his three partners. He asked for bids to start above the reserve price. A hand went up at the back of the room and instead of stating a price, the person wanted to know if there was any possibility of the lot being split up.

"No there is not," came the firm answer from the auctioneer.

There was a pause afterwards which felt like the longest span of time for the four buyers. The auctioneer looked around the room, saw no interest in other faces, announced the sale was going for the upset price and crashed his gavel down. The four looked at each other as if to say, *"Is that it?"* Lalji was then surrounded by three individuals who wanted to know if he would split the land and sell smaller plots.

CHAPTER FIFTEEN

PELTING RAINS WITH occasional hail arrived in Nairobi without much warning. It seemed they were here to stay. It could rain for hours at a time with flash floods of red Nairobi soil washing away down the roads. Bulging blood-red streams fed into the Nairobi River, which burst its banks. There was mud everywhere, making it almost impossible to move goods around. The public struggled to walk in the slippery sludge.

Thankfully there were almost no mosquitoes. The swarming termites provided their own kind of nuisance, flying almost blanket-thick around lamp posts. It was during one of these downpour days that the car of Khimji Bhagwanji got stuck in deep mud near Mohan's shop. There was a lot of commotion and cries of 'Har Ambee' as passers-by tried to free a sunken wheel from the soft mud. The car was eventually released and the driver headed for his destination, wiping the cold rain from his face and ears.

Lalji asked Mohan about Khimji Bhagwanji. According to Mohan he was wealthy businessman from Mumbai who had set up a business in Tanganyika ten years before. He had acquired Trade Licences in a few towns in German East Africa. He supplied uniforms and timber. Khimji Bhagwanji had arrived in Nairobi having turned his back on German East Africa. He was looking to buy land for agriculture. He realised the policies of the British and the German sarkars (governments) meant that the odds of him buying land were slim, being Indian. Mohan added that it was rumoured that he intended to head further inland. Somewhere past the White Highlands where he may stand a better chance of acquiring land.

Khimji Bhagwanji, who liked to be called "KB", was a qualified civil engineer who had graduated from university in his home city of Mumbai. He liked to refer to Mumbai as 'Bombay' and had managed to get admitted to a

Parsee Gymkhana Club in Mumbai. He was always immaculately dressed in western business suits. His tall stature and handsome looks had once given him the title of the most eligible bachelor in Mumbai.

Having a successful civil engineering firm in Mumbai, he decided in his mid-thirties to find a more challenging pursuit. He was influenced by Joseph Pullen, the Chief Planning Director of Mumbai. Pullen was returning to Scotland after completing an extensive tour of duty in British East Africa and Mumbai. Of the same age and both bachelors, they had spent many evenings together at the Gymkhana Club. They mused over life, politics, and the economic powers of states.

The two came from starkly different backgrounds. Pullen's father was a docker and could hardly manage to provide for his family unless he worked overtime. KB's father had been a wealthy businessman who sent his children to study abroad. Pullen never finished high school. Joseph Pullen also loved his single malt whilst KB was a teetotaller. KB was also a strict *Vaishnav* (follower of Lords Vishnu, Ram and Krishna), remaining a strict vegetarian with his only vices being small cigars and a penchant for well-cut suits.

Not content with his success, KB believed all educated Indians had to attain positions in society of political or economic power, or both. He knew he needed to change his life's trajectory to achieve this. He saw economic freedom also as the way forward for all Indians to achieve freedom from the Raj. Joseph Pullen, or 'Joss' as KB referred to him, advised his friend to head out to Africa. There he would find what he was looking for in life he advised.

"There is something to be said for the new continent. It's rugged and beautiful at the same time. Everything is new, waiting to be touched by the hand of modern development. The climate is both harsh and seductive, the people fearsome and warm," he would reminisce.

KB decided to turn his back on engineering and rejected the notion of settling down with a high society wife. His calling to Africa, the challenges and the prospects of making it big enticed him. He had decided after much research that the opportunities were better in German East Africa. Much against Joss's advice as his friend did not trust the Germans. Once there, KB set up a small factory in the coastal town of Tanga. With contacts from the Mumbai commercial world, he started importing material for garments. A local German agent procured for him three *Pfaff* sewing machines. His business was an instant success with the German *sarkar* who needed uniforms for their African recruits for the police and armed services. Uniforms were also required for other government employees. With the help of a young designer from Mumbai, KB had made a roaring success of his first venture within three years. He became popular and well known in the local German community.

Within the same compound of his factory, he set up a sawmill and started supplying timber for construction. With a permit allowing logging in local forests, he had a small gang of local men trained in spotting mixed hardwood species. Within six years he had a major timber operation and he saw his wealth rise. His German *sarkar* contacts were happy with his products and saw his factories as essential to their mission. They coveted him by presenting him a *"Favoured Trader"* title. He also supplied prisoner uniforms for prisoner gangs who were forced into labour.

One day Khimji Bhawanji saw a diligent employee of his in the ranks of a prisoner gang. On further inquiry, he learnt that the man had been incarcerated for stealing fish from the market. He had denied the accusation and the evidence was flimsy. Khimji Bhagwanji tried to have the man released, even offering his personal surety, but his efforts fell on deaf ears. He later learnt his employee had died in a police camp before his trial. Rumours were rife about violence and executions of prisoners in camps. His respect for the German *sarkar* was to suffer a further dent when they introduced an enforced cotton growing policy for the locals. This came coupled with a "head tax." People had to grow cotton and sell it to the *sarkar* to be able to pay the head tax.

Within the African people there was intense hatred of the Germans and Khimji Bhagwanji could sense the beginnings of a rebellion. Sure enough, within months there was a serious uprising against the forced cotton growing and the head tax. The *Maji-Maji Rebellion* was crushed ruthlessly. A scorched earth policy followed the crackdown, and the resultant famine added to the genocide count. In the end, hundreds of thousands of those who had rebelled lost their lives alongside innocent non-participants. On the German side, a few hundred African riflemen and a handful of their German officers were killed.

KB had approached the *sarkar* to be allowed to buy land for agriculture and much to his surprise this was flatly refused without discussion. It was made clear to him that as an Indian he would not be allowed to hold land, or to farm. When he applied for tax clearance to visit Mumbai for a month, it was denied. The *sarkar* needed him to keep supplying uniforms for prisoner gangs, under new 'emergency regulations.' Feeling trapped and fearful, KB saw his position to be similar to the local Africans, ensnared in the administrative whims of the colonial administration.

KB saw the *sarkar's* greed for more produce and tax lead to chaotic ruling. Young civic administrators and military commanders, fresh from graduating in Germany, started to push their weight around. KB had surmised that the Germans nursed a deep inferiority complex and resentment in relation to the British. He thought the British had a head start, using their Indian subjects to further enhance their colonial ambitions in Africa.

KB decided to quit and cut his losses. He packed two trunks and secretly boarded the *vaan* of an Arab trader he knew well and landed in Mumbai four weeks later. There he spent a few months reassessing his life. His desire to return to Africa rekindled, as nowhere provided him with the same excitement of fresh opportunities. Remembering his friend Joss's words of not trusting Germans, he decided British East Africa was likely to be a better place. He cursed himself for not taking Joss's advice earlier. Joss convinced him the British were investing better, first building the Uganda Railway, and then encouraging white settlers to farm. But Joss had once said in a drunken rant that you should *'never trust an Englishman unless you can see his hands!'* He never understood what that meant and Joss had never elaborated, but the remark had stuck in his mind.

KB knew the British reserved farmland ownership for white settlers only. But he figured that the railway stretched well past the White Highlands into Uganda, which had attracted much fewer white settlers. This was partly because of the distance from Nairobi and the pesty mosquitoes. It was there, where the British had first tried to start a Zionist state, that he saw his prospects of acquiring cheaper farmland. He had learnt the country was lush and fertile.

A socialite by nature, once in Nairobi KB had made contacts in the British *sarkar* (government) after first looking up contacts that Joss had recommended. His stories of German East Africa and its administration were popular in the smoking rooms and bars of the Norfolk Hotel or the New Stanley Hotel. He learnt more about the "Zionist Scheme" from Ken Marchant, a middle grade civil servant from the Administrator's Office, with whom he had struck up a good friendship.

When the Jews rejected the scheme there was jubilation amongst the settlers, who had opposed it from the beginning. At the same time, it was a major disappointment to the *sarkar* who were desperate to see settlements in Uganda after the completion of the railway. Having failed to attract white settlers and then the Jews, they had not considered any further options.

It was then that KB decided to pay the area a visit. Having boarded the train in Nairobi, he spent a few days heading up country learning about the land, climate, and people. He stopped at Nakuru in the heart of the White Highlands to get a better impression of how the white settlers were managing. The talk in Nairobi was of a lack of reliable labour and constant disputes with 'squatters' in the region, making it difficult to get farms established. KB had seen an advertisement in the paper for a bed and breakfast in Nakuru, and had sent a letter to book his room in advance.

The house, embraced by a veranda full of flowerpots in bloom reminded him of a garlanded bride, the red painted roof like a red sari veil over her head. He pulled the chain for the bell at the front door. A large dog started barking inside and a tall slim white woman, her hair in curlers, came to the door.

Opening the door, she held out her hand and welcomed him in with a broad smile. She asked a servant to chain up the dog. She had very pale skin and tried to draw attention away from it by a generous application of rouge on her cheeks, and cherry red lipstick.

"Your room. Available?" asked KB. "I wrote you a letter," he explained.

"Yes of course Mr Bagwanji, come in." She pronounced his name perfectly. The house was warmly furnished with carpets and a small stone fireplace in the living room. There was a zebra skin rug on the floor.

"Please, sit down." She indicated an easy chair to KB and sat herself down opposite. "How long would you like the room for?"

"I am passing through on my way to Uganda. One or two nights."

There was no mistaking his Bombay accent. She introduced herself. "I am Dorothy McLeod. My husband works for the Agriculture Department here in Western Province and he often goes to Uganda. You are from Bombay if I am not mistaken?" she asked.

Surprised, KB answered he was.

"You see, I was born in Delhi and lived many years in Bombay. My father was in the British Army stationed there. So, what brings you to Nakuru, and Uganda?"

"I am looking to invest in a business," answered KB, avoiding any talk of buying land. "Right now, I am looking to see what is possible. You see, this is my first visit to this area. I spent many years in German East Africa."

"Oh! That must have been interesting. You will need to speak to my husband who knows what there is to know about Uganda. I am sure he will be delighted to speak with you when he gets here this evening."

"Thank you, Mrs McLeod. I would also like to talk with him. Right now, I will drop my case here and go to the shops to look around. Can you tell me what the charge will be for the room?"

"It's one rupee, four annas for the night, including hot water and breakfast. If you want supper, it would be an extra six annas."

"That's fine. No supper thanks. I am vegetarian."

"Fine. Let me show you the room and the bathroom," and she led the way to the side of the single-story house.

***

KB returned to the house before sunset. He had made acquaintance with a small trader, a Tulsidas Moolchand who invited him home for supper that evening. There he also met Atma Singh, the railway station master at Nakuru. Atma Singh had initially arrived as an indentured labourer to work on the railway. Unlike most of his Sikh compatriots, he had opted to stay on after his English supervisor asked him. He had better education than most from his group and managed some English words.

Tulsidas and Atma Singh were deep in conversation. They were thrilled to speak to the stranger and share their knowledge of the changes along the route to Uganda, the peoples, climate, wildlife. They mentioned there were some white settlers who wanted to grow tea and coffee in the cooler climate of the western escarpment. Further west towards Lake Victoria and Uganda the fauna changed to dense grassland. Atma Singh was surprised that an Indian wanted to travel inland to Uganda. He had travelled to the end of the line to Kisumu, then onwards on the *SS William McKinnon* on Lake Victoria to Kampala. He talked excitedly of Uganda, saying it reminded him of the *haryali* (lushness), of Punjab. Those words stuck in KB's mind.

On returning to the McLeod house, his approach was announced by the loud Alsatian held on a chain by a tall *askari* (watchman), seated on the front veranda. Mr McLeod opened the door and greeted KB, inviting him in with an outstretched hand. "Geoffrey McLeod, but call me Geoff." He was holding a tumbler of whiskey and invited KB to sit with him for a sundowner, offering KB a glass. KB explained he did not drink. They sat on a floral-patterned sofa in the lounge. Mrs McLeod joined them opposite the fireplace and brought in fresh pineapple juice for KB and herself.

"I hear you are on your way to Uganda, to check the place out. Good neck of the woods. Needs more people like you. Good people, the Bagandans. Plenty to do there. Depends what you have in mind?" Geoff inquired with raised eyebrows, swirling his whiskey glass. KB noticed he only spoke in short sentences, like announcements.

"Well, I am open to any opportunities. I had a factory in Tanga making uniforms and a timber mill."

"That's jolly good! We could do with your sort of expertise here. Anywhere in British East Africa really. How did the Germans treat you?"

"The Germans were honest in their dealings with me. Also, generous. But I didn't see any long-term future there."

"Too right. Can't trust them. Are you a family man KB?" inquired McLeod after another swirl of the whiskey glass.

"No, sir. I am single."

"That's good show, my man! You would do well. Nothing holding you back then." He turned pink after glancing at his wife who was eyeing the ceiling.

They talked of life in Nakuru, the Rift Valley, building of the railway and how the settlers were getting on. They discussed Bombay where the McLeods had first met. Finally, KB mustered up his courage and ask the direct question.

"Is there any prospect of purchasing agricultural land in the areas beyond the White Highlands, towards Uganda?" asked KB.

Geoff was not expecting the question and fumbled for a moment, whiskey ceasing to swirl. "I am not sure of that. It's all Crown Land now. Depends on what the Crown decides I guess," he replied with a chuckle.

Mrs McLeod, who had been silently listening, interjected. "Darling I was speaking to the Commissioner's wife at the last Women's Association meeting and she was saying how disappointed the Commissioner was that the Jewish scheme had not worked out. She said he was concerned they were not able to attract enough settlers."

KB studied Geoff's face.

"You may be right, dear. Can't say really. Not my area of work," replied McLeod.

"Maybe you could introduce this gentleman to the Commissioner," she suggested.

"Yes, yes. He would be interested in what the Germans have been up to. Splendid. I will see what I can do," was his response, the whiskey spinning energetically again. He took down KB's details and said he would write to the Commissioner in the morning. Mrs McLeod looked most satisfied.

CHAPTER SIXTEEN

WORD SPREAD QUICKLY in Nairobi that the Habib brothers' properties had been acquired by the four young men from Porbander. It became the main topic of conversation amongst the Indian community but barely got any attention elsewhere. The acquisition, using a bank loan, also inspired a great deal of interest.

For many, it was a step into the unknown. Some wondered who Lalji was, the leader of the four. Was he clever at business or had he been hoodwinked by the English bank manager? Dragging his three compatriots with him into a trap? What would they do with such a large chunk of land? How would they pay the loan back? Unable to fathom out the answers, most were not hesitant in making predictions. 'They will be back in India before the end of the year after bankruptcy.' Or 'What can young men know about how a business is built up piece by piece?' Or 'They must think the rest of us are fools'. The opinions at the tea houses and at the barbers emphasised how the land was useless for farming or building, from many who purported to know. "If it was that easy the Habib brothers would have done it a long time ago."

Mohan informed Lalji of the rumours doing the rounds and how most thought the acquisition was a risk too far. He even mentioned how they had become the brunt of jokes. Lalji shrugged it off, with not even a fleeting concern the critics could be right.

"In business, there are always options," he told himself.

Apart from the parcel of land for the bank, they had two potential buyers who had expressed interest in plots. The process of finalising the sale would take three to six weeks. There was much to do with more bank and legal documents, municipality permissions and registering the land in their names. The four of them had discussions but all looked to Lalji for advice and leadership, and his final word if there was disagreement. They started to study the land on the map and made site visits. It was clear that the lower areas near the river were more appropriate for growing crops while those near the town were more attractive to build on.

Firstly, they had to define how much land and where they wanted to retain some for themselves. Secondly, they needed to sell some land to bring in cash. They started talking to those interested in plots. What remained would be the greatest challenge: how to put it to good use. Within days they had promising conversations. First, an established businessman called Popat Ibrahim came to discuss a land swap. He had four prime plots in the vicinity of Victoria Street and Government Road. Two were built on. One housed a furniture and timber shop on Government Road, while the other had a hardware outlet on Victoria Street. The two further unbuilt plots were on Government Road. Originally from Surat, Ibrahim had a large family of brothers and nephews. They were looking to merge their interests into one outlet and at the same time expand their business space. Besides making furniture, they wanted to sell tools from Europe.

Lalji realised the Ibrahim sites were in prime commercial spots, ideal for retail trade. Lalji and Ramji knew the two buildings, which were falling into disrepair. They realised that the ideal use of these sites would be to establish new stone buildings with shops on the ground floor. On the one or two floors above there would be offices. They had no capital to build immediately, but the existing outlets could be temporarily used as they were. Nairobi was expanding and there was likely to be a shortage of both office and retail space in prime locations soon. They also realised that the price of the two empty plots would need to reflect their inability to develop or use them initially. Lalji was confident that he could negotiate a price that was workable for them and fair to Popat Ibrahim.

They received a second proposal which came from Mr Edwards at the bank. He had become aware that there was a shortage of storage space in Nairobi. A lot of cargo brought in by the railway needed road transport and dispersal to final destinations after handing over to the owners. Roads could be impassable for days at a time, especially in the rainy season. The railways authority provided limited and expensive storage space which was not well secured. Mr Edwards suggested to Lalji that he should think about building storage space and making it available for commercial use.

"Yes, I see there is a need and an opportunity," replied Lalji, "but we need to be able to pay all the bills at the end of the month. At this rate there will not be much left over for construction."

"Have you enough finance to build your own business space?" asked Mr Edwards.

"I don't think we do right now."

"You can't afford to wait long as the debts will start to build up."

"Yes, Mr Edwards. We are talking to others to sell plots and exchange some land for better sites in the town centre, around Government Road."

"That is good news Lalji!" exclaimed Mr Edwards with a big smile. "You must come and talk to me about that another time. Today I have a proposal for you which I want you to hear. That is why I sent for you."

"Yes, Mr Edwards, I am listening."

"The Army moves supplies along the railway as you know. A lot of gear is unloaded in Nairobi to go north or south. This is a regular route for them. They use their own lorries but these are taking a beating on the roads here. Many more have broken down than are in use, awaiting spares."

"Yes, a difficult situation, Mr Edwards."

"Quite so. I was talking to the C.O. at Nairobi barracks who was inquiring if I knew of any space available in Nairobi for storage. I told him there was not at present but a certain group was looking into building on land in Nairobi for commercial use."

"I see."

"He was keen to learn more and I said I knew the party and that I would speak to you. When I told him, like you say, finance might be a problem, he suggested one year's rent could be arranged in advance through the Empire Office in London. I think that's a helpful idea. What do you think?"

"That sounds good. When can we meet the C.O.?" responded Lalji, immediately.

"Wait Lalji, why don't you talk to the others. You need to know the rough costs of building something like this. I will find out what the C.O.'s budget is for the year and we can then see what size is affordable to build to make it work for everybody. Hopefully, his budget will be bigger than his needs," said Mr Edwards with a big smile.

"That is good. Good *principle* as my partner would say," chuckled Lalji and made Mr Edwards laugh out aloud.

***

Nizar obtained more detailed maps of the area from the Public Map Office of the Nairobi Survey Department. Water, future electric supply and proposed roads needed to be considered to decide how the land was to be managed, let or sold. Every evening at Mohan's shop after closing the four would lay the plans out on a table and discuss matters further. Nizar liked charts and maps and had traced the outline of the land on the charts in red.

Firstly, they marked the land the Bank had asked for. The area near the river was soft but well drained. It would do well for small scale produce of cash crops. There was always a need for fresh food produce in Nairobi. From the river and further towards the town a few small workshops had been set up and the area was starting to look like a mini-industrial area. This was also the area of interest to Popat Ibrahim. There was a narrow dirt track connecting with the western end of Government Road. The land for the Army would need to be near this section to restrict their heavy lorries to the top of the road.

Nizar was keen that one of Popat Ibrahim's existing shops on Government Road could be an outlet for their own business. The sales would be more retail than wholesale from that location. Ramji still required a workshop to start carpentry and building work. The options for him were to build a small workshop on the new land or occupy the remaining Popat Ibrahim shop on Victoria Street. Lalji suggested they occupy and share one of the two shops while they were getting going and the other property let out to bring in some income. All agreed.

Within a month they had made firm decisions. Further site visits followed. Mr Edwards came on a couple of visits to familiarise himself with the issues. Mr Edwards suggested a Parsi attorney by the name of Pherosha Pestonjee to do all the legal work for the four partners, and for their sub-leases. Pestonjee agreed a good reduction of his fees in the hope that the bank would pass more clients to him in the future. The bank's own lawyers were Roberts McDonald, whose head office was in South Africa.

Pestonjee was a middle-aged lawyer, short with a pale complexion. He had a copper-beaten skin, scars from childhood smallpox. He was well dressed, polite and spoke Gujarati with a Parsi accent. That was a big advantage for the four as they did not need to trouble Mr Edwards to get legal matters explained. Pestonjee had a tiny office with one window, housing three small

desks and two typewriters, situated on Queensway near the Courts. He shared the space with four other lawyers, three Parsi and one Bengali from Calcutta. Two black advocate gowns hung on a wall, shared by all for attending court.

On Mr Edwards's advice, the four were going to set up fifty-year business leases having acquired the freehold in their names. All the legal paperwork was prepared, signed and lodged with the relevant authorities over a few days. Mr Edwards handled the banking and funds transfer for all the parties. The bank had already fenced off their plot and a billboard outside announced the future opening of the new bank.

The arrangement with the bank was the first to be completed and the easiest. No sooner had they finalised the legal documents when surveyors and architects were seen on the site. The land swap deal was more complicated and took longer. The final picture saw Popat Ibrahim swap his four central Nairobi properties for a single plot almost equal to his four. There were four sets of papers to be lodged with the City Municipal Council and applications made for the utility supplies. Popat Ibrahim was a patient man who had grown to admire the four young men. He regarded the deal as a winner for them all, even though he had to give up his plots at below market price. For his extended family to be working out of the same premises was a big plus.

The Army was the slowest to come in with their agreement. London took its time with the matter discussed in various committees. They kept coming back with more questions. Finally, they gave their go ahead after realising there was nowhere safe or large enough in Nairobi to store incoming weapons and equipment. Especially after the heavy rains closed country roads.

CHAPTER SEVENTEEN

THE AFRICAN STANDARD, May 1905

HURRAH!
The Zionists decline- without thanks
The Zionist Executive Committee at Vienna have decided to recommend to the Basle Congress that the British Government's offer of land in East Africa should be declined, as exclusively pastureland was unfit for Jewish Emigrants.

***

THE AFRICAN STANDARD, July 1905

The New Promised Land
The Zionists are waiting with eagerness the report of the small commission which they sent out to East Africa to examine and report on the new land of promise, the plateau near the Uganda Railway offered them by the English Government, says the Manchester Dispatch. The result of this investigation is expected to be known immediately. There appears, however, to be some doubt whether the Guas Ngishu plateau is best suited for pastoral or agricultural occupation. If agricultural, the 5,000 square miles would support a much larger number of people than if they were pastoral. In any case, there is no dispute to its being an ideally beautiful country. English travellers agree that it resembles the more hilly portions of Great Britain. There are green-wooded downs, roaring Scotch burns, meadows of blue forget-me-nots and pink and white clover, and such characteristically English flowers as violets, daisies, and buttercups vie with more tropical flowers. As to climate, it is of perennial sunshine pleasantly varied by April showers. It is, therefore, even more difficult to understand the reluctance of the Jews to settle there. It

is curious that though there seems to be difficulty in inducing them to go to East Africa there is none in getting them to go to the Cape. According to statistics, there are 20,000 Jews in the Transvaal. The figures for the census of 1904 are 19,537 in Cape Colony, 1,616 in the Orange River, and 585 in Rhodesia, and there are estimated to be at least 1,700 in Natal, or a total of 45,000 for South Africa. The explanation is, of course to be found in the superior attractions of gold and diamond to the pastoral pursuits of the ancient race.

***

On his return from Uganda, KB stopped once again in Nakuru and booked the room at the McLeods. He had taken the Lake Victoria boat to Kampala where he rented a room above a Gujarati tailors' shop. He spent three days there, looking around the small town of Kampala and the surrounding areas.

He saw many differences from Nairobi and Tanga. The local Africans were more interested in agriculture and had skills in growing crops. Fishing was commonplace. In many ways the locals resembled the Luo people around Kisumu, on the Kenyan side of Lake Victoria. Also, they were welcoming and less suspicious of outsiders. The country was lusher, especially around the many scattered lakes which fed the dark soil. The Kingdom of Baganda had a monarchy, at the head of it was the Kibaka, respected and treated with great awe by his people. He was locked into an arrangement of "protection" from his enemies by the colonial *sarkar* (government), in return for access to his land. KB was familiar with this protection model from Indian Maharajas who had signed similar treaties.

With abundant lakes in Uganda came mosquitoes and malaria. Most of the lakes were infested with crocodiles. Children fell prey to both crocodiles and snakes frequently.

On his return to the McLeods in Nakuru, KB rang the bell at the front veranda. The familiar barking of the dog followed until Mrs McLeod opened the door. Once again, she was dressed smartly in a flower printed cotton frock and her rouge, as before, was overdone.

"Good afternoon, Mr Bhagwanji."

"Good afternoon, Mrs McLeod," greeted KB tipping his black hat. "I was inquiring if you could accommodate me for another night or two?"

"Yes, of course. The room is unoccupied. Bring your things and come in."

Once KB was in, she pointed to the room and asked, "Why don't you drop your things in your room and join me for a cup of tea. I have just made a fresh pot."

"Thank you. That is most kind."

Tea was served in the rear veranda overlooking the garden. Abu, who was the cook, butler and domestic worker, served it with home-made banana bread and fruit jam.

"Mr McLeod is coming home earlier today. He has a reception to attend in the Town Offices to discuss some new proposal from Lord Bellingham. His Lordship has acquired land near Njoro to start farming wheat," she informed him. "Oh! I almost forgot; Mr McLeod has spoken to the Commissioner about your interest in Uganda. Mr McLeod says the Commissioner was most interested and suggested a meeting when you returned."

KB noted the formality with which she referred to her husband. "That would be excellent!" he stated, feeling elated.

The next afternoon KB was seated on a wooden chair in the Commissioner's Office next to Geoff McLeod. The room was pungent with the smell of pipe tobacco and the Commissioner, a tall man in a uniform of khaki top and shorts, was seated behind his desk. He greeted them, extending his arm. "Good afternoon gentlemen. I am the Commissioner of Western British East Africa. Major William Roger-Benfield is the name. Geoffrey McLeod and I know each other of course."

After KB introduced himself, they sat down. "I hear you left German East Africa and are here to purchase agriculture land. For what purpose might I ask?" the Commissioner inquired, revealing tobacco-stained teeth of various hues, brown to yellow, in different states of disrepair.

KB was pleased with the direct approach. At least he was not going to be sent out after a polite conversation and a cup of tea.

"I have experience of running a timber mill in Tanga. My main business was producing uniforms for the Colonial Government. I am looking to buy land for agriculture in Uganda. I intend to try out a few crops first, to see what will do well in the soil there," announced KB.

"Anything particular in mind as a crop?" asked the Commissioner, his eyes focusing on KB. For the first time KB noticed the icy blue eyes.

"Well, I have a few thoughts. I would need to take advice from people like Mr McLeod here to find out what the experience has been so far for other settlers. I have contacts in British India at the Poona Horticultural Institute, who are experts in tropical fruit and plantation crops."

"Are you thinking of introducing something new in that case?"

KB knew this was the make-or-break question, "Yes, something which suits the climate, the soil and resistant to local disease. *Something different from the crops of the settlers already here,*" emphasised KB slowly and clearly.

There was a fast nodding of the Commissioner's head after a sigh. "Any initial thoughts, having spoken with your contacts in Poona?"

"Well sir, I was thinking of trying sugar cane first, and maybe cotton," replied KB.

The Commissioner's eyebrows flicked up in admiration and Geoff broke into a smile. "Yes, that sounds like a sound proposition" responded the Commissioner. "What would you want from us apart from the land?"

"Well sir, the area needs a good new crop to open its commercial scope. The terms of sale of the land need to be right, at least the same as offered to other settlers."

"Of course," agreed the Commissioner.

"It would be important to include the option to be granted more land in the future if the crop is successful to start a useful export trade." KB watched the Commissioner who sat up straight in his chair. He went on, "And favourable rates on the railway for the exports."

There was a pause as the two men studied each other. "Is there anything else?" asked the Commissioner.

"Yes, one more thing. The land needs to be in an area where there are no land disputes with the locals. If there are, then the disputes need to be settled first so there is no need to resort to force later."

"That's quite some demands, Mr Bhagwanji."

"You will find it's not too different from what was offered to the settlers invited to start the Zionist State. And for my part, I will not be treading on anyone's toes from the established settlers."

The Commissioner was surprised at Bhagwanji's knowledge of the settlers' entitlements and privileges. He liked that, there was a glint of admiration in his eyes.

"Let me consider your proposals further and I will contact you in Nairobi. Meanwhile, will you drop me a note of your proposals. I don't want to miss anything out," said the Commissioner. KB responded by handing him an envelope which he removed from an inside pocket, smiling.

" I can see why you did not stick around in German East Africa," commented the Commissioner with a reciprocating smile, standing up to see the two men to the door.

CHAPTER EIGHTEEN

WITHIN WEEKS OF the legal work being completed, the four *jehajis* (travellers) had decided to adopt the name of *'Porbander Stores'* as their business title. It was a requirement of the bank that they had a business identity. The bank account would be managed by Lalji.

In the end, the land exchange with Popat Ibrahim happened without a hitch. The four partners of Porbander Stores decided the Victoria Street premises would be the shop for Nizar and Ramji. The front would house Nizar's hardware outlet and Ramji's timber yard and carpentry workshop would be in the back, accessed from the side. The Hindu priest from the temple came to perform prayers to bless the business and the auctioned land.

Construction workers had moved into the bank's plot and started digging the foundations. The Municipality agreed to widen the dirt track for the Army trucks to access their land. There followed a period of inaction while they waited for fencing materials to arrive which the Army wanted. Plans for their *godown* (warehouse), drawn by the same firm of architects and surveyors that the bank used, downsized the storage area to allow a covered space for vehicles. Approvals were obtained from all parties. More importantly, the cost was within budget, met from the annual rent received in advance.

All this had a healthy impact on the finances of Porbander Stores. There were two other potential purchasers who wanted small plots but only for an outright sale. The partners decided since their cash flow was manageable, they would rent out the remaining land instead.

Ramji agreed with Popat Ibrahim to do all the carpentry for his new outlet. The builder who was going to start the construction was short of a carpenter and was willing to allow Ramji use of his workshop. Within days Ramji realised there was a need for decent quality wood for building. Existing supplies were erratic and the quality variable. He realised he needed to secure regular supplies of quality timber and arranged for Nizar to go with him on a visit to a sawmill outside Nairobi. The journey into a dense forest ten miles from Nairobi brought them to *'Richter von Dyke Sawmill and Timber Merchant.'* An overweight middle-aged man with a long greying beard, wearing dungarees and a leather hat was busy sawing planks of wood in the middle of the compound. He was being helped by two African workers and he stopped the mill when Ramji and Nizar approached. After the clattering died down, they heard the fast-flowing river behind the compound which drove the mill.

Introductions were made in English despite all parties having a poor command of the language. Richter was Afrikaans, his wife had died from malaria two years before, within months of him starting the sawmill. With a good knowledge of African trees, he had invested in this spot to start a mill. The intention was that his late wife would have helped him to sell the timber in Nairobi, while he concentrated on running the mill. Unfortunately, after her demise he had ended up doing neither well. He was still training his key workers in spotting the right trees and when they were ready for felling.

He showed them what he had in stock and in response to Ramji's inquires showed him the native trees it came from. He went through a demonstration of strength, density and durability using a few tools and a pail of water. Nizar was lost but Ramji seemed to comprehend very well. Soon Richter and Ramji struck up a conversation of the advantages of some varieties of the softwoods and where each was best used. They seemed to agree. Ramji placed an order for what he needed and arranged to pay Richter on delivery.

After the first delivery Ramji placed a further order for more stock of wood having decided which was better for his needs. Richter was pleased with the choice as most of his customers chose cheaper varieties which rotted quickly. Before long, Ramji had started to supply other carpenters in Nairobi. Richter became a willing participant in the arrangement, which allowed him the freedom to concentrate on his sawmill.

Lalji and Bhasker continued their work with Mohan. The shop remained as busy as ever. Nizar found time to call in and help with the bookkeeping, releasing time for Lalji to concentrate on other matters. Supplies had to be chased up, new suppliers met, late payments chased. Sometimes Ramji would ask to borrow Njenga from Mohan's shop to help him sort timber out in the yard and assist with cutting wood.

A household goods supplier, *E. Lewis Supplies* based on Government Road, was experiencing financial difficulties. It was an established shop that had started out selling basic items of glassware, crockery, and cutlery. Eddie Lewis was a hardworking individual who found it difficult to say no. He had over the years managed to squeeze into his shop more imported items for which he became a local agent. He seldom declined an offer to take on a sole agency and ended up becoming a retailer for all manners of imported products. These varied from smoking pipes, cigars, perfumes, propriety medicines, cosmetics, umbrellas, to hunting gear and knives. To manage the extensive range, he had engaged an elderly couple from Goa: Mr Ribero helping on the shop floor and Mrs Ribero writing the accounts.

Trade was good until a second-hand market in household goods started to thrive by courtesy of the auction house. It seemed failed settlers when leaving the Protectorate sold their household items at the auction house.

Eddie had a gregarious wife Sybil, who loved afternoon tea at the Norfolk Hotel. He had three daughters who were at boarding school outside Nairobi. Despite Mrs Ribero nagging that cash flow was poor, Eddie remained oblivious to the reality of his declining business. The day came when Eddie could not pay the girls' school fees. All his wealth was stacked up on the shelves of the shop and the goods were not shifting. Eddie asked for a personal loan from his bank and when that was refused, he asked Sybil to reduce her afternoon teas and kitty parties. On learning the fees for the schools were unpaid, Sybil packed her suitcase and left for Mombasa with the girls. They took the first steamer back to England.

Eddie went looking for Popat Ibrahim as a neighbouring shopkeeper to see if he could buy out the business. Having moved on from the area, Popat Ibrahim was not interested but introduced Eddie to Lalji, as the new owner of his shop. Lalji and Eddie got on like old friends. Eddie was clearly unhappy and a little distressed at feeling he was failing as a father, husband and businessman. Lalji felt sorry for him and looked at the business with Bhasker before discussing it with the other two partners.

It was clear that only about a quarter of the lines in stock had any reasonable turnover. This was the glassware, crockery, and utensils. The rest of the stock was gathering dust. Lalji had felt obliged to see the shop, out of curiosity and kindness to Eddie. He then suggested to Eddie he could take the household goods off him but not the rest. Lalji planned to sell them at the second shop premises, a hundred yards up Government Road.

Much to Lalji's surprise Eddie agreed to his proposal straight away. Lalji asked him to come up with a figure for the stock while he consulted his remaining partners. He inquired of Eddie what he would do with the remaining stock and Eddie replied he would travel up country and sell to other retail outlets. Whatever remained he would auction. His shop was rented so he had no worry about selling the premises. He planned to turn everything into cash and follow his wife and his daughters back to England. There, he could join the family business of Sybil's father, who was a master butcher in Liverpool.

***

The four partners of Porbander Stores agreed to the deal. Their second shop was on its way to becoming established, dealing in imported household goods. They talked to Mohan who requested that Lalji or Nizar continue to give him part-time help with his books. A sum was agreed with Eddie for his goods and he agreed to take payment in three instalments. The stock was moved to the new premises on Government Road. A prominent sign above the shop, in red with white lettering, announced 'Porbander Stores'. The other shop managed by Nizar and Ramji had been named 'Porbander Timber and Hardware Supplies.' The four celebrated their new ventures with a meal at a *bhajia* (snack) house on Bazaar Street.

There was goodwill and excitement amongst his three partners that day. But Lalji was keen to sit them down and discuss the risks in the steps they were taking. He informed them they stood most exposed at that stage with large liabilities while the two shops were starting to get going. Soon everybody's mood changed. Bhasker pointed out they had been lucky with the Army contract. Nizar commented how the Popat Ibrahim swap had resulted in two empty retail premises, in prime locations. Ramji suggested they move into the empty space above both shops for both convenience and to save rent. The suggestion was agreed by all. Within days they had set up two 'homes' above each shop. A common kitchen for all four was set up in Lalji and Bhasker's accommodation.

One morning Pestonjee the lawyer walked into Lalji's shop. After greetings he introduced KB, who had come along with him.

"This is Mr Khimji Bhagwanjee, a businessman from Mumbai who was in German East Africa before," he announced to Lalji and Bhasker. Lalji recognised the black car parked outside the shop.

"Jai Shree Krishna," greeted Bhasker and Lalji in chorus, both with joined hands in front. KB responded in kind.

"Khimjibhai is in Nairobi for a short while. He is shortly going towards Uganda to start a project there. We are awaiting official papers from the Administrator General's Office. In the meantime, I thought I would introduce you gentlemen as you are all at a similar stage in your businesses." Turning to KB he went on, "Laljibhai here has two other partners apart from Bhaskerbhai. They have two shops and other interests as well. They all hail from Porbander as you saw from the sign outside."

The two visitors were invited to the back office for a cup of tea which was declined politely. On inquiries from Lalji, KB explained his interest in farming crops for export. They chatted about the land permits, taxes and the lack of help for Indian traders or would-be farmers. KB explained he was hoping to get help while Uganda remained an unpopular destination.

"Laljibhai has land not far from here, some of which they are renting to the Army," stated Pestonjee.

"Why don't you consider producing some food on the rest?" asked KB.

"We were considering food items like vegetables, fruits and pulses from India for the local Indian market. Not of much interest to white settlers!" he laughed.

"That sounds like the right thing then. I have a trip coming up to Poona to the Horticultural Institute to discuss crops for my farm. If you want, I can make some inquires for you?" asked KB.

"That would be very helpful Khimjibhai. I can give you a list of what we are thinking about," replied Lalji.

"And soil samples. I need to take some samples from the land for analysis. Can you supply me some?"

"Yes, Khimjibhai but we have no experience of farming or having tests done on soil. I imagine it would be costly?" inquired Lalji.

"The man running the Institute is a close friend of mine from college. I am sure costs will be minimal. If something from your list is right for the soil, I can bring back seeds for you."

"That is especially good of you, Khimjibhai. Thank you."

CHAPTER NINTEEN

Geoffrey McLeod sent a letter to KB, informing him of Major Roger-Benfield's imminent arrival in Nairobi. He requested KB attend a meeting with the Commissioner. The note was brief, specifying the day and time at the Administrator General's Office.

KB sensed this was to be his opportunity to finalise the Uganda deal. He set off with his brief case containing documents he knew would be required at some stage of the process. These included a 'Certificate of Financial Means' from his bank in Mumbai, stamped by the Colonial Office. He carried his Engineering degree in the file and cuttings from Mumbai newspapers praising his success in German East Africa.

Walking up the steps to the Government Offices he noticed the dark interior of the mahogany-panelled entrance hall. A large chandelier hung from the ceiling which contained no less than thirty candles, all burning. There was a desk on the left with a typewriter behind which a bespectacled middle-aged woman sat. Her desk plate announced her as 'Mrs J Murray' but not her role. She peered over her brown-rimmed glasses and looking up and down at KB asked, "Yes?" with raised eyebrows.

KB realised it was rare for an Indian to be within these walls. "I am here to see Major Roger-Benfield, the Commissioner of Western British East Africa" he replied with a straight back.

"Yes, I know what he does. Have you an appointment?"

"Yes. My name is Khimji Bhagwanji."

"Take a seat there Mr *Bhaaji*," she pointed with the back end of her glasses which she had removed.

A tall blonde man in a striped double-breasted suit appeared after a few minutes and introduced himself to KB. "Mr Bhagwanji, this way please."

In the office was a large, walnut table with tall portraits on the walls of military men, old men with gold chains, medalled chests wearing red gowns. Beneath the frames were their names. At one end was seated Major Roger-Benfield, studying papers in front of him. On his left was another man in a striped suit also reading. KB was shown to a chair opposite by the man who had just ushered him in.

"Good morning, Mr Bhagwanji," greeted the Commissioner, yellow teeth visible. "On my left is Mr Peter Bennet who is Assistant to the Administrator General and you were shown in by Mr Andrew McDonald, also from the Administrator's Office who will take notes."

"Good morning, gentlemen," KB acknowledged each with a nod. Bennet continued reading without looking up.

"I have briefed the Administrator General about our meeting in Nakuru. About your interest in land in Uganda for starting a new agricultural crop, with an eye on export," stated the Major. Mr Bennet, who represents the Administrator General, is going to ask you some questions."

"That's fine, sir."

"My dear *sir*," Bennet addressed KB, fixing his eyes on him. "Are you aware that *Indians* are not allowed to own agriculture land in the Protectorate?" The sarcasm and put down was obvious.

KB decided not to lock horns unnecessarily. He knew the Major would have a bigger say in any decision. "What the Protectorate needs is to start development of agriculture in Uganda. The land and railway are underutilised," he answered.

"But allowing anyone who comes along would hardly be a sound policy for the Administration, you understand."

"It would be an outright purchase, unlike the situation for European settlers who need to bring a little capital and be granted land. I intend to buy the land and use my left-over capital for the farm. I only need the option of a grant of land *later*, if the project is a success and there is a need to expand," explained KB.

The Major saw which way the interview was going and interjected looking at Bennet and then KB. "The conditions approved for the proposed Zionists settlement were more generous than what Mr Bhagwanji is asking for, as we know. Mr Bhagwanji is proposing a purchase now and a land grant in the future if things work out."

"Yes, I see that," responded Bennet, irritated. "Something like this needs a change in the regulations. We can't change regulations every time someone new springs up with a plan."

"Regulations evolve," responded the Major gently. He turned to KB and asked how he intended to pick the right crop and what he had in mind.

"I would get the soil analysed at the Poona Horticultural Institute. They can advise what may be suitable crops for the weather and local conditions. I would also get the first seeds from there."

"What experience do you have of farming, Mr Bhagwanji?" asked Bennet.

"Not of farming but I ran a successful timber and sawmill business in German East Africa. If things do not work out, I can always go back to producing timber."

"And did you purchase land in German East Africa?" asked Bennet.

"No, sir, it was not possible," replied KB, noticing a wry smile at the corner of Bennet's mouth. He went on. "I saw that as an opportunity lost for both parties. The role the German rulers had in mind for me was not of further interest to me."

Bennet sat up and realised he was dealing with an individual with intelligence. He had turned his back on a running concern in German East Africa, and was now willing to put his money into a project which he believed in.

The Major asked for any documents or credentials KB may have brought and KB handed over what he had. Mr McDonald put the Certificate of Financial Means in front of Mr Bennet and tapped on the figure of KB's holdings to draw his attention to it. Both knew that on the White Highlands settlers with 1,000 British pounds in assets could receive 1,000 acres for free. There was a slight rise of Bennet's eyebrows on reading the figure on the document. He pushed away the press cuttings, as if of no interest.

When all the documents had been read through and the details noted by Mr McDonald, the Major asked KB if he had anywhere specific in mind in Uganda.

"I would like to be within easy reach of the railway. Somewhere the locals have an interest in growing crops and where there are no land disputes with the local people," replied KB. "A fertile place of course," he added.

"How well do you know Uganda?" asked Bennet, more contrite in his tone.

"I have travelled there recently and surveyed the maps and rainfall patterns at the Public Map Office."

What remained unsaid was that it should be sufficiently far away from the white highlands, so as not to tread on any toes. Unsaid, but well understood by all round the table.

"Well, if that's all, I think we can let Mr Bhagwanji go, gentlemen," announced the Commissioner. There was a large, friendly smile on Mr McDonald's face and finally eye contact with Mr Bennet who was trying to force a smile. KB sensed he had won this round two to one.

"We shall be in touch Mr Bhagwanji. This must have the blessings of the Administrator General. If he is agreeable, we willl talk further," said the Commissioner, extending his hand to KB.

CHAPTER TWENTY

TIMBER STARTED TO arrive from Richter's sawmill. Soon Ramji and Nizar had a small following of customers. Nizar paid attention to the retail side of the shop. Ramji was still on-site at Popat Ibrahim's, putting up shelving, doors, and cabinets.

Nizar had seen an advertisement in the Mombasa Times from a firm of toolmakers in England. They were looking for agents in Africa. Nizar made contact and in return, he received samples of ironmongery, nails, screws, bolts, and nuts. The letter accompanying the parcel said they needed agents in Africa, excluding South Africa where they had an agent. The terms of credit were favourable and after Ramji had tried out a few of the products the two of them consulted Lalji and Bhasker. They also asked Richter his opinion and he was encouraging about the quality.

Letters were exchanged to be appointed as agents and a Bank reference provided. The exporter was willing to undertake clearance of goods at Mombasa and pay the rail freight to Nairobi for the first year. Soon after the agreement had been reached the first crate of goods arrived with steel nails, screws, and door ironmongery. Hammers, chisels, and saws followed in the next batch. Within a short time, the business had become well established and successful. They needed more help so they brought over Njenga from Mohan's shop to help in the yard.

In the meantime, Lalji and Bhasker had started to accumulate the chosen stock from Eddie Lewis's shop. Eddie managed to connect them up with his suppliers in London and France. Credit terms became generous when Lalji emphasised they were still willing to continue selling a limited range despite Eddies difficulties.

Bhasker, with his jovial nature and big smile, became popular with the customers. His English started to improve and his sales technique provided amusement for many. He repeated catch phrases like *'only the best'*, *'most superior quality'* and *'the best of the best'*. But he earned the respect of customers because of his honesty and reliability. He would not sell a product if he thought it was inferior in quality and would chase up orders from exporters.

The domestic situation was not so successful. Bhasker was the main cook and his repertoire was not expanding. Furthermore, any dish he cooked tasted different each time. Occasionally Nizar or Ramji had a go at cooking without much success. On Sundays, they ended up eating at a *bhajia* (snack) house. At least once a week they went to Mohan's where his sister baked soft hot *rotis* (flat breads), something they all looked forward to.

One day Nizar asked Lalji if he had made any plans of getting married and bringing Janki to Nairobi.

"Not something that's crossed my mind recently," replied Lalji. "Why do you ask?"

"It's just that you used to say early on that you would be going back to Porbander near the end of the first year to get married. But you have not mentioned it recently."

"With the business situation and getting things settled, I have not given it much thought. I should check with Janki and her family before I inquire about the costs. But first, we need to send more money to our families now things are running smoothly again, what do you think?" asked Lalji.

"Yes, that is so. I was checking the figures and if things continue as they are now then we should at the end of this month be able to send more money than before."

"That's good."

"When you are ready to travel, *and Jankibhabhi also,* then you should take the steamer to Mumbai and then the train to Porbander we think. Similar trip when you return of course," suggested Nizar with some nervousness.

"Oh, so you have all discussed this already?" Lalji asked with a smile.

"Yes, Laljibhai. We know you have everyone's interests at heart, and in the businesses. The businesses will get busier with time. See how things are progressing."

"Why the steamer? It's more costly as you know," responded Lalji.

"It would be safer. For you and especially for *Bhabhi* (your wife). And more comfortable. Also, you can be sure it leaves on time."

Lalji laughed aloud and Nizar followed suit. Bhasker and Ramji walked in, wondering what was responsible for the joviality. Lalji explained he had just learnt of their plan for him to return to India, get married and return with Janki, using the steamer for the journey. Bhasker said they had considered what was going to be safer and more comfortable.

"Yes, I know, and I must say I had not given it a thought but it seems the right thing to do," responded a chuffed Lalji.

Ramji, who had not said anything, spoke with a straight face. *"Nizar and I think you coming back with Jankibhabhi* (your wife Janki) *may be the only way we will get proper food again!"*

Everyone was in fits of laughter, including Bhasker.

Over the next four weeks, Lalji gave his trip more thought. He wrote to his father Parshottam who discussed the prospect of the wedding with Janki's family. Lalji also wrote to Janki who replied she was ready to take up her role as his wife and travel to Nairobi with him. Then a new kind of impatience came over Lalji, something he had not felt before. The *S.S.Ludhiana* was leaving for Mumbai in a few weeks. With a fortnight's stay in Porbander, Lalji thought he could be back in Nairobi within seven weeks.

In the meantime, Ramji and Nizar were approached by a man who wanted to rent some land near the Nairobi River. His name was Hashimbhai Janmohammad who had been a millet farmer in Gujarat. He wanted to set up supplying basic cash crops like pulses, grains, fruits, potatoes and greens. He was looking for a quarter of an acre to start. The four *jehajis* (travellers) agreed for him to rent a small strip parallel to the river, accessible from the end of a dirt track.

CHAPTER TWENTY-ONE

THE AFRICAN STANDARD, August 5th 1905

H.H.AGA KHAN

....

ARRIVES IN MOMBASA

....

ENORMOUS SUMS OF MONEY COLLECTED FOR HIS BENEFIT

....

S.S. BOHEMIA FLIES THE RED FLAG

....

IMMENSE ENTHUSIASM

....

Two Hours at the Mosque

....

Leaves for Zanzibar

....

Early on Monday morning before daylight, the Khoja community of this city were astir, finishing off the decorations and completing the arrangements for the reception of their esteemed chief H.H.Sultan Mahommed Aga Khan Shah.

The community had been most lavish in their subscriptions to the Entertaining Fund with over thirty thousand rupees having been subscribed. The sum was raised to be spent in the city and has no connection to the contributions to the Religious Fund, which H.H. Aga Khan controls. It is estimated several lakhs of rupees will be raised for the later fund in Zanzibar and East Africa combined.

....

RECEPTION

As the Austrian Lloyd S.S. Bohemia steamed into Kilindini harbour, flying at the mast head the red flag in honour of the illustrious passenger, a special train, conveying the leading members of the Khoja community, estimated at some four hundred, left Mombasa Station for Kilindini Pier.

At 10.30 a.m. H.H.Aga Khan, accompanied by his suite, landed at the pier head and met with a reception such as can only be accorded by an Eastern people; at times the enthusiasm of the welcome approached frenzy.

At 10.45 H.H. entered the train awaiting him and was quickly conveyed to Mombasa.

The scene as His Highness stepped onto the platform was indescribable; with a most surprising suddenness the whole available space was swarming with people, children, young men and old men, all striving together to get a close view of the chief they loved to honour. It would have been an impossible task for His Highness to have reached the Victoria awaiting him at the station gates had it not been for the influence of his presence.

Immediately the carriages were occupied, a procession was started through the city to the Khojas' Mosque, close to the market, where a religious service was held lasting 2 hours. At 1.30 the procession was reformed and proceeded to Mr Jeewanjee's Bungalow, MacDonald Terrace, where the party partook of Luncheon. During lunch several speeches were made and many congratulations passed.

Alladina Visram during his remarks thanked Mr Jeewanjee for his generosity in placing his Bungalow and premises at the Khojas' disposal.

....

DECORATIONS

The decorations were excellent, carried out by an influential committee under the superintendence of Alladina Visram, a well-known and much respected merchant. Over the Entrance to Jeewanjee's House an arch was erected and the following words were inscribed thereon: 'Welcome H.H. Sultan Mahommed Aga Khan Shah.'

The special train which conveyed to and from the landing pier was covered with flags and bunting of various hues and the carriage in which H.Highness and suite travelled was lined with delicate silk and hung with drapery.

The Bazaar was alive with colour, each Khoja trying to out-do the other in their welcome.

....

NOTES ON THE VISIT

Prior to leaving for the S.S.Bohemia which left for Zanzibar on Monday after-noon, H.H. Aga Khan visited the Sub-Commissioner of the Province at his residence in Mombasa.

....

The two white horses harnessed to His Highness' carriage were especially imported from Zanzibar for the occasion.

....

It was found the Victoria could not traverse the narrow street in the bazaar adjoining the mosque without the removal of certain dwellings. These were promptly demolished and the owners duly compensated.

....

The Police lined the street on the route from the station to the mosque and an Inspector accompanied the party in a carriage. Excellent order was preserved.

....

An enterprising citizen secured an excellent snapshot of Aga Khan. It shows him in a well-cut black frock coat and Astrakhan Fez like that worn at the Persian Court.

....

H.H. Aga Khan is a British subject of immense influence. The local Swahili described him as Karibu Mahomet. Who's Who of 1902 gives the following: -

Aga Khan, Aga Sultan Mahomed Shah, K.C.I.E.; cr. 1898; b. 1875; Brilliant Star of Zanzibar, 1900, 1st Class; 1st Class Prussian Order of Royal Crown, 1901; has travelled a great deal; has many religious followers in East Africa, Central Asia, and India; head of Ismaili Mahomedans. Address: Aga Hall, Bombay. Club: Marlborough.

CHAPTER TWENTY-TWO

THE STEAM SHIP 'Ludhiana' was berthed and loading up cargo for its journey to Mumbai. It was a passenger and cargo ship, rusty and rat infested.

The facilities depended on the class of ticket. The cabins of first class, set on the upper deck and ocean facing, provided plentiful natural ventilation. There was a dining restaurant and a cabin cleaning service. Second class was on the deck level and the cabins non-ocean facing. Meals were taken in the restaurant after the first-class passengers had finished. The third class was below deck and comprised cabins with no porthole windows. Passengers had to bring their own rations and cook for themselves in designated areas on deck. There was constant noise and vibration from the ship's engine room. There one also heard the sounds of rodents scampering along steel pipes. The atmosphere was rancid and stifling from lack of ventilation. Lalji was impressed with the first sight of the Ludhiana at the harbour and by its size. Having done the journey by *vaan* (dhow), Lalji felt adventurous enough to try his hand at staying in third class. Soon he would vow never to put himself through the experience again.

He had a shared cabin with two bunk beds, the place just big enough to take his bedding and his luggage. The two latrines for the third-class passengers were close by. The clattering of the metal doors made it almost impossible to sleep until the early hours of the morning, when the latrine queue had died down.

Lalji's cabin mate was a young Sikh man on his way back to the Punjab after the end of his contract as a construction labourer for the railway. Parmatma Singh was his name. Having done his three years for the railway, he was heading back to help his family run their small farm holding. His father had retired from the Army after having been injured. He had two elder sisters and a younger brother. His first preference had been to join the Army like his father and grandfather. But his father had talked him out of that citing poor pay and lack of facilities. His foray on the railway construction had not been easy, catching malaria once and dysentery twice.

Lalji had collected rations for the journey in Mombasa. He had a mixture of ready to eat items from Premlal Joshi's food shop where he had spent a night after reaching Mombasa. He also carried a ration of *khichdi*, a premixed combination of moong and rice for boiling to make a hot meal. A few items of fruit he had picked up near the ship he shared with Parmatma Singh. Before reaching the harbour, Lalji had bought rolled up bedding for the journey and a blanket. Parmatma Singh had no bedding and slept on the hard bunk, something he said he was used to.

After setting sail the ship's horn blasted so loud and long it evoked a feeling of excitement in Lalji. He finally felt he was on his way back home, to return to his family and friends having achieved success. He had never been nervous of his business abilities and his trepidation of leading others had now disappeared. His excitement was further enhanced knowing his return journey would mark another major step in his life. That of a married man with householder responsibilities. Two major life events in the space of two years contrasted with his previous slow and hopeless life in Gujarat. He now had time to reflect on his father's secret ambition to send him to Africa and felt deeply grateful for it. His father had seen a dream for his son and gone about trying to make it a reality.

Like Lalji, Parmatma Singh was also likely to get married and settle down once he reached his family. He was grateful that there was enough family land to sustain their needs. He had no experience of famines like those in Western India. He admired Lalji for venturing out with his three compatriots and for making his mark in a foreign land. His job allowed little time to find out more about the country he had left behind, let alone make any plans to settle. Like other Jat Sikhs from his district of Punjab, they had come to do a job. It was expected they would return to take up their family and farming roles. Their recruiting agents knew this and seldom mentioned there was an option to stay on to start a new life in Africa.

They decided to put effort into learning each other's language. It would help while away the free time they had. Neither spoke Hindi well and Parmatma Singh knew very little English. His passion was for singing Punjabi folk songs.

His singing would lead to a discussion of the meaning of the poetic words. In return Lalji would read aloud tales from a Gujarati newspaper or magazine and explain the meaning of the text. In the evenings they would sometimes recite poetry, Parmatma Singh of love and separation and Lalji of patriotism. Soon the two had become close friends and were walking, talking and eating together.

Three weeks later they docked at Mumbai. Lalji and Parmatma Singh headed for the railway station after Lalji had sold off his sleeping kit at the docks. The two checked their train times, exchanged addresses, and said their farewells.

***

As the train pulled towards Porbander station, the sound of the carriages clattering on the rails seemed to intensify from echoes reflected off close buildings. A loud engine whistle preceded the brakes and Lalji leaned out of a window. Up ahead on the platform he saw groups of people waiting for the arrival of their guests. For the first time since setting off from Nairobi he felt an unexpected nervousness. "Maybe it's just that I haven't had time to think much about home," he thought to himself.

No sooner had the train stopped, he jumped out with his case. He started heading towards the exit thinking he would grab the first ricksha he found. Suddenly he was face to face with Thakorbhai, the village *Sarpanch* (elected leader) who was waiting with outstretched hands in front of him.

"Welcome my boy! Welcome to your home, traveller!" he bellowed.

Lalji then noticed the group of people behind him including his father Parshottam and his brother Naran. He realised they were one of the groups he had seen from the train. He was not expecting to be met, let alone have a welcoming party on the platform. Hugs were exchanged, feet of elders touched, and 'Jai Shri Krishna' greetings exchanged with all. A commotion started with the *Sarpanch* cracking orders to youngsters whom Lalji did not recognise. They were to carry Lalji's case and call up the rickshas.

Lalji saw his father Parshottam quietly wipe away tears while he was talking to others. His brother Naran asked about the ship and the voyage, the train ride and if he was glad to be back. Realising there would be the time for these questions later he announced to Lalji, "*Baa* (Mother) has stayed back to prepare your favourite food. But Jankibhabhi is here."

Lalji realised he had completely overlooked a smaller group of women at the back of the main group. His heart started to pump faster and his first glance connected with Janki's eyes. Both broke into an instant smile with eyes lingering and studying the other. Her friend Mukta was with her and prompted her to move forward. Janki stepped forward and tried to touch Lalji's feet but he stopped her, bending forward, noticing the tattooed dots on her ankles. His hands briefly touched hers and he felt closely connected. They had only once held hands when he had gone to say goodbye. Both corrected themselves instantly with a 'Jai Shri Krishna,' clasping hands in front of their chests. A brief waft of flowery perfume passed by Lalji, making him feel light-headed with excitement. Suddenly they realised the others had gone quiet and people had been watching them. When Lalji looked around he saw a few expectant faces, expressions changing to disappointment when nothing more intimate happened.

He saw Noormohammad, Djiraj and Karsan together in a small group. All three greeted him and took turns to hug him. Noormohammad kissed Lalji on the forehead and addressed him as 'my brave son'. All three had tears in their eyes and for the first time Lalji realised how much faith they must have had in him to keep the group together and safe. Dhiraj held Lalji's hand and would not let go, having burst into sobs on Lalji's chest when he embraced him. Ramji, also emotional had gone mute and could not find words to speak. Lalji told all three how well their sons were doing in Nairobi.

On the way home Lalji saw the landscape was still as barren as when he was last there. The one difference was the occasional tufts of grass and bushes were greener, a sign that the rains had been and left early again. The heat was stifling and the animals looked lethargic and beaten, eyes reflecting hopelessness.

On reaching home, his mother Rambai rushed out followed by a couple of ladies from the neighbourhood. Lalji bent down to touch her dusty feet and she embraced him, eyes shut and whispered, "Welcome home my son."

All the other rickshas ended up at Parshottam's and before long there was total mayhem as news spread of Lalji's return. Shopkeepers left shops unattended and farmers rushed from the fields, each to catch a glimpse of Lalji. Only Janki's ricksha had diverted to her village taking her companion with her. Lalji was looking around when Naran realised what was on his mind and said, "Jankibhabhi had to go home."

"I was looking for my case," Lalji stated, unconvincingly.

"It's in the bedroom. Shall I get it for you?"

"No, I will get from it what I want."

Lalji stepped out of the bedroom and into the back yard where the visitors were seated on two *palangs*, light bedsteads with string-tied tops. He handed out three presents to the fathers from their sons in Nairobi.

Ramji's father opened the brown packet held by string and inside was a long letter addressed to him, his wife and the remaining five children. There was a bundle of rupees in a separate envelope and a small block of wood from the timber yard. No doubt the significance of it would be in the letter.

Noormohammad also discovered similar items in his package. There was an envelope with money, a few yards of material for his siblings and mother. For him there were two yards of white cotton for making shirts.

Dhiraj opened his parcel which also contained a separate envelope of rupees. Like the others there were pieces of cloth for the family and a letter.

Lalji sat on a chair in the middle of the gathering and was bombarded with questions. Everything was asked about, from the journey, the land, the people, the *sarkar* (government), other settlers, living conditions, the price of food, expenses, the weather and the dangers. The yard was packed, with some perched on the low boundary wall. Having exhausted most people's questions, Lalji excused himself so he could go to rest and the villagers dispersed.

When they were alone Parshottam asked Lalji if he had any concerns or regrets.

"No, so far things have gone very well. We have worked hard and been lucky. It's a new country, much different from here. The land is lush and beautiful. The local people are good but new to the ways of the world. They have their own beliefs, more are becoming Christians and obtaining education. There are many local languages but the main one is Swahili, which isn't difficult to pick up."

"Are there opportunities *Bhai* (Brother)?" asked Naran.

"Yes plenty. But one needs to be careful as it is easy to get tempted by big ideas which go nowhere. A lot of white settlers are disappointed with their experience. They are moving on elsewhere in Africa or back to Europe. It's a country which wants to become modern. One must spot the right opportunity," replied Lalji, before adding: "The railway is a bonus. It has opened many new opportunities."

"I hear the railway workers were Indian," stated Parshottam.

"Yes, they were from Punjab. One of them was travelling back to Mumbai with me and we became friends. The railway took longer than expected and it has turned out to be much more expensive."

"Are there many Gujarati folk there?" asked his mother, Rambai.

"Quite a few and many from Kutch too. All are interested in making a life there unlike the railway workers who came on contract. But we do not have the full variety of foods and spices. On our land in Nairobi a farmer has started planting different vegetables from India."

Rambai made a mental note to discuss this with Janki.

"Do you feel safe there, son?" asked Parshottam.

"Yes, we do. The *sarkar* (government), like here, is keen to keep the best for the white settlers. They need to make the railway pay for itself but it has not been easy to attract enough Europeans. That means there are more opportunities for us," explained Lalji.

Turning to Naran Lalji asked, "How are you getting on with the shop?"

"I have maintained everything the way you did *Bhai* (Brother)," responded Naran, sounding defensive. He added, "The trade is much like before. We had a slight increase after the short rains but it looks like there will be another famine."

Parshottam, who wanted the conversation to remain upbeat said with a big smile, "We can talk about these things later. First, it is time for lunch and afterwards we are expecting Janki's parents to call to discuss the wedding."

CHAPTER TWENTY-THREE

LALJI WAS PLEASANTLY surprised how much had already been planned for his wedding. Nine days hence was the big day, fixed after consulting the priest for the most appropriate and auspicious time for the Vedic ceremony. The *kankotri* or wedding invitation, had been printed and was ready to send out. Naran and his parents had drawn up and agreed a guest list —essentially most of the village and a few relatives from elsewhere as far as Porbander. Naran and a few of his friends had decided there had to be a *dhol* (two sided drum) player to announce the arrival of the groom along with his *jaan-baarat* (groom's entourage) at the wedding.

The venue was going to be Janki's house. Her parents, Gopalbhai and Valbai, had been planning the arrangements for a few weeks. They had arranged the priest, who in turn managed the flowers, decorations and the *mandavo* (wedding canopy). Moreover, the walls were whitewashed and where necessary any outstanding repairs around the house undertaken. Extra cows had been hired for the wedding day to provide enough milk.

Lalji brought out his presents for the family. He turned to his mother. "Here *Baa* (Mother), this is for you from Mombasa."

"What is it, son?"

"Just something you can have made into what you like," he said, handing over a large piece of Japanese printed cotton. His mother's eyes lit up.

"And for you brother," handing Naran more material, this time in Khaki fabric.

"Thank you Laljibhai," he said, sliding his fingers over the material, unimpressed.

"And for you Bapu, a small item from Nairobi."

He handed Parshottam a Westclox pocket watch in its new case. Parshottam creaked it open to expose a brilliant white clockface. The time was set correctly and he put the watch to his ear, beaming a reassured smile when he heard it ticking.

"God bless you, son. I have never had a watch before. We still do not have a clock in this house. But I will carry this always. Look how well it is made and the numbers are so clear."

Lalji then showed his family different pieces of cloth material he had bought in Nairobi for the members of Janki's family. Everybody approved. Naran wanted to know the prices of everything. Janki and her parents arrived, in good spirits. Gopalbhai embraced Lalji who in turn touched his feet and those of Valbai. Janki looked on shyly, until tea was offered when she scurried into the kitchen to help prepare it. It was clear the four parents had met before and were sorting out outstanding issues. Out of courtesy, they tried to involve Lalji who did not want to take an active role. He was content to leave matters with the four of them and Naran. He had once been told by one of his married friends, "Don't get too involved in your wedding. Your job is to turn up. The rest is fun and joy for the two families. It's their day."

Getting up, Lalji ambled to where Janki sat near a calf which she was trying to feed. "How are you, Janki?" were his first words.

She looked up and studied his face. "I am well. Have you been well in Africa?"

"Yes, apart from the odd cough. Nairobi gets cold at night."

She smiled.

"And the others?"

"They are all fine. Settling into a routine with the business and learning to look after themselves."

Janki giggled at the thought. She wondered how successful they were.

"Here, I have something for you," he announced, pulling out of his pocket a strung-up packet wrapped in crinkly purple paper. The kind used by all *sonis* to pack jewellery. She beamed an excited smile and asked if she should open it straight away.

"That's up to you," Lalji replied.

"Very well then. I will open it when I am alone," she replied, tucking the small packet into her bodice. Lalji wondered how soft her breasts must feel, seeing the packet had fitted under her garment without any hint of it externally. Janki realised what she had done and became embarrassed, looking down.

Everyone else was involved in conversations and had not noticed them. Lalji put his hand on hers and said, "It's time for us to start our life together. I love you and I want us to be together now."

"That is also what I want, and quickly," Janki replied, looking into his eyes, squeezing his hand tightly.

***

Janki could not contain her excitement and as soon as she reached home, she opened the small package from Lalji. She gasped so loudly that her Aunt Lalbai in the next bedroom heard and rushed in.

"What happened, Janki?" she asked urgently.

Janki was overjoyed at seeing a pair of silver *payals* (anklets), which she held across one palm, looking at the detail of the intricate design. Lalbai's eyes lit up and she gasped, "Waah, what beautiful *payals*. The silver is so beautiful. Put them on, let us see what they look like," making space for Janki to sit on the floor.

Both struggled to fasten the soft metal, carefully placing the small hooks into their delicate clasps. As soon as they were on, Janki jumped up, held her dress shin high and stared at her ankles, taking small steps then long ones to get the tiny bells to jingle. With each step her joy multiplied and she was grinning more and more, with sounds of admiration from her aunt in the background.

Lalji had acquired the pair of *payals* (anklets) thanks to Mohan and his four partners. They were all in Mohan's shop one day when Arjun Jetha called. He was a travelling *soni* from Surat in Gujarat who frequented Nairobi annually to sell his latest designs. Nairobi had yet to get a soni shop although Mombasa boasted four. Mohan was contemplating buying something for his sister and was looking at some gold bangles. He asked Lalji if he would like to buy something for his future wife and Lalji declined. He had never bought any jewellery in his life. The only jewellery he had ever touched was his mother's bridal ornaments.

Lalji's lack of interest made Nizar and Bhasker go over and take a closer look. Bhasker asked the soni if he would show them something for a young bride-to-be. Arjun Jetha opened his metal trunk and from somewhere in the depths brought out a cloth bag and loosened the strings. He put a red piece of velvet on the counter and brought out a few pairs of silver *payals*. None of them recognised what they were, so Arjun Jetha demonstrated how they were worn and showed the workmanship. He held up and shook them to produce the soft sounds of the tiny bells.

On everyone's insistence Lalji had a look and was about to walk away when he noticed one pair of interest. It had its little bells hanging from three tiny spheres, arranged in a triangle. He remembered Janki's ankle tattoo of three dots. He touched the anklet and wondered how it might look on Janki's ankle. The others noticed and Bhasker immediately volunteered, "I think this will be an ideal gift for your future wife."

A chorus of agreement followed from the others and Lalji bought the anklets with cheering from all.

***

All the Hindu rituals were well known to Lalji as he prepared himself for the two-day event. There were items to be bought for the various ceremonies which required a few visits to the shops in Porbander. Following the wedding there would be just two more days before Lalji and his new bride would be leaving to catch the steamer from Mumbai.

The next morning Lalji stepped into the shop at the front of the house. The stale air of the place brought about a sensation of *deja-vu*. This was immediately replaced by a sinking feeling in his heart when he saw the same items for sale, at the same price. The place had not moved on at all. Even the weights of the weighing scales looked as always, their oxidised grey surfaces covered in grease and dust. His year away had been so eventful that coming back to the shop was like entering a stubborn dream, unchanging and refusing to move on. It was then that he made up his mind of what the next step was for the family.

Naran was at the door observing him. Lalji had been unaware of his presence.

"Things are much the same as when you left, *Bhai* (Brother)," stated Naran, looking down.

"Yes, and the stock looks the same."

"We have the same customers. Nobody spends unless they must."

"Are you still running errands on the bicycle and collecting payments?"

"Not as much as you did. I do some deliveries as before. The high tax means people don't spend."

"If business cannot come to us so we will have to go to the business," Lalji said. Naran looked puzzled as did Parshottam who had just joined them. "What I mean is the business is not here anymore but it is in Mombasa, Nairobi and Uganda. It is time for you to join me in Nairobi."

Naran had given the matter some thought before Lalji's return. He agreed instantly.

"You are right *Bhai* (Brother). If you had not sent the funds when you did, we would not have been able to manage. It has been of much help, especially in getting your wedding organised. I also want to join you in Nairobi."

"Good then. We must start making plans," said Lalji. "I would suggest you follow after winding things up here."

"It will not be necessary to close things here," interjected Parshottam, "The shop will keep me active and it's a service to the villagers."

"I thought you and *Baa* (Mother) may want to join us," suggested Lalji.

"I am not sure your mother would be happy to move. We are better here," said Parshottam.

"As you wish, *Bapuji* (Father). But here, this is for the general expenses of the wedding and the household expenses," said Lalji, handing over a wad of rupee notes to his father.

"Thank you, son. I am proud of your success."

The following seven days went by fast. First, there were the visitors and neighbours who came and went as they wished. Everybody was welcome all the time. All wanted to know how the preparations for the wedding were going. All wanted to contribute in some way, especially their opinions. Lalji was a great one for delegating, unlike Naran, and things started falling into place. The four of them went to Porbander to get their clothes sewn and to buy presents to give to Janki's family.

The day before the wedding in the afternoon, Lalji perched on a stool in the courtyard of his home. He was dressed in pure white, surrounded by only the womenfolk of the village and extended family, ready for the *pithi* ceremony (pre-wedding ceremony when the groom/bride are anointed).

The ritual anointing of the groom at his home with a yellow paste consisting of turmeric, oil and perfume was mirrored by the same ritual conducted for the bride at her home. The invited ladies were charged with the task of painting the groom's face yellow and luminous before he started to prepare for the wedding. With much merry making, joking, and singing he had his cheeks and forehead rubbed with the yellow paste. His mother was the first, followed by other senior ladies who each blessed him with a fingertip touch of yellow on the forehead and both cheeks. As the event moved on and as the participants got younger the *pithi* paste started to get applied more liberally. Onto the forehead, neck and shoulders. A generous and flirtatious application by one of the young ladies led to Lalji grabbing some paste for himself before retaliating with his dollop smeared on her face. There was much clutching, pushing and laughter with paste flying in all directions, hair and clothes smeared in yellow. The laughter and singing continued until the last anointer had finished her turn.

After washing and a change into fresh clothes, the ladies returned in the evening with their families. It was to be an evening of folk and wedding songs and *Ras Dandya* (Gujarati folk dance). The clothes had turned more colourful, hair tidily set and jewellery visible. Badru and Gulbanu, with an array of local musicians, arrived early to set up. Their instruments were unpacked before a quick rehearsal as they had not performed with the musicians before. Tea and snacks were prepared on a coal stove and kids ran helter-skelter adding to the sense of chaotic excitement.

***

The morning of the wedding day was the religious start of the proceedings. The family were all up before dawn preparing for the first of the ceremonies. The most opportune times for the day's ceremonies had been checked by the priest in his astrological calendar.

By the time Lalji was ready his parents were seated on a carpet in the back-yard. They sat aside of the old priest who was busy preparing and arranging flowers, threads, *vermillion* and *gulaal* (traditional coloured powders). Alongside were water containers for the *mandvo* ceremony. The ceremony was to invite Lord *Ganpati* (*Ganesh*) into the wedding canopy and to negate any obstacles. The old priest had brought along with him a young assistant to help in the preparations. He had started to have an assistant because of his poor hearing and eyesight he said. But all knew he was getting forgetful and needed some prodding.

The area was beautifully decorated with large banana leaves and flowers in the four corners of the prayer area. In the centre of the area on a wooden plinth was a *loto*, a copper container with a lipped top containing water. Around the top were adorned five mango leaves, and in the middle stood an upright coconut.

"*Jai Shree Krishna* Panditji," Lalji greeted the priest, touching his feet. The old priest placed his right palm on Lalji's head, closed his eyes and blessed him.

"This is a good day for a wedding. The month is favourable, the moon is waxing and the stars are right," announced the priest, a big smile on his face exposing pink toothless gums.

"We are grateful for all your guidance in these matters," replied Parshottam, Lalji nodding. The priest did not acknowledge the compliment.

"I hear your in-laws had a large celebration last night," the priest informed Lalji. "The cow-herders were talking this morning. We are now ready to start the ceremony."

Once the priest started recounting ancient *slokas* (prayer verses), he was lost to the world. Reciting with eyes shut, he would open them only to give instructions to Lalji and his parents, the three participants of the ceremony.

After what seemed an endless ninety minutes, the priest finally signalled the end of the ceremony. He gave permission for the participants to stand.

Gifts were handed to the priest and payment in the form of *dakshina*, a gift of gold or money offered to him for his services by Parshottam and Rambai. Like any Brahmin priest, he did not specify a fee and had left that up to the discretion of the householder. His was not to ask but to respectfully accept what was given.

The afternoon saw a gathering of the groom's friends and relatives, in preparation for the wedding *jaan-baraat* (grooms wedding entourage). That was going to walk to Janki's house where the wedding would be held in the evening. At the head of the *jaan-baraat* would be the *dhol* (two sided drum) player and Lalji on a horse, followed by the wedding guests. At the appointed hour, Lalji emerged from his room. Dressed in a new wedding outfit, he looked every bit the accomplished groom. No longer did he look like the young man heading off the Porbander sea in a *vaan* (dhow) towards the unknown. Instead, he stood tall and looked confident with strong features. In his off-white *dhoti* (traditional attire for men) with bright red borders, his tunic embroidered in gold and his turban tall with its tail trailing to his mid-back, he looked like a minister of the Maharajah.

The *jaan-baraat* was ready to proceed. Lalji bowed down to his mother to receive her blessings before heading out to the waiting horse. He was flanked by his brother and the rest of the male members of the party. As tradition dictated, the groom's mother did not attend the wedding. She stayed back in the company of other senior ladies, keeping vigil at home and to prepare for the return of the *jaan-baraat* after the wedding.

Once Lalji mounted the decorated white horse the *dhol* player burst out into a loud rhythmic repertoire of wedding beats. Not happy at being the only invited musician, he had roped into coming along with him a *shenai* (flute) player and a keyboard harmonium player. His accomplices followed his cue straight away, prompting the young men in the front of the group into a frenzy of dancing to the wedding tunes. On reaching the village border the musicians stopped playing and Lalji dismounted to continue on foot. Horse riding did not appeal to him.

Approaching the small lane to Janki's house, they could see the decorated walls and entrance to the house. Flags, bunting, and banana leaves adorned the approach. There in attendance was an equally enthusiastic band of musicians. Upon hearing the *jaan-baarat* musicians, they commenced their feverish version of wedding music. Neither group wanted to be outdone by the other into conceding inferiority. Lalji mounted his horse again.

The *jaan-baraat* was welcomed by a group of men and women from close families. At the head of the group were Janki's father Gopalbhai and the *Sarpanch* (elected leader) Thakorbhai. Both wore identical turbans. Customary greetings and embraces were exchanged, and the guests served cool aniseed sherbet. At the gate Lalji was greeted formally by Janki's mother Valbai. She conducted a small welcoming ritual to allow him through the threshold and to dispel any unwelcome omens.

Within minutes Lalji was seated on a low platform in the wedding *mandvo*, (four-poster canopy for the wedding rites). The officiating priest was seated on one side, a *havan-kund* (receptacle for the *Havan* fire) situated in the middle of the canopy where the *havan* (ritual fire used in Hindu ceremonies) would be lit. Next to Lalji was an empty seat for the bride. The priest demanded silence from the unruly guests and the wedding rites started. First the traditional washing of the groom's feet by Janki's father. Soon after the bride was

145

brought in, fully veiled with the red and gold sari covering her head. She was accompanied to the *mandvo* by her maternal uncle and seated next to Lalji. Again, the priest recounted in Sanskrit further slokas for the greeting from the bride to her groom. Then followed the couple garlanding each other.

The wedding slokas followed. Janki's parents participated in the initial rites leading up to the *kanyadaan*, the ritual gifting of their daughter to the groom. Both the bride and groom participated together in offering *samagri* (mixture of grains) into the *havan* fire during the proceedings. Then followed the *mangal pheras,* four rounds of walking around the havan fire. Each walk around the fire was initiated by prayers endorsed in turn by the bride's father for the first round, the bride's brother for the second round, her maternal uncle for the third and lastly the groom's father. With the four rounds completed, the formal part of the wedding was ending.

What remained was the exchange of gifts from both sides and speeches. On their completion, the bride and groom, now tied together symbolically with a knot linking her saree and a shawl that had been placed on Lalji's shoulders, stood up and walked out as man and wife. Together they took their first seven symbolic steps as man and wife, promising each other seven virtues of married life.

The newlyweds met the elders of both families and took blessings from them before others greeted and blessed them. By now the priest had lost all authority to keep silence. Both sets of musicians exploded into a frenzy of musical battle, each out-playing the other. The traditional wedding meal was served to the guests seated on the floor on mats. Men and women had their own seating areas. Lalji and Janki sat together with their parents.

Before the *jaan-baraat* left for Lalji's home there was one last and important undertaking. Most of the local guests had left, the rest were waiting for Janki to appear from her room for the onward journey. The atmosphere had turned heavy, people silent or talking in soft voices in small groups.

On her appearance, escorted by her aunt, a tearful Janki approached first her mother and then her father for a final embrace to say goodbye. The crying of the three of them led to a chain reaction of sniffling and tears amongst the small crowd. Very soon there were no ladies left with dry eyes, each one recalling their own *vidai* (bride departing) event. Even the teenage girls, many of them engaged and yet to marry, were overcome. Meanwhile, Lalji waiting aside of these proceedings, looked uncomfortable and guilt-ridden, like a newly sentenced convict. After much sobbing and embracing, the crowd followed the newlyweds to a decorated oxcart waiting outside. On the cart, the newlyweds were joined by a few uninvited folks who held out they were unable to walk by reason of age or infirmity.

On reaching Parshottam's home, around four in the morning, they were met by Lalji's mother and a handful of the ladies who had stayed back. Lamps and lanterns showed the way towards the decorated threshold which was lit up. An earthen pot filled with rice stood on the threshold. Janki carefully lifted her saree and knocked the pot over with her right foot spilling the rice on the floor for good luck. Clapping and cheering followed and she walked in where Rambai welcomed and embraced her, blessing her with a long-married life.

Strong tea was served and the newlyweds seated together on a mat on the floor. They took part in a traditional game of *koda-kodi*. This involved a competition where they had to retrieve a gold ring submerged in a round tray filled with water, milk, colours, and flower petals. The ring was thrown into the tray with a fistful of coloured beads and seashells. Both the bride and groom made a grab for the ring which proved elusive and raised cheers and laughs from the onlookers, especially when a bead or shell was pulled out or the couple wrestled fingers under the water to grab the prize. A large cheer went up for the winner and the game continued for three or five throws, to decide the ultimate winner, who took the ring. It was insinuated that the winner would become the dominant partner in the marriage and so the competition to win was fierce.

CHAPTER TWENTY-FOUR

THREE DAYS LATER the newlyweds embarked on their journey.

Janki had been excited and was looking out of the window during the train journey to Mumbai. That was her first train ride, and she felt excited and inspired. She was travelling through Gujarat, the names, language, and script all familiar. On reaching the harbour in Mumbai and seeing the *Malabar*, a massive ship, she realised the onward journey was into a new phase of her life, into a strange land. Lalji saw she had become pensive, and she looked vulnerable.

He gave her a reassuring smile. He showed her their sea view cabin in second class and took her on a tour of the steamer. She found the stairs frightening with their slippery metal grills and the passages narrow. She held onto Lalji's hand so tightly he had to ask her to let go after a while. Everywhere she went she wore the anklets Lalji had bought her; the soft tinkling made Lalji feel warm and loved.

There were a few other 'passenger' emigrants on board, mostly young men or couples like them. Some had children with them, most having left them back with family until they had settled in Africa. They were emigrating of their own free will, paying themselves for the passage. Unlike indentured labourers who signed a ten-year contract to serve the master paying for the passage.

Janki seemed to cope well with the listing and the noise of the ship. They spent time taking walks, playing cards, talking, and reading. Janki had a copy of the *Bhagavad Geeta* (Hindu scripture, words of Lord Krishna). She would read the Sanskrit words aloud in the morning. She would then discuss the Gujarati explanation with Lalji. She loved to sing and had a voice for it, but not having had encouragement to learn, she remained reluctant to sing in front of others.

"I want you to tell me everything about Nairobi. I want to hear about the place, you must tell me about your work, your home, what you buy, what you eat. Also what Ramjibhai, Nizarbhai and Bhaskerbhai are like. How do you men spend your time, what is there to see in Nairobi, how close are the wild animals, have you seen lions and crocodiles yet?"

Her string of questions made Lalji laugh at her impatience. Every answer led to further questions followed by quiet periods of reflection. It was after all the first time they had spent so much time together. Lalji was surprised at how well Janki remembered everything he told her.

Getting to know each other's thoughts, emotions, and reactions, was an exciting time for both. Time seemed to fly past. The physical and emotional bonds that were forming between them, becoming rooted into trust and friendship. They were committed to each other, despite not knowing each other well. Neither realised while they were forging a partnership they were gradually falling in love. Janki had found her way to obtaining daily fresh drinking water and arranged a regular slot on the communal stove on board to cook . She started preparing simple meals from their rations. She watched Lalji eat, enjoying her cooking and occasionally complementing her food. She felt a sense of accomplishment and delight at this.

The ship made one stop in Karachi before heading south towards Mombasa. Once again, at the Socotra crossing, passengers offered prayers and coconuts to the sea. Janki said special prayers in Sanskrit before the two of them cast their coconut gently into the sea.

On the morning of their arrival in Mombasa harbour Janki was up and ready from dawn. She was studying the scene ahead, sipping her tea. Lalji joined her.

"There it is, Mombasa. The port of our new country," he announced.

"There are so many *vaans* and small boats here. I did not expect so many people."

"It is always busy because Mombasa is the entrance to British East Africa. Everyone and everything arrives here first, and from here it gets sent inland. Look over there on our left, that large building with pink walls, that's the *quila* (fort) built by the Portuguese when they ruled this part. It's known as Fort Jesus."

Suddenly the ship's horn blasted so loud Janki pressed her fingers into her ears. It prompted sea gulls to fly away in alarm from various vantage points on the steamer. It also induced sudden activity at the harbour where men appeared from nowhere. They launched small boats in a hurry to row up to the ship to sell their goods.

***

After disembarking from the *Malabar*, Lalji hired a porter and they walked up to Premlal Joshi's VC restaurant.

"You have just come on this morning's steamer?" inquired Premlal Joshi after greetings were exchanged.

"Yes, from Mumbai. This is my bride, Janki. We got married recently. We will be taking the night train to Nairobi today."

Premlal called his wife to introduce Janki to her.

"You are welcome as always. I expect you will want to have a proper wash and something fresh to eat then," he said.

"That would be good."

They boarded the overnight train to Nairobi in the evening. Janki had already had a lengthy conversation with Premlal's wife, acquiring tips about running a home in British East Africa. By the time she boarded the train she had been shown and knew the local names of various vegetables and fruit. To Lalji's surprise, she had also learnt how to say 'hello', 'come in' and 'wait here' in Swahili.

Lalji had noticed she was not nervous of the locals like other new arrivals. Janki had a cheerful disposition with strangers. As a child, she had come across an African Siddhi man when she was little. She remembered him well and his occasional visits to their village, offering tool and knife sharpening services. His name was Kanha, and he sang strange tunes she did not recognise. To frighten the children he would put his hand into the stream of sparks emitted from the grindstone, and then laugh at their amazed faces.

Despite the number of passengers coming off the *Malabar* there was room on the evening train to Nairobi. Lalji had managed to get a second-class cabin with two bunk beds and Janki had arranged a tiffin for the evening meal courtesy of Premlall Joshi. Night fell soon after the train departed and they both alighted at the tomb of Seyyid Baghali to pay their respects.

They slept together on the lower bunk, any discomfort from the cramped space negated by the chilly night breeze and the cosiness of their warm bodies touching. Lalji kissed Janki tenderly on her forehead and cheek, like he had done so every night since their wedding. This time Janki turned her head and her open mouth met his in a passionate kiss. Once again, they made love; this time Janki seemed more relaxed and confident.

Dawn brought the sound of the train horn going off intermittently as the driver tried to alert the animals on the tracks. Janki was at the window, hot tea in hand, watching the spectacle of Africa rushing past the window. She sat silent and mesmerised, but also excited.

Arrival in Nairobi was noisy with groups of traders and their staff jostling for space to collect cargo. The Europeans from the first class were met by first-class porters, tall uniformed Mkamba men in red coats wearing Fez hats and white cotton gloves. Lalji and Janki climbed down to the platform with their belongings. There a shout of "There they are!" It was the voice of Bhasker from behind a group of porters. Lalji turned to see Bhasker and Nizar striding towards them, all smiles. Both embraced Lalji in turn, before turning to Janki.

"*Namaste* (Greetings), *Jankibhabhi, welcome to Nairobi,*" Nizar said on seeing her. "I am Nizar," clasping his hands in greeting.

"Yes, I know Nizarbhai. *Namaste.*"

"*Jai Shri Krishna Jankibhabhi*, I am so happy to see you," an ebullient Bhasker announced bowing, with hands clasped in *namaste*.

"*Jai Shri Krishna Bhaskerbhai.*"

"There are rickshas waiting right outside. We can get going. Any more luggage?"

Nizar and Lalji walked ahead and Bhasker accompanied Janki. "I hope your journey was not too tiring?" asked Bhasker.

Janki smiled, "I am glad we are here. Nairobi looks so pretty with the green hills in the distance. The bright green and the red soil look so very attractive together."

"Yes, it is pretty. Not dry and dusty like Porbander. Also, much cooler. You will have to wear warm clothes as it can get very cold here in the evenings."

On reaching home, Lalji showed Janki around the place. Bhasker had vacated his room and moved in with Ramji and Nizar to give the newlyweds privacy.

Having looked around, Janki brought out packets and letters for the three of them from their families. The three men were busy discussing the shops when Janki interrupted, "Can someone take me to the market today to buy fresh supplies?"

"Yes of course Jankibhabhi," responded Nizar.

"I will have tonight's food ready by seven. Lunch will be ready at one every day," Janki said, looking at Lalji for approval.

"That would be just fine," responded Lalji, adding, " We may also need some groceries. Perhaps you could have a look around the kitchen first."

"Yes, I have already done that and we do need a few things," she confirmed.

The other two looked elated at the prospect of having proper home-made hot food, cooked by a woman.

***

Before sunset, all four of the *jehaji bhais* (brotherly travellers) were at Lalji's place. Janki had taken her first walk to the Central Market and brought back fresh vegetables. She had picked up spices, pulses and *dahls* (lentils) from the ration shop nearby. Bhasker, who had accompanied her, paid and carried the shopping.

Ramji came with Nizar from the timber shop.

He greeted her, *"Namaste, Jankibhabhi. "*

Janki looked up from the coal stove on the floor where she was stirring a *dahl (lentil dish)*. The familiar aroma of home cooking was back and it brought a spontaneous smile on his face.

"Food smells good," he remarked.

"Jai Shri Krishna Ramjibhai. You have lost weight from the last time I saw you."

"A little. I think because the work is getting busier. I do not seem to find much time to cook and we have to eat Bhasker's cooking, which is the second reason!"

They both shared a laugh. provoking a coughing fit for Ramji, turning his face red. Janki offered him some water which settled the cough.

"Nairobi water. Have you tried it yet, Bhabhi? It's very pleasant."

"Yes, I have, it's sweet. That cough you also had back home I think," she inquired.

"It comes and goes. The timber yard is dusty which brings it on. Nothing to worry about, I am sure."

Dinner was served to the four seated cross-legged in a row on the floor. Janki insisted on cooking and serving hot *roti* (flat bread) off the stove while they were eating. She had her own food after. There was complete silence while everyone was eating. Janki just about kept up with the regular demand for her *rotis*.

After a while Lalji piped up, "If you don't say anything, Janki may think it's not up to your taste!"

The other three burst out into a chorus of compliments and apologised for their absent-mindedness and their bad manners. All mentioned how the food reminded them of home. Janki flashed a smile of gratitude at her husband.

"Tomorrow I will get more supplies. Later you can all let me know what food you have been missing from home and I will see if I can make it," she said.

The next morning, just before sunrise, Janki heard Kijana from Mohan's shop outside. He was getting prepared to fire up the copper *bumbo*, a wood-fired water urn for their supply of bathing water. Within minutes the acrid blue smoke was wafting across the yard and made him cough and splutter. Janki left Lalji sleeping and went outside.

"Jai Shree Krishna," she said out of habit.

Kijana turned and saw her, stood to attention, and saluted.

"Jambo Mama," he greeted her with a big smile.

"Jambo." Pointing at herself she announced, "Janki."

"Ndio, Mama." Nodding, he confirmed he knew with a massive smile of flashy white teeth which endeared him to Janki straight away.

Kijana's next job was to help Janki clear up. He removed all the enamel plates and cups from the night before and took them in a bucket to the standpipe in the yard. There he proceeded to wash them, carefully scouring each one with a mixture of soap and sand. Having left them to dry in the morning sun, he gleefully accepted a mug of tea from Janki before setting off to Mohan's shop.

Before he left, he turned to Janki and said, *"Chai hiko mazuuri sana, Mama.* The tea was very good, Mama."

Janki smiled at his compliment.

"Jai Shri Krishna." It was Lalji at the bedroom door.

"Jai Shree Krishna. The tea is ready. And Kijana has been. The hot water is ready for your bathing," said Janki with an efficient look and a smile, sari and hair tied tightly. She looked as if she was in a hurry to get going with her chores. Lalji found it hard to look away from her body and shape, slim and tall like a chiselled marble statue.

"We need to hire a separate domestic worker to help you," stated Lalji. "Kijana has been helping with basic things to keep us going. But you will need someone else who has more time. And someone with experience."

"That would be good. Someone like Ramukaka (Uncle Ramu) at my parents' house or Gangabai at your parents. Someone who can help with the shopping and in the kitchen."

"Yes, precisely. We should ask Mohan if he knows anyone. That reminds me, Mohan and his mother will be calling to meet you in the afternoon. Along with his brothers and sisters. I am sure they will have tea."

CHAPTER TWENTY-FIVE

DESPITE A FEW weeks away from Nairobi Lalji was pleased how well things had been progressing. The construction site for the new bank had progressed to the point of completing all the walls and partitions. The Army depot was already functional and saw more traffic coming and going. The fence was deliberately high to prevent onlookers and loitering.

Ramji had finished at Popat Ibrahim's who was pleased with the workmanship of his shop fittings. Ramji was starting to receive orders for further work. Meanwhile, he had been making cabinets for their own hardware shop where Nizar was organising the English tools. They invested the proceeds from Popat Ibrahim's work into further stock from England which was generating more interest. Bhasker was occupied running Porbander Stores on Government Road. He had managed to buy more goods than had been pre-ordered by customers. His chatty nature had ensured that he picked up information from European customers about what was popular. Some items being new to Nairobi, he had negotiated a full year's credit for Christmas orders.

Mohan Lalvani was managing well on his own at his shop. Bhasker managed to get to him most days to lend a hand in the evenings. They had been considering what to do with slow selling goods. Lalji persuaded them to sell them at auction rather than selling up country. Khimjibhai Bhagwanji (KB), was in Nairobi having paid a visit to the Horticultural Institute in Poona. When he heard Lalji had returned he came to see him at Porbander Stores.

"Welcome, Khimjibhai! Did you have a good trip?" asked Lalji.

"*Jai Shree Krishna,* Laljibhai. Yes, my trip was successful. I hear you have also been to India and back."

"Yes, I returned yesterday."

"And I hear you have come back with your wife. Congratulations."

"Thank you. Will you have some tea?"

"That would be welcome, thank you. I have brought some reports and a few seeds for your land by the river," he said, passing a large cane basket to Lalji.

Lalji opened an envelope and looked over the reports. There was a lot of technical information in it including the type of soil, composition, water content, amount of nitrogen and minerals. It then went into detail about the sort of crops which would do well in the soil subject to weather issues. Lalji turned his attention to this section.

There was a list of plants suggested that would be suitable for the soil. Most kitchen garden plants were recommended and the soil quality was reported as excellent for them. In addition, the report mentioned food trees and shrubs which could do well. It listed mangos, guavas, passion fruit, loquats, and roots such as potatoes, sweet potatoes, and cassava. KB was also carrying a small tin within which there were sample seeds of many items neatly packed in small paper bags.

"This is so helpful, Khimjibhai. There are many suggestions here for us to consider. Tell me, how did you get on for your own project?"

"Well, I have been told to consider coffee, tea, mangos, and passion fruit. Also, bananas, pineapples and sugar cane. When I get to Uganda I will start planting a few of these to see how they do. Right now, I will concentrate on what can be harvested soonest for the market."

"Of course. But you will see how the rest do?"

"Yes. The weather is quite stable unlike in the white highlands."

"And labour?"

"That is another issue. The people there are already used to small-scale farming for themselves which helps."

"When are you heading that way?" inquired Lalji.

"I leave in the next few days. Waiting for the right paperwork from the Administrator's Office."

The two talked at length about the general political climate and what was going on in the Protectorate. Neither addressed the political scenario, only the consequences of it on their livlihood as Indian traders. Their chat was about the latest government hurdles, and how to best prepare for them, to minimise any harm to their businesses. Politics was not an arena open to them, not a luxury they could afford to spend time on. The politics of British East Africa was about the Colonial Office, the British India Office, the Settlers, and the

Administrator General. It was a white man's arena. The Indians worked within the system, trying to minimise any impact on themselves and their livelihood. Even as taxpayers there was no direct representation of their interests. They were wanted for their taxes but only tolerated in other walks of life.

As far as the local Black population was concerned, the concept of representation and influence was absent. The Africans were treated with suspicion and hostility. For them, it was a case of trying to avoid having their land grabbed and made refugees in their own country. Of avoiding imprisonment, or worse, if they dared to resist.

***

Within six months the four *jehaji bhais* and Janki had settled into a set pattern of life. The men worked every day except Sunday. They ate twice a day together at Lalji's. Janki had a domestic help called James, a cousin of Kijana. James was a great boon for Janki: not only did he clean and wash but accompanied her to the market and helped in the kitchen.

James had a zest for learning. It did not matter what the source was, he just wanted to absorb and learn. He had not been to school so found print and books fascinating, to look at and to hold. He had learnt what numbers were and could recite them in Kikuyu, Swahili, and English. He was also learning to count in Gujarati from Janki.

With no previous experience of being a domestic help, he picked up his role quickly and started to take an interest in Janki's Gujarati cooking. The two would often have chats on topics ranging from culture, cooking, religion, learning, language, Gujarat, and local politics. Janki picked up most of her Swahili from James and he learnt words of Gujarati from her. They made a list of words common to both languages. Words like *kitab*/book, *kalam*/pen, *kata*/cut, *safar*/journey, *dunia*/world, *hesab*/calculation, *pesa*/money, *lekin*/but, *tayar*/ready, *rang*/colour, *gadi*/vehicle, *dukan*/shop, *chai*/tea, *sarkar*/government, *sandhuk*/box. In Swahili, many of these words had an extra vowel added at the end. Janki could not read or write in English so she wrote in Gujarati. James would struggle to spell in English, writing in an exercise book which he carried constantly, holding it low by his side, gripped by his palm and fingers. It was in the manner of pupils at school standing in assembly.

James' fault, if at all, was his intense resentment of the white man. He was easily provoked into anger when talking about them or even when spotting them in the street. His face would contort with eyebrows almost touching and words came out as if he was hissing. Kijana informed Janki it was something to do with an argument James had seen as a child between his late father and a white settler. Following the argument his father had been jailed, where he died unexpectedly. For Janki, the most disconcerting side of James' anger was when he would swear oaths on the white man in everyday conversation. His *'haki ya muzungu'* was not a 'swear to God' but a 'swear on the white man'. Unwittingly he would say the phrase in the street or in the marketplace, getting nasty looks from any passing *askaris* (constables).

The two businesses of the partners were doing better by the month and profits were re-invested into newer products. Offers to become agents came regularly. It was Lalji who assessed any offers of interest. To convince him, the salesman had to know the product well enough to answer all his queries. He had to be prepared to offer new lines of goods on a sale or return basis and provide generous credit terms. In Lalji's reckoning, if the product did not fly off the shelf from demand, then it was not worth having. Products that occupied a shelf for a time and were in low demand were returned never to be seen again in the shop.

Lalji was strongly against sending staff or partners 'up country' to try selling products at low prices to local shops. He was happy to provide cheaper wholesale rates for anyone who came down from 'up country' and who bought in bulk. He emphasised to his partners their role was not just to sell but also to develop an understanding of the market.

"If you know your market, you will know the right product," was his mantra.

One morning Hashimbhai Janmohammad came to see Lalji. He had leased the quarter acre near Nairobi River to try out cash crops. He had been in arrears with his rent from the beginning, a source of annoyance for Bhasker.

"Why did he rent the land if he has no way of paying?" Bhasker would complain to the other three. None of the others minded as they knew Janmohammad was still experimenting with crops and had nothing to take to the market. But he attended promptly at the end of each month and requested further grace for his arrears. Usually, he would bring with him a sorry looking crop from the land as a peace offering.

On this occasion, it was not the end of the month which surprised Lalji. Half expecting a tale of woe or a declaration that he was folding up his experiment, he surprised Lalji with his opening words. Handing over a large bunch of fresh radish and carrots, moist with sticky dirt on the sides, he declared, "Laljibhai, I wanted you to be the first to know the crops are doing very well now."

Lalji smiled, "Come and sit down, Hashimbhai and thank you for the vegetables. Janki will be pleased."

"Yes, I know. I brought these for you knowing she cooks well."

"Good to hear the crops are working out."

"Laljibhai, I will be paying rent this month and will slowly clear my arrears." Lalji nodded. "As soon as I do that, I would like to rent another larger plot," he said.

"Another plot?"

"Yes. Two things have happened. Both are to do with you Laljibhai."

"Me?"

"The seeds you gave me from Poona have worked, the carrots, tomatoes, herbs and cucumbers have done very well."

Lalji had forgotten about them after handing them over. "That's good news. What was the second thing that you were going to say?"

"Laljibhai, I have tried hard to get things to grow. I know the soil is fertile. After you came that day to show your new bride the plot, and she handed me the box of seeds, everything has changed. All the seeds have started to grow. Allah's mercy is upon us."

"Maybe the Indian seeds are more suitable than the European ones," suggested Lalji.

"You are right. And your young bride has brought good blessings to the plot. By Allah's grace may you both be happy always."

"I will tell her. She will be very pleased. Now, what's this about more land?"

"As soon as I have paid my rent and arrears, I will be ready to cultivate more as the new crops are doing much better. That's why I will need more land."

"Have you got buyers, Hashimbhai? For your crops?" asked Lalji.

"I will be able to sell them off at Nairobi Market to the stall holders."

"You will need time to work in the field, harvest and take the produce to the market, every day. You are going to need help, are you not?" Lalji asked.

"You are right. I should get the present crop ready first and see how it goes."

"I have heard next month there is a show where farmers can bring along their crops for buyers to see. Why don't we get your name down as one of the vegetable producers? You should be able to meet some buyers who can take your crops directly from the field if you are lucky."

"That would be perfect. I can then concentrate on getting the crops to grow and harvest." A wide smile had broken out on his wrinkly old face.

***

"W. Aitcheson Wines and Spirits" was an old established liquor store on Government Road. The old man, Walter Aitcheson, was born in Strathclyde and spent his life in Africa from the age of ten. His business, which he ran with his son, had been established for fifteen years and was known for its fine wines, champagne, and Scottish malt whiskey. A lifetime in Africa had not diluted his thick Scottish accent which was difficult for most people to understand. To compensate, he had developed a booming voice. He presented a military image of wearing khaki shirts, shorts, and stockings held up with garters. The image finished off with tan-coloured brogue shoes. Often, he wore a white sola topee and carried a rhino whip tucked into his belt. He looked hunting-ready every day, completely out of place in a shop.

Recently he had suffered a serious stroke, which left him initially unable to speak, and just about able to walk. He had a reputation for heavy drinking and was often seen being carried to his car by staff or his son after closing the shop. Both father and son had different interests. Walter loved shooting and hunting while his son Andrew was into fishing and opera. Mrs Aitcheson had died in childbirth in Rhodesia and Walter never remarried. Andrew had spent years in boarding schools where he picked up his love of opera and Roman architecture. After the stroke, Walter had become concerned about his son's ability to handle the business after his death. He did not believe that Andrew could make a success of the business. He felt Andrew would make bad deals and risk losing everything. Walter was looking to sell up and send his son to Bible College in Scotland to become a Missionary. Something they had both agreed on.

Walter came in to see Lalji one day; his presence at the shop threshold was an unexpected sight. Lalji had never spoken to Walter but always acknowledged him in the street with a polite nod of his head, despite the gesture never being returned. Lalji asked him to take a seat seeing he was struggling with his stick and his stiff right leg. He took the seat and declined tea. Lalji asked about his health.

"Beh-ter but noht walk-ing well," he managed slowly.

"Did you want something for the house?" asked Lalji looking up at the shelves and Bhasker who was looking on.

"N-no! Your biz-nez ok?"

"It's improving," replied Lalji, non-committedly.

"I wan-t to sell m-mine. Wo-od yu be int-rest-ed?" The directness surprised Lalji.

"Why are you selling, Mr Aitcheson?"

"I wa-nt to re-ti-re an go to Scot-lan-d."

"I see. Why did you think of me?"

"I see an kno-o the way you ru-n you-r shop-s."

"I don't know your business but we can talk after I see it. I need my three partners to see also."

"It-s like an-y biz-nez. Co-me an' see. Mee-t my son."

"Fine. Tomorrow afternoon, ok?"

"Ok f-or me" said Walter before clambering out of his chair, turning awkwardly, and hobbling off.

The next day Nizar accompanied Lalji to Aitcheson's shop, fifty yards up from Porbander Stores. Neither had been in the shop before and neither had any clue about any alcoholic drinks, both being teetotallers. Nizar had a religious objection but assured Lalji he was happy to look at the books and check out the business worthiness of the shop. If there was a purchase of the business, he said he would opt out of selling in the shop.

"Co-me een gintil-men," Walter greeted them at the door. He pointed his stick at his son and introduced them. He showed them around, hobbling along the shop floor, stock room, and back office. He could not manage going down to the cellar so his son led the way for Lalji and Nizar. The cellar housed some barrels and kegs. Nizar found the smell offensive and heady.

Andrew knew the stock but had little knowledge of the overheads of the business. He could not identify their biggest risk but knew what sold best. He admitted he had not negotiated any discounts from the suppliers after his father had left him in charge. Walter was quite amenable and opened his ledger and accounts for examination, using his left arm and hand clumsily. Lalji noticed Andrew stood back, not attempting to help.

Lalji asked about the regulations around liquor licensing. Walter informed him that the Liquor Ordinance had granted the business a licence to import, store, supply and sell wholesale and retail. Soda, tonic water, and ginger ale did not need licences. Walter had always had his licence renewed on request and assured Lalji it was easy to transfer it to a new owner.

"When does your licence finish?" asked Lalji.

"In a year's time," answered Andrew.

"Mis-terr Lal-jee yu look unn-hapi."

"I am thinking that the licence is a big risk for us." Nizar was nodding his agreement. "No Indian business has a liquor licence except Alladina Visram. In his case, the Governor requested him to start importing good quality liquor and gave him a licence as nobody else was able to do it. He had the money to start."

"Aye, I see. Let mee make in-qui-er-rees," said Walter.

CHAPTER TWENTY-SIX

THE MOMBASA TIMES carried an announcement from the East Africa Agricultural and Horticultural Society, about their upcoming Fifth Annual Show at Nairobi, to be held at the Naranjee Market. Producers of 'Vegetables, Fruits, Flowers, Economic Products, Dairy Produce, Cattle, Sheep, Pigs, Donkeys, Manufactured Articles and Horses' could apply to exhibit. A charge was payable for the stall and application form could be obtained from the Honorary Secretary in Nairobi.

Without a second thought, Lalji sent a messenger to the Honourable Secretary to obtain a form. The handwritten reply asked for details of the farm and the farmer before application forms could be issued.

***

The Honourable Secretary was chairing the meeting of the Horticultural Society.

One other voting member out of four was present. The Chairman had the fifth casting vote. Most meetings were inquorate, it being difficult to get farmers down to Nairobi unless they were passing through.

The Honourable Secretary's wife Betty was taking minutes.

"Let's turn to 'Any Other Business.'"

"The Committee needs to consider whether to admit as an exhibitor at the Annual Show a Mr Hashimbhai Jan Mohamed. He has made an application and sent the fees," announced Betty.

"What does he want to show?"

"Kitchen vegetables of various kinds grown along the Nairobi River."

"What is the farm called and is he the owner?" asked the Honourable Secretary formally.

"There is no name or title of the farm. He has rented a quarter of an acre from Mr Lalji Par-shottam, owner of Poor-band-er Stores."

"Sounds like an allotment to me. What do members think?"

"Yes, it is a *coolie's* (derogatory term for Indian person) allotment," said John Hunter, a maize farmer from Ngong Hills, the only other elected member of the committee present.

"Remind me what the policy on allotments is?" the Chairman asked Betty, pretending ignorance.

"The policy states any acreage of under one acre is classified as an allotment and cannot become a member or exhibit at the Society's shows."

"Are we agreed the application to exhibit is declined and the fees returned to Mr Hash-boy?"

"Aye," was the response from John Hunter.

"Carried unanimously. What's next?"

***

Osmanbhai Naranjee, the owner of the new Naranjee Market, walked into Porbander Store. A middle aged and soft-spoken man, his reputation as the richest man in British East Africa was well known. He had been the chief supplier of the indentured labourers for the construction of the Uganda Railway. He took an interest in the labourers, ensuring their working conditions reflected their contract. He ensured those who were returning to India at the end of the construction, were given the passage and severance they were entiltled to receive from the Protectorate. His appearance at the door unannounced was a surprise.

"*Salaam* (greetings) . Are you Laljibhai?" he asked in Gujarati.

"*Salaam*. Yes I am. And you are Osmanbhai Naranjee I know. How nice of you to come to our shop. Please sit down here in the office. How can I be of help?"

"You have a fine shop here. Hope the business is good. You have done well in the short time here."

"Thank you. That means a lot coming from you Osmanbhai. I have three other partners from the village."

"And you are from near Porbander."

"Yes, a village near there."

"I like to see our people succeeding. Also, I admire it when they share their good fortune with others."

Lalji smiled, wondering where the conversation was heading.

"Who is Hashimbhai Janmohammad?" asked Osmanbhai.

Lalji explained he was renting a small plot to try his hand at growing local produce. He was a tenant of theirs.

"I hear from the Mosque that you have helped him with seeds and are not forcing him to pay his rent arrears."

Lalji sat up, nodded his head.

"That is laudable. There is opportunity in British East Africa and we must not let those behind us struggle needlessly. The odds are stacked against us Indians, so what you are doing is good. There is plenty for everybody."

"That is very true."

"And the Africans. They need help to learn modern trade and farming. First, they need education of course."

"I fear that may take a very long time," suggested Lalji.

"It will be two or three generations, I think. But the *sarkar* (government) in making them landless or 'tenants' means they are destined to fail. They will struggle to come out of poverty to join the business community."

There was a long pause as both men allowed the conversation to sink in.

Lalji asked, "Can I offer you some tea?"

"Just water thank you." Lalji got up and brought him a glass.

"I was at the Horticultural Society Office yesterday to discuss their arrangements for the Show at the market. I own the market as you may know. I saw by accident your application for Hashimbhai to show his produce."

"Yes."

"Well, I know they are going to refuse the application. But I am here to help you and Hashimbhai to get his crops seen and sampled.

"How do you know they will refuse? Why would they?" asked Lalji.

"For us as traders, it is not necessary to question the ways of those in political office. As I said, things are not fair for any of us. But we have the know-how. And we have each other."

"What can we do?"

"I own the market but this is their show. I could interfere, but there is a better way. Just before the entrance to the show there is an empty space where he can exhibit his crops. It belongs to me. I want him to show his produce there, like a regular stall holder. I hope he has something to make us proud."

165

"That will be perfect. I will make sure he has good crops and plenty for those who need samples. I am most grateful. And the rent?"

"There is no need for rent right now. The space is unused and Hashimbhai needs it. Please bring him to the Market Office tomorrow morning to sign the papers."

"I will. This is very kind and generous of you."

Osmanbhai smiled and turned to go, disregarding the compliment.

"Keep in touch Laljibhai. *Salaam* (greetings)."

"Salaam, bhai (brother)."

***

The next Gazette carried a notice under the heading 'Liquor Ordinance.' The Wine Merchants and Grocers Licence application made by Lalji Parshottam of Porbander Stores, transferred from W. Aitcheson Wines and Spirits, was listed to be considered by the Nairobi Licensing Court. Walter and his son attended along with Lalji and Bhasker at the Provincial Commissioner's Office at *'10 o'clock in the forenoon'* as announced.

Before the proceedings began, a bespectacled clerk with glistening oily hair and moustache, wearing a civil servant's striped black suit, came over to Walter Aitcheson and asked if he could have a private word. Walter obliged and, with Andrew, followed the man into the office. A few murmurings could be heard at first, until suddenly there was a large crashing sound of Walter's walking stick smashing on a desk. Then the sound of an angry man shouting, incomprehensible at first but distinctly Walter.

"I wi-will sell me buz-niz to who I bludy like and yo-ou caan piss orf," he shouted.

More murmurs and mumbles followed by the sound of water pouring into a glass.

"Ann I don-no want any furr-thar shite, und-er stood?"

Then the office door opened and out walked a red-faced Walter with an embarrassed Andrew following, avoiding all eye contact with the occupants of the room. No sooner had Walter sat down the clerk came back, ahead of the Provincial Commissioner, and stood aside the desk at the front of the room where the Commissioner would sit. The clerk looked like he had just seen a ghost, all colour having left his face in stark contrast with Walter's blood-red appearance.

The tall Provincial Commissioner, in khaki uniform and tan knee-length boots, followed looking miffed, eyebrows almost touching, and sat down at the desk. Lalji wondered if that was his natural appearance or if it had to do with Walter's outburst. The proceedings started with no eye contact between the Provincial Commissioner and Walter. Lalji's application was swiftly dealt with first, even though it had been listed as third in the morning's business. The transfer of licence was allowed. The matter concluded, the Commissioner looked at Walter for the first time, an expression of contempt indicating he should leave.

Outside, Lalji and Bhasker thanked Walter and Andrew. They arranged to meet again at Walter's shop the next day. Walking back to their shop, Bhasker asked Lalji if it was a risky step to go into a business governed by regulations and restrictions.

"Yes, it is and always will be. The risk means you can command a better profit. To survive in the long term, we must ensure we become indispensable for those who oppose us now," replied Lalji. Bhasker nodded, wondering what Lalji was planning.

The next day the four *jehaji bhais* (brotherly travellers) met Walter and Andrew in the wine shop. Nizar had been through the accounts of the business with Lalji and they were both satisfied. The terms of business with the European suppliers were generous and supplies obtained easily. There was a lot to learn for the four teetotallers about alcoholic beverages, having previously thought all alcohol was the same. Walter suggested they never disclose to any customer that they did not drink.

They had to learn the different storage requirements and understand how to display the products. The four partners had decided to buy the shop with the entire stock. They were to use the cellars for stocking bottled products only, as no one was able to deal with the stench of alcohol from the barrels. Bhasker would be the partner at the business, while Lalji managed Porbander Stores. They kept the trading name, 'W. Aitcheson Wines and Spirits', uncertain about how the European clients might react if they used an Indian name. Bhasker would start to spend his mornings at the shop to get acquainted with it.

Walter stated a sale price. He knew the four partners were going to discuss the price and get a loan from their Bank. Lalji, Bhasker and Nizar went to see Mr Edwards, all the paperwork neatly presented in a soft, beige file. Having looked at the papers and checked with the three partners their plans, Mr Edwards asked for more time to consider the matter. His immediate comment was to ask why they were considering investing into further premises while the Nairobi River site had enough land to build on.

"This type of business needs the high street," explained Nizar.

"Yes, I know. The business is sound. If you had made use of the river site you may not need a loan at all. I know you have not had the time to do much there yet," pondered Mr Edwards.

"If we develop plans for the river site, would that help?" asked Lalji.

"I can't say just yet. Let me consider it more and we shall talk again. Let me see, are you able to come back on Friday morning?"

"Yes, we will," responded Lalji. "What do you think of the price?"

"It seems in the right region. Mr Aitcheson has taken a fancy to you. For good reasons he may drop the price further for you."

Lalji smiled.

***

On the morning of the Horticultural Society show Hashimbhai had arranged to take his produce to the Naranjee market with Lalji. They were to meet Mr Naranjee there in the morning. At ten in the morning Hashimbhai turned up at Porbandar Stores with a cart full of his produce. Bhasker saw him first and could not resist quipping at him about his produce.

"That's a fair amount of produce, Hashimbhai. And there you were telling us all along you could not get much to grow."

"This is not all mine. I had to get some from other producers to fill the market stall. But yes, the crops are doing better. I told Laljibhai I will be paying the rent this month."

"Don't forget the arrears."

"Yes, yes. That also," responded an annoyed Hashimbhai.

"The crops look healthy I have to admit."

"All blessings from Allah. And *Bhabhijaan*."

"*Bhabhijaan?*" inquired Bhasker, unaware who he meant.

Lalji appeared at the door of the shop.

"Ready to go Hashimbhai?" he asked.

"Yes, Laljibhai. I was going to explain to Bhaskerbhai how suddenly the crops started to do well after the new seeds brought by *Janki-bhabhijaan*."

"Oh! I understand now," was Bhasker's response who then turned and went back into the shop shaking his head. Lalji laughed at Bhasker's reaction.

At the market, Mr Naranjee showed them around and introduced them to other stallholders. Most of them were European owned but manned by African staff. There was the occasional Indian stallholder. No local African stallholder, just one Arab with produce from the coast and Oman. The temporary entrance to the Horticultural Show was up and decorated. A few European ladies were arranging flowers and sheaves of harvested wheat onto hooks on the walls. Everyone was engrossed in their work. Hashimbhai's presence as a new competitor did not seem to raise much interest. The presence of Mr Naranjee had a reassuring effect.

The next morning Hashimbhai was at the market at six in the morning when the show opened. He unpacked his produce, all chilled from the cool night temperature. He wiped away dew that had settled on the tomatoes and sat down, waiting for his first customers. He had learnt many buyers and hoteliers would turn up for the show so he had made a special effort to smarten up. A brown belt held up his brilliant white cotton trousers; his beard trimmed; on his feet a pair of polished black leather shoes without socks.

Around eight o'clock people from the Horticultural Society started to turn up. Most of the livestock was arriving in the morning. Last-minute arrangements were needed in the pens for the few animals that were going to be displayed. Hashimbhai had noticed a small group of stall holders and Horticultural Society members chatting and looking in his direction.

"What price are the tomatoes?" Hashimbhai's gaze was interrupted by a short, balding, middle-aged man in a white uniform.

"Twelve cents a pound," he responded in his best English.

"I will take five pounds. And the cucumber, carrots, and spring onions, how much?"

Hashimbhai struggled with some of the prices but happily jotted the prices down on a scrap of paper. The buyer was joined by a red-faced, plump, white lady, in her twenties, and an African assistant carrying a large basket.

The young lady spoke to the buyer, "Have you been to the other stalls yet, Roberto?"

"No, I don't need to go there. I know what they sell. This man is a new seller and his tomatoes are perfect for my pomodoro sauce."

"Yes but…"

"I am the chef. I know what I want. Today I want to try out this man's vegetables. *You capirsi?*"

The young lady nodded her head. When Hashimbhai had served all the chef wanted he totted up the bill and the young lady paid. The goods were transferred to the large *kikapu* (basket).

"You will be here tomorrow signor?" he asked Hashimbhai.

"*Inshallah* (If Allah wills it). Yes, yes, I will be."

The man nodded his understanding with one brisk nod and walked off, followed by his two assistants.

By late morning Hashimbhai was left with a few carrots, some bunches of coriander, and a few pounds of potatoes. Trade had been brisk and he put it down to his prime position near the entrance. What he had not done was to check out the quality of his competitors.

He was packing up when Mr Naranjee approached him.

"All well Hashimbhai?" he asked.

"By Allah's grace all has gone well today. And thank you for this stall. The position has helped me a lot."

"Don't get too used to it. You are only here for a short time until you have big customers who are willing to pick up the crops from your land."

"Yes, yes, Mr Naranjee," eyebrows raised in expectation.

"I see you have met the head chef from the Carlton Hotel today."

"The gentleman in white who came with the red-faced lady and a servant?"

"Yes, Mr Roberto. He comes every morning."

By the time the Agricultural and Horticultural Show ended Hashimbhai had run out of stock. He had two other contacts like Mr Roberto who were looking for steady supplies and others who had requested samples from his next harvest. Mr Roberto had been back every day to buy his tomatoes and try out other crops.

At Mr Naranjee's request, they had a meeting in his office with Lalji. Most of the information came from Mr Naranjee who had been approached by prospective buyers. The crops and their quality had been well received with buyers keen to set up regular purchasing.

"These people need to have a firm commitment from you Hashimbhai. That you will supply them what they need in the quantities they need. Which means you must be able to produce more than you do now," Mr Naranjee explained.

Hashimbhai looked unsure, then said, "I have asked Laljibhai for more land. Then I will be able to provide more."

Lalji intervened. "Hashimbhai, even if you have the land, you will need workers. It's not a job for one man."

Hashimbhai looked uncomfortable. "I know my crops will be the best quality if they have my attention."

"Well, what if we find you someone to learn from you and help you? You are going to need someone to see to the customers as you cannot manage on your own. You will need more labourers, especially if you need to rent more land," suggested Lalji.

"Yes, I see. It will be better for the business. But where can I find such a person?"

"I will look around, and let you know if there is someone suitable," said Lalji.

"Thank you. Thank you both for thinking of my welfare."

Within a fortnight two people were recruited. Ramji had previously dealt with someone who was training to become a carpenter and had worked for his father. His name was Laxman and he had been in Nairobi six years. Laxman's father was a stone mason and wanted him to become a carpenter to complement his business. Laxman had farmed in Kutch and his heart was in growing crops and vegetables. Ramji suggested to Lalji that he could become Hashimbhai's right hand man if they were going to enlarge the plot.

In the meantime, Mr Naranjee had recruited an experienced Kikuyu man, Mwangi, who had been working for a farmer from the white highlands. Mwangi was in charge of the market stall of his white boss, but his pleasure was in growing. He had farmed his father's land before it was handed over to a white farmer by the *sarkar* (government). Mwangi had accepted the situation and believed his father's land would return to him some day.

Lalji with his three partners agreed to a doubling of the plot along the Nairobi River on the south side, fenced off and farmed on their behalf by Hashimbhai, with help from Laxman and Mwangi. Hashimbhai's skill was in growing crops. He found managing money and rent difficult to grapple with. The four partners offered him a regular wage as they did for Laxman and Mwangi. Hashimbhai agreed with the new arrangement and the land was prepared, making sure to remain within acreage regulations as Indians were not permitted to own farms.

Lalji suggested Ramji and Nizar, being closer to the plot would oversee the new venture, named *Porbander Kitchen Garden*.

CHAPTER TWENTY-SEVEN

JANKI HAD BECOME acquainted with the *Sanatan Dharma Mandir* (Temple where followers of all major Hindu Gods attend) after meeting the priest on her weekly visits to the temple. She liked the wide denominational observations of the *Mandir*, something she was used to back home. She started to get involved in festival activities and struck up friendships with many of the women.

Her involvement also helped her to learn more about Nairobi and the life of people in the Protectorate. Some had been in Nairobi for ten or even twenty years. The husbands of some were in employment, others were in business, and a few were on short-term contracts from India. Janki realised early on there was a close union between the ladies of the *Mandir*. Their realisations and experiences were quite different to those of the menfolk.

The group managed to follow religious calendar activities. They shared recipes for locally grown food. They shared their knowledge of home and Ayurvedic remedies. They were aware of trends in supplies and knew appropriate home products. They knew which untrustworthy shopkeepers to avoid, knew the school and its teachers. No one person had all the information and the cross pollination of information created a low-level buzz when they met. Some would be hand-sewing clothes for the Deities of the *Mandir*. Some made fresh flower garlands, some wicks for lamps and others cooked at festivals. Whatever their activity, the group of eleven would ensure each one was appraised of latest developments.

The *Mahila Mandal* (ladies' group), as they became known, were not just a support group for each other. They also helped resolve domestic disputes. Usually these were between warring wives of brothers living under the same roof. Sometimes issues stemmed from older in-laws unwilling to change for new entrants to the family after marriages. Janki was the youngest in the group but never felt out of place. It felt like home again where her mother and aunt would sit in the yard discussing and gossiping the latest goings on in the village. As a repository of information, new and old, the group rarely failed to satisfy.

Within three months Janki had complete knowledge in all matters of a Nairobi household. From where to buy, what to cook, who to seek help from, who to employ. She had complete control of the domestic scene and household expenses. The other ladies in the group joked that Janki was the ideal daughter-in-law but lacked a mother-in-law who could have appreciated her. Someone else responded there was no such thing as a satisfied mother-in-law, initiating a fit of further giggles. Lalji appreciated Janki's efforts to gather information which eased their living in Nairobi. He especially enjoyed her cooking.

Of the *jehaji bhais*, Bhasker was the closest to her and talked more about the businesses with her than Lalji did. Janki prayed regularly at the *Mandir* that the *jehaji bhais* would remain close and always look out for each other. Every now and then she would remind Lalji that when it was opportune, he needed to plan for his younger brother Naran to join them. Naran had made her promise she would keep reminding Lalji. Lalji was waiting to find something suitable for Naran to do. Although Naran had run Parshottam's shop since Lalji left, Lalji knew the limited breadth of his experience. Naran was a slow learner and lacked confidence which would undoubtedly improve with experience. But he also had a strong sense of pride and confidence which inhibited him from asking for help.

Lalji wanted for him a role which would expose him to making business decisions, and in the process learn how to navigate the regulations and laws of colonial Africa. He thought that having Naran join as his assistant would make him dependent, which would not be a long-term option.

The wine and spirits business had taken off slowly. Some customers were displeased with the ownership change. However, when the Regimental Commander of the local Engineers Company found out it was run by the *jehaji bhais* he started to order supplies from them. His impression of Lalji's helpful nature from when the Army rented the land alongside the Nairobi River had a lot to do with his decision. In addition, Roberto, the Head Chef at the Carlton, started to place orders for wines to be imported from Italy and

France. The business had sole agencies for French Cognac, Portuguese Port Wine, French Champagne, Scottish Malt Whiskey, and Irish Stout. Bhasker ensured stocks were well controlled so as not to disappoint customers. Invoices were paid in time to build up goodwill with the suppliers. Mr Edwards had not been able to lend the full amount of the loan to the business. What he could lend was forty per cent of what the partners required. Lalji accepted the loan as it would get them started and decided they would run with lower stock levels at first. At least the business would be secure and the opportunity would not be lost he thought.

One day KB dropped in unexpectedly. He made it a point of seeing Lalji whenever he was in town.

"How are you settling down in Uganda Khimjibhai?" asked Lalji.

"Things are a little difficult at present but we have started to clear land for planting now that we have a farm," he said with a smile.

"So pleased to hear that. Where in Uganda? Is it near the railway?"

"Yes, a hundred miles before the track terminates in Kampala. I have come to sign further papers with the Administrator and to recruit staff."

"What kind of staff?" inquired Lalji.

"I need a general manager and an accountant to start with. The accommodation is basic, so it might suit someone younger and unmarried."

"You may be looking quite some time then. Maybe recruiting directly from India might be better."

"I know that is the better way. But right now, I could not afford their wages. Also, there is no guarantee they would stay if they came on a contract from India. I need someone who is young, adaptable and will not leave easily. Someone who would grow with the business."

"If that is the case, why two people? Could one not do the job?" asked Lalji.

"I thought it may be too lonely for one person."

Lalji reflected for a moment, before narrowing his eyes on KB.

"Khimjibhai, I have a proposal for you. My own brother, back in Gujarat, is looking to come here to settle. He has recently turned eighteen. He has been running my father's store but is keen to join me. I am thinking, he is young, fit, and intelligent. His maths is good for a manager, not like that of an accountant. Would you consider him?" asked Lalji.

"Now that is interesting. I do not have a brother to turn to for help. But if he is willing to learn and is committed to staying in Africa then he sounds good. Has he got a business-brain?"

"Let us say he would be fifth generation as a trader, like me. He can read and write fluently in Gujarati. His English is basic but like me he will pick it up."

"Sounds good. Let's talk after I return from the Administrator General's office."

"Tea?"

"When I return, Laljibhai."

***

Ramji seemed to have lost more weight. It was Janki who noticed his appetite had waned and his cough was more irritable. Once again, he brushed it off as dryness from the dust at the sawmill. One day he went into a fit of coughing at work and passed out. Nizar brought him back to the house and alerted the others.

Janki got there first with Lalji. Ramji was lying on his bed in a darkened room, sweating profusely, coughing and spluttering. He had a high fever and Dr B K Shah was sent for. The doctor diagnosed pneumonia and had him admitted to the Nairobi Clinic.

The prescription of twice-a-day morphine injections and fresh air started to show slight improvement after two weeks. By then Ramji had dark circles around his eyes, his cheeks had hollowed and his legs had lost strength. Gradually his appetite started to return. His cough and fever improved but one morning he coughed up a dollop of blood-stained sputum. From then on, the blood stains became frequent. Dr Shah brought a colleague to concur and they both agreed that Ramji had signs of tuberculous pleurisy. He was advised fresh air, fresh fruit and vegetables, and boiled turmeric milk with honey. The injections were stopped and he was allowed home.

Ramji was confined to his room and the backyard. Janki came three times a day with his fresh hot meals and persuaded him to sit outdoors in the morning sun and get fresh air. Lalji and the others saw him every day, sometimes twice a day. Dr Shah's advice was to avoid close contact. Ramji started to wear a handkerchief covering his mouth and nose when anyone entered his room.

The other three *jehaji bhais* were floored by the whole episode. Ramji's ill health seemed to have come on suddenly and none of them expected it. None had direct experience of serious illness. His cough seemed to have always been there and they had stopped noticing it. Dr Shah suggested Ramji's trade and the dust may have a lot to do with getting the infection. He said it would have been made worse by the cold damp conditions of the recent rainy season.

Lalji suggested and all agreed to get Ramji to Mombasa for three months. It was Dr Shah's advice for convalescence. It would be warmer and the sea air would help his lungs. Nizar volunteered to accompany Ramji. He would arrange accommodation near Premlal Joshi's vegetarian restaurant and daily help. When they spoke to Ramji, he agreed.

"I think it would help. The sea air on the *vaan* (dhow) coming here was good for my cough. It had almost gone," observed Ramji.

"I will stay until things are in place," Nizar said.

"Thank you. I will need to let my family know."

"Do that as soon as you get settled in," suggested Janki. "That way they will worry less."

"Yes, you are right, *Jankibhabhi.*"

"You should take your *tablas* (pair of percussion instruments, played together) with you and polish up more *taals* (formulae of beats)," joked Bhasker.

Ramji smiled at the mention of his *tablas*. "Yes, but in three months I will be so far ahead you will never catch up!"

"As long as you promise not to sing. Leave that to me," joked Bhasker.

***

The overnight journey on the Mombasa train had been uneventful for Ramji and Nizar. Ramji seemed tired and slept throughout the journey. Nizar woke him up twice to offer him water as he was running a fever. Each time, he changed his shirt which had become soaked in sweat.

"We are almost there," Nizar greeted Ramji in the morning. "The air is already humid."

"Yes. It seems so long ago we were going the other way. Have you slept?" Ramji inquired.

"A little. The train stopped twice for animals when the hooting woke me."

"Oh!"

They hired a ricksha from the train station to Premlal Joshi's restaurant. Premlal was out and his wife showed them into a room and offered breakfast and hot water for bathing. Before Nizar could answer Ramji had laid down on the bed and was drifting off into sleep, waking with bouts of coughing.

When Premlal returned he came to greet them but Ramji was still sleeping. "My wife tells me your friend is not too well."

"Ramji has had a cough for some time. The doctor suggested sea air to help him recover. I was wondering if you know somewhere near the sea, we could hire. Something small."

Premlal looked at Nizar closely. "Are you concerned about someone catching it?"

"That and making sure his strength and mind remain strong."

"I will ask around. But you need to be able to cook and clean. It would be like setting up a home."

"I know. My brothers in Nairobi have asked me to take as long as we need to get Ramji well. It's difficult to know when he will start to get better."

"You could stay here. I will arrange two rooms close by so you do not need to share. We can provide the kind of food he needs and the room is cleaned daily. It's not necessary to worry about setting up a home when you have Ramji to look after."

Nizar looked lost in thought, looking past Premlal into vacant space. "Do you know any doctor nearby?"

"Yes, there is Dr Pinto. I also know of an Ayurvedic doctor and a hakim."

"And the rent with food?" asked Nizar nervously.

"I will charge you for the meals only. In return, will you write up my accounts? I hear you are good with figures."

"Yes, of course, I will. That is a big weight off my mind. I can put my energy into that and getting Ramji better. Thank you, Premlalbhai."

"And from here the Mosque is near for you."

Nizar smiled at Premlal, thanking him again.

Ramji slept most of the day. He hardly ate anything and drank little. His eyes looked sunken. Towards the evening his speech was slurring and Nizar started to get concerned. He asked Premlal if the doctor could be sent for.

Dr Pinto, a thin wiry man in his sixties with ivory-coloured hair and dark-rimmed glasses attended. He examined Ramji and administered an injection for the fever.

Outside the room, he confided to Nizar and Premlal. "The next two days are crucial. He has developed pneumonia on the same side where the TB is. I would suggest twice daily injections and sponging to control the fever. If he loses consciousness then we should move him to the hospital."

No sooner had he left Nizar broke down and sobbed in front of Premlal. It was as if a dam of held-back emotions had released. He spoke to Premlal about how the four had come from Porbander and quickly got involved in making a living. He was remorseful about not spotting Ramji's ill health. Looking back there had been signs of something wrong.

"Have you had to look after someone sick before?" asked Premlal.

"No."

"Do you miss your family?"

"Yes, but it's important to make a success of life here. Things are better now Jankibhabhi has joined us. At least we eat proper meals every day." Nizar blew his nose and wiped his tears. "I am afraid I will not know what to do if he dies."

"We are here to help. First, though, you must send two telegrams in the morning. One to Ramji's family and one to Laljibhai in Nairobi."

"Yes. Yes, you are right."

That night Ramji had a high fever and Nizar, Premlal and his wife took turns to sponge him. His coughing bouts seemed to improve and were less explosive. Towards the morning he coughed less but his breathing was quicker and shallower. He was in deep sleep most of the time.

Nizar managed a few hours of sleep. In the morning he went straight to the Telegraph Office. On his return, he met Dr Pinto who was examining Ramji.

This time the Doctor spoke in front of Ramji. "His pneumonia has taken hold. It will be hard to save him now. I will call again in the evening but let me know if you are worried about anything new."

A couple of hours later Ramji's breathing became shallower. He seemed to miss out occasional breaths. On one of these pauses, his breathing failed to restart. Nizar shook him.

"Breathe Ramji! Wake up! Wake up, breathe," Nizar shouted at him, shaking him. But there was no response. Premlal spoke loudly into Ramji's ear to wake him. There was no response and the breathing did not restart.

Dr Pinto came and confirmed death. He issued the death certificate and gave instructions on the procedures to follow.

Nizar felt a strange peace come over him. There was numbness, but also relief after witnessing his friend's struggle. Ramji had become unwell so suddenly and unexpectedly. His death seemed similarly hurried. But for Ramji, he was thankful that the end came quickly.

CHAPTER TWENTY-EIGHT

JAMES HAD LEARNT his chores quickly around the house. Janki admired how keen he was to learn new things. Often, he would observe her cooking.

"Mama, what is the green grain you are boiling?" he would ask, in Swahili.

"This is *moong*, to make *dhal*," Janki spoke in a poor mixture of Swahili and Gujarati. He understood it all.

"Here are the chopped vegetables."

"Pass me the oil. I will show you a different way to cook them today, without tomatoes." She loved to show him even though he was not likely to be cooking for himself.

James obliged, adjusting the coal in the stove. He was intrigued by her way of cooking — her frying, boiling and her roasting the thinly rolled out *rotis* (flat breads). Most of all he was fascinated by her use of spices of different colours and the different smells and tastes from them. He wanted to know about the *dahl* (lentil) grains, the flours, the spices. At times Janki felt he looked up to her as a mother, despite their similar ages. He loved tasting the result, remembering how it was made, and trying to ascribe each taste to the different ingredients used. He was fascinated by Janki's ability to turn out perfect dishes without tasting them. To him, that was the sign of a true craftsman.

One day she asked him about his family.

"I have three brothers and two sisters. All live in the rift valley with my mothers."

"That's not a large family. Are the others younger?" she asked.

"Yes, all of them. I must provide money for them."

"You said mothers."

"My father had two wives. One brother and sister from the younger wife."

"And your father?"

His face contorted into a painful expression. "My father is dead. The *muzungu* (white man) he worked for at Njoro killed him," he stated impassively in a loud voice.

"Why was he killed?"

A long pause followed as if James was grappling with a decision of what to reveal.

Without any eye contact he said, "He worked for the white farmer who had taken his land. At first everything was fine until the *muzungu* found out my father owned the land before him. His Arab foreman told the *muzungu* my father lived in the 'squatter' camp where all the displaced lived."

Janki listened in silence, having stopped what she was doing.

"One day the police *askaris* (constables) came to arrest him. They said he had stolen money from the *muzungu* and demanded to see his *kipande*, his identity card. My father told them he was waiting to receive his from the government. They took him away with his hands tied up and beat him to confess to stealing. According to one of the guards, while being beaten he accused the *muzungu* of stealing his ancestral land. The beatings continued into the next day until he passed out. The following day they sent for my mother to come and collect his body."

"*Oh Maa!* How horrible. How old were you?"

"I was twelve. My mother collected us and took my father's body to the colonial house where the settler farmer lived. Along the way many people joined us when they heard what had happened. When we got to the colonial house the *muzungu* was sitting on a chair on the veranda, smoking his pipe. His rifle was on his lap and his three big dogs were tied near the entrance. He was angry, his face the colour of blood. He aimed his rifle at us and shot in the air. Everyone stopped, we were frightened. He called his Arab man to tell us to go home or else he would get us arrested by the police."

"Go on," said Janki.

"The next morning, we buried my father. When we returned home my mother asked us to pack our things and to get ready to leave. We walked all day to another 'squatter' camp where my father had a friend."

"Is that where you grew up then?"

"At first. I used to graze the goats for my father's friend along with my brothers. Then he started to beat us for little reason and my mother would stop him. Then my mother started to cook for him, even though he had a wife. After that I left when I saw my mother was pregnant."

"And your second mother?"

"She never came with us. She was young and asked my mother to take all the children and look after us."

"Where did you go after you left?"

"I walked to the big road and a petrol tanker picked me up. The driver took me to Nairobi. Here I applied for a *kipande* and started to look for work. I stay with Kijana whom I knew back home."

"So, you are angry with the white people, the *wazungu*," Janki asked, getting the pronunciation right.

"They take your land; they take your cattle and they build their colonial houses with verandas. They have guns and dogs. They can get your arrested and killed when they want. They are not good people. Only *Mungu* (God) can punish them.

"Do you believe in God, in *Mungu*?" asked Janki.

"I know my ancestors' *Mungu* may not be strong. That is why I go to Church and ask the God of the *wazungu* to punish them. I think their *Mungu* is fair and can punish them. The father at the Church is a good man and talks about being kind and gentle with everyone. I like that. The white farmers go to their own Church but I don't think they listen to the father or their God."

That evening Janki told the others about James' story.

"The *kipande* is a big problem," said Lalji. "If it is lost, they get sent back up country or jailed. Even as an employer there is only so much you can do. If you go to the police, they will accuse you of employing someone without a *kipande* and take you to court."

"So, what can you do?"

"We keep a record of the *kipande* and its number. The white superintendent at Nairobi Central accepts our records. He arranges for a replacement."

"But this only happens if you know someone is in custody and before they are trucked up country, Bhabhi," added Bhasker.

There was a knock at the door. Lalji opened it and there was a post-man with a telegram.

"It's from Mombasa, from Nizar," announced Lalji, ripping open the envelope hurriedly.

Everyone stopped speaking as Lalji announced, "*Hey Bhagawan*! Ramji is no more," and sat down heavily on a chair, letting out a deep sigh.

The telegram from Nizar was so brief it did not state how Ramji's health had deteriorated quickly on reaching Mombasa. The cremation was going to be that afternoon. Premlal Joshi had made all the arrangements. By the time the telegram reached Nairobi it would be over. Nizar had added that he had sent a telegram to Ramji's parents. He would be returning to Nairobi by the following day's train and would bring Ramji's ashes with him.

Lalji, always the leader with words of experience and wisdom, felt bewildered and helpless. Their plans and aspirations had featured all four of them moving ahead together. The loss of one of the partners was never contemplated.

On Nizar's return the word spread around Nairobi of Ramji's death. Lalji closed the shops for the day and people started coming home to pay their respects. Mohan was the first and brought along Kijana in case he could be of help. In the evenings for the next 13 days, they had further prayer meetings where Janki or one of the other ladies from the *Mandir* (Temple) read from the *Bhagavad Geeta* (Hindu scripture, words of Lord Krishna). *Bhajans* (religious songs) followed the readings.

Janki and James had moved the furniture, little as it was, out of the main room at Lalji's and placed soft mats on the floor for the visitors. People trickled in at odd times, sat solemnly and listened to the texts being read aloud. After the reading, people would talk about the last time they had seen Ramji. They talked of his personality, the difficulties of his work and the associated risks. If the general mood allowed it then the conversation would divulge to other matters like the prices of goods, the poor roads and transport. Or often it was politics and the state of the Colony.

The hot topic of the times was that the white settlers had successfully lobbied the Foreign Office. The Protectorate was to get its own currency, the Schilling. The Indian Rupee, before now the ubiquitous currency of the Indian Ocean, would no longer be used. Non-white ownership of land in the White Highlands of Kenya was formally banned. Another victory for the white settlers.

"Make no mistake. They will do to us what they have started in Natal," someone said.

In Southern Africa, the government was to introduce the Asiatic Registration Bill, later to be dubbed the 'Black Act' by Mohandas Gandhi. The bill was part of the attempt to limit the presence of Indians in the Transvaal. They were to be confined to segregated areas and limited in their trading activities. The political weapon being wielded against the commercial know-how of the Indians was legislation. Even without the Black Act, the Indian traders were already subject to rampant discrimination. The law was blind to the injustices.

Someone read from a South African newspaper, about trading licensing. *"The licencing Officer is the servant of white storekeepers. He knows their views, and whatever his opinion may be, he can hardly be expected to sacrifice his appointment by opposing those who employ him."*

He went on. *"Indian traders face tremendous hardship because of the racist application of the law. That danger was illustrated when Ebrahim Moosajee's application for a retail licence was turned down by W.H. Acutt, licensing officer of Indwedwe, Southern Africa. His appeal was heard by a three-man Board chaired by Acutt. They upheld the refusal. Moosajee took the matter to the Supreme Court, where he argued that the Board was not legally constituted because Acutt, as licensing officer, was prejudiced since it was his decision that was appealed against. In effect, Acutt sat in judgement on his own decision. While Judge Gallwey opined that this was 'most undesirable,' and considered the practice 'irregular,' he could not overturn the decision because it was legal."*

Bhasker would get visibly enraged at the excesses of white privilege. The developments in one part of Africa were repeated with regularity in others.

"See, they make more laws to keep power and wealth, all for themselves," he would say. "They need us but they don't want us."

"Things are not so bad here," someone else would say.

"Not yet Bhai (Brother). Just because they have not given us a *kipande* does not mean they like us. We Indians are not welcome anywhere. Not even in our own country."

"I hear the Uganda Railway workers are being urged to go back to India," observed someone.

Once the musicians were ready, the *bhajan*s (religious songs) started and the conversation died down.

***

After any discussion of politics, Bhasker would unleash his choice expletives at the white man, provided Janki was not in earshot.

"Bhaskerbhai has a short temper," Janki observed one day. "I hope he is fine with the white customers."

"He is a shrewd businessman," said Lalji. "He knows it's strictly no politics in the shop. But he is not just all talk," Lalji continued, provoking a startled look from his wife.

"What do you mean?" asked Janki.

Whispering he replied, "Along the river there have been some incursions by Kikuyu fighters. They oppose the *kipande* laws. They hold meetings to organise opposition against the white settlers. Our land has been used as a hideout by some."

"And Bhaskerbhai?" asked Janki, also whispering.

"Bhasker has known about it for some time, I think."

"But that's so near the Army supplies! He has not mentioned it to us," responded Janki, her colour draining away.

"The *askari*(watchman) at the shop knows some of the Kikuyu. The police call them terrorists. They have lost everything to white farmers who threw them off their own land, some even left their livestock behind. They are fighting to get it back. Bhasker is sympathetic to their cause but has not said anything to me. He may have granted them permission to pass through our land. I guess he does not want us to know in case anything goes wrong."

"Is that all?"

"As far as I know. But there may be more."

"What do you mean?" Janki asked.

"I don't know if he helps in any direct way. I see him having long whispered conversations with the *askari*(watchman)."

"Is this not risky? Should we not ask him?"

"Mmm. If he is helping in any way, are we not sympathetic to these people who have been thrown out of their homes?"

"But the risk..."

"He has kept his dealings restricted to whatever he discusses with the askari(watchman). And the two of them have not involved us."

Janki was lost in thought for a while.

"He is not just a simple businessman, is he?" she observed.

CHAPTER TWENTY-NINE

RAMJI'S FATHER HAD sent a telegram acknowledging his son's death. He had asked for the ashes to be brought back to India if they had not already been immersed in water. Lalji had sent him a detailed letter after Nizar's return. Ramji's father responded that he was willing to send his second son Khimji to take Ramji's place. Lalji wrote back saying there was the need for Khimji to take his brother's place, provided he also had Ramji's skills. He advised he should start preparing without delay.

In the meantime, KB had arrived in town for further administrative business with the land authorities. He dropped in to express his condolences.

Lalji and KB had previously talked at length about the Uganda farm. KB had a few false starts with his crops and was desperately short of skilled manpower. Unlike in Tanganyika, he had a large amount of land to handle. The recruitment of labour was proving difficult. So far, he had with him a tall Arab from Mombasa called Abdul, who did most of the engaging and training of local workers. Abdul was not school educated, but he was intelligent and a good supervisor.

"Have you given further thought to taking on my brother Naran? He would make a good right-hand man on the farm," asked Lalji.

"If he could stay on the farm that would be of great help. It's not going to be the same as Nairobi, the place has no roads. The people need a lot of training but they are good people, willing to learn."

"I shall write to him immediately," said Lalji. "I think I know the answer will be positive."

"Excellent. I take it he can handle basic accounts?"

"Yes, and he had more schooling than me."

"That sounds good. Please keep me informed. I will be back to fetch him when he gets here."

"I think he will need to spend a short time with us first in Nairobi, to get familiar with things. It's not like Porbander as you know," Lalji said with a laugh. "We are also arranging for Ramji's brother to come as well, to continue running Ramji's timber yard. He is also a carpenter."

"That reminds me, I am going to need a carpenter very soon on the farm. I will wait until he gets here."

Both the young candidates were happy to travel straight away. Lalji's mother, Lalbai was less than enthusiastic about sending her second son to Africa. She was concerned he would be further inland from Lalji and Janki. She questioned how much he knew about running a farm. Naran was keen to get going and dismissed her worries. For him, the adventure he had waited for was about to begin.

When the time came to book the passage, Lalji had sent funds and instructions for the two young men to take the steamer from Mumbai. They would join the ranks of 'passenger emigrants' to British East Africa.

Within a fortnight Naran and Khimji were on their way to Mumbai.

The ship was delayed because of protests in Bombay and Poona against the Partition of Bengal announced by the Raj. Security was tight and the two travellers were grateful to have found lodgings. Many owners were reluctant to take in strangers, especially young men. Since the announcement of the Partition Plan in July 1905, the country had meandered into a series of protests, political rallies and riots against the Raj. The claim that partition of India was necessary to improve administration in the country was not accepted by the public. It was no secret that the Viceroy Lord Curzon was seeking two separate provinces to divide Hindus from Muslims in Bengal under the guise of reforms. His Home Secretary had said, *"Bengal united is a force, Bengal divided will go in different ways. Our principal motive is to weaken a united party against the government."*

It took three attempts for Naran and Khimji to finally board the ship. At every attempt, they met barricading groups of young men along the way shouting slogans and '*Vande Mataram*'. Both were naïve to the situation they encountered. They had never seen any street protests. They realised their welfare lay in echoing the slogans, raising their fists in unison with the crowd.

The nearest they had ever come to witnessing political unrest was when someone at the village *Panchayat* meeting started to shout at the leader, having been told to sit down.

***

The arrival of the two young men brought about an atmosphere of celebration and happiness. Lalji had gone to the train station in Nairobi to meet them.

"*Jai Shree Krishna,*" he greeted them both.

"*Jai Shree Krishna Bhai* (Brother)," Naran responded.

Khimji, who looked bewildered, eyes darting left and right, was like a younger version of Ramji, with a similar walk and identical voice. He greeted Lalji with tears in his eyes.

At home, Janki was preparing hot *parathas* (fried flat breads) to serve with ginger tea, spicy potatoes, yoghurt and mango pickle for the travellers.

"*Jai Shree Krishna*, welcome to Nairobi," were her first words to them at the door. The young men entered in single file, hands clasped in *namaste* and greeted her, then touched her feet as they had done with Lalji at the train station. Janki realised for the first time that although they were of similar age, the respect they held for Lalji and her was like that for a more senior person.

Kijana had come in earlier than normal to prepare hot water for the travellers' bathing. He had laid out *thalis* (metallic plates) on the kitchen floor, where the men sat on shallow wooden platforms. The hot breakfast was served by Kijana while Janki was occupied with frying the *parathas.*

"How was the journey and your ship?" Janki asked.

"The crossing was fine. We were lucky we only had two days of rough sea," replied Naran.

"And the food?" she asked.

"We managed on our rations," replied Khimji. "We could not eat every day and only managed small meals most days. So, we have brought with us whats left of our rations."

"The food is delicious Bhabhi. It's like we never left Porbander," said Naran.

Janki laughed before adding, "Well I am going to need help in the kitchen from another woman soon, to keep everyone fed."

"That would be Nizar first to bring his bride," said Bhasker, who had walked in with Nizar.

"And what's wrong with you getting married? Planning to stay a bachelor for life?" retorted Nizar, making everyone laugh at his irritation.

"I don't mind who is first as long as you all bring your brides to make your life complete here," Janki added.

***

Nizar took Khimji under his wing and showed him around the timber yard. Khimji, like his late brother, was a competent carpenter and within minutes had checked out the tools and the timber. He was intrigued by the colours and different textures of the African wood. Nizar had arranged Richter to come and meet him and explain the different qualities of the wood. Khimji collected a few small blocks of different woods and a chisel to take home with him. He could not wait to get to know the wood for himself.

Meanwhile, Lalji showed Naran the two shops and explained how the wholesale supplier system worked.

"You have a lot of products imported from England. Some from Europe," commented Naran.

"We depend on what can be imported by the English wholesalers. But they will try to get other products on request. The restrictions are not too bad."

"The farm you wrote about. Have you seen it?" asked Naran.

"No, I have never been that far. It is the largest farm owned by an Indian, who is well thought of by the *sarkar* (government). His name is Khimjibhai Bhagwanji, from Mumbai. He likes to be known by his initials, KB. He is setting up the farm and will be a good man to work for. He has a lot of experience of Africa and has already made a mark in German East Africa."

Lalji sent a telegram to KB that Naran and Khimji had arrived and could travel to Uganda.

CHAPTER THIRTY

Events elsewhere were taking an ugly turn against Indian settlers. In Southern Africa, the Government of Transvaal drafted a new law to control Indian immigration. The *sarkar* announced controls on their businesses and also where they could live. The law made it compulsory for all Indian males over eight years old to be registered and have fingerprints recorded. After the end of the Anglo-Boer war, the Indians had hoped for better treatment from the British. For the Indians in British East Africa, the repercussions of the Black Act in South Africa spelled uncertainty and danger.

The news in Nairobi was dominated by Mohandas Gandhi's efforts to stand up to the law. Gandhi's movement of *Satyagraha* (path of truth) was formed to inspire and challenge the law through passive resistance. Nine days after a mass meeting of Satyagrahis organised by Gandhi, the law was passed. People in Gujarat became nervous about emigrating to Africa and a deep distrust of the British became endemic. Where large families had planned to emigrate together it became the norm for some to stay behind to keep hold on any family land.

Bhasker stated, "*Bhai* (Brother), we should not invest further now. We have already done quite well."

Lalji read the situation differently.

"Why are you so afraid, Bhasker. If they make us go, who will look after the services we now provide?" Lalji asked. "In any case, it is the Boer *sarkar* who is responsible for the South African laws, not the British."

"Laljibhai, there is no difference between the Englishman and the Boer for us. Even though they fought a war," said Bhasker. "Look what the British *sarkar* did to Mohandas Gandhi and our people in South Africa. You cannot trust the British. They say one thing and do another."

"You are right not to trust either one. But for the British, business and revenue always comes first. Whether it is the Boer, African or Indian, we are all slaves to feed their greed."

"Who gets ahead or left behind does not concern the British," Nizar said, joining in the conversation.

"After their war with the Boers, they needed to give them something to stop them rising again, or else another war would break out. And the British *sarkar* simply cannot finance another war," added Lalji. "Here they need us. They have invested in the railway and want to reap the rewards from it. The white people from England find it hard to live here, while the Indians are getting things running. I think they need us more than they would admit."

"True," agreed Nizar. "If you look at the Mombasa Times you will see as many English people returning home as arriving here. Some are going to Southern Africa where they have more white people, white schools and businesses. Others who came from India are returning to the Raj."

While the discussion was ongoing, the two newly arrived listened intently, without expressing any view. Before leaving Gujarat, they had no idea of the uncertainties or issues they might face in the new world, which would be their future. Now it all sounded daunting.

***

Three months after Naran had taken on the role of KB's right-hand man, he had set up a new farm office. The office was next to the entrance of the farm. It had adjoining living quarters. Khimji spent a month constructing the wooden structures. The whole building stood on stilts to avoid flooding and keep out termites, rodents and snakes. Although there was a tin roof, there was no door to the office and only one desk and chair.

The fertile area around Baganda was proving to be an agricultural gift. Whatever KB tried on the land would grow. After further discussion with his agricultural advisers in Poona, KB decided on a sugar cane plantation. There were to be smaller areas for pineapples and plantains. The cane could have two harvests a year and required little more than rain once planted, of which there was plenty. It was a hardy crop with few issues of disease. Naran agreed with KB to recruit more workers and became involved in training them with Abdul, the Arab foreman. KB had brought from Mombasa tools and *pangas* (machetes) for a hundred men. It was not long before the first crop of sugar cane was harvested. It was pressed to get its ruddy brown juice, and then boiled into a thick sludge, ready for export to London for refining.

Soon after the harvest KB decided to travel to India to recruit engineers and order machinery from Europe for refining the sugar on site. The finished product would be cheaper to transport and fetched a much higher price.

One day in KB's absence an Italian settler by the name of Lorenzo Giovanni visited the farm. He asked to see the owner and Abdul brought him to see Naran.

"*Bonjorno.* I am Lorenzo, 20 miles up the railway," he announced, pointing westwards. "I grow tomato, and olives on my farm."

"Hello. Myself Naran. Boss KB. Gone to India. I am manager," explained Naran with a broad welcoming smile, extending his hand.

"*Si*, good. I see you are planting sugar cane."

"Yes. Just to try," answered Naran suspiciously.

"Good?"

"Yes. Good," Naran said with a slight shrug of the shoulders as if to convey less than full certainty.

"You are making sugar for export?"

"Yes, export."

"Not liquor?" inquired the Italian.

"Liquor? No, no."

"But you have strong smell of alcohol here."

"Yes, very strong. Natural. From the sugar."

"Oh. When does the boss return?"

"Next month."

"I will come to see him."

"Yes, I tell him. Myself Naran, Manager."

"*Si*, you told me. Goodbye."

Naran was doubly chuffed at his ability to get by with his simple English, and secondly as it sounded good to refer to himself as manager.

Abdul, who had been standing in the doorway the whole time looked unhappy with a grimace. Naran asked him what the matter was, and he stated stoutly, "*Alcool, No! Alcool haram!*" (forbidden by Islam) before storming out.

The work on the farm continued smoothly under Naran and Abdul. Wages in their pockets, and being able to buy goods from the few shops gave the workers a new pride in their jobs. Soon crowds of young men started to gather outside the farm looking to be employed. Many were relatives or brothers of incumbent workers. Naran was sure he could not afford more staff just yet, but it was reassuring that there was a potential workforce out there. Abdul would ask them to return when the crop was ready for harvest, only to find the same faces arrive the next day, asking if it was harvest time.

***

When KB returned from Mombasa he came with good news. He had recruited an engineer who would join a month later and had secured a deal on machinery to start their own refining. While in Nairobi, he had visited the Commissioner and had been received well this time by him and his English Secretary.

"Come in Mr Bag-waan-jee and take a seat," the Commissioner had greeted him.

"Good afternoon, Commissioner."

"So, what brings you to Nairobi? I hear you are busy planting sugar cane in Baganda."

"Yes. I went to Poona to recruit an Engineer. I have machinery coming from England for processing the sugar juice."

"Good to know, good to know," growled the Commissioner tweaking the end of his moustache. "I hear good things about your product."

"Oh. How is that then?" inquired KB.

"That first shipment you sent to England has invited inquires to my office here from English Agents. We have referred them to you of course. I am glad you are here as I wanted to discuss something with you."

"Yes, sir."

"There is an *Ey-talian* farmer not too far from you, -Lorenzo something. He has taken a fancy to your sugar cane and wants to produce alcohol from it. For industrial use although he wants to try making some for drinking. Would be dreadful stuff to drink if you ask me."

"So, he wants to buy some?" inquired KB.

"He wants to grow it for himself, he tells me."

"Oh."

"I have told him we can't licence more cane plantations as yours is enough for the moment. I have told him to buy the juice from you. I believe he has met your manager."

"Thank you. That is fine."

"It seems to me the time is right for us to consider your expansion of the land. Your new machinery and an engineer should allow you to increase capacity, am I right?"

"Yes. We are going to need more land. The crop has taken well to the local soil."

"And you now have a farm manager, brother of Mr Lalji?"

"Yes, sir. He has settled in fine."

"Good pedigree, Porbander Stores, what?"

"Yes, definitely," responded KB visualising Lalji's family as good canines.

"Do you think you are ready to expand KB?"

"That's the plan, Sir. With the manager, engineer, and the new machinery. We have trained up over a hundred Baganda men to harvest the crop."

With raised eyebrows and a smile, the Commissioner responded, "Do you now? That is indeed good news. How is the labour situation there?"

"The Baganda are an agricultural people. Hard working and keen to learn. We have no shortage of recruits."

"Excellent! We will need to talk with the Kabaka about leasing more land. He is a decent fellow. If you employ his people, he will be cock-a-hoop. Why don't you return to see my assistant here in the morning and discuss this further and I will see what can be done."

"Thank you, sir."

KB could not believe what had just happened. He went straight to Lalji to discuss it.

"I didn't expect he would turn down the Italian farmer and offer the land to me in the same conversation, Laljibhai."

"Why does that surprise you?"

"Well, for a start I am not European and secondly, I am still trying out different crops."

"You had a business in German East Africa which was successful. You have studied the soil and the climate and obtained seeds. Things are slowly working out and you are recruiting more workers. You have not shot anybody in a local land dispute and your product was received well in London. What more can the Commissioner want?"

"The way you put it, Laljibhai, makes sense. Thank you for your encouragement."

"This may be spearheading the Commissioner's reputation for all you know," Lalji chuckled.

KB burst out laughing. "Now you are having me on Laljibhai."

Lalji's gaze was unmoved.

"Have you ever known me to joke about business? Anyway, how is that younger brother of mine getting along? Let's talk at home, Janki will have made lunch."

CHAPTER THIRTY-ONE

NAIROBI WAS SHAKEN by the murder of a white farmer and his family fifteen miles to the north. The British settler farmer, in his fifties, his wife in her thirties, three children aged between five and twelve, their two dogs, their cook, and their *ayah* (nursemaid) were all slain in daylight at Flame Tree Farm. The raiders took cash, two rifles, a pistol, ammunition, knives and tools. Unusually, no livestock was taken, a sign of change in tactics by the 'terrorist' raiders.

The white community was outraged and demanded the perpetrators be brought to justice and hanged. The white farmers started setting up all white vigilante patrols in the area. The police responded by rounding up all employees from adjacent farms for questioning. All were detained in camps. Two casual labourers from Flame Tree Farm died in custody during interrogation.

***

In Nairobi, a meeting of leading Indian businessmen was arranged by advocate Cyrus Banatvala. It was to discuss possible sanctions by the *sarkar* (government) against Indian businesses, if they were implicated in helping African terrorists. Forty-nine people attended, representing thirty-four businesses. Lalji and Bhasker went together.

The meeting was called to order by advocate Cyrus Banatvala.

"My fellow Gujaratis, and Mr Nath Sethi and Mr Tarlok Singh from the Punjab," he said addressing the audience.

Some took the few seats available and the rest stood.

"I am here today to bring you information and take soundings from you. It is about the general security situation following the murders at Flame Tree Farm. Many of you may know I have practised in the Nairobi Courts for the last two years and have an office in Government Road. In my work I meet the Authorities from time to time and I am happy to say my relations with them are very helpful for my clients."

People shuffled in their chairs to be able to see better.

"The police have been questioning some people to find out if any businesses had contact with the culprits. You may know that one such businessman is Moosa Ibrahim, an Arab importer in partnership with Somnath Samjee, the furniture maker.

"The police are looking for other businessmen who may have been involved in helping the terrorists. So far there have been no further arrests and both Mr Ibrahim and Mr Samjee have been released without any charge. It transpires their name came up in some paperwork on the farm because they had delivered bedsteads."

Everybody was too serious to laugh. Cyrus continued, "I am concerned about any backlash from the government. Areas such as licence renewals, planning applications and approval of Indian residential plots. It seems the government suspects Indians of aiding and financing terrorists. Hence the proposal to sanction *all* Indian businesses if that turns out to be the case."

"You may know that white settler farmers have called for confiscation of property and deportation of anyone involved. Anyone found guilty would get a severe sentence from the courts."

"I have been asked to make this clear to the Indian businesses and to encourage anyone with information to come forward without fear of arrest. You may do so through me as your lawyer and I will ensure the process followed is fair and correct. Any Indian involved with these sorts of crimes should desist straight away. I will take questions and invite your comments." Cyrus finished his speech, before sitting down to face the audience.

Speaker 1: "What is the proof Indians take part in helping these terrorists?"

Cyrus: "It is only a suspicion."

Speaker 2: "That is outrageous! The *sarkar* (government) suspects us of involvement without proof. And threatens us with losing our businesses and driving us out. We have put our roots here and helped the *sarkar* to make Nairobi an important trading centre."

Speaker 3: "These threats mean that we must now start to report suspicions about each other."

There was a general buzz of conversation in the room. Cyrus did not comment.

Speaker 4: "It may be possible, that someone could be involved. I personally don't know anyone who could ever be involved in such a thing. I don't know anyone in this room who would take such a thoughtless course of action."

Speaker 5: "I agree. Indians are unlikely to be involved. We do not have a history of promoting bloodshed. We would have nothing to gain providing support to the African terrorists. What could be the reason for anyone of us to have anything to do with this?"

Cyrus: "The police think some parties may be providing help in kind, like food, shelter, or even money."

Speaker 3: "In return for what?"

Cyrus: "Not for any material gain. Maybe for ideological reasons or to make trouble. You see the police are suspicious of nationalist sympathisers from India who have an agenda to spread discontent in all parts of the Empire. To start a revolution. It is thought these anti-Empire seditionists work through the Indian business community. Already entry to Mombasa is refused to known seditionists. Some revolutionary magazines have been intercepted at Mombasa post office."

Speaker 3: "We are always an easy target. We get blamed despite working within the law and regulations. We still stand to lose what we have built up. I ask why any Indian would risk losing such a lot for no good reason?"

Speaker 2: "What sort of magazines Mr Cyrus?"

Cyrus: "These arrived by sea mail but have not been claimed. They are all past copies of an anti-British publication in Bengali."

The audience burst into spontaneous laughter, unsettling Cyrus.

Speaker 1: "Bengali! Does the *sarkar* understand there may be nobody in Nairobi who can speak Bengali, let alone read or write it?"

There was further jovial laughter and shaking of heads.

Speaker 5: "Maybe we should report those who are literate in Bengali!" encouraging further laughter.

Cyrus, emphatically: "The *sarkar* takes this very seriously. A large amount of seditionist publications are written in Bengali."

Speaker 6: "Can we be sure there is nobody who may sympathise with the position of the African? Let us be honest with each other, do we not see the lot of the African is to give up his home and ancestral land? Then be sent somewhere far with no mention of compensation, persuaded by the barrel of the gun."

Speaker 2: "Sympathy is different from taking part or assisting. I sympathise with the position of the African, as I am sure you do."

There was general clapping and cheering. Then there were angry shouts of, *"We know how inhumane the sarkar is; they treat the African worse than stray dogs; they have stolen the land from the Africans."*

Cyrus, forehead sweating, appealed for calm. Struggling to be heard, he shouted, "It is such careless talk which can lead to trouble with the *sarkar*."

Speaker 7: "I have listened carefully to this debate. Are we blind to the possibility that the anger of someone declared a squatter in his own land, and forced to leave may result in such horrific crimes? Can we not see how such crimes can be committed by those who would never have thought of violence before? What does such a man feel when his family go hungry and the farmer owner of his land has plenty for his family but will not share? Where is the rightful compensation?"

Cyrus was craning his neck to get a better view of the new speaker.

There was complete silence. People were lost in their thoughts.

Speaker 5: "You are right sir, there is much to understand about the African's plight. This conflict is like that of a householder who is trying to defend his home against a powerful thief. Only the thief has papers to show he has become the rightful owner of your house, even if you have lived there for generations. The thief has become owner of your land, property and livestock. The only thing he has not asked for is your wife and children."

Angry murmurings of agreement filled the room.

Speaker 6: "And if you object then the rifle will be pointed at you and your family."

Speaker 8: "We Indians are bystanders watching this unravel. In our case, we are being warned. A warning which the African was not given. But still, our lot is not much different from theirs."

Speaker 1, looking at Cyrus: "Why are we being dragged into this? We have wives and children. Businesses to run. Why would anyone of us get into this dispute, no matter what our sympathies? We do an honest day's work and pay our taxes. Why would anyone think we could ever be involved when we are at the mercy of a powerful *sarkar*? Remember, it was the same *sarkar* in Bharat which passed laws and collected taxes at the end of a gun barrel. Those taxes drove our fathers to poverty and brought us here to start a new life."

Cyrus: "No one is dragging you into a conflict. The *sarkar* wants to ensure the terrorists don't have sympathisers within the Indian community."

Speaker 2: "If they have proof of anyone involved, they should arrest them. What is the point of calling a meeting like this and threatening us without any proof that someone from here may have anything to do with this crime?"

Suddenly there was angry shouting by the attendees, "*Why suspect us? Why threaten us? Where is the proof of our involvement?*"

Bhasker had been listening seated next to Lalji. His fists were clenched and his palms sweaty. He went to stand up to speak but Lalji pulled him down to sit.

"No, Bhasker. We are here to observe, not to be observed." Red-faced and dry-mouthed, Bhasker sat down reluctantly. Mohan, sitting on the other side of the row, noticed and leaned forward to signal to Bhasker to stay seated. Bhasker calmed down and wondered if Lalji and Mohan were aware of his activities.

Speaker 3, stood up and appealed for calm before asking: "Why are you here advocate Banatvala? Who has sent you to warn us?"

Cyrus: "I am here as an advocate, who understands the law and am concerned about the present situation of *lawlessness*. I am here to inform you that the *sarkar* will take strong stance against Indians if anyone is found to be helping the terrorists."

Speaker 3: "See that is the difference between you and us, sir. You also call them terrorists, but nobody here has used that term. You say you are informing us but in reality you are warning us, are you not?"

Cyrus: "Informing, warning — let us not argue about words? I am assisting you by letting you know what could happen."

Speaker 2: "And you will gain clients if that happens."

Cyrus, irritated: "That is unfair! I could have chosen to not bother."

Speaker 2: "But you have been chosen to speak to us. You must also have been asked to find out the mood of the Indians to relay back?"

Cyrus: "I am doing this voluntarily to help......."

Speaker 7, shaking with anger: "If you were a true friend of ours and wanted to represent our interests you would have made it clear to your contacts in the *sarkar* that holding us all responsible, in case there is ever someone found here to have helped terrorists, would be grossly unfair." He stood up, spat on the floor in front of Cyrus, and walked out.

Cyrus: "Of course I told the Commissioner it would be challenged in court."

Speaker 2: "Challenged in court? Are you unable to say it would be monstrous and wrong?"

Speaker 8: "Mr Cyrus, it seems to me your real purpose here today is to get information for the *sarkar* whose courts you work in. You are also making sure that any case against anyone here goes to you to represent in court. Am I right?"

Speaker 3, interrupting: "We are mostly ignorant of the law here. We do our work and are building our livelihoods diligently and honestly. We have no time or inclination for politics, or to get involved with court cases. We see the lot of the African and his plight. We see him as a fellow human being. We can understand his anger even if we do not accept his tactics. His response is that of a desperate man. Without any alternatives. We see that. We understand that."

Speaker 2: "Cyrusbhai, are you here to help us or spy on us? Please answer truthfully."

Cyrus: "I am here voluntarily to give information and help prevent any problems for the Indian community."

Speaker 2: "You speak to us in Gujarati, which is also your mother tongue as a Parsee. And you keep saying you are here to help the Indians but you are not listening to us. You seem to see yourself as different from us, maybe because of your position and education. I must be honest with you, it would worry me if you were talking on my behalf, either to the *sarkar* or in court."

There was loud clapping and a general buzz of agreement with the last speaker. Most avoided eye contact with Cyrus and started to leave before the meeting closed.

CHAPTER THIRTY-TWO

LALJI HAD NOTICED a remoteness in Janki and unusual moodiness. He had assumed it would be tiredness or her painful periods and thought nothing of it at first. He realised it was more when she rebuffed him at night. He also noted her friends from the *Mandir* (Temple) dropping in for a chat more often than usual, giggling and whispering.

One day Lalji noticed Janki looking sideways at herself in the mirror, her petticoat lower than usual under her sari. He looked puzzled which evoked a giggle from Janki when she caught his eye.

"Mr Porbander Stores, what are you looking at?" she teased him.

"Uh, nothing."

"You are wondering if you wife is changing are you not?"

"I guess. Are you all right?"

"What do you mean?"

"Well, you look fine but…"

"But what?"

Well, sometimes, not always, you are remote."

"What makes you say that?"

"Ugh. Not much I guess."

"Tell me."

"Well, you don't seem interested in what I tell you about the shops. As I said, you seem remote."

"And?"

"No nothing else, just…."

"Tell me."

"Well, we don't seem to be close in bed like before. I'm sorry, I don't need to say that."

"Well, Mr Porbander Stores, I have never felt better and thank you for asking. But you need to know something."

"Oh!"

Lifting her sari up draped around her forearm, above her head like a curtain, she said," Your dear wife is carrying your first child."

"What!"

"You are going to be a father soon." She dropped the sari, revealing a beaming smile, cheek dimple fully visible.

Lalji stood there rooted to the ground, as if not comprehending the words.

"But how do you — I mean, should you not see a doctor? How can you be sure?"

"Mr Porbander Stores, a woman does not need to see a doctor to know. How do you think your mother knew she was carrying you?"

"Yes. But what do we do now?"

Chuckling loudly at her husband, Janki teased him further. "Well, try and look less shocked and maybe smile in happiness!"

Lalji burst out laughing and sat down. He laughed more at his own reaction than the happiness of the occasion. He was out of his depth, and Janki, his delicate wife for whom he made most decisions, was now in charge of something of which he had no experience. He felt a new feeling inside him, a mixture of awe and humility. His dear Janki now represented the presence of the power of nature and he wanted to hold and squeeze her but was not sure if that was safe or appropriate. He continued laughing until he was in tears and started sobbing. Janki, standing next to him, held his head in her hands and pressed it against her stomach until he stopped sobbing, gently caressing his hair.

***

Within days the pregnancy was making itself felt with morning sickness and lassitude. She managed to cook for the men but relied more on James to help in the kitchen than before. With James serving the hot *rotis* (flat breads) at lunch as well as rolling them out, it became clear to the menfolk that Janki was struggling.

Nizar dropped in to Porbander Stores after closing.

"Laljibhai, I wanted to have a chat," he said when the shop was empty of customers.

"Yes Nizar, what is it?"

"*Bhai* (Brother), we often see Jankibhabhi tired and she does not look well."

"Oh. It's fine. She is expecting."

"Yes *Bhai* (Brother). That is good news. For her the next few months are going to be tough."

"She has already spoken to some of the ladies from the *Mandir* and they have all offered help."

"Does she need to see a doctor?"

"She tells me she doesn't and it's all quite normal. One of the ladies at the *Mandir* is well experienced and is overseeing her progress. I have no knowledge of what should happen, so I accept what she says."

"*Bhai* (Brother), I am thinking with the pregnancy, then the baby, she is going to need more help."

"Yes. She tells me one of her friends has a good *ayah* (nursemaid) who can assist once the baby arrives."

"I believe she would be better off if she had another woman in the house."

"Yes, the *ayah* (nursemaid)— unless you mean ....?" He looked into Nizar's eyes.

"Yes. My father has been asking for some time for me to return and get married. They have chosen a distant cousin, Husnara. I am told she is good in matters of the home."

"Nizar that is good news. I did not know. I am sure it would be good for Janki to have someone to share the home responsibilities with. But how can we...?"

"I should take the steamer to Mumbai, go home and return before the month is up with Husnara. Khimji is already familiar with the shop and the yard. I can let everyone at home know to prepare for the *nikaah* (Muslim wedding ceremony)."

"That seems too hurried. You have not seen your family since you left Porbander. Yes, let us prepare but you need to spend a little longer at home don't you think?"

"Maybe a little longer. But we have a big delivery coming from England in two months and Khimji will need me."

"And Husnara. Will she be fine living here and being away from family? There is only Janki here until she meets others."

"I am told she will be fine. She cooks well, mainly vegetarian food. She will blend in well into our family."

Lalji felt a sense of pride to hear Nizar refer to their group as 'our family.' When Janki heard she was overjoyed. She had more knowledge of Muslim wedding customs than Lalji.

"Well, Nizarbhai, I hear you have been keeping a secret," she teased him.

"I am not one for secrets, Bhabhi. Just happened so fast. The last letter from my father informed me. I have not read it to you yet," he confessed.

"Well, in view of this happy development, I expect to receive a suitable new saree from Porbander!"

"And you'd better practise to become the senior lady of the house!" said Nizar, evoking a loud laugh from Janki.

"You only have a short time. We need to start getting some presents ready for your family back home and for your bride, don't you think?"

"I was thinking, Bhabhi, would you mind coming to the soni and the *saree* shop to help me choose?"

"Nizarbhai, you menfolk always talk about commissions and profits. You do realise I will need a commission for that?" she said with a smile.

"Of course! I am beholden to your demands," said Nizar, laughing and walking away shaking his head.

***

The Official Gazette carried a list of plays licensed for performing in the Protectorate. It quoted the author, date of the licence and the number of performances allowed. To celebrate the return of the newlyweds, Janki had organised tickets for the family. It was the first performance of *'Sunheri Khanjar'* by Munshi Mohammad Ibrahim Muhasar.

It was a major event in Nairobi. The arrival of a stage company from Mumbai on a tour of Africa. It was the talk of Nairobi. Local fliers were printed and posted up. There were write ups of the author, the artistes and their fifteen-strong troupe. The company carried their own screens and light props with them, and included two musicians. One of the cast also functioned as a comedian to fill in the gaps when sets or costumes changed.

The front three rows had been reserved for important people. These included the Commissioner of Police and a high-ranking officer from the Administrator General's office. A large group of Parsi lawyers with their families, all dressed in traditional Parsi clothes were also included. The lawyers had abandoned their western suits for the evening.

Two observers, both white, from the administrator's office were sitting at the end of the first row. They had a small writing pedestal in front of them, to take notes of the performance. They were there to also listen for any disallowed words, seditious language, or anti-authority behaviour from the crowd. Quite what they understood of Hindi or Urdu was anybody's guess. But the presence of the Authorities was there to be seen, ensuring His Majesty's peace remained undisturbed.

The performance started with the National Anthem to save the King. Most of the audience stood in silence not knowing the words sung by a group of school children. That was followed by speeches given by the Commissioner of Police and a senior member of the Parsi community. Both were drowned out by a general hum of conversations and the Commissioner's speech was severely challenged by a Parsi child in the second row. The baby seemed hell-bent on howling his irritation at being there, unable to be pacified by his mother.

One of the two officials taking notes stood up red-faced and remonstrated with the bewildered Parsi woman. The woman neither understood the man's English nor was able to control the child. She burst into tears which seemed to have a temporary calming effect on the child. The child turned and saw the angry, white official and promptly restarted his howling with greater gusto. The official returned to his seat, shrugging his shoulders and muttering under his breath to his colleague. A couple of the senior Parsi men went to talk to the woman who was persuaded to leave to pacify the child somewhere outside.

Janki and Husnara were thrilled at being there. Neither had seen a Mumbai *natak* (play) before. The sight of the mock walls of the set, the clever use of drapes and music to create the mood, had them both mesmerised. They sat at the end of the row together, whispering and pointing out things to each other. The performance lasted a full three hours, the play interrupted often with stoppages for changing costumes and scenes. The comedian was entertaining, but he found it difficult to hold the noisy audience's attention. The atmosphere was like a primary school outing.

The Indian community in Nairobi was most complimentary after the first show. Everywhere people seemed to be talking about the *natak*. The remaining shows sold out after the first performance. It seemed everyone Indian, even the non-Gujarati speakers came. The actors were feted wherever they went, and one afternoon a few of them dropped into Porbander Stores, much to the delight of Lalji and Bhasker.

The official report of the Commissioner's Office was that the play was largely as in the plot. The performance was disorganised, the audience unruly and uncivilised. They recommended the Administrator issue future licences with conditions on limiting audience numbers. The performances should be of limited length and with strict adherence to fire and safety rules. And the King's anthem should be played by the police band.

***

Janki's morning sickness settled as suddenly as it had come. The initial tiredness was replaced by a breathless feeling when she did anything strenuous. Husnara's arrival provided a welcome change in their lives, the two women able to share each other's perspectives and provide mutual support.

Husnara was gregarious, chubby-faced and chatty. Jet black hair with soft waves on the sides made her look older than her years when she was not wearing a head scarf. She wore her scarf to go outdoors which seemed to make her look like a teenager, her fresh looks accentuated by her mascara. She had to learn and get familiar with Africa and Nairobi's ways. She found the climate cold but was thankful for the small numbers of mosquitos. Like Janki, she excelled in cooking and both shared long conversations and recipes. They compared the different styles of cooking they had been brought up with. Husnara had helped her sister through two pregnancies and was reassuring for Janki to have around.

"You need to rest more Jankibhabhi," she would say when Janki got short of breath.

"I know, but I need to also remain active. Show you more of Nairobi before the baby arrives."

"Nizar will show me Nairobi. Right now, we need you to get the baby delivered. There will be time for everything else later."

Towards the time of the delivery, Janki found it difficult to be active. She was troubled with back ache and leg aches which landed her in bed for long periods. Husnara and James managed the household chores, shopping and cooking together.

One day James came to Janki and asked her, "Mama, I see that the arrival of *Mungu's toto* (God's child), is near?"

"Yes, James. We may get busier then," sighing.

"*Mama kidogo* (younger Mama), will also get busier in helping with the *toto*."

"We will see how it goes," replied Janki, wondering where this was leading to.

"I will be able to manage all the cooking on my own, Mama. The two of you can look after the *toto*."

Janki had been feeling unusually emotional in those days, suddenly burst out crying at James' kindness. A shocked James lost his composure, not comprehending Janki's reaction.

"If that is fine with you Mama. I don't want to say anything wrong, Mama. I apologise Mama."

Husnara arrived when she heard Janki crying. "What is it, what happened Jankiben?" she asked worriedly.

"It's nothing. James here was telling me how excited he is at becoming an *uncle*," Janki replied, looking at James with tenderness in her eyes. "I found it touching."

James looked down at his feet, not understanding his own emotions or Janki's response, for a moment not sure if he had said something wrong. Then he felt a rush of emotion and goodwill at being addressed as an uncle of the unborn child, not daring to make eye contact with Janki, wiping away a tear.

"Oh! Yes, that is good," said Husnara. "Now you must rest more. These final days are physically and emotionally wearing."

CHAPTER THIRTY-THREE

KB WAS AN early riser, and often went for long walks after dawn. Sometimes he walked with the farm dog. One humid morning, he left alone with little water in his flask and during the walk he needed to get it refilled. Not far from his trail was a small river where he had stopped for water before. It was possible to reach a small pool among the rocky bank where he could fill up. The sounds of the African forest, including baboons barking and parrots whistling, made him want to sit and rest a while.

The rocks were wet from overnight rain and the water's edge was covered with fresh moss. He stooped with his right hand reaching for the water when his feet slipped on the moss. He nosedived and landed with force four feet below, hitting the side of his head on a boulder.

The alarm was raised when KB did not return for breakfast. Naran and Abdul arranged a small search party. Within an hour they had reached the river and the dog located KB's body. Arrangements were made to retrieve KB from the rocky site using gravel to cover the slippery rocks. Naran felt compelled to wash the bloodied rock, as if to deny the rock a trophy.

Wood was collected for a funeral pyre and Lalji was sent a telegram later in the afternoon. Vikram Banerjee, the engineer, and Naran cited verses from the *Bhagavad Geeta* (Hindu scripture, words of Lord Krishna) before the cremation. All the farm workers attended. It was the first time they had seen a cremation.

***

When Lalji reached home, there were three ladies present from the *Mandir*. One was in the kitchen making tea and boiling water and another was in the bedroom, with Janki who was in labour. The third lady was scuttling from kitchen to bedroom and responding to orders given. Husnara was at Janki's side holding her hand and assisting. She saw Lalji come in and take off his black hat before sitting down on an armchair.

"The baby is on its way," she blurted out to Lalji in a panicked voice. "The water broke this afternoon."

"What's broken? Shall I get it fixed?"

Husnara stared at him blankly, then realised Lalji had no clue and burst out laughing. The other ladies caught on and soon everyone, including Janki, were laughing. Lalji realised it was to do with childbirth and what he said must have sounded ridiculous. He too saw the funny side and started to laugh. Nizar, who had followed Naran, volunteered to go to Dr Shah's dispensary to inform him.

Late in the night, the sound of a baby chocking and crying out angrily replaced the shrieks of Janki. Lalji and Nizar, seated in the living room looked at each other and smiled. The lady who had been doing the running and fetching came out with tears rolling down her cheeks, announced to Lalji that it was a girl.

When Lalji was finally handed his daughter, he held her tight and felt a mix of emotions welling up inside.

"Please don't squeeze her so tight, Laljibhai," the lady was telling him. But he was lost, staring at his newborn daughter, oblivious of all around him. He saw how perfectly she was formed, red-faced and flat-nosed, with a thick growth of hair. He sat and enjoyed his sense of awe while Nizar went to inform Bhasker and Khimji.

Realising his absent mindedness he asked, "How is Janki?"

"She is fine, Laljibhai. Tired and needs to sleep. She just fed the baby. Give us a little time while we give her a wash and make her comfortable. Meanwhile, you are in charge of your little *Laxmi!*"

Lalji realised how bizarre it sounded to refer to a delicate baby as *Laxmi*, the powerful Goddess. He felt a strong desire to protect the baby. Lalji handed the baby to Nizar when he returned with the other two partners. The three men then started to fuss over the new-born who had fallen asleep.

Lalji went to see Janki when he was allowed. He kissed her forehead, held her hands in his and sunk his forehead between them. Both started to cry.

CHAPTER THIRTY-FOUR

LALJI AND NIZAR were sitting in the grand lobby outside the Commissioner's Office. The meeting had been called for ten in the morning and they had arrived early. People seemed to go into the Administrator's office and not come out again. They were different faces they had not seen before, all European. Some acknowledged the two Indian men by a nod of the head or wishing them good morning. Others walked by without a glance. They were served tea while waiting although they had not been asked. Lalji had removed his black Gujarati *toppee* (hat) and placed it on his lap. They wondered what the meeting was about, having received a written notice of appointment the day before.

They were led into a huge room with dark mahogany panels. On the walls were portraits of bearded white men, taller than a standing person. Grey busts of other old men stood on pedestals in the corners. Their feet sank into the deep soft carpet. Nizar almost tripped trying to walk normally until Lalji told him discreetly, "Lift your feet up, like in the mud after the monsoon."

They were seated in the middle of the room, and across the desk was the Commissioner with three members of the Legislature on either side of him. Each had a name plate in front but the Commissioner still introduced each one to Lalji and Nizar.

Nizar felt under dressed in his shirt, slacks, and *chappals* (open slippers) under his feet in front of black woollen suits, greased moustaches and cuff links. Lalji was wearing a new, white cotton shirt, pantaloons and leather shoes without socks.

"Mr Laal-jee, I wanted to discuss the sad situation which has arisen after Bag-wan-jee's accident and his death. My compatriots here are from the Assembly and we need to look at the situation and find a way forward," announced the Commissioner.

"Yes, sir. The farm is still running and crops are being harvested. My brother—"

"—Yes, we know all that. It is fortunate your brother is continuing with the good work of Bag-wan-jee."

"Yes," Lalji wondered what was coming next.

"You see, Bag-wan-jee had no will and the paperwork for the Estate had not been finalised at the time of his death."

"Oh."

"Yes. And most of the land was going to be leased to him by the Crown. He owned only a small part of it."

"The project was doing well. He brought machinery from England."

"Yes, yes. And a fine thing too. His first produce was received well in London."

Lalji started to feel more comfortable now but had still not worked out where this was leading to.

"I think, we all think, the project as you called it should continue since it has started well."

"Yes, sir."

"Your brother is settled well and has engaged an engineer I understand."

"Yes."

"Bag-wan-jee left no will but he had lodged with my office a Power of Attorney in case he was absent from the country. He had named you as his Attorney."

"*Power, attorney*. Sorry, I don't understand," responded Lalji, evoking a wave of laughter around the table.

"Yes, I thought that might be the case. Did Bag-wan-jee say anything about this to you?"

"No, sir."

"Well, in simple language it means you will have to run the Estate from now. Unless you refuse outright of course."

"Sir my brother is there and knows more so he is best at managing it. I am running stores in Nairobi."

"Yes, but your brother is employed at the Estate. You will have to take the legal responsibility for the Estate, from what I understand. At least until the Court decides."

Lalji looked nervous and before he could ask the Commissioner had read his mind.

"There will be a peppercorn rent, so to speak, for the lease. Nothing that should bother you much. It is a twenty year lease."

"What is *pippercor*, sir?"

"It means a small charge so that documents can be written up and everything made correct in the law."

"How much *pippercor*, I mean the charge, sir?"

Looking around the table and receiving nods from all present on his side of the table the Commissioner said, "One English Guinea, in other words, twenty-one English Schillings."

"Twenty-one Schillings a month?" responded Lalji, getting warm to the idea.

Another wave of laughter around the table before the Commissioner responded.

"Twenty-one Schillings a year, for the next twenty years!" announced the Commissioner, leaning forward and looking at Lalji through his glasses perched at the end of his sun-burnt nose.

Lalji nodded slowly, thinking. There was complete silence in the room. Nizar thought Lalji had not understood but before he could say anything, the Commissioner interrupted the silence.

"Well, what do you think, young man?"

"I think it is good to continue with Bhagwanji's project. Yes, what you say sounds good. I need to have a little time to think and discuss. With my partners."

"Very good. Let me know by the end of the week your answer."

"Yes, I will come back. And discuss further."

The Commissioner stood up and extended his hand to Lalji. No one else shook hands and Nizar followed Lalji out of the room, taking care to lift his feet up high at every step.

"Well, gentleman, I think he will bite," the Commissioner said after they had left the room.

"What does Lloyd Edwards have to say about him?" asked John Derricks, a self-styled opposition person in the legislature. His job was to ask questions without revealing his position.

"He says Lalji is a shrewd and capable *business-walla*. Sings his praises."

"And the Italian?" asked Derricks.

"Buggered off gorilla hunting to the Congo I hear. Left his place in a state with a local *signorina* expecting his baby."

"Oh."

"No one from these parts wants to go so far inland. No schools or facilities, except for the railway. And the Colonial Office wants to see more land in agriculture use if we are to send the train to the end of the line."

***

The baby was named Ganga, after the family priest back home had proposed what letter the name should start with: '*gah*'. The priest had consulted astrological texts and arrived at the suggestion from the time of birth. Lalji's had no sister, so a cousin sent possible names starting with the initial letter. It was the traditional way, the paternal aunt's prerogative to name the new-born. Janki was relived there was a choice of a few names. She had heard of mean sisters-in-law who insisted on one unattractive name to spite the parents.

Husnara and Janki spent time chatting and giggling. Nizar often wondered aloud if they would ever run out of topics to chat about, to their amusement. Ganga had become the star attraction in the lives of the men. All wanted to see her every day and hold her, probably wondering how long it would be before they would hold one of their own. She had taken on quite a presence in the family, with the evenings taken up entertained by the baby. Lalji was a proud father. He could not wait to get the baby to the new photographer's studio on Regal Way, but Janki kept postponing the appointment.

Bhasker had taken to visiting toy shops in the Indian Bazaar and selecting toys for Ganga. Often, he over-estimated Ganga's abilities and brought back something appropriate for a much older child. Janki and Husnara were in giggles when he produced a massive wind-down spinning top. His response was to set it spinning in front of the child who showed little interest. He went back to catching the baby's attention by playing *taals* (formula of beats) on his *tablas* (pair of percussion instruments, played together) which evoked cooing and smiles from the three-month-old.

***

Lalji left for KB's Estate and arrived after a hot and exhausting journey lasting almost two days. He was picked up at the railway stop by Naran.

"*Jai Shree Krishna,* Bhai (brother)."

"*Jai Shree Krishna,* Naran."

"It is a tiring journey from Nairobi."

"Yes, but I was fascinated by the sights along the way. Here it is so much greener than Nairobi."

"True, and it is more fertile. KB was right to choose this place for the farm."

"I see that now. He told me crops did well here with little effort."

"How is Jankibhabhi, and little Ganga?"

***

Lalji sat behind the table in KB's office. Naran and Vikram the engineer sat across the table.

"I have had two meetings with the Commissioner in Nairobi," said Lalji. "He has asked for KB's documents of the farm to be brought back to sort out what happens next."

"All the documents of the farm are in that leather briefcase," said Naran, pointing to a brown satchel nested between bundles of papers on a table to the side. The papers were neatly piled up in wooden trays which were labelled. "What do you mean 'what happens next'?" asked Naran anxiously.

"We will discuss in more detail later. But first I need to know how the farm is getting on and what are Vikram's plans," replied Lalji, trying not to sound too mysterious.

"I am settling down fine here, Laljibhai," replied Vikram. "The crops are coming on well and the cane harvest had to be brought forward by a month. The yield is good."

"Yes, and the workers are hardworking. We have sent wagons of the cane syrup to Mombasa and Vikram is getting the refining process up and going. That still has some way to go," added Naran.

"Yes, a few adjustments are still required to get the right colour. By next harvest we should be sending not syrup but grain sugar," said Vikram proudly.

"Good. I will let the Commissioner know. If you stay behind, Naran, we need to discuss a few things."

Vikram took the cue and departed.

"The Commissioner informs me KB only owned part of the estate. The rest was leased to him," said Lalji.

Naran was sitting forward, listening intently.

"He had no will but left legal papers to nominate me to run his affairs in his absence."

"Oh?" Naran raised his eyebrows, the pulse on his thin neck pulsing faster.

"I was also not aware until the Commissioner told me. It seems that the Commissioner and the *sarkar* (government) want us to continue running the estate. I must sign papers to pay for the land rent."

"Do you know what that will be, Bhai (Brother)?"

"Yes, it's very nominal to encourage us to stay. For your part, how do you feel about continuing?"

"I am happy to continue, *Bhai* (Brother). You sent me to the right place to learn about Africa and start learning the business of the farm. When you say KB nominated you, that can be you or your family, right? Whoever you choose?" asked Naran, a worried look on his face and breathing faster.

"These are matters of the *sarkar* in Nairobi I need to clarify. In the first place, I will need to sign the papers to take responsibility. You need to stay and continue your work here."

"Oh," responded Naran, sounding dejected.

Lalji looked at Naran. There was an unfamiliar look on Naran's face, a mixture of annoyance and arrogance which quickly passed in a flash before he smiled again.

"Yes, of course, *Bhai* (Brother)," said Naran. But his gaze had averted and he was no longer listening to Lalji.

Lalji felt the discomfort of the interaction. He decided to leave further discussion until after he had seen the papers. He also realised he needed to allow Naran more time to understand the new reality. More time also for himself to understand Naran, and how his mind worked.

***

The negotiations with the Commissioner were rapid. It was a case of listing what Lalji wanted. The response was a yes or no. There was little discussion. If the Commissioner was unsure, he would usually say no. Lalji saw him as a military man with little knowledge of business. The Commissioner liked to make things happen, usually immediately. He lost interest in prolonged discussions and became impatient. Lalji kept things simple for the Commissioner and one tactic he used was to ask for some of his needs to be met in the future. This worked each time in his favour.

The final lease agreed included options to buy the land at any time in the future, reduced freight costs, a police post near the estate, and reduced taxes for the first ten years. After five years there would be the prospect of acquiring further new land with the same conditions of lease. Lalji also asked for and got the assurance of first option for local land disposals in a radius of fifty miles. For the Commissioner, it was nothing more onerous than what he could achieve with a stroke of his pen, on land most Europeans did not want to travel to. The only thing he had to deliver immediately was a police post.

Lalji ran through the agreement with Lloyd Edwards, his banker. Edwards looked at the draft document and kept quiet.

Lalji asked nervously, "Any problem Mr Edwards?"

"Problem is not a word that comes to mind. I am wondering if this Lalji is the same man, fresh from Porbander who came to me asking for a business loan in the past." A smile was revealed on his face.

"You think all right then?" asked Lalji, smiling back.

"It's more than all right! How did you get the old goat to agree to this? It's good, very good Mr Lalji. And you did it on your own."

"See, if you say so, then it's fine. What you say is important to me. I am now happy to sign Mr Edwards."

***

When the papers were signed and witnessed, Lalji sent a telegram to Naran to inform him of the news. After the signing, the Administrator General had asked Lalji and his attorney, Rustomjee, to stay behind for tea.

He seemed unusually twitchy that day. Having sat down on his office veranda where tea was served, he turned to Rustomjee and started talking.

"Rush-tomm, I want you to impress on Mr Lal-jee here what a big step the Government has taken in entrusting him with the land and project of KB."

"I will explain to him, sir."

Lalji intervened, "I know this is big step for the *sarkar*. For me, it is also same."

Rustomjee looked down into his cup.

"Yes. I want to express my best wishes to you in this venture. You see there are those who would say I have put too much trust in someone with no background in farming. KB of course had the knowledge and experience."

Lalji looked straight in the Administrator's eyes, who looked away. He continued, "I know that after KB's untimely death his wishes would have been for you to continue with his work."

"Thank you. We intend to do our best and make it a success," affirmed Lalji confidently.

"Of course, I am not always going to be around so I hope any expectations you may have from me are restrained. Many will be watching to see how things turn out."

Lalji understood this to mean that not all was well in the *sarkar* (government). He suspected there had been opposition despite the apparent unanimity when he was informed he would be required to run the estate. He appreciated the hint.

"Sir, I thank you for being frank. You are a busy man and it will help me to save time also, knowing this I mean."

That brought a smile to the Administrator's face. Rustomjee was still looking down slurping his tea and listening, unaware of the subtle exchanges.

CHAPTER THIRTY-FIVE

JANKI AND HUSNARA had devised a system to send food parcels up country to the Estate for Naran and his engineer. Every fortnight they would do a major cook of *theplas* (spicy fried Gujarati rotis) and *achars* (pickles), Gujarati snacks and send them on the train. Both men on the farm had basic skills in preparing food but relied more on Abdul to cook them fresh produce.

Janki had written to her in-laws in Porbander suggesting it was the right time for Naran to get married. To have a wife with him on the farm would ensure he had home-cooked food daily. The reply she received was positive and she mentioned it to Lalji. When they next saw Naran, on one of his trips to Nairobi to pick up supplies, they discussed the details. Naran agreed at once. Jaya, Naran's betrothed from the age of eleven, was ready to travel having heard so much about the adventures of living in Africa. The wedding date was set after steamer tickets were booked. Within weeks Naran was crossing the Ocean once again, still in his first year of arriving in Africa.

On his return with his bride, Naran left for the estate within two days, leaving Jaya with Janki and Husnara, to learn the tips of surviving in this new continent. The Lalji household had never been so busy, with a kitchen functioning through the day. Meals were prepared for four men, three women, four staff and numerous droppers-in whom the menfolk brought to lunch. Often those who dropped in had come for a day from upcountry to collect supplies and stock. Some were acquaintances and others customers. Lunch times were a hive of activity, of conversations to catch up on and exchanging news. Occasionally, the visitors came with spouses or children which added to the general buzz and commotion. Life seemed to have settled in its own way into a pattern which worked well. So far, Lalji thought, we have managed to stick together as partners and life has been harmonious. However, he had a feeling that things would not remain so for long.

It was since Naran's arrival that Lalji had begun to sense a change in the dynamics within the group. Naran, although diligent, found it difficult to accept advice in matters of business. It was a departure from the fellowship of the partners where there was mutual respect and reliance. Lalji had noticed Naran talked down to Khimji, in a dismissive way. Khimji had remained polite but felt the affront. Nizar, having also noticed, suggested to Lalji he was the only one who could speak to Naran, which he decided to do on Naran's return to pick up Jaya.

"I see the crops on the estate are doing well. What you are sending to Nairobi by rail we sell locally and the rest goes to Mombasa. The local Europeans have complimented the refined sugar," said Lalji.

"Yes, *Bhai* (Brother). We have good workers and a good engineer in Vikram. He ensures every load is processed properly," responded Naran.

"Naran, you had not had much of a chance to settle down when you were handed this responsibility. And now that you have Jaya, more responsibility will follow."

"Yes, but I am happy as things are progressing well. I have learnt much since I came. The farm has potential to produce more and we can expand to buy more land."

"Let's walk before we start running. We need to ensure we have got the farm working to full capacity. Try out two or three cycles of crops and get familiar with the climate, see how-"

"-I am already familiar with these things. I believe expanding quickly will give us enough security in the good times so we can manage any hard times."

Taking a deep breath Lalji responded, "These are issues for all of us to discuss, Naran. We need everyone's agreement," provoking a quizzical look from Naran.

"Surely if the engineer and I are confident, we can progress to expanding?" There was irritation in Naran's voice.

"It needs to be timed correctly. The other businesses must not get disturbed. All options need looking at."

"Yes *Bhai* (Brother), you are the brains in the group. Everything happens as you say." The sarcasm was hard to miss.

"We have always had agreement between us partners in everything we do. What we have achieved so far, we were familiar with. It was business and trading. It's in our blood. The farm came our way by chance and everybody appreciates your hard work and faith in it, but farming is a new area for us. We do not understand all the risks."

"Does everyone include Bhasker and Khimji?"

"Of course. They are part of the group as well. We have done everything together as a group of four when Ramji was alive. Khimji replaced him as you know."

"Khimji is young with little experience. He arrived with me."

There was a distinct tone of superiority in Naran's voice. Lalji let there be a pause, keeping his eyes fixed on Naran, not responding to the bait.

"Well, I think my views should be taken into consideration because I run the farm."

"Of course, they are. The rest of the businesses are interdependent and we have loans from the bank. Everything needs consideration when new investments are discussed."

"Fine."

"Which means that all who work in the Porbander businesses are consulted and listened to," Lalji said, looking straight into Naran's eyes.

Naran rose to take his leave, looking unhappy and shaken after the chat. He had not seen this side of Lalji before. He expected more autonomy and some favouritism.

Later, Nizar asked Lalji if the chat had gone well.

"As well as could have been."

"Oh."

"Naran has taken on responsibility quickly. If KB were alive, he would still be learning under his guidance. The success of the Estate has gone to his head. He has not considered how farming is a chancy business. He thinks everything will happen in a predictable way. Tell you the truth, he worries me."

"I agree Laljibhai, we must see how things work out. Let us keep a close watch on things."

***

Husnara had decided not to observe the month-long *Roza* fast. Nizar, as always, was going to fast. Lalji thought nothing of it, even though Husnara was the more pious of the two .

One evening, Nizar met Lalji at Porbander Store.

"*Bhai* (Brother), I need to talk with you about something," he said when they had closed. Lalji had got accustomed to Nizar's private chats after closing, just the two of them, usually about something significant.

"Yes, Nizar."

"It's Husnara. She is expecting."

"That is very good news!"

"Yes, by the grace of Allah it is good indeed. You may know she has not been fasting for *Roza*, it's because of the pregnancy."

"Oh! Now I understand. If Janki knows, she has not said anything to me."

"*Bhai* (Brother), you are like my elder brother. My father always insists I take advice from you before doing anything. He seems to trust your advice more than his own."

Lalji could not help letting out a chuckle. He took a long breath.

"I think Husnara and I should have our own place before the baby is born. It is fine we have stayed with you all this time while Husnara was learning from Jankibhabhi. We have been very happy to have spent time with you."

"Then stay longer. What's the hurry? Will Husnara not need Janki around her while expecting?"

"*Bhai* (Brother), please do not misunderstand me. We have lived together all this time and are in business together. Both of us are grateful. But we would like the child to grow up in a *Musalmaan* (Muslim) household. It is a question of the having the right cultural start for the baby and their learning."

"Hmmm."

"Our Gujarati culture, our life as a big family is perfect for the child who will grow up alongside Ganga. But the *Musalmaan* education needs a household which is all *Musalmaan.* Otherwise, the child might grow up confused. I hope you understand."

"I do Nizar, but I must admit I had not seen things that way. But you are right, and I understand. You already have a house above the hardware shop and we can move Bhasker and Khimji into our place for the two of you to set things up your way. It's hardly a problem."

"Thank you, *Bhai* (Brother). I was hoping you would understand."

"Tell me Nizar, how long have you been considering this?"

"Well, I started to think about it after listening to a visiting Mullah at the Mosque. He was knowledgeable about the *Hadith* (traditions of Prophet Muhammad) and keen that we create the correct ambience for bringing up children in a *Musalmaan* family. Then, when Husnara became pregnant it seemed to become more important."

"Let us talk to Bhasker and Khimji tonight and arrange things. You better let Janki know your good news as well. She will feel the separation from Husnara, they get on so well."

"Jankibhabhi already knows about the baby. I thought she might have mentioned it. But she does not know we are thinking about moving out."

***

Nairobi society learned that the partners of Porbander Stores and Porbander Timber & Hardware Supplies had acquired farming land in Uganda. There was a steady stream of inquisitive callers dropping in at the shops. Everyone wanted to know how the partners had done it. On realising their role was that of replacing KB, who was the brains and financer, they seemed satisfied they had not missed a trick.

But, the questions were replaced by requests for loans. These were initially for credit on goods purchased from the partners, but later here were requests for loans of cash. Usually, the partners had allowed a month or two-month credit extension as it meant their goods occupied other peoples shelves.

When requests were made for help to pay school fees, a trip to India for family matters, or medical bills, Lalji and his partners obliged. A verbal agreement of when the loan would be repaid was noted into Nizar's accounts. Thankfully, absconding was rare.

Then came those who wanted to invest or expand their business or build a home. Many were reluctant to approach the bank for a loan. They ran too small a business, had poor literacy and understanding of English, or their business case was weak. Lalji found these the most difficult to deal with. He was not a money lender and despised those who were. But he was learning fast how they fulfilled a role to help people aspire in times of need.

"Laljibhai, that man Ladhabhai came to the timber yard again today asking for a loan," said Bhasker. "He needs to get a proper roof on his shop as the rain keeps soaking his stock. I told him such requests are best discussed with you."

"We never say the decision is a joint one between the four of us, otherwise we would never hear the end of these requests. We always say it's your decision, Laljibhai," said Nizar with a laugh.

Khimji, new to the fold and a little nervous of his place, kept quiet.

"Do we know if he has other needs or is it a genuine desire to get a roof?" asked Lalji.

"His shop and roof are in a terrible state. His shop has more rodents than ever before," replied Bhasker.

"And his trade?"

"Busier since a new ricksha stop set up outside. He has had to ask his son to work with him. Taken him out of school."

"He is buying more frequently than before, *Bhai* (Brother)," added Nizar, "selling the products to customers, not just feeding mice!"

"Very well then. If you ask him to come and see me, I will see how much he needs."

"I will tell him."

"With all these requests for loans we must place a limit on how long they take to repay," suggested Nizar. "It does not look good in the books to have too many debtors."

"I agree. But the difficulty arises when they have a genuine need and we are their only hope," replied Lalji.

"Maybe we should charge them interest, like the bank?" suggested Bhasker.

"The moment we do that we become money lenders. It becomes a business, rather than favours," said Nizar.

"I don't want us to become money lenders. Then you cannot stop all kinds of people coming to you. You must then take something of the right value as security, and we don't want a business like that," said Lalji.

"Yes, there would be sleepless nights," agreed Bhasker.

"I would find it hard to lend money on interest, *Bhai* (Brother). It would be considered *haram* (forbidden by Islam) for me," said Nizar, startling everybody.

"What about borrowing from the bank? Is that not also *haram*?" asked Bhasker.

"Yes, it is. It is more *haram* for the lender than the receiver. We should pay up the bank as quickly as we can for that reason."

Everybody was quiet.

"When we arrived here nobody would have financed us to start. The bank loan was a necessary arrangement then," said Lalji. He went on: "Now our fortunes are different, we can live within our means. If we can afford to help small starters with interest free loans for a short time, then we should."

Everybody was nodding their heads. Lalji felt relieved the issue had been agreed.

"I think the one thing to add is that we should limit lending to an amount we could afford to lose if repayments are not received. I do not want to deal with lawyers and courts. Nizar can work out what would be the right amount after checking their accounts," said Lalji.

Everybody nodded their agreement once again.

CHAPTER THIRTY-SIX

RICHTER FROM THE sawmill was visibly upset at Ramji's demise. He felt he had lost a colleague and a skilled artisan, someone who had got to know his woods. Despite their language barrier, neither being fluent in English, they had become friends. They would spend a good hour chatting while timber was loaded for Ramji's yard. They talked about children, their faiths, and of training their workers. Occasionally Richter would confide in a low whisper looking in Ramji's eyes, "Don't trust the British!" whenever it came to getting permits or licences. Ramji never asked him why, for fear of upsetting him.

After Khimji's arrival, Richter had turned up at the timber yard to meet him. Khimji was not busy so sat down with him over a cup of masala tea. They discussed the woods, like Richter had done with Ramji. He stayed two hours and explained the qualities, uses and prices of the different woods. By the time he left they had struck up a friendship which left Khimji grinning for the rest of the day.

Ismail Habib, a successful furniture maker, had been purchasing wood from Nizar and Ramji for some time. One day he dropped in to see Lalji at the shop.

"*Salaam* (greetings) Laljibhai, I am Ismail Habib Velji," introducing himself, his flowing henna-stained beard pointing to the floor.

"*Namaste* Ismailbhai, yes, I know the name. Welcome."

His name literally meant 'Ismail-son-of-Habib-son-of-Velji', in Gujarati tradition. It also informed Lalji that Ismail's father Habib had converted to Islam as his own father's name Velji was Hindu.

"You probably know in that case that apart from my furniture factory, I take a keen interest in the politics of British East Africa," he said.

"Yes, I see your name in the newspaper from time to time." The acknowledgement seemed to please Ismail who stroked the orange beard gently like a pet cat.

"You may know in that case the fortune of us Indians here is better than in Southern Africa. But still, it is not right."

"I had heard."

"Over there, in all four colonies the *sarkar* (government) has passed laws to limit the trading and residing rights of Indians."

"Hmm."

"Now they must carry passes. Already they have been forbidden to walk on *pavements*."

"One cannot understand the minds of these people," said Lalji, shaking his head.

"Here, they are going to appoint Indians to sit on the Legislative Council soon. One seat for Arabs and two for Indians."

"I see."

"I would like to see an intelligent young Indian, with ability to be appointed for one of the seats. I think that person should be you."

Lalji was taken aback by the directness of the approach and left speechless for a moment.

"Why me, Ismailbhai?"

"As I say, you are young, intelligent, successful."

"But I have no ability or interest in politics. There must be others who would be better suited."

"Yes, there are. But they want power and influence. What the *sarkar* is offering is seats to sit in opposition, not in government. A kind of counterbalance to white settler ambitions."

"I see."

"There would be no power, and little influence. It needs someone with dedication and energy. Someone intelligent. It would be a thankless task in many ways."

Lalji laughed at the man's frankness.

"Then what would be the point, may I ask?"

"Yes, well if we do not fill the seats, we will lose them. The white settlers will say Indians are not interested in civic matters and deserve less, as in Southern Africa. We will remain at the margins forever."

"What would such a person be doing on behalf of the Indians?"

"Well, for a start we need land. The restrictions on where we can live or work are unfair. Then we need our own schools and hospitals. We need to be able to bring our relatives from India to escape the economic situation there. Allowing our people to come here is probably going to be restricted or stopped unless we fight for it."

"Ismailbhai, are you going to be the second candidate?"

"I could be if nobody else cares to stand," averting his eyes briefly. "I would see my role as a mentor for the young candidate with my previous experience. That is why we need someone young, someone with a growing family, someone who lives in Nairobi and has a business."

"Ismailbhai, I must be honest with you. I have never considered such a role as I have no interest in politics. Secondly, I would not consider something like this without consulting my three partners — I am sure it would take my time away from the business."

"I understand. Any other objections?"

"Fundamentally, and forgive my frankness, I cannot see the point of sitting in a powerless role arguing with old white men. They are only interested in grabbing land, using us as a token to validate their actions. They will continue to exclude the African from any say of what happens in their own land."

Lalji surprised himself with his own eloquence. He felt something passionate within, something he had not felt before. It was not anger or frustration. It was the voice of his conscience. He was verbalising the powerlessness of anyone Indian or African to do anything about the political situation.

"You make your points like a true politician," said Ismail with a smile. "And I cannot argue with your last point."

"There is already one politician from Porbander in Southern Africa. A thorn in the side of the *sarkar*. He is a London-educated lawyer and still he faces imprisonment time and again for speaking up. What chance do I have?"

"You are right, Laljibhai. But we cannot all be Mohandas Gandhi and he cannot be everywhere. But we must start somewhere."

"Let us talk again after I have spoken to my partners."

"Of course."

Any fleeting interest in politics that could have sparked in Lalji was promptly snuffed out as a waste of time in his mind. He was a businessman at heart. But his conscience surfacing spontaneously in the conversation made him think he would need to be successful first. Before he could think of influencing the *sarkar*.

"*The lasting salvation for us Indians is in economic strength,*" he thought. "*The African needs to become politicised. They have the numbers, and the country belongs to them.*"

After a few days, Lalji politely declined the invitation to be appointed, without consulting his partners.

***

Over the following months, Nizar and Lalji reported to their partners that profits were healthy. They predicted the partners would be able to pay off the Bank within a few years. They started to plan their future expansion and goals.

The arrival of commerce in Nairobi had driven up the need for centrally located offices and shops. Lalji was keen to construct a stone building with a hard roof, three or four stories high on the land they owned at the end of Government Road. He envisaged shops on the ground floor and offices on the floors above. The top floor would become four residential flats for the partners. He had architect plans drawn up for a four-story building at the end of Government Road. It would be the tallest block in Nairobi. He had started to explore construction costs with builders. Meanwhile Husnara was about to deliver, and Naran's wife Jaya was also expecting. Janki and Lalji had insisted she come and stay with them in Nairobi until the baby was born.

Husnara delivered a healthy baby girl Memuna at home. Janki started to spend more time in assisting her. Every morning she would walk to Nizar's home, clutching Ganga who looked like a rag doll with outsize clothes, heavy *kajal* (mascara) under her eyes. Usually, James accompanied her to carry any shopping. Janki's attendance at the *Mandir* (Temple) was suffering since the babies had arrived. Soon after, Jaya delivered a baby boy after a troublesome four weeks of her pregnancy with backache and swollen feet. Naran came down to Nairobi and spent a fortnight with Jaya and the baby. The arrival of his son seemed to inject new confidence and optimism in him. They named the baby Dhiraj.

Lalji seemed to be surrounded by nursing mothers and babies. The evenings were taken up by visitors dropping in to see the new arrivals. There was a continuous cycle of feeding and changing. He reflected how quickly life had changed after settling in Nairobi. Everything had transformed rapidly from an existence of bachelors, to husbands and then family men. Getting into bed after settling Ganga in her baby hammock, Janki noticed Lalji had already fallen asleep. She missed talking to him. Even for her, the family life had become a blur attending to baby needs. She was unable to give her full attention to Lalji's plans to expand. Conversations were short-lived. She looked at him with admiration as she lay down next to him, pressing his head into her bosom. He reacted by embracing her but did not wake up.

CHAPTER THIRTY-SEVEN

THE YEARS FLEW past with flawless regularity. Lalji and Nizar had young expanding families. Within the next five years, Lalji and Nizar had two further children each. Bhasker seemed to remain the free-spirited bachelor. Lalji's second born was a boy they named Jagdish. The third, coming twelve months later was a boy, Kishore. Nizar and Husnara had two boys, Habib and Yunus. Get togethers remained unruly, with the noise of babies crying, needing feeding or changing.

In parallel, a steady stream of white and Indian settlers arrived in Nairobi as the infrastructure took shape. Job opportunities for skilled workers were plentiful, especially in construction and municipal services. Banks, commerce and civil service were recruiting furiously from the Empire and Britain. Those with families from Britain were usually on a few years contract. Some chose to stay on, especially if they had excelled in their chosen field.

The colonialist's life was luxurious with good weather, inexpensive food and servants. The outdoor existence lent to the charm of being from the white ruling class. Activities like fishing, hunting, riding and safari-travel remained their privileges. Their residential areas in Nairobi were not only on prime land but supplied with utilities before anywhere else.

In contrast, the Indian community attracted economic migrants and semi-skilled artisans. Mainly Gujaratis and some Punjabis. The economic migrants, usually young men, followed family members or other close connections. The passage was eased by better steamer ship services. On arrival they sheltered under the wings of their contact. Nobody it seemed spent time without work. Everybody found a spot in the machinery of the colony's structures.

Lalji had made good his intention to build a grey stoned four-story building at the end of Government Road. It was on the corner of Sixth Avenue, known as 'Mombasa House.' The entrance was imposing, with cemented floors and Nairobi's first elevator inside. Before the building was completed, it had already been let with four shop units on the ground floor. Two of the ground floor shop units were combined for the Grindlay and Co Bank. There were offices on the two floors above let out to insurance firms, law firms, and architects. The partners occupied the top floor. There were four flats, one for each partner.

Naran had experienced a cycle of spoilt crops from heavy rains and a slow recovery. With Vikram's help, they planned and built better drainage on the estate. The constant bane of his life was nightly visits from herds of marauding elephants who had acquired a taste for sugar cane and bananas. He had tried different tactics, from placing bonfires, to employing Masai warriors as night guards. But what worked best was the sound of rifle fire to scare off the beasts. Naran had also had an addition to the family, a daughter named Shanta, once again born in Nairobi.

One Sunday after lunch Nizar and Khimji asked to speak to Lalji and Bhasker. Lunch was slowly cleared and babies fed before their afternoon nap.

"*Bhai*, we do not seem to have much time for proper discussions these days," complained Nizar.

"Yes, our time is no longer our own with the children," agreed Lalji, with a smile.

Nizar looked nervously at Husnara who had entered the room to get something.

"For the children, we need to plan their education and futures."

"Yes, of course. What do you have in mind Nizar?"

"You see *Bhai*, all children are different. Some need handling differently from others. Each needs to be able to bloom in their own way."

"True."

"And as parents, we need to be able to respond to their different needs. We as adults work together and our lives are dependent on each other. We are similar in so many ways…."

"Which has been the foundation of our success Nizarbhai," Bhasker interrupted.

"True. No doubt our closeness has made us successful as four partners. That is a formula which has worked while we were starting off our lives in Africa."

"And it will be different for our children. Is that what you are saying?" asked Lalji.

"Precisely. Their future needs are different."

"How?" asked Bhasker.

"Well, for a start we may want different things for our children. Some will study, go to schools and colleges. Others would need to acquire skills for their life ahead. Some will go into business; others may become professionals."

"And the girls?" asked Bhasker.

"That is a good question. You see, I cannot educate Memuna like the boys as we would never find a husband who would accept a wife more educated than himself. In another fifteen years, we will have to let her go to start her married life."

"What do you think should happen, Nizar?" asked Lalji.

"*Bhai*, I think we should realise we have different lives to lead in the future, for our children. We need to take different directions, go our separate ways running our own businesses and bringing up our families in our preferred ways."

There was stunned silence. Even the women, who appeared to have been engrossed in their own conversation in the adjoining room, became quiet.

"Hmmm. And Khimji, you are of the same opinion?" asked Lalji.

"Well, Laljibhai, I know how the partners have made progress. I mean before my time. We are now involved in different areas of business and some areas suit certain individuals better than others. Like I am more interested in the sawmill and timber than construction or retail. If we could all concentrate on our own areas then it would be good."

"What do you think Bhasker? Have you also discussed this with Nizar and Khimji?"

"No, this is the first time I am hearing this."

Lalji took a deep breath. "Let us all pause and think about this. It seems to me both of you are thinking about going your separate ways but I am not sure I have fully understood the reasons. However, we must consider going our own way sometime, so no matter what the reasons we should give it a thought."

"That would be good," responded Khimji. Nizar looked down between his knees, not saying anything.

***

Janki had sensed the conversation with Nizar and Khimji had hurt Lalji. She knew this from his expression and the fact he had become quiet and preoccupied. She allowed him time alone with his thoughts, even after he declined a chat when they got to bed.

Bhasker had left earlier with a grey look on his face, merely saying to Lalji at the front door "I am with you, *Bhai*, I am not going anywhere," before leaving. Lalji had tapped the back of his shoulder in gratitude.

The next morning Lalji was up early and left without waiting for breakfast. He headed to the legal chambers at Mombasa House who were his tenants. He met Pestonjee who was opening his office.

"Good morning, Laljibhai," greeted Pestonjee. "It's unusual to see you here so early."

"*Jai Shree Krishna*, Pestonjee. Today I have come to consult you for advice and help in a delicate matter."

Pestonjee saw the crowded furrows on Lalji's forehead and realised there was a serious matter on his mind.

"Come into my office and we can discuss it."

***

The four partners sat down at the lawyer's chambers and were each handed a bundle of legal papers by Pestonjee. Lalji sat on one side with Bhasker on his left and Nizar sat opposite Bhasker. Khimji was clearly confused about where to sit and was shown into a chair next to Nizar by Pestonjee.

Despite their brotherly relationships, the atmosphere was heavy and formal. Pestonjee spoke first.

"I have taken instructions from Laljibhai that he wishes to divide up the partnership. The purpose is to allow Nizarbhai and Khimjibhai to quit with their share of the assets. Free to pursue their desires and wishes as they see fit."

Nizar and Khimji looked uncomfortable. Bhasker had started flicking through the paper bundle, looking down.

"Laljibhai wants it understood that this follows the wishes of Nizarbhai and Khimjibhai which they expressed at his home. I am thankful to Nizarbhai for sharing the latest business accounts, bank statements and an estimate of the stocks held in the businesses. That gives me the ability to put a global number of what the partnership owns, less loans, adjustments for creditors and debtors. You will see on page three there is at the bottom the final figure of what is the net worth of the partnership. Just above are the figures for the various businesses owned by the partnership and their net worth alone. You will see the overall figure at the bottom of the page is a total of the various businesses held. Any questions so far?" asked Pestonjee.

Nobody spoke, each was looking at the papers except Lalji who knew the figures.

"It is proposed that the assets are divided equally four ways between the four of you here today," added Pestonjee.

"What about something for Naran, does he not get anything?" asked Khimji.

"Naran was never a partner and he started working for KB where he had been receiving wages," said Lalji.

"And the farm in Uganda…."

"The farm was part owned by KB. The rest is land rented or granted by the *sarkar*. They could take it back at any time. What we invested in was machinery using small loans. There has not been much profit as you know. KB's land would pay off the loans. It is easier to leave it aside as something free-standing with no impact on the partnership," explained Lalji. "Nizar will confirm that is the case," he added.

Nizar nodded in agreement.

"Good then. I would suggest everyone reads the paperwork and I will answer any questions you have. On the last page, everyone signs the division of assets as agreed. The date is the end of the month," said Pestonjee.

"That is next week," exclaimed Nizar, surprised.

"We can change the date to suit you all by agreement," said the lawyer. "But before that, we need to know if everyone agrees to the arrangements."

"Arrangements?" asked Bhasker.

"Yes. It is proposed that Nizarbhai keeps the hardware shop, Khimjibhai the timber yard. Bhaskerbhai and Laljibhai the remaining two shops. Mombasa house flats that you own individually remain in your hands. Laljibhai is prepared to buy from all of you your share of the Mombasa House rental business if you wish. Or you can leave your share in it and remain partners with him. It does not have to be all four of you."

"The timber yard and hardware shop have less expensive stock as we know," said Nizar.

"Laljibhai and Bhaskerbhai will recompense you the difference in stock value. That will be paid into your individual bank accounts which Mr Elliot, your manager, has agreed to open. You will need to sign the forms at the bank."

Nizar was taken aback by the statement. He looked at Lalji and asked, "*Bhai*, you do not have the funds…?"

"Mr Edwards has agreed to a loan. His suggestion, not mine," said Lalji, raising his hand, to say no further discussion was needed.

"Lastly there remains the matter of land held near Nairobi River. It is proposed the undeveloped land is also split four ways between the partners. The sections rented to the Army and others are available for anyone of you to buy from the others, or left as a joint asset at present," said the lawyer.

CHAPTER THIRTY-EIGHT

THE WAR WHEN it came to East Africa was a relatively tame affair as far as Nairobi and Mombasa were concerned. German East Africa to the south was poorly supplied or supported by Germany. But the resolve of their commander Lieutenant-Colonel Paul von Lettow-Vorbeck was unmatched.

The British of East Africa, the Belgians from the Belgian Congo and the Portuguese from Mozambique had become allies. Allied to fight the German presence in East Africa. British suspicion of Belgian colonial ambitions led to an uneasy relationship. The Portuguese were thought too weak to be a threat to British interests.

The fighting was rural and centered around gaining territory. The British added to their strength with troops from India and South Africa. Lettow-Vorbeck was intent on keeping the allies engaged in a costly campaign. His aim was to divert troops from the European theatre. His tactics of withdrawing from confrontation when outnumbered and regrouping elsewhere paid off. His crack *Schutztruppe* was a small but highly effective fighting force. Well versed in defensive guerrilla tactics.

The war was fought on land, at sea and on the Rift Valley Lakes to gain territorial control. Early successes of the Belgians saw them despatched back to their new gains of Rwanda and Burundi by the allied commander General Jan Smuts. Smuts thought a post war settlement with Germany would be difficult if the Belgians occupied a large section of German East Africa. Lettow-Vorbeck's African *askaris* (soldiers) proved an effective fighting force alongside the *Schutztruppe*. At times massively outnumbered, the *Schutztruppe* still prevailed in many battles.

By the end of the war the allies had lost 400,000 personnel including troops and 600,000 African porters. Lettow-Vorbeck and his small army, managed to escape to Portuguese Mozambique. Twice as many died from disease as enemy action. At least nine porters were recruited for every soldier who served. Porter recruitment followed tribal lines.

***

The British war effort required massive supplies to be available for the front. Lalji and Bhasker were summoned by the Administrator's office at the start of hostilities, to discuss supplies for the troops. They sat in a meeting room and waited.

The Assistant Administrator entered with a small entourage of black-suited men he referred to as secretaries. The Commander of the Army Supplies Depot was also present who smiled and shook their hands.

"Mister *Laljee*, we wanted to talk with you about our requirements. To help with the war effort," announced the Assistant Administrator.

"Yes, sir."

"We need your help."

Lalji looked visibly worried which the Assistant Administrator realised.

"We do not need fighting men. We are looking for dependable suppliers of provisions for the front. That includes imported goods and local produce. You see, we want to appoint preferred merchants, people that we have worked with, can rely on and trust."

"We will do our best to meet your requirements, sir," replied Lalji looking at Bhasker who nodded quickly so as not to appear disunited. "Let us know what you need."

"Good show. I want to talk to you about another matter as well."

"Yes."

"You hold land near the river. Some you farm on and much of it is unused."

"We have projects in mind, for the future."

"Yes, well we need more space for supplies next to our Supplies Depot. We need to expand the size of the existing depot and provide for parking more vehicles. The site is central enough for us."

"How long do you need it, sir?"

"Until the end of the war my man!"

Lalji did not respond and looked pensive. He was finding the meeting uncomfortable. It was not like a dialogue, not like with the Commissioner who had a different manner of talking.

The Assistant Administrator interrupted his thoughts.

"I know what you are thinking. I need the land *pronto* and we will double the rent per square foot we pay to you at present. We need an area four times larger than the present site and maybe more in the future. What say you, Mr *Laljee*?"

"Sounds good, sir."

"It is good my man! I don't want to requisition the land against your wishes which would mean we do not pay you much. It's better we agree now."

"*Requisition*, meaning sir?"

"Means I don't want to do it without your agreement although I have the power to do that."

"Yes, I see. And what about the supplies contract? When can we discuss that so we can help the *sarkar* (government)?"

The Assistant Commissioner burst out laughing and the others in the room smiled.

"You don't miss a thing Mr *Laljee*. I like your directness. I am not surprised everyone speaks highly of you. I am going to an engagement but the others here will supply you with a list of what the requirements are. If you cannot do it, we will need to ask for tenders from the marketplace."

"Sir, if we can agree prices, we will try to meet all your requirements."

"You are sharp. I like you Mr *Laljee*."

The Assistant Commissioner left with two of his secretaries. The others seemed to relax in their chairs, shifting and pouring glasses of water.

***

That day Lalji bought a copy of the Official Gazette. It was full of official notices, retractions of Powers of Attorney, appointments under the Native Authority Ordinance, legal and probate notices, currency notes cancellations, official food prices and Court schedules. The part of interest to Lalji was the Tender Notices put up by the Central Committee of Supplies. He recognised the name at the bottom of the notices, that of one of the Secretaries present at the meeting with the Assistant Commissioner. His name was Lt Col A H Jenkins.

After the meeting, Jenkins had asked Lalji to see if he could get food items from a list, which he handed him. He said the items would be sent to the war front. He was happy to wait a few days for a response, adding that rail transport would be the responsibility of the government. Lalji noticed the food tender invitations in the Gazette were for the Uganda Railway and the European School. There was no mention of any requirements for the war front. He guessed that under Martial Law, the *sarkar's* dealings with him were going to be off the record. As a preferred supplier, there would be no compulsion to adhere to the food prices stipulated in the Gazette. The prime focus was on procurement and uninterrupted delivery.

The first list was a test run. Lalji expected it was likely to include a few items impossible to obtain to assess him. The thought made him smile.

CHAPTER THIRTY-NINE

Naran had arrived in Nairobi with Jaya and their son at Lalji's invitation. The brothers had much to discuss after Nizar and Khimji's departures.

"I see from your books you are making good progress on the estate," stated Lalji.

"Yes, and the best crops are sugar cane, plantains, and pineapples. They do well in the climate there."

"Here we have agreed a lucrative contract to supply the Army's requirements for the war. The profits are healthy. The business needs another pair of hands to keep up with the demand. I was thinking about getting you here as the third partner."

"That sounds good," responded Naran with a smile. "What would we do with the estate though?"

"How about having a manager at the estate? We cannot abandon it, but we could appoint someone suitable. We would still need to oversee the business side, from here."

"That could be a solution, yes. The right person would not need much training as the engineer and foreman run most things."

"I have discussed it with Bhasker. It would also mean being in Nairobi you will be close to us and better facilities, including the school."

Naran paused at the mention of Bhasker. He still felt there should be a special place for him, being Lalji's brother. Lalji noticed the hesitancy.

"I am going to be guided by you, *Bhai*. I am sure Jaya would be keen. She finds the estate very lonesome and the mosquitoes difficult."

"Good. Let us talk in more detail later."

The postman arrived, knocked on the open door bearing a telegram from Porbander. Naran went pale at the sight of the envelope bearing the telegram.

Telegrams carried news of disasters or deaths. He wondered who it could be that might have died and started to shake. Lalji noticed and put the envelope down, pouring him a glass of water and pulling a chair up for him before opening the envelope.

The news was indeed heart-breaking. Parshottam had passed away suddenly that morning and arrangements were in hand for the funeral later that day. Reading the short message again and again, Lalji felt numb and disconnected from his surroundings. As if trying to exorcise the words and wish them away.

"Who *Bhai*?" asked Naran.

"*Bapuji* (Father). This morning."

Lalji wanted to escape somewhere quiet and be alone with his own thoughts. He felt his eyes filling up. Naran was already sniffling, filled eyes looking out at the street.

"Let us lock up and head home," said Lalji. "Janki will want to organise prayers."

Between Janki and Jaya, they managed to organise prayer evenings every day for fourteen days for well-wishers to attend. The children remained as active and noisy as ever, unaware of the goings-on. In an odd way, their noise and levity provided an escape from the melancholic atmosphere.

Lalji's regret was that he did not manage to get his father to visit Nairobi. Although they had discussed the trip in their letters the arrangement seemed never to materialise. After the grandchildren were born Lalji had hoped to arrange a trip for his parents, but the war had disrupted normal travel.

***

By the end of 1917, the British forces had land control down to central German East Africa. Whilst trying to engage the elusive Lieutenant-Colonel Paul von Lettow-Vorbeck, the British authorities started to look for traders. They needed them to settle along the German railway line from Dar-es-Salaam to Tabora.

A notice in the Official Gazette of British East Africa invited merchants and firms to apply to the Senior Political Officer in Dar-es-Salaam for traders' licences, in all towns along the route. The traders would need to make their own arrangements for shipping, landing cargo and leasing premises. Railway space for cargo was subject to space being made available by the Army, whose own requirements for the war came first.

Lalji was approached by JWH Parkinson, the new Administrator General. Parkinson wanted to know if he would be interested in starting a wholesale supplies business in Dar-es-Salaam or Tanga. The offer of a wholesale licence to an Indian was unheard of. Lalji undertook to investigate and paid a visit to German East Africa.

The circuitous journey was difficult. First, the train journey to Mombasa. This was followed by a steamer to Dar-es-Salaam. Here was met by a Political Officer called James Hughes. Hughes went with Lalji on the German Railway as far as a stop called Morogoro. There the journey ended because of army travel restrictions. Lalji was glad. He was not impressed and realised why he had been offered the wholesale licence. On his return, he went to see the Administrator General.

"So, what is your view about starting something in German East Africa Lalji?" he asked.

"The country is not as advanced as British East Africa. There are fewer farmers and little trade.

"They have a good railway, the *Usambara*."

"The railway is good but few people use it. The farms are large and remote. Sisal seems to be grown everywhere. There is coffee and rubber starting, little else."

"If you had stores and supplies along the railway, the place would open up, don't you think?" asked the Administrator General.

"I don't think it will help," said Lalji bluntly. "There is not much happening there at present. And there are too few customers."

"Hmmm."

"It will take time. There is little farming for food, so the railway is not used every day."

"The railway has followed an old trade route," Parkinson said absent-mindedly.

"Yes, sir," said Lalji looking down, "It was mainly ivory and slave caravans when the Sultan of Zanzibar ruled."

"Yes. Well, Lalji I thank you for paying a visit and checking it out. I will have to inform the Army not to get their hopes up too high."

"There could be merchants interested in Gujarat if they receive some incentives."

"I see," said the Administrator General, looking away.

Before the war the Germans had tried to recruit merchants and craftsmen from India using agents but failed. They were not a familiar colonial power for Indians, who did not trust them. Lalji knew better than to voice the fact that the German *sarkar* (government) did not have a vast hinterland of labour from an Empire situated the other side of the Indian Ocean. British East Africa had fared better with its cohort of Gujarati settlers. They had filled up the economic middle ground with their commercial acumen.

"The Germans had that essential ingredient missing: the Gujarati settler," thought Lalji.

As if he had read his mind, the Administrator General looked at Lalji and nodded his head.

CHAPTER FORTY

By the end of the war, it was clear that Lalji, Bhasker and Naran had done well from the Army contracts. The lease of the extra land near the Nairobi River was likely to continue. Reversing procurements was not something the Army did well, if at all. Besides, they had used the land more extensively than expected. They ended up building massive stores and workshops for repairing vehicles. There was a look of permanence around the site.

The Administrator General introduced a 'Soldier Resettlement Scheme' for those white soldiers tempted to put their roots down after the war. At the same time, he introduced a major boost for farming by announcing 999-year leases for farms. An extension of the railway into the fertile areas of the Western Highlands was nearing completion. That would facilitate more agriculture.

Having learnt a thing or two about the Indians, he allowed bidding from European and 'Asiatic British Subjects'.

"Who are 'Asiatic British Subjects'? asked Naran, reading the announcement in the Mombasa Times.

Bhasker laughed, always a cynic of *sarkar* announcements. "It means anyone of Indian origin, who has been accepted for British Nationality — all ten of them —and they all work as barristers in the courts."

Everyone laughed.

Having recently met the Administrator General, Lalji was not so cynical.

"I think Parkinson is a cunning man. He would not stop anyone of us bidding but expect us to become British Subjects if we win the bids," said Lalji.

"*If* we win the bids, *Bhai*," said Naran.

"*When.* They have more land to give away than they can manage. The *sarkar* wants it to be used for agriculture and there are not enough Europeans who have settled. As before, so many keep returning home within a few years of getting here."

"So why not just say all 'British Indians and Chinese'?" asked Bhasker.

"There are not any Chinese here. This is aimed at us. This way it gets through the complex colonial regulations in London without attracting too much attention. Parkinson gets his farms occupied and the Indians get a chance to get into agriculture if they wish. Parkinson turns them into British subjects. All done without a mention of *Indians*."

"Few of our people want to run farms," said Naran.

"True. I think he is casting his net wide at this stage, to test us out. He knows most Gujarati's would sooner run businesses than farms," said Lalji.

"He may want Naran to bid because of his success of the Baganda farm," joked Bhasker. "Why did he not instead allot factory sites in Nairobi to any Indians, I mean to *Asiatics*? We can manufacture just as well as the Europeans."

"Again, it is to do with what London can digest. At present very few places in the Empire allow locals or Indians to own or run factories. Or do wholesale business, even in India," said Lalji.

"You are right, *Bhai*. They know what could happen."

***

The children's requirements became routine. The elder ones had a regular need for uniforms and shoes as they grew. The younger ones were easier to cater for: they only got the chance of a new purchase when the hand-me-downs did not fit or became too worn. Janki and Husnara were competent with their sewing skills to make small alterations and get an approximate fit. To be taken out for a fitting of new clothes or shoes was a rare event for the younger ones. In fact, the sharing and recycling were routine to the extent where a pencil lost was soon replaced with one which had been cut into two, from another child's school bag. Toys, if available, were a communal commodity, and any possessiveness was short-lived if one wanted to have access to the toys of others.

One evening Lalji was met by an anxious Janki while he sat telling stories to the children. He knew when Janki was uneasy as she would bring a load of washed clothes, drop them on the cement floor where she would sit crosslegged. Then start folding them silently with a fixed frown on her face.

"Something the matter, Janki?" asked Lalji.

"Well, I have some worries."

"Tell me."

"It is about Ganga. She is growing up fast. I mean, we should be looking to her future now."

"Oh. She is only ten, Janki."

"When I was ten, I was already engaged. I know that does not happen in Africa but we should have some plan, don't you think?"

"When she is older, maybe 16 or 18, we can go home and find a groom for her. That is what people do. Then she and her husband can stay there, or we can bring them both here to work and live in Africa."

"Yes, but you are always so busy. Will you find the time? Nizarbhai and Husnara have got Memuna engaged already, so even if work holds him back, they have a groom who will wait for her, or travel here to marry her."

"Yes, but you know in their culture that's how it is."

Janki frowned without responding.

"Is something else the matter? Something you are not sharing with me?" asked Lalji.

"Well, you might as well know. Your daughter is a woman now. Her periods have started," Janki said in an irritated tone.

Lalji took a moment to let it sink in before bursting out laughing, to the annoyance of Janki, who walked out in a huff with her bundle of folded clothes.

***

Lalji's elder boy Jagdish was already showing signs of ambition. He loved going to the shop or talking with Lalji and Bhasker about the business. His younger brother Kishore was physically delicate with asthma, with a tendency to cough and wheeze in the morning chilly air.

The troop of seven children would be taken out on Sunday afternoons by their fathers, Lalji, Nizar and Naran. The mothers stayed back in Mombasa House for an afternoon nap and a long natter over a cup of tea. Sundays were also visiting days in Nairobi. Friends dropping in unexpectedly was the custom. The womenfolk often ended up entertaining guests while the men were out with the children.

Going out in families was usually a rare event and usually involved weddings. A rare and unique occasion was the screening of *Raja Harishchandra*, the first

Indian cinema film. It arrived in Nairobi five years after its release in 1913. A large hall had been booked and the projector with its Italian operator hired from the European Theatre. A large, white cotton sheet was suspended at one end of the room and the projector stood plumb in the centre of the room, directed at the wavy white screen.

The occasion stood to be so over-subscribed that those on seats became outnumbered by children seated in the front on the floor. Latecomers stood wherever they found space. The Italian projectionist was frightened that his equipment would be knocked over. He got annoyed if the children came close to him.

Eventually, the doors were locked after the observers from the Administrator General's office were seated. The lights were put out. The opening scene was met with an audible drawing in of breath by the audience. Then an excited chorus of screams and clapping from the children.

Eyes gawped; the audience froze into a catatonic state. The children kept looking back at the projector and the dancing light coming out of the lens at the front. They were trying to figure out if the metal box contained miniature people, horses and buildings. Little children wet themselves with excitement. Older ones watched stupefied, some sat with jaws open, drooling into their laps.

The projectionist had sunk back into a low chair and lit a cigar. His face was a fixed smile of pride and achievement, his temper cooled. Those who noticed the heavy curls of smoke coming from the projectionist's cigar wondered why the patterns they made did not disturb the image ahead. Like it did when someone trespassed or stood up in the path of the light. The occasion was exciting and new and so enthralling that everyone in that overcrowded room would remember it for the rest of their lives. For others it would be a source of huge inspiration. To see moving Indian images on a big sheet at one end of the room was the start of being able to dream about the future, of elsewhere and of India.

While Kishore sat staring throughout the film, Jagdish decided halfway through the film he would one day build his own film house in Nairobi. Just like the European Theatre, which he had seen only from the outside.

CHAPTER FORTY-ONE

OSMANBHAI NARANJEE, THE market owner dropped in at Porbander Stores. With him was a well-dressed man in white shirt and black trousers, hair swept back neatly over his head.

"*Namaste*, Laljibhai," greeted Osmanbhai.

"*Namaste*, Osmanbhai. What brings you here after such a long time? Everything fine at the market?"

"Everything is fine. Your man Hashimbhai is doing an excellent job and providing good quality vegetables."

"Yes, we are pleased with his success."

"I have come by to introduce you to Jagatlal Patel, who comes from Surat."

Lalji clasped his hands in greeting and was met by an extended arm for a handshake. Pleasantries were exchanged before Osmanbhai resumed the purpose of his visit.

"Laljibhai, I know that Ismailbhai Habib spoke to you about the Legislative assembly seat. I have known him six years."

"Yes, a fine man with good intentions."

"I know you have no interest in politics. But there will be times your support may become necessary for the good of our community."

"Yes of course. I have offered my support to Ismailbhai Habib."

"Jagatlal here is a law clerk and a senior member of the East African Indian National Congress. He has some good ideas to help our flagging Congress Party. He is keen to start a newspaper for us and we need your support. The newspaper is going to be important for sending out information from the Congress Party. We need to create dialogue amongst the Indians here."

"How can I be of help?"

Jagatlal spoke for the first time. "Laljibhai, we need funds to start the paper. We have collected enough funds to buy a printing machine but we need sponsors and advertisers for the first few copies to get the business going."

"I will be happy to advertise. Please let me know what more you need and I will see what is possible. I will also speak with my partners."

"Thank you, Laljibhai. We were wondering if you have any contact with anyone local who has political ability?"

"Local?"

"Yes, there is a young Kikuyu named Gichuru who is bright and I hear speaks well."

"I am sorry, I wouldn't know."

"Maybe your partner Bhaskerbhai can help. His shop is near the river, and he meets people."

"I shall ask him."

"Thank you. We would like to meet Gichuru to discuss his views, as he has a mind for politics. For now, we must take leave as we have to call on others."

"Will you stay to have tea?"

Both visitors declined and stated they would be in contact.

***

Across the ocean, Mohandas Gandhi had reached India and was making ripples the *Raj sarkar* (British government) felt unhappy about. He had been successful in galvanising support for his stance against the Rowlatt Act. The Act would decimate the rights of Indians to protest against the excesses of the Raj. A national momentum was building up with agitation in Bengal and Punjab on a regular basis.

Two of Gandhi's compatriots had been arrested and their whereabouts were unknown. On Sunday 13th April 1919, a hastily arranged protest was planned in Amritsar in an open space. People had gathered not only to protest but others had come with children for a Sunday afternoon outing. Many were there to celebrate *Baisakhi* (spring festival) which fell on that day. Others wandered into the ground after a nearby *Baisakhi mela* (Baisakhi funfair) closed early.

Over lunch, the local British commander Brigadier General Dyer heard that a crowd was gathering. When the protest meeting started later in the afternoon, Dyer arrived with ninety soldiers. They blocked the main exit from the enclosed park with armoured trucks.

Without warning the crowd to disperse, he ordered his men to open fire into the crowd.

The firing continued until they exhausted their ammunition. Women and children were also shot in the indiscriminate firing. Over 1,000 died and a similar number were injured from the shooting and the stampede. A water well in the centre of the park was the end of 120 people who died from gunshot wounds or drowning.

The *Raj sarkar* set up a Commission of Inquiry. After its findings were published, no action or court martial was set up to prosecute and convict Brigadier General Dyer.

Winston Churchill, in the House of Commons debate of 8 July 1920, said, *"The crowd was unarmed, except with bludgeons. It was not attacking anybody or anything… When fire had been opened upon it to disperse it, it tried to run away. Pinned up in a narrow place considerably smaller than Trafalgar Square, with hardly any exits, and packed together so that one bullet would drive through three or four bodies, the people ran madly this way and the other. When the fire was directed upon the centre, they ran to the sides. The fire was then directed to the sides. Many threw themselves down on the ground, the fire was then directed down on the ground. This was continued to 8 to 10 minutes, and it stopped only when the ammunition had reached the point of exhaustion."*

Sir Rabindranath Tagore, a Nobel laureate, received the news of the massacre by 22nd May 1919. He decided to renounce his British knighthood as 'a symbolic act of protest'.

In a letter to the Viceroy he wrote, *'The enormity of the measures taken by the Government in Punjab for quelling some local disturbances has, with a rude shock, revealed to our minds the helplessness of our position as British subjects in India. The very least that I can do for my country is to take all consequences upon myself in giving voice to the protest of the millions of my countrymen, surprised into dumb anguish of terror. The time has come when badges of honour make our shame glaring in the incongruous context of humiliation.'*

***

Jagatlal Patel launched the *"East African Post"* amid excitement within the Indian community. Soon, there was disappointment that the weekly was only in English and carried a strong political flavour.

After its launch, Bhasker arranged for Jagatlal to meet Harry Gichuru, a young Kikuyu typesetter. Gichuru worked for the settler paper *The Vanguard*. The two talked at length and found much common ground in their politics. Gichuru needed capital for a press to start printing a newspaper for Africans. Jagatlal offered his printers *pro bono* and so they started their collaboration with the launch of Gichuru's paper *Rafiki*. Bhasker and Lalji were happy to have arranged the connection between the two men. As always, Lalji insisted on keeping their role confidential, away from spying eyes and ears.

Three years later Gichuru would be arrested and jailed for his political views, having founded 'The African Society'. The Society was a political association opposed to the *Kipande*. The *Kipande* was housed in a small brass case and required to be worn around the neck by all African males over the age of fifteen.

Two days after Gichuru's arrest, a crowd of supporters had gathered outside Nairobi Police Station. They had come to protest at his arrest and demand his release. The police replied by opening fire on the demonstrators, killing over twenty-five, some shot in the back. White settlers had joined in the shooting against the protesters. With Gichuru in jail, Patel used the *East African Post* to continue to voice African concerns in his editorials. Two years after Gichuru's imprisonment, Patel would also be arrested and jailed, for participating in a campaign to boycott a poll tax.

CHAPTER FORTY-TWO

KISHORE WAS LALJI'S youngest son and required more attention than the other children put together. His asthma was troublesome almost daily. It seemed he was also prone to coughs and infections which invariably led him to Dr Shah's door. Janki did her best for him, keeping him wrapped up in the mornings against the Nairobi nippy air. At the slightest hint of a cold, he was banished to staying indoors. Then followed nightly drinks of hot turmeric milk, which he reluctantly gulped down with Janki standing guard over him.

On one of the visits to Dr Shah, the doctor turned around and asked Lalji if he was well.

"Yes, doctor. I seem to have caught the boy's cough. It should settle and I will be fine."

"Laljibhai, you are looking a pale colour since I last saw you."

"I have not been getting out of the shop much. The days at work are getting longer ever since Nizar left, and I have also started doing the books."

"Are you sleeping well?"

"Not these last two weeks since the cough started. It can be irritating sometimes and keep me awake."

"Let me check things out while you are here."

Having examined Lalji the doctor had a worried look on his face.

"Laljibhai, to me you also look like you have lost weight. Look, your ribs are sticking out."

"Hmmm. Janki keeps saying I look thinner. I told her it was my new shirts; they are a size larger. Is everything all right, doctor?"

"Lalji, I want you to see one of the specialists at the hospital. I do not think you have what Kishore has here. You have inflammation in the chest which is causing the dry cough."

"Is it something to worry about, doctor?"

"It could be something serious, but whatever it is, it should be at an early stage. Apart from young Kishore, is there anyone else at home with a cough?"

"No."

"I will arrange for the new physician at the Mission Hospital to see you and give us the benefit of his knowledge. He is highly spoken of and well known in his field."

***

Dr Hamish Meldrew confirmed pleurisy of the left lower lung. He prescribed fresh air and sunshine in a warm seaside location for three months. Lalji was to adhere to a diet rich in protein and fresh fruit. The doctor's suggestion of meat, eggs and fish in the diet was not acceptable to Lalji, who had always been a *Vaishnav* (follower of Lords Vishnu, Ram and Krishna) vegetarian.

It took a couple of weeks to organise everything. Janki and Kishore would go with Lalji for his stay in Mombasa. Arrangements were made for renting a small dwelling of two rooms and a kitchen. At home Jaya would look after the children. Ganga, Lalji's eldest, could help supervising the younger ones.

Handing over the paperwork of the businesses was more complex. Bhasker had little interest or aptitude for it and suggested Naran take on Lalji's duties. Nizar, who lived next door in Mombasa House, would help with the accounting. For the Bank and official matters a power of attorney needed to be drawn up handing over control of the business and assets to Naran while Lalji was away.

From what little he knew about powers of attorney — the Mombasa Times was full of announcements of cancelling them — Lalji was sceptical of appointing one. But after discussing it further with the Bank Manager and Nizar, Lalji agreed. Naran found himself in his elder brothers' shoes, with complete control over the businesses and assets.

***

Lalji was in Mombasa when news came that the East African Protectorate would be administered under different names. The Protectorate, had been amalgamated from the previous British East Africa and the annexed German East Africa after the war. It was to be renamed 'Colony and Protectorate of Kenya'.

The Colony was the main body of the country and the Protectorate was a narrow strip of land on the coast. This was administered by the Sultan of Zanzibar. To the south, German East Africa had been turned into 'Tanganyika Territory' after the German defeat. It was to be administered by the British. To the west, the 'Protectorate of Uganda', often referred to as part of 'British East Africa' was also administered by the British.

With one eye on the politics of South Africa, the white settlers in Kenya had been agitating for an elected Legislative Council. They adopted the American Revolution war cry, *'No taxation without representation'.* Their demands fuelled the Indians to ask for elected members on the two seats reserved for them.

Reservations arose when the Indians also asked for new barriers to immigration be eased. They also wanted to be allowed to buy land in the White Highlands. Fearing an expanding Indian population alongside the poor retention of settlers from Europe, the white settlers opposed the Indian demands. Their leader, Lord Delamare, was looking for autonomy from London. He wanted to establish a white minority government, like in Southern Rhodesia and the Union of South Africa.

Jagatlal Patel the publisher of the East African Post, was lobbying against the white settlers. He spoke with ferocity on the exclusion of the African in the settlers' plans and their refusal to share power. He saw what was happening in southern Africa as a dangerous precedent. He said that would wipe out all rights of Africans in their own country. His views on Indian immigration were equally robust. He argued that the future of the Colony's development, and upliftment of the common man, could only happen if the Colony had a liberal immigration policy. He wanted to allow artisans, skilled labour, and merchants from India to settle. He believed the white settlers feared the Indians more than the Africans whom they had banished to reserves. He said the Africans did not need to fear the Indians, who only wanted to trade. They were not interested in displacing anyone from their ancestral land.

'We Indians know what it is like to live under the British Raj. We oppose them in their quest for domination in Kenya Colony, just as we oppose their domination in India,' he wrote.

CHAPTER FORTY-THREE

LALJI RETURNED FROM Mombasa feeling stronger. Three months away in the warm climate and the sea air seemed to have settled down his cough. Janki was not so sure. She accepted the cough hardly troubled him but she was concerned he had not regained his weight and seemed to tire easily.

Dr B.K. Shah gave Lalji a clean bill of health with caveats.

"Laljibhai, your chest sounds better but there is scarring. Remember your improvement will hold if you do not throw yourself into long hours of work, and poor eating habits. You must have fruit in your diet and keep up with the walks in the fresh air," advised the doctor.

"I agree, and all that will happen. My brother Naran has been managing well in my absence and I intend to let him continue with more responsibility. Poor chap, ever since he landed in Africa, he has had to take over other people's responsibilities, first KB's and now mine," said Lalji.

"Learning under pressure is the quickest way, Laljibhai."

"Yes, that is true."

"We doctors think we know it all when we graduate. Then when we take responsibility for *real* patients, we realise what we learnt at college never fully prepared us for the real world of medicine. Pressure and responsibility are good teachers," said Dr Shah, chuckling.

Naran and Bhasker persuaded Lalji to take the afternoons off after his return. Naran insisted he could manage with less help from Lalji, now the war had ended and the Army demands for supplies were reduced. Lalji was glad for the respite. He could concentrate on planning for the future. The Army contracts had been lucrative and he now had his sights on further land investments. All their debts, including those at the Bank, had been cleared thanks to the lucrative Army income.

Office and shop buildings interested him. Mombasa House had been a major success and he had his mind on further developments in the same sector of Nairobi, not far from Government Road. The film industry in Mumbai was taking off in a big way and going to the picture house was becoming a popular family pastime. There was the need for a picture house in Nairobi to cater for the Indian Community, and his son was constantly suggesting to Lalji to think about building one.

In the overall hustle after his return from Mombasa, the issue of retracting his power of attorney seemed to get overlooked.

***

The white settlers sent representatives to London to demand white minority rule in Kenya, as well as wanting to restrict the White Highlands for white settlers only. They also wanted to restrict Indian migration into the colony. The Indians sent their own delegation to put their case against the demands of the white settlers. A third delegation was sent by the missionaries who were suspicious of white minority rule and wanted safeguards for the Africans.

On 23 July 1923, after deliberation on *"the Indian question"*, the British cabinet agreed on a political fudge to settle the issue. It confirmed that the right to impose immigration controls from India vested in the colonial government in Britain, and not with the settlers. Immigration restrictions imposed locally by the white settlers' *sarkar* (government) on Indians would be removed. At the same time, the Cabinet also continued to restrict Indian ownership of land in the White Highlands.

In a White Paper published later, known as the 'Devonshire White Paper', it stated that in the *'administration of Kenya His Majesty's Government regard themselves as exercising a trust on behalf of the African population, and they are unable to delegate or share this trust, the object of which may be defined as the protection and advancement of the native races."* It allowed for the formation of the first African Political Party, the Kikuyu Central Association, stating that 'the Imperial state would protect the interests of Africans'. The paper affirmed 'the continuance of white control of the Kenya Legislative Council.' This was perceived as a victory by white settlers throughout Africa.

The Indians were granted five seats on the Legislative Council, increased from two.

***

Indirect rule from London was blended with a degree of local power wielded by the colony's *sarkar*. Initially, the white settlers felt alienated by London and blamed the Indians for 'creating trouble'. As if to underpin their mistrust of Indian merchants, and as a retaliation for the Devonshire White Paper, a new tax on profits of four per cent was legislated against Indian businesses. In addition, the writing of accounts in Gujarati was banned. The first legislation was passed in Tanganyika, but the trajectory and aim were obvious.

The East Africa Indian National Congress called for a *hartal* (strike), a stoppage of all business activities. The political stakes were raised and the Colonial *sarkar* was nervous about the *hartaal* spreading into the rest of British East Africa. Meetings of the Indian National Congress were monitored closely and leading figures were followed.

Jagatlal Patel, leading the Indian National Congress, was trying to hold an open meeting for Indian businessmen in Nairobi but permission was denied by the Town Council, citing fire regulations. Mr Naranjee arranged for his market building to be made available on a Sunday afternoon. He had recently had his Fire Department Public Safety Certificate renewed. The new Inspector of Police, a young Glaswegian called Rory Sullivan, wanted to know in advance the numbers attending, the purpose of the meeting, and the names of organisers. He wanted to be assured that no 'trouble' would ensue and of course, there would be observers to ensure nothing 'seditious' was said or planned. There should be no call for a *hartaal* he warned. He asked to be given the agenda of the meeting in advance.

Among the speakers listed was Harry Gichuru from the Kikuyu Central Association as the chief guest. Jagatlal Patel and Osmanbhai Naranjee were to address the meeting, which was to be conducted mainly in Gujarati, except when Harry Gichuru spoke.

Two police *askaris* (constables) were stationed at the front door and a further six were in the marketplace. A small desk for the Official observers was placed facing the makeshift stage where the speakers were seated. The two white observers in police uniform, were accompanied by a new face in civilian clothes, a plump middle-aged white man with dark hair and a grand moustache, smoker's pipe held in his left hand held closely at the side of his chest. Rory Sullivan sat in a police van outside with six armed *askaris* in the back.

People arriving for the meeting started asking nervously why there was such a large police presence. A father who had brought along three young children turned around and headed home, sending his apologies with a friend. Harry Gichuru arrived with an elderly Kikuyu woman and his younger brother. One of the two *askaris* at the front door stopped him while the other went inside and returned with the plump, white man, holding his pipe.

"Good afternoon, sir," he greeted Harry.

"Good afternoon."

"May I know the purpose of your visit here today?"

"May I know who is asking?"

"Yes of course. I am Harry Thwaites, new Inspector of Police, CID."

"I have come to attend this meeting organised by the East African Indian National Congress, on invitation by its leader, Jagatlal Patel."

"*Tame Gujarati Bhasa bolo cho?* (Do you speak Gujarati)?" asked Harry Thwaites.

A puzzled Harry looked blank. Those around him went quiet. The atmosphere became tense, all eyes on Harry.

"*Namaste.* I am learning Gujarati so I am here to listen."

"Are you planning to address the audience?" Thwaites asked in English.

"If I am asked to, I shall."

"You see that's the problem. You don't speak Gujarati and these Indians don't speak much English. Seems to me you are here to brew up trouble."

"I am a guest and not here to make trouble. I am here to listen to the meeting and understand the concerns of these Indian people, not all of whom are Gujarati or speak the language."

"As long as that is all you do. If you attempt to address the meeting, I will have you arrested."

"Is that all?"

"For now, yes."

"*Jai Shree Krishna,*" said Harry Gichuru.

"*Jai Shree Krishna,*" was the CID Officer's reflex response, visibly irritated that he had been tricked into responding to the greeting.

Inside the meeting, the organisers had been distributing a leaflet to the attendees. Within minutes at least four hundred had assembled and the large central space of the market looked barely able to contain the crowd.

The two observers had both got hold of the leaflet, printed in Gujarati in red ink. They were looking around anxiously at the front entrance to see if they could spot Harry Thwaites coming back in. One *askari* had been dispatched to the police van with a copy for Rory Sullivan.

On being handed the leaflet Harry Thwaites went a deep shade of red. He summoned Jagatlal Patel and asked him what the meaning of the Gujarati leaflet was.

"It's our programme for the evening, Sir," replied Jagatlal.

"Yes, but it's in Gujarati. And the letters are in grotesque red ink! Looks more like a wedding invitation than a meeting agenda."

"Our audience mainly speaks Gujarati, sir. What else can we do?"

"Yes, but you did not clear this with us before the meeting."

"We cleared the English version as you know. Most of you don't speak or understand Gujarati, but it's the same document. You can check if you wish."

"And this red colour?" asked Thwaites, avoiding the invitation to compare the two versions.

"It's the appropriate colour for anything printed with *Ganesh* and the *Swastika*. There at the top you see in Gujarati it says '*Shree Ganesh Namah*' (I bow to you Lord Ganesh) flanked by two *Swastikas*. You will see it is on the English version here."

Thwaites' bulging eyes met those of Harry Gichuru standing next to Rory Sullivan, who had also arrived and witnessed the exchange. There was nothing further to be said and Sullivan turned briskly to head out to his vehicle.

On seeing the interaction, Osmanbhai Naranjee decided to insert into the programme an impromptu item. He asked Bhasker to obtain his *tablas*, to start the afternoon off with a *Ganesh bhajan* (religious song praising *Lord Ganesh*). Bhasker left as fast as he could, pursued by two aides, one of whom played cymbals in the *Mandir* and the other who could sing. All three arrived back in time to start the programme. Within minutes of the music starting, Thwaites had decided to leave for a smoke and a chat with Sullivan. The two official observers in the audience, feeling exposed sat dutifully at their desks looking straight ahead trying to mentally absent themselves from the *bhajans* (religious songs).

When Jagatlal Patel addressed the meeting, Thwaites was back and seated. He was providing a whispered running commentary to the two observers who wrote down his translated dictation for their record. Patel initially outlined the *sarkar's* (government's) new tax aimed at Indian businesses. There were loud murmurings in the audience and Thwaites stood up from his chair and turned around to glare at the audience. Silence followed.

Someone asked if the tax was going to be aimed at non-Indian businesses. Patel replied there was no mention of that, with one eye on Thwaites who was translating for the recorders. Someone else asked if Kenya Colony would be hit by the same tax as in Tanganyika. Again, Patel replied it was not mentioned. But this time he added, "But we should prepare for the change in law, just in case."

Someone suggested it was premature to be concerned as the tax was probably only going to be imposed in Tanganyika where they needed rebuilding after the war. Maybe it would be temporary. Was it not their duty to help the country recover? Further speakers exchanged views and speculated as to whether or when a similar law may come to Kenya Colony.

Having seen the audience through their discussion, Patel decided to move the meeting on. He was reassured that Thwaites had heard nothing alarming so far and was beginning to gain a normal colour on his face.

"The *sarkar* are also introducing a law about writing of business accounts," he announced.

There was silence. He continued, "Writing your account books in Gujarati script, in red ink will not be acceptable anymore."

There was a chorus of shouting '*why?*'

"If we are to submit our accounts to the *sarkar,* they need to be in a language they can read," replied Patel. "The colour of ink on official documents is black," he added.

The statement was met with angry shouts and cries of defiance. Harry Gichuru looked uncomfortably at Thwaites, whose eyes were darting from side to side trying to mentally pin the shouts to faces.

Raising his hands to ask for calm, just as it looked as if Thwaites was agitated enough, Patel went on. "There is clearly misunderstanding here. I would not think anybody can expect the entire Gujarati business community to become fluent in English overnight. Just as we do not expect the *sarkar* to have armies of Gujarati-literate inspectors," he said with laughter from the audience. Thwaites's face turned red again. "Some may understand Gujarati, even speak it but to read and write is another matter." The audience continued laughing and Thwaites' face looked like it would explode. Patel and Naranjee calmed things down.

Patel continued. "We in the East African Indian National Congress will seek urgent meetings with the *sarkar* to sort things out. As things stand, none of this makes sense. There has got to be a *misunderstanding* of course and we hope to get it cleared up at the earliest opportunity."

"What will meetings do? It is clear they have cast aspirations on our honesty and want to penalise us. They are jealous of our business ability and want to tax us again. I left Bharat because we could not bear the taxes there," a middle-aged Bohra man said.

There was general agreement and consensus with this view in the audience. A couple of Punjabi men speaking in Hindi agreed that the laws were being introduced to stifle the Indian business successes.

The mood was slowly getting angry. Patel changed tack.

"Brothers, reach into your pockets and bring out any currency note you have, and hold it up for all to see," requested Patel. Suddenly, Thwaites stood up and signalled to the *askari* (constable) close to him to be ready.

"Look now at the picture of our beloved King on the note."

Everyone held the note between two hands and stared at the King's image.

"Look below the image of the King, underneath the English writing. What does it say there?"

Suddenly there was an explosion of laughter and the gathering erupted into a frenzy of cheering and shouting. Thwaites fumbled for his wallet to look for a currency note, looking around to see which denomination was the subject of the commotion. There were all the denominations there, waving cheerfully in the air, with laughter so loud it shook the walls of the marketplace. He pulled out a five schilling note, looked at the King's image and below where in Gujarati script it said '*Panch Schilling*'. At least his Gujarati literacy extended to being able to read the basics. Thwaites looked to his side and saw Harry Gichuru looking him in the eyes, pity written all over his face.

At that moment, Thwaites wished he had paid more attention to his Gujarati mother teaching him reading and writing after Missionary School. Fishing, hunting and riding with his English father had led him to a middle-grade commission in the army, followed by the Colonial Police Force. Being transferred from Colony to Colony, like his late father in the King's Army, he had cursed his mother for not being white, and developed a hatred for all natives.

CHAPTER FORTY-FOUR

BOTH LALJI AND Jagatlal Patel were invited to the opening event of the Ismaili Jamatkhana in Nairobi. From the laying of the foundation stone to its opening took precisely two years. The palatial blue-grey building, also known as the 'Khoja Mosque', was the tallest building in Nairobi. The four panelled front doors, twice the height of a tall man, were extraordinarily imposing on the corner of the Government and River Roads. With a massive clock tower above roof level, it was a visible landmark for miles around Nairobi.

The speed of building, the architecture and the skills of the craftsmen raised eyebrows in Nairobi society. The white settlers realised that despite the limits placed on Indian businesses and land ownership, they had a flair for commerce. Limiting the arrival of Indians was the perennial demand by white settlers who felt the competition was unfair. It was a live issue, and not just in East Africa but along the entire length of the east coast of Africa below the Sahara. In political circles it was widely perceived that if Indian migration was left unchecked, it would lead to the erosion of British commercial might. That would endanger their hold on economic and then political power.

The Governor of the Colony confided over a state dinner to a visiting official from the Colonial Office, "They [Indians] are remarkably astute at making good their ambitions, no matter what barriers you put their way."

To the concern of Jagatlal and the Congress, the various communities of the Gujarati diaspora were putting down firm roots in the Colony. This was despite the hostility of white settlers and the suspicions of the *sarkar*. The Congress Party was looking to improve the representation of Indians in the political structures of the Colony. They wanted to form alliances with groups like the Kikuyu Association to pursue a common agenda. For Jagatlal, Indian economic strength built on a shaky political foundation spelt disaster for the future. But to talk about fair representation in commerce or politics seemed futile with the Gujarati diaspora. They had all within their lifetime experienced famine and hardship back in *Hindustan* (India). Lack of political opportunity was not a novel experience and did not cut it for them. They could survive despite the odds. The opportunity to advance and set up their own schools, hospitals and places of worship provided an incentive. They were focused on business, at the expense of extramural political aspirations.

"Politics is for the privileged. Our priority is the get the basics for our children and for their future," Jagatlal was once told by a small trader.

"You seem preoccupied, Jagatlalbhai," inquired Lalji. "Something on your mind?"

"What can I say, Laljibhai? It seems as soon as we make some progress the *sarkar* aims another weapon at us."

"What is it this time?"

"I have it from good sources the new Governor, who just opened this building, has in mind to introduce a poll tax, aimed to hurt us," said Jagatlal.

"So, winning the Indian immigration battle led to this?" asked Lalji.

"Exactly. He may have opened this magnificent building but he has gone away with envy in his eyes. And the settlers have his ear."

"I see. They needed us, indeed wanted us, to help open Africa. Now that we have exceeded their expectations, we are no longer welcome," said Lalji.

"Laljibhai, tell me who you think they are," asked Jagatlal.

"The two *sarkars*, here and in England."

"I wish it were just that. I used to think that way but I don't anymore."

"Explain."

"Well, it is those two. But it is also the Monarch in England, the Viceroy in India and the Empire Office in London. Then you have the nobility and the military — once again British, Colonial and Indian versions. You see, nobody has full control, and yet everybody has control."

"Hmmm. Then perhaps our way is the best in these circumstances," said Lalji.

"Meaning?"

"Meaning, guide your small vessel to ride out the waves of every storm, but stay true to your destination. Like we have always done."

Jagatlal sighed. "You may have a point."

***

Lalji's cough seemed to return overnight. His improvement after returning from Mombasa had reached a plateau. He managed well despite the occasional night sweat and daily tiredness.

An irritant cough at bedtime woke him halfway through the night. It made breathing difficult. Janki brought him a hot water bottle and made him hot turmeric milk with honey. Having exhausted all she knew; she woke Nizar and Bhasker in their flats and asked if Dr Shah could be called. He diagnosed pneumonia and suggested transfer to the hospital. Once there, the morphine seemed to take effect and Lalji could speak without provoking a bout of coughing. He asked Janki to return home and to bring the children to see him in the morning.

Janki realised he was profoundly ill from the way he spoke with urgency. His speech interrupted by breathlessness, she saw fear in his eyes for the first time. She held herself together and smiled reassuringly, holding his hand which felt ice-cold. Lalji asked Nizar to return in the morning with Naran and Bhasker.

When they left, he asked the nurse for a pen and paper.

In the morning Janki returned after dawn. Naran and the children followed later. The nurse informed them that Lalji had required two further injections of morphine in the night.

Lalji refused any food but sipped tea. Although more communicative he was clearly unwell, his breathing still laboured. When Nizar arrived with Bhasker, Janki left with the children to get them to school. Jagdish remained back on Lalji's request.

"I want the four of you to be aware of my wishes in case I do not survive this illness," said Lalji, his words interrupted for taking breaths of air.

"But *Bhai…*" protested Naran, then promptly hushed up when Lalji raised his hand to silence him.

"I have known for some time this illness is still with me," he said. "I have a young family like the two of you. We have done very well after arriving in Nairobi. Very well indeed."

"Very true, Laljibhai, and a lot of credit for your decisions," said Bhasker.

"*Our* decisions, Bhasker."

Naran looked and felt distinctly uncomfortable.

"I have written my wishes on this paper which I want you all to follow to the letter," said Lalji.

"Of course, *Bhai*," said Naran.

"Nizar, you will need to function as my representative to ensure everything happens as I intend. You know I would do the same for you."

"There is no question, everything will happen as you wish, Laljibhai," said Nizar.

"Good. Jagdish here is only fifteen," said Lalji, holding out his arm for Jagdish to get close for a hug. "He stands to inherit a lot at an early age and will need a lot of guidance."

"We are here, *Bhai*," spoke Naran, slight tremor in his voice.

"Naran, you hold my power of attorney at present. You need to change the name on my account at the bank, which is held jointly with Bhasker, to continue in my place. You should do that without delay. Are you in agreement, Bhasker?"

"Yes, *Bhai*."

"Then the question of my assets. First, Bhasker will get his half share of the business and assets. He has the option to continue as a partner with Naran if he wishes."

"I understand, *Bhai*," said Bhasker.

"Understood, Laljibhai," said Nizar.

Looking at Naran, Lalji continued, "You will inherit a quarter of everything I own, which is half of the rest after Bhasker has had his share. The other quarter will go to Janki and to my children."

"Understood," said Naran with the others nodding.

"Out of that, Janki will inherit fifty-five per cent and the children fifteen percent each. My daughter Ganga will be given her share, either in cash or gold, after she gets married. The two boys will inherit their share, including properties, on reaching their eighteenth birthday. In the meantime, Naran will hold their inheritance on trust, with you, Nizar, being required to agree to any divisions in a fair way in the future."

Lalji needed time to catch his breath after a bout of sudden coughing.

"All seems very sensible and fair, Laljibhai," said Nizar.

Naran was preoccupied for a moment but then he re-joined the conversation. "I hope none of this comes to happen and you get back home again. Like you did after your rest in Mombasa."

"Somehow I doubt that," said Lalji, looking into his son's eyes which had welled up with tears, pulling him closer. "It is fine whatever happens to me, and you, my son, may have to grow up quicker than we thought."

Jagdish had started to sob and Lalji asked for his pen and papers.

"Here I have everything written out. I want you Bhasker, Naran and Nizar to sign underneath my signature. It also says that we have agreed this in front of young Jagdish here, but he does not have to sign because of his age."

Nizar checked the paper to ensure what he understood was within it and signed. Naran scanned the document, signed it and then read it to refresh his mind of what had been agreed. Bhasker signed without reading it.

Dr Shah had come in to see the patient and agreed to sign as witness.

"Thank you all. Nizar, you have the task of getting this officially lodged with an attorney as my last will. Please would you do that today."

"Yes, of course."

***

It was a sunny Tuesday morning in Nairobi and the shops on Bazaar Street had started to open. The tea stand at the *bhajia* house had emptied, having lost its customers to the shops where they worked.

What sounded like a commotion interrupted the sleepy start to the day. Shops at the Government Road end of the street started to close with their owners putting shutters back on. The disturbance led to neighbours coming out to the front to see what was happening.

"It's Laljibhai from Porbander Stores. News has come that he was admitted to hospital three days ago. Early this morning he passed away. We are shutting down out of respect for him. We will go to the funeral."

The shops closed like falling dominos along the street. This led to a steady stream of owners and staff hastening their way to Mombasa House. The English Bakery shut its doors fearing a riot was about to break out. The news reached the Inspector of Police on duty before the first group had arrived at Lalji's flat. He dispatched a small group of *askaris* (constables) to investigate and report back.

The crowd gathered outside Mombasa House and exchanged news and rumours until Bhasker came down and confirmed the news. He said Lalji had died after a short illness and his wife and elder son were with him in the clinic.

He announced the funeral would take place at 2 pm at the cremation ground. He invited those who had gathered to come upstairs to sit and pray for the departed soul. Sitting space was available in both Lalji's and his flat.

Many came and sat vigil in front of a *diya* (lamp) placed between a grainy photograph of Lalji and *Shivji* (Lord Shiva). Others headed home to fetch their wives. The ladies, clad in white saris with all make up and jewellery removed, sat around Janki. Most men chose to arrive at the cremation ground directly. The body was conveyed in the new hearse donated by Porbander Stores to the Town Council earlier in the year. As was the custom, no women or children attended except for Jagdish, who would light his father's funeral pyre.

The cremation ground had never seen so many people attend in the past. It seemed the whole of the Indian community was there, and everyone joined in the chant to *Shree Ram* (Lord Ram). Mr Edwards, the Bank Manager, attended with a member of his staff. It was his first attendance at a Hindu funeral. He was smartly dressed and wore a black tie in respect. Next to him was the police inspector on duty that day, with a black band tied around his short sleeve. The Inspector had never met Lalji, but after he heard back from his *askaris* that Indian businesses had shut for the funeral he chose to come.

Harry Gichuru's son was in Nairobi that morning, having arrived to see Lalji to collect rations for the Missionary Clinic in Kikuyu Village. Lalji had paid for the clinic to be built the previous year out of his own funds. The nuns, with Gichuru's son, would arrive monthly seeking supplies. The two nuns who had accompanied Gichuru junior, one Dutch and the other Indian, also came to the cremation, being the only two women present. Kijana from the shop, tears rolling down his cheeks stood away from the main crowd, with other members of staff from the shops. Pembo, still employed as a night watchman, stood a distance away from the crowd in his long coat, eyes shut in meditative trance.

The *Pandit* (priest) started chanting his *shlokas* (religious chants) as soon as the body had been placed on the pyre. Further logs of timber were placed to enclose it. When ready, he asked for Jagdish to come forward and Naran brought him forward, protective hands on the boy's shoulders. The pyre was fully alight within minutes.

The ashes were immersed in the Nairobi River after the pyre had burnt itself out and cooled. A small crowd of close friends and relatives accompanied

Jagdish and Naran with the *Pandit* for the purpose. Janki had sent fresh flowers to be immersed with the ashes.

Everybody returned to their respective homes afterwards to wash and a change of clothes. Many returned to provide their support to the family at Lalji's flat. They joined in a simple communal meal, the first of the day for Naran and Jagdish.

The reading aloud of the *Bhagavad Geeta* had begun and Janki, seated on the floor weeping quietly, was trying hard to comprehend what had happened. She was trying to catch words from the reading which she hoped may help to make sense.

CHAPTER FORTY-FIVE

MR LLOYD EDWARDS asked to see Nizar and Bhasker and both arrived together before the appointed time. It had been just over a month since Lalji died, and the businesses were just settling down after the initial disruption.

Family life had become a dwindling stream of visitors in the evenings, still coming to show their solidarity. Janki, who had not set foot outside the front door, appreciated these distractions which provided relief. It also reduced the dreadful feeling in the pit of her stomach when she thought about the future. It was her lifeline to the real world outside. She generally refrained from taking part in the conversations, but looked forward to each evening's proceedings.

"Please come in, gentlemen," announced a smiling Lloyd Edwards at the door to his office.

"Thank you for coming to the funeral of Laljibhai, Mr Edwards," said Bhasker.

"That's all right, you don't need to thank me for that. We all know we lost a fine man too soon. A jolly good businessman and lately a good philanthropist."

"What is a philan....?" asked Bhasker.

"A generous man, a man who cared about others and provided for them without wanting anything in return."

Bhasker nodded in agreement.

"Thank you for your kind words, sir," said Nizar.

"Gentlemen, we go back a long way as you know. I remember the day you came to see me with Lalji for your first loan. I remember it as if it was yesterday. And with Lalji's leadership and the hard work of you all, you have accomplished what you set out to do, and much more."

He went on, "For my part, I saw in you all determination and a strong will to succeed. I knew you would never let the Bank down. Indeed, you have made good your words and done better than we thought possible," said Edwards.

Nizar and Bhasker looked at each other.

Nizar spoke, "Sir, since you asked to see us, is there something troubling you? Anything we have missed out? Maybe after Laljibhai died?"

"No, not at all. You gents are doing fine. But I wanted to talk about the businesses and a delicate matter."

"Yes?"

"I know how Lalji and the four of you did your business. Naran, Lalji's brother, whom I have only known for a short time, I do not know him well."

"Yes?"

"Without breaking any bank rules, I need to be open with you, as far as I can. Naran has asked to borrow a large sum against the assets of the partnership. He wants to buy agricultural land near Mount Kenya. I expect you know about this?"

"No sir, we do not," answered Bhasker. "But half belongs to me and half of the rest to Jankibhabhi and the children. So, Naran's share is only a quarter of everything."

"Yes, I see. I am not sure what Mrs Janki knows."

"It is not likely she knows anything, like me," said Bhasker, agitation in his voice.

"I don't think she knows, otherwise she would seek our advice," said Nizar. "But in any case, I am supposed to make sure things go the way as in Laljibhai's will."

"Yes, and I would suggest the will is acted on as Lalji wanted. Very soon."

"Is there a risk to those assets?" asked Nizar.

"Well, it's a straightforward matter of land purchase financed partly by the assets. I understand it includes those of the children, and the rest financed by the loan."

"How much loan, sir?" interrupted Bhasker.

"Well, I am not able to give you details, but a substantial loan. Larger than what you have ever borrowed as a partnership."

Nizar gasped. Bhasker was getting more agitated, sitting on the edge of his chair.

"And the land is for?"

"Agriculture. Naran tells me his farming experience in Baganda was very successful. I have verified that is the case with the Commissioner's Office."

"Is it already planted? Is it sugar cane?"

"No, it's grassland ready for development. Some surrounding farms have grown wheat or corn but not all have succeeded. I know a white settler who returned home after his crops failed for two years."

"Is it not fertile?" asked Nizar.

"It's fertile enough. But prone to frost and heavy showers. It is ideally suited for dairy or animal farming, but Naran is thinking of crops."

"Are you happy to lend?"

"From the Bank's point of view, the amount of capital put forward is enough and the land will remain in our charge until the loan is paid off."

"But?" asked Nizar.

"But I have not seen the determination in Naran's eyes like I saw in the four of you when you first came to me. I don't see Lalji's understanding or focus, although I see a good amount of confidence in Naran."

"Hmm."

Bhasker, looking shaken asked, "He has no right to do this. He has not even mentioned this to me as his partner in business. If the children's share is not there, will you still lend what he needs?"

"That is a good question. We would need to do all our calculations again. My feeling is we would decline the loan," Edwards said looking at Bhasker, raising his eyebrows.

"When is this all going to happen?" asked Nizar.

"There is still time before lawyers start drawing up loan contracts. At present, it is with me to decide on."

"You see, Mr Edwards, I need to consult a good lawyer to make sure all can be done according to the will. If things don't work out all that Laljibhai built could get destroyed. And his children will lose their share," explained Nizar.

"Quite so," agreed Mr Edwards nodding his head. "Have a chat with Mrs Janki and if you need a good lawyer, I can recommend one to you."

"Thank you, Mr Edwards."

"Of course, gentlemen, you understand I asked for this meeting with you, because of our long standing relationship. I know where you all started from and I respected Lalji very much. I would not want to see all your hard work go to waste."

"Thank you, sir. This meeting will remain confidential," said Bhasker, by now seething with anger.

***

The qualities that were attractive in Bhasker according to Lalji were his strong conscience and lack of greed. He had trusted Lalji implicitly and his loyalty exceeded that of most men. He would do for Lalji where others refrained.

For him to show anger was rare; he usually treated contentious issues in a matter-of-fact way. But he hated dishonesty and injustice, the two things most likely to enrage him. For him the treachery of Naran was incomprehensible. He confided in Nizar that as a business partner he shouldered the blame for allowing Naran too much control, too early. But the deceit towards Janki and the children he found unpalatable.

Seeing Bhasker troubled by anger and guilt, Nizar asked, "Bhasker do you think Lalji had no idea about Naran's character?"

Bhasker looked stunned, unsure of what Nizar meant.

***

Nizar had called for a meeting at his flat after informing Naran that both he and Bhasker were aware of what he was planning. Janki and Jagdish were present. Bhasker and Nizar sat on one side and Naran opposite.

"Naran, it is barely just over a month since Laljibhai passed away. As you know he has left instructions in his will about the partnership and the distribution of assets after his death. It has come to our notice that you may have started to make changes even before the legal paperwork has been finalised," said Nizar looking at Naran.

"Nizar, I know my duties and my role. I am also like my late brother. I already have plans and ambitions for this family. What I am trying to do is to improve our position for everyone's future. For Jankibhabhi, the children, and all of us," replied Naran, casting a glance at Janki and Jagdish.

"Did you discuss any of these plans with Laljibhai before his death?" asked Bhasker, "You have not discussed them with me."

"I was going to ....and also with Jankibhabhi. "

"What are these plans?" asked Bhasker.

"I thought we should invest in land. We should go into farming while the price of land is cheap. I have found an area near Mount Kenya where most farmers are white settlers and the owner is willing to sell to us."

"Your experience in farming is limited, Naran," observed Nizar.

"Yes, but it has been long enough for me to be able to spot fertile soil and understand what crops would do well there."

"And if it fails?" asked Bhasker.

"It is unlikely to fail. The area is lush and rich in vegetation. In the worst case, we could sell the land and recoup our money."

"What does the present farmer plant? And what will you plant?" asked Nizar.

"Nothing at present, but the neighbour farms maize and wheat. I think we could start sugar cane and plantains."

"When were you planning to discuss this with us?" asked Bhasker, anger in his voice.

"Once I have negotiated a good price for the land," replied Naran defiantly.

"How is it to be funded?" asked Nizar.

"Well, first we could use our cash and borrow against our buildings, after renting the shops. Otherwise, we could sell some of our properties to reduce the loan."

"But you have not asked any one of us, Naran. It is also not what Laljibhai wanted us to do," said Bhasker, eyes bulging.

"Yes, Laljibhai was not aware but I am certain he would have liked the idea, and the plan. If you don't like it, you can take your share and keep running the business here in Nairobi."

There was stunned silence while everyone waited for Bhasker's response to the provocation. Instead, a new and calmer voice of Jagdish spoke up.

"*Narankaka* (Uncle Naran), does it not make sense for you to take the loan out with your share and move to this farm you have in mind?"

Naran was first taken aback by the voice, by the confidence and calm logic of the young man. Sniggering, he replied, "Well, you need experience in business and farming to do what I am trying to do. These things are not taught in school."

"The loan you will need, is it something arranged on your share or against the partnership and the assets?" asked Bhasker.

"It would be against the assets because it is a very large farm, the second largest in the district," replied Naran, pride swelling his chest.

"So, you have in mind to farm, raise money from our properties and assets, obtain a loan and add newer crops to make the farm productive. Meanwhile, none of us have been consulted."

"I was going to ...."

"What other steps have you taken, *Narankaka*? (Uncle Naran?)" asked Jagdish, his voice polite and his manner sounding more like his late father's.

"Am I to respond to the questions of a child?" reacted Naran angrily, looking at Janki.

"Just imagine I am asking the same question," said Nizar.

"In that case, fine. To keep the businesses going I had transferred the funds from the business to a separate bank account in my name."

"How dare you?" reacted Bhasker, in a rage now.

"Someone must take steps otherwise everything would grind to a halt. The paperwork from the will may take a long time. If you are so concerned, how come you have never once asked about the bank situation, Bhasker?"

***

Janki had sleepless nights after the meeting. She was concerned about how the meeting had gone. She had not expected Naran to start making decisions of his own so early after her husband's death, and without consultation. She realised Naran thought her unworthy of any business ability because she was a woman. What worried her more was that Naran did not seem to show any insight or regret in the steps he had taken. Lalji would never take unilateral decisions on important matters without consulting his partners. He would usually have talked it through with her first.

You don't know how much your brother trusted my opinion, she thought, looking at Naran. There was also a small degree of comfort for Janki in the way her eldest Jagdish had conducted himself. She did not know how much he knew about business, but he showed the calmness and determination of Lalji.

At the next meeting Bhasker and Naran were barely on speaking terms, the ill feeling between the two palpable.

Nizar spoke first, "We have had discussions about what you said at our last meeting, Naran. We have made decisions you need to know about."

"Yes?"

"Jankibhabhi and Bhasker are not in favour of uprooting from Nairobi or ready to consider a life on a remote farm. They want the businesses and assets not sold but divided according to Laljibhai's will."

"I see."

"You are free to leave to pursue your interest in farming. The business funds you have transferred to your own account, using Lalji's power of attorney, can remain with you to help you get started. When the actions from the will are finalised, they will buy out all your property holdings. They will pay for your share in cash. At present all the properties are in the names of Lalji and Bhasker, as you know."

"Hmmm."

"Do you have any questions?" asked Nizar. Bhasker and Janki had been looking down all the time. Jagdish had eyes fixed on his uncle, studying his face.

"You are kicking me out then. I did not expect this from you, *Bhabhi!*" he retorted, eyes bulging at Janki.

"It is not my mother's decision, *Narankaka*. She has remained neutral. It is the decision of the three of us and my late father," said Jagdish.

"What nonsense. How did your late father decide with you?" a red-faced Naran demanded to know.

Bhasker turned to Nizar and said, "Please tell him *Nizar*."

"Naran, the morning when we all signed up to Lalji's wishes and his will, I stayed back as he asked me to do. He handed me a signed instruction that his Power of Attorney which you held was being revoked. It has been with the lawyers and only remains to be notified by printing it in the press."

"But why would he do that?" asked Naran.

"Laljibhai did not trust you fully. However, he still wanted you to have a share of his assets. I was instructed to use it only if you strayed from his planned will. So, you see the actions you have taken in transferring the business funds to your own account can be reversed by using this document in court. But Jankibhabhi has asked that we leave things as they are. There is nothing to be gained in going to lawyers and courts. I am sure Lalji would have thought the same," explained Nizar.

For the first time, Bhasker looked up to meet Naran's eyes.

"Jankibhabhi and Jagdish will join the businesses and we will run them all together," said Bhasker.

Looking pale and out manoeuvred, Naran hung his head low and said, "I was only trying to do the best for everybody. You have all misunderstood my objectives."

No one responded.

EPILOGUE

THE FOLLOWING YEARS brought changes to Nairobi not seen before. The town expanded at an unprecedented rate. Solid constructions in stone and cement started to go up. The edifice of a capital city started to take shape.

Halfway along the Mombasa Railway to Nairobi the Sikh staff of the railway had built the first *Gurudwara* (Sikh Temple). A clear sign of confidence and establishing their presence in the new country. Schools, hospitals and places of worship started to spring up under the initiatives of Indian communities. With minimal help from the *sarkar* (government), these started to form infrastructure of the new colony. Newer migrants from India, known as 'passenger migrants', followed by steamships in the wake of further development. The chain reaction had ignited. A quiet revolution of establishing a new society in a new land had taken hold. The *sarkar* was relegated to bearing witness to the economic and civic capacity of the second tier. Not something in the original blueprint of the Empire builders.

The Indian problem had become the Indian solution.

The colonial *sarkar* was preoccupied with unrest. It was busy legislating land grabs under pressure of the white settler class. It ran native reserves, collected hut and poll taxes. It was in no position to pay attention or be involved in the quiet transformation taking place in the fabric of Kenya society.

Commerce, like civic society, was stratified into three tiers. Factories, wholesalers, land sales, automobile and heavy machinery was reserved exclusively for European operators. Indians and Arabs were allowed commercial activities within strict licences so as not to compete with white businesses. The local Africans were entitled to serve and labour.

Jagdish picked up the business quickly. His will and determination reminded Janki of Lalji in the early days. Janki had initially started to come to the shops in the afternoons to write the accounts and keep an eye on Jagdish. Soon it became clear her concern was misplaced. Jagdish was stepping into Lalji's shoes comfortably.

Bhasker was relieved his role was less active again. He was a creature of habit and content to continue with his music in the evenings. One of the first things he did for himself was to build a music school, the *Sharda Music Academy*. He wanted to help children learn music, dance and singing. He engaged visiting teachers from India. He chose a plot of land near the Nairobi River, not too far for the students to attend in the daytime. But remote enough to provide a secret rendezvous for political activists in the evenings.

Mr Edwards started to meet Jagdish regularly to talk about the businesses and to mentor him. Impressed by the boy, he thought Jagdish had a meteoric future ahead of him. He was impressed by how well-read Jagdish was about commerce in the British Raj. Despite giving tips to the young man about possible opportunities, he noticed Jagdish was not rushing into anything. He seemed to be waiting for something big, something special.

The first move Jagdish made was to build a magnificent cinema hall, his childhood dream. The timing was perfect with Indian cinema audiences in Nairobi, who could not get enough of the films.

Naran had decided to buy his farm near Mount Kenya and moved there with his young family. He had to settle for a smaller farm and used the rest of his funds to buy a plot of land in central Nairobi. He planned to build on it in the future when his finances allowed. But after two crop failures, Naran was forced to quit. He had barely enough left to pay back his loan. The central Nairobi plot of land was auctioned and picked up by an anonymous buyer at a generous price. Janki did not let it be known that she was the purchaser.

Naran headed home to Porbander with his young family. He never felt able to meet Janki or Jagdish again. He also refused to meet any of Lalji's ex-partners. Jaya, his wife, was not so inclined and met with Janki secretly to say farewell before they left.

The Baganda farm was a partial success. Initially there were healthy harvests but without Naran being present the place fell into a steady decline. When the engineer returned to India at the end of his contract, the *sarkar* decided to take back the farm and sold it to a white settler.

Mr Edwards retired to England to be near his aging mother and to play village cricket. He read years later in the bank newsletter that a young Indian entrepreneur had taken Nairobi by storm. He had interests in real estate and property development, cinema halls, importation of luxurious European goods and small machinery from Japan. The young man was asked if he would ever consider political office, and his answer was 'no'. Asked why, he responded, "My father came to Africa from humble roots. He wanted to do business and through business to benefit others. Every transaction in business is done by consent on both sides, and both sides win. But politics is different. In politics, consent is often missing. Someone usually loses, while someone else gains. So no, it's not for me, I cannot see myself in politics."

On reading the name of the individual, Mr Edwards roared with laughter on his deck chair on the village green. Faces around him gave him startled looks.

Made in the USA
Las Vegas, NV
16 October 2024

96935400R00163